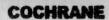

The Cl...

Born in Gainsborough, Lincolnshire, Margaret Dickinson moved to the coast at the age of seven and so began her love for the sea and the Lincolnshire landscape. Her ambition to be a writer began early and she had her first novel published at the age of twenty-five. This was followed by twenty-eight further titles including *Plough the Furrow*, *Sow the Seed* and *Reap the Harvest*, which make up her Lincolnshire Fleethaven trilogy. Many of her novels are set in the heart of her home county but in *Tangled Threads* and *Twisted Strands* the stories include not only Lincolnshire but also the framework knitting and lace industries of Nottingham. Her most recent novel, *Jenny's War*, was a top twenty best seller.

www.margaret-dickinson.co.uk

Plough the Furrow

Sow the Seed

Reap the Harvest

The Miller's Daughter

Chaff upon the Wind

The Fisher Lass

The Tulip Girl

The River Folk

Tangled Threads

Twisted Strands

Red Sky in the Morning

Without Sin

Pauper's Gold

Wish Me Luck

Sing As We Go

Suffragette Girl

Sons and Daughters

Forgive and Forget

Jenny's War

Margaret Dickinson

The Clippie Girls

PAN BOOKS

First published 2013 by Pan Books
an imprint of Pan Macmillan, a division of Macmillan Publishers Limited
Pan Macmillan, 20 New Wharf Road, London N1 9RR
Basingstoke and Oxford
Associated companies throughout the world
www.panmacmillan.com

ISBN 978-0-330-54431-3

1 3 5 7 9 8 6 4 2

A CIP catalogue record for this book is available from
the British Library.

Typeset by SetSystems Ltd, Saffron Walden, Essex
Printed and bound by CPI Group (UK) Ltd, Croydon, CR0 4YY

Visit www.panmacmillan.com to read more about all our books
and to buy them. You will also find features, author interviews and
news of any author events, and you can sign up for e-newsletters
so that you're always first to hear about our new releases.

For my loving husband, Dennis

Acknowledgements

On a visit to Crich Tramway Village, the Home of the National Tramway Museum, I saw tram number 264, which had been damaged in the Sheffield Blitz of December 1940. Now beautifully restored, along with many others, this tram inspired my story. I am very grateful to the staff of the museum, who have been so helpful with the research for this novel. I also wish to express my thanks to the staff of the Sheffield Local Studies Library, who kindly helped with my researches in the newspapers of the day, most notably *The Star*. And as always, many thanks for the continuing support of the staff at Skegness Library.

Thank you to Pauline and Mervyn Griggs, Margaret Trigg and Marjorie Payne for all their memories of and information on Sheffield.

A great many sources have been used for research, including: *Sheffield Transport* by Chas. C Hall (Transport Publishing Company, 1977); *Clippie* by Zelma Katin (John Gifford, 1944); *Sheffield Tramway Memories* (South Yorkshire Transport Museum Trust Ltd, 2010); *Sheffield's Date with Hitler* by Neil Anderson (ACM Retro Ltd, 2010); *Then & Now: The Sheffield Blitz – Operation Crucible* by Alistair Lofthouse (ALD Design & Print, 2001); *Sheffield Blitz* by Paul License (Sheffield Newspapers Ltd, 2000); *It's a Bit Lively Outside*, compiled by Joyce Holliday (Yorkshire Art Circus, 1987).

And last, but never least, my love and thanks to my

family and friends for their constant support and encouragement, especially to those who read the typescript in the early stages, David Dickinson and Fred Hill; to my agent, Darley Anderson and his staff; to Trisha Jackson, Natasha Harding, Liz Cowen and everyone at Pan Macmillan and to Tory Lyne-Pirkis and Clare Motte at Midas Public Relations.

One

Sheffield, 3 September 1939

Mary Sylvester switched off the wireless, the smell of warm Bakelite still lingering in the room as she glanced round the table at the worried faces of her three daughters.

Peggy, the eldest, was the first to speak. 'Oh, Mam – whatever are we going to do?'

Hastily Mary dashed away her tears, hoping the girls hadn't noticed. She smiled bravely. 'We'll cope, just like we always have done.' But the smile, which she was striving so hard to keep, faded as she murmured softly, 'Though what your poor dad would have thought, I don't know. He fought in the last war and now it's going to start all over again. All those brave young men slaughtered in the trenches and now we're going to lose another generation of wonderful boys.' She met Peggy's steady gaze.

Mary's eldest daughter was the one who was most like her: curly brown hair, soft brown eyes and dimples in her cheeks when she smiled. And, more often than not, Peggy was smiling. But not at this moment. Not when they'd just listened to Mr Chamberlain telling the nation that Britain was now at war.

The girls, of course, had no memories of the Great

War – the war that had been supposed to end all wars. Peggy had been born in February 1918, when Mary and Ted had been married for nine months.

'A honeymoon baby,' the neighbours had cooed, but Peggy's mother had muttered sourly, 'Thank goodness it wasn't early. I couldn't have borne the gossip.'

Ted Sylvester had arrived home severely injured early in 1917 and Mary, despite her mother's foreboding, had insisted on keeping her promise to her fiancé and marrying him at once.

'You'll be nursing him for the rest of your life,' Grace Booth had warned.

'I love him, Mother,' Mary had insisted. 'And he says that my letters and the thought that I was here waiting for him were what kept him going through all the horror. I can't let him down now, even if I wanted to. And,' she'd added firmly, with more conviction in her tone than she was feeling inside, 'I don't.'

Ted – fair-haired and blue-eyed – had been an out-going, jolly chap before he'd marched to the Town Hall to enlist in the Sheffield City Battalion with the rest of his mates soon after war had been declared in 1914. He'd marched off with a jaunty step and a merry smile and Mary had been so proud of him – so proud of them all. But he'd come back a changed man; he was no longer cheerful, but sat for hours sunk in gloom, hardly speaking, scarcely seeming to notice anyone around him. But at least he had come back, Mary comforted herself. So many of his pals had not returned from the carnage on the Somme in 1916. So many Sheffield mothers, wives and sweethearts – even children – had been left mourning the loss of the men in their lives. Ted had survived all that, only to be wounded as soldiers on both sides faced another bleak Christmas, with no sign of an end to the war.

'He'll be better when you're married,' Ted's mother had said when he was safely back in England. 'When you're in your own little house, he'll be better.'

'I – I don't know whether we'll be able to afford to rent a place of our own, Mrs Sylvester. I mean – Ted won't be able to work for a while yet, will he?'

'If I know my Ted, he'll be back on his feet in no time.'

Mary had stared at her future mother-in-law in amazement. Didn't she realize the extent of the damage to Ted's left leg? The surgeon had even warned that he might never walk again, but Ted's mother resolutely refused to believe it.

Mary bit her lip. 'We might have to live with my mother and father for a while—'

'Oh no. Not that. I don't hold with youngsters living with in-laws. No, you need your own home. You'll manage. You're a sensible girl, I know that.'

Mary was indeed 'a sensible girl' and frugal with her money. After their marriage, she kept her job in a city centre store, even though it hurt Ted deeply. 'I should be able to look after my wife,' he'd grumbled.

'It's – it's only for a while, darling. Just – just until you're well enough to work again. When you joined up they promised they'd hold your job for you at the bank, didn't they?'

'Pigs might fly,' Ted had muttered morosely.

'But you're a wounded soldier, surely . . .'

'And have you seen just how many wounded soldiers are wandering the streets, begging on street corners? A land fit for heroes! Don't make me laugh.'

Mary had bitten her lip, afraid to tell him that she already suspected she was pregnant. But soon she'd been unable to hide it any longer and the 'few weeks' living with her parents had turned into months and then into years.

And they were still living in her mother's house when another war began.

'Does Gran know?' Rose asked, bringing Mary's wandering thoughts back to the present. 'Where is she, anyway?'

'Up in her room,' Myrtle, the youngest and the quiet one of the three sisters, murmured. 'She said she didn't want to hear it. I'm surprised, though, because she's a glutton for reading the newspapers or listening to the news.' Despite the gravity of the situation, the family exchanged amused glances. Every evening there was a lot of 'shushing' from Grace when the news came on the wireless.

'Don't worry, love,' Mary said. 'Your gran will soon be out buying every newspaper that's going. She'll not miss a thing. She's just shocked at the moment, I think.' Mary could remember how her mother had followed the news avidly during the last war. She couldn't believe that Grace would be any different this time around. Mary smiled at her youngest daughter. Myrtle, with ash-blond hair and hazel eyes, was, at fifteen, studious and conscientious. She was regarded as the clever one in the family. At least, that's what her two older sisters told her constantly. 'Thick as two short planks nailed together, me,' Peggy would say cheerfully. 'But you stay on at school and try for college or university, Myrtle. Just think how proud we'd all be.'

And Rose would butt in too. 'Then you can get a marvellous job and keep us all in our decrepit old age.'

Myrtle would smile quietly and say nothing, but deep inside she hoped her sisters' teasing would one day come true. She loved learning and next year she would sit her School Certificate. After that, she wanted to stay on into the sixth form and go on to further education. But now it looked as if her hopes and dreams might be shattered. The future would be very uncertain for all of them. She glanced around her family and was surprised to see Rose's eyes gleaming. 'Do you think they'll be looking for women conductors to work on the trams?'

Where Peggy was calm, level-headed and responsible, Rose, with unruly curly fair hair and bright blue eyes like her father, was outgoing and impetuous. When she set her heart on something she could be very stubborn, but her family loved her for her undying cheerfulness and her bouncy personality, even though her untidiness drove them all to despair. But she was the one who could always be relied upon to find a silver lining to every cloud. Even now, when they were frightened by the news and fearful of what was to come, it was Rose who could find a spark of hope in the darkness. Her one ambition had always been to become a conductress on the city's trams, and now she might just get her chance.

When rumours of an impending war spread, Laurence Bower, an inspector at the Crookes tram depot, had approached his superior, Mr Holmes. 'I think we ought to start thinking about recruiting women to be conductresses. We had them in the last war. I reckon we're going to need them again.'

His manager had frowned. 'Tram motormen and, I

presume, conductors too will be reserved occupations. Do you really think there's any need?'

Laurence had shrugged. 'You know how it was last time. There'll be a lot of the younger men wanting to volunteer. Are you going to stop 'em?'

Mr Holmes had looked thoughtful. Then he'd sighed. 'I suppose not. If they want to go, then I suppose we'll have to respect their wishes. But I'm not sure the Transport Committee will agree to us taking on women before we really need to.'

Laurence, who was on good terms with Mr Holmes, smiled. 'If I was you, I'd think about getting a few girls trained up ready and worry about "permission" afterwards. The bosses'll be panicking the minute war's declared and only too happy to find you've jumped the gun. Women will be drafted into all sorts of occupations that the men leave behind when they either volunteer or are called up. You mark my words.'

'Have you anyone in mind?'

'Oh yes,' Laurence had said airily. 'There are one or two in the canteen who'd make excellent clippies.'

Now Peggy smiled at Rose as she told her, 'Mr Bower's already asked me if I'd like to train to be a clippie if war was declared.'

Rose's eyes widened. 'And?'

'I said I would.'

'Oh! How wonderful!' Rose clapped her hands. 'I'll ask him tomorrow if he'll take me on.'

'I think he's got enough recruits at the moment. They're training fifteen to start with, he said.'

Rose's face fell, but only for a second. 'But when all the fellers start leaving, he'll want more then, won't he?'

'I – suppose so.'

'And *then*, he won't be able to refuse me, will he?'

To this, no one answered. Only Grace was heard to mutter sagely, 'It's an ill wind . . .'

Two

Grace Booth's house was on a street leading downhill from Northfield Road. The front door led into a small hall, with the best front room to the right. Straight ahead, beyond the foot of the staircase, a door opened into the living room, where the family spent most of their time. It was the warmest room in the house with a fire that burned constantly in the range. And, although there was a modern gas cooker in the back kitchen, Grace still liked to use the range oven for baking. In one corner of the living room beneath the space left by the stairs on the other side of the wall, a door led down into the cellar, where coal and coke were kept, delivered through a chute from the street. Beyond the living room was the kitchen with a deep white sink and draining board with a blue-and-white check gingham curtain covering the shelves beneath it. Beside that was the gas cooker. The family still used an outside lavatory – known to all as the 'nessy' – in the small back yard, which led to a communal yard backed onto by several houses. Upstairs, there were two bedrooms and a bathroom on the first floor. Grace had the best bedroom at the front of the house. This room was distempered in blue and the wooden bedstead was covered with a blue satin eiderdown to match the walls. Mary and Peggy occupied the two single beds in the back bedroom and up another flight of narrow stairs was the attic bedroom decorated in pink, which Rose and Myrtle shared. In comparison with many of the houses in the city, it was a spacious, well-kept home, but with five grown-ups it could still feel crowded at times. The favourite room for each member of the family was, perhaps, the bathroom, where they could wallow in the deep white bath and lock the door against the commotion of the house for a while.

Grace had moved into the house as a young married woman and had lived there ever since. Her husband, Daniel, had been employed at various banks in the city after leaving school and had worked his way up to be chief cashier at the Yorkshire Penny Bank Ltd by the time he retired at the age of sixty. While he was there he had nurtured several young men and set them on a promising career. One of them had been Edward Sylvester, known to all his family and friends as Ted. Ted had been a diligent pupil under Mr Booth's tutelage and Daniel, having taken a real liking to the young man, had no qualms in inviting him to his home. There, of course, Ted had met Mary and, if such a meeting and what followed had been what Daniel had hoped for, then his aspirations were realized when Ted and Mary began courting.

Grace was not keen on the match. She had planned to keep her only child under her thumb. Now Mary's marriage might thwart Grace's plans for being cared for in her old age by her daughter. But Grace could be devious and manipulative when it suited her and the Great War had played into her hands. It suited her to suggest that the young couple should live with the Booths. Daniel, after he'd retired, doted on the three baby girls, proudly wheeling them out in the cumbersome, second-hand perambulator around the streets where they lived. It was while he was out with six-month-old Myrtle in the pram one freezing December morning in 1924 that he suffered a fatal heart attack. The screaming baby, tipped over in the pram as Daniel fell, alerted passers-by and they rushed to help.

'I know him,' Mrs Parkinson, running out from her house, told the gathering. 'It's Mr Booth. Him 'as used to work at t'bank. He lives in t'next street. Oh poor, poor man. There, there, my little love.' The woman had turned her attention to the wailing child, sensing that there was no more any of them could do for the man until an ambulance arrived.

'D'you know where he lives then?' one of the men asked. 'Because if you do, I reckon you'd best take the child home and tell his folks.'

'Aye, I will. Mary'll come.'

'Who's Mary? His wife?'

'No, his daughter. Mother of t' little 'un here.'

'Then you'd best fetch her.'

'Has anyone sent for an ambulance?'

'Yes,' another man, panting from running, said, 'I've just phoned from the box on the corner.'

'It'll be a while.' The first man looked around at the gaping faces. 'Can anyone fetch a blanket out? Keep him warm – just in case there's any chance . . .' His words petered out. They could all see that there was little hope for poor Daniel. No one there was qualified to pronounce him dead, yet they all feared the worst.

'He's a gonner I reckon,' the man, who'd asked for the blanket, said as he laid it gently over Daniel. 'But we've got to try.'

Mary came running, flinging herself to her knees beside her father. 'Oh, Dad, Dad!' She felt his cheek, but it was icy cold. She looked up, pleading with the faces above her. 'Can you carry him? Bring him home?'

'Best wait for the ambulance, love.'

'Oh, but—' Mary had begun to protest, but at that moment they heard the clanging bell of the ambulance and real help was at hand.

Having found out where they were taking him, Mary sped home pushing Myrtle, who, sensing something dreadful had happened, was still crying. Ted met them at the door.

'Dad's collapsed in the street,' she panted.

'We guessed that,' Grace snapped from behind Ted. 'How is he?'

Mary hesitated. 'He – he doesn't look good, Mother. The ambulance's taken him to the Royal.'

Grace had shaken her head impatiently. 'I told him not to go out. Too cold for the baby, I said, but would he listen? No. Just because she was yelling and wouldn't stop and he thought he could get her to sleep. And now I suppose he'll expect me to go traipsing to the hospital.'

'I'll come with you, Mother—'

'You can't leave me with the kids,' Ted protested, limping back to the chair by the fire.

'Peggy's at school and if I feed and change Baby before I go—'

'I can't handle Rose. You know I can't. She's so wilful and naughty.'

'She's spoilt. That's the trouble with that little madam.' Grace nodded sagely. 'You let your father spoil her, Mary. You—'

'I'm not getting into an argument about that now,' Mary snapped, anxiety making her unusually short-tempered.

Both Grace and Ted stared at her, but she lifted her chin and returned their glares. 'When Dad might be – might be—' With a sob she turned away. 'I'm going to the hospital whether you like it or not. If you've any bother, get Letty from next door. She'll help with Rose.'

And with that Mary squashed her hat onto her head, wound the thick woollen scarf around her neck and turned to her mother. 'Are you coming or not, Mother?'

Grace stared at her for a moment and then dropped her glance. 'You go. Find out how he is. I'll go this afternoon – at visiting – if . . .' She turned away, her attention caught by Rose. The four-year-old was climbing on to a chair and reaching across the table towards a jug full of milk.

'Get down, you naughty girl. You'll spill the lot.' Grace smacked the child's bare leg and Rose began to howl. Ted, in his chair, closed his eyes and groaned. With a sigh and a shake of her head, Mary left the house. It was over a mile to the Royal Infirmary from where they lived, but Mary walked quickly along Springvale Road, now and again taking little running steps in her anxiety about her father. Arriving at the hospital breathless and agitated, it took a while for her to find anyone who could tell her what had happened to him, but at last she was told by a sympathetic sister that the man, who'd been brought in after collapsing in the street, had been dead when he'd arrived.

'I'm so sorry, my dear, and I'm afraid that we'll have to ask you to identify him.'

Mary shuddered and bit her lip, but nodded bravely. She was trembling as the sister led her to where her father lay. He looked surprisingly peaceful – as if he was just asleep. She fancied that at any moment he might open his eyes and smile up at her. But poor Daniel would never again smile gently at his daughter and lovingly dandle his granddaughters on his knee. Or take them for walks. If only he hadn't gone out that bitterly cold morning. Grace had been right and now Mary knew she'd never hear the end of it.

And she was right, for Grace's first words on hearing that her husband was dead were to lay the blame. 'If he hadn't been wheeling out your crying baby, he'd still have been here. And now what are we supposed to do with three screaming brats and an invalid?'

'Peggy's no trouble, you know she's not, and the baby's a good little thing – most of the time.' Mary hesitated to say anything about her middle daughter. Rose was a handful, there was no denying it and Grace certainly wasn't going to. She sniffed and muttered, 'But that Rose makes up for it. Well, I'll tell you something, Mary. Now he's not here to spoil her any more, she needs taking in hand and if you won't do it – then I will.'

With that, Grace had turned away and retreated to her bedroom, leaving Mary to make all the necessary arrangements for Daniel's funeral.

It was a sad day. Tears streamed down six-year-old Peggy's face and even Rose, at four, seemed to realize that her beloved Grandpa wasn't coming back. She cried loudly standing at the graveside and refused to be hushed.

'Funerals aren't the place for young children,' Grace told Mary tartly. 'You shouldn't have brought them.'

Only a few months later, in the summer of 1925, Ted's war wounds, which had never healed properly, became infected and he died of septicaemia five days before Rose's fifth birthday. Mary mourned the loss of the man her husband had been before the war, but he had come back so very changed and had suffered so much that she couldn't help feeling a sense of relief that he was now at peace. So, the household became a family of women with no man to influence the growing children or soothe the inevitable tensions between Grace and Mary.

They settled into a routine. Mary returned once more to her work at a department store in the city, leaving a reluctant Grace to look after the baby. Myrtle was a placid child and Peggy biddable and, at seven coming up to eight, did her best to be helpful about the house.

Trouble only erupted when Rose came home from school.

Three

The three girls grew at an alarming rate and the furniture, which Grace had bought during the early years of her married life, soon began to look shabby. But she was not going to replace it whilst three young children rampaged through the house. Besides, there was little money for such luxuries as new furniture, but as the children grew older and more respectful of her belongings, Grace managed to pick up second-hand furniture in auction sales. Dressed in her dark coat and felt hat, she loved the excitement of bidding for a piece and winning. In the living room, where the family spent most of their time, two easy chairs were set either side of the range, which Grace resisted all attempts to have removed. The dining table and straight-backed chairs and the square of carpet – all had been shrewd purchases in the salesrooms. Even the wireless that stood on top of the sideboard, close to Grace's chair, was second-hand.

Between them, Grace and Mary redecorated the rooms when they needed it, hanging serviceable green wallpaper in the living room.

'It'll not show the smuts from the fire as much as a pale wallpaper would,' Grace had decreed.

'But we saw a nice beige wallpaper we could put in the front room. We don't use that room much,' Mary pointed out. 'Only on special occasions.'

Grace's best front room had a three-piece suite covered in light brown moquette with a flowered motif. A crewel-embroidered fire screen stood in the tiled fireplace and a glass-fronted cabinet housed Grace's precious china tea set, which had been a wedding present.

'True,' Grace had agreed, 'though I like a fire lit in there now and again – specially in winter – to keep it aired.'

Mary was thrifty with her money, but was hard pressed to keep her three daughters clothed and shod. By the time dresses, coats and shoes reached Myrtle, they were so worn that Mary often had to relent and buy new ones for her.

'So I get all the hand-me-downs,' Rose grumbled, 'and Myrtle gets new ones like our Peggy.'

'I'm not buying you brand-new clothes.' Mary smiled. 'They'd still be torn and dirty in no time.'

'That's true.' Rose had to agree and she did so with a merry smile. Rose was the tomboy of the family. Always laughing and always in some scrape or other. She played football and cricket with the boys next door rather than with dolls and tea sets.

'I don't know why you let her run wild, Mary. That girl will come to a bad end, you mark my words.'

So, whilst Peggy dutifully helped around the house and Myrtle, even from an early age, applied herself to her studies, Rose ran free. Peggy was of average ability academically, but she had no desire to stay on at school longer than the statutory leaving age. As soon as she could, she left school and found work in the tram workers' canteen. Two years later Rose joined her and they worked side by side. The sisters were popular with their work mates and especially with the tram drivers and conductors, who flirted outrageously with all the canteen staff.

But there was one, quieter than the rest, who seemed to have his eye on Peggy. Bob Deeton, with light brown hair and hazel eyes, was a solid, dependable young man, who'd been selected to train as a driver earlier than most and he came into the canteen regularly. He always contrived to have Peggy serve him, though at first he seemed tongue-tied, too reticent to strike up a conversation.

'I reckon he likes you.' Rose nudged her sister.

'Don't be silly. He's never even asked me out.'

'Would you go, if he did?'

'I might.'

Rose glanced thoughtfully across the room to where Bob was sitting eating his dinner. 'Well, I would, if he asked me.'

Peggy laughed. 'Don't be daft, Rose. He's not your sort. Far too quiet for you.'

'He's shy, that's all.' Rose defended the young man. 'I like that. I'm fed up of all the flirting that goes on here.'

Peggy gaped at her. 'But you love the banter. I've heard you giving back as good as you get.'

'Well – yes, I suppose I do, but I realize it's all insincere. If I was to take any one of them seriously, they'd run a mile. No, Bob's nice. He's kind too. Have you seen how Mr Bower always puts the young trainee conductors with him? That's because he knows Bob will look after them and help them.'

Peggy chuckled. 'I think it's you Bob ought to ask to go out with him, not me.'

Rose shrugged. 'It's not me he's interested in.'

Peggy could not fail to hear the note of wistfulness in her sister's tone.

Slowly, as time went on, Bob plucked up the courage to ask Peggy to go out with him. At first she refused him gently, but the young man was nothing if not persistent and the invitation was repeated every Saturday he was not on duty. For a while Peggy still resisted. But, in the end, her excuses sound lame even to her ears. At last she said, 'Yes,' and Bob almost danced around the canteen with delight.

'Hello, Bob,' Rose greeted him, when he arrived to take Peggy out for the first time. 'Come on in. She's still upstairs titivating, making herself beautiful for you.'

'She's already beautiful,' Bob said gallantly.

'By heck, you have got it bad,' Rose teased as she ushered him into the living room. Myrtle was seated at the table, her schoolbooks spread around her. Mary was sitting with a pile of darning on her knee and Grace, closest to the fire, was reading a newspaper. The older lady was small and wiry. At home, she was always dressed in her pinafore, with her grey hair pulled severely back from her face into a bun in the nape of her neck. She wore round steel-rimmed spectacles, behind which her sharp, pale blue eyes missed nothing. In contrast, Mary took her pinafore off as soon as she'd finished the household chores. Her hair was cut short, with curls and waves close to her head and nothing – except the smart, close-fitting hat worn at a jaunty angle when she went out – was allowed to cover her hair.

'This is our mam.' Peggy gestured towards Mary and

then nodded towards Grace. 'And this is Gran. Don't take any notice of her, her bark's worse than her bite.'

Bob shook hands politely with the two women and sat down in the chair which Rose pulled out for him.

'Like a cuppa, Bob?' Mary asked, half rising from her chair.

'No, no, please don't trouble, Mrs Sylvester. We'll be off as soon as Peggy's ready.'

There was an awkward silence for a moment, whilst Mary bent over her sewing, Grace rattled her paper and eyed the young man over the top of her round spectacles. 'Been working there long, young man?'

'I started in the repair shop until I was old enough to train up to be a driver.'

Grace grunted and shook her paper again. 'Mm.'

There was another awkward silence before Rose, trying to fill the gap, asked, 'What are you going to see?'

'I don't know. Whatever Peggy wants.' Bob hesitated a moment before saying generously, 'You can come with us, if you like.'

Rose threw back her head and laughed. 'What? Play gooseberry? No, no, I wouldn't do that to you, Bob.'

At that moment, there was a noise on the stairs and Peggy came into the room.

'Guess what?' Rose teased saucily. 'Bob's asked me to go with you.'

Peggy smiled and nodded. 'That's fine. Hadn't you better get your coat then? It's time we were going.'

For a moment Rose looked startled, then she spluttered with laughter. ''Course I'm not coming. Get on with you,' she added, shooing them both out of the room, but as the door closed behind them, Rose's merriment faded. Had she imagined it or had there been a look of disappointment on her sister's face when Rose had refused Bob's invitation? But then she shrugged off the thought and turned to go up to the attic bedroom she shared with Myrtle to play records on the wind-up gramophone.

As she put her foot on the bottom step, Grace's voice from the living room reached her. 'Rose, there's the washing up to do.'

Four

'I need some help with the blackout when you get home tonight,' Grace warned them all at breakfast the morning after the Prime Minister's sombre announcement. 'I'm not climbing up stepladders and on chairs at my age.'

As Mary had predicted, once Grace had got over the initial bewilderment as to how and why the governments of all the countries involved had been so foolish as to allow another war to come about, she threw herself into organizing her own 'home front'. Now she accepted that, as more than one journalist had already suggested, the armistice in 1918 had not really ended the Great War. The intervening years had merely been an extended truce. But now the dictator who'd risen to power in a demoralized Germany and was invading country after country with his jack-booted army had to be stopped.

'Your mother's going out today to get the blackout material, and Tom from next door has given me some wooden battens and plaster laths in case we need to make frames for the windows instead of curtains. I should have got it organized before this,' she muttered, more to herself than to the others. 'But I just didn't want to believe it was really coming.'

Mary was dressed smartly for going into town. She allowed herself few clothes; what money there was had always gone on her daughters, but those she had were of good quality and lasted well. Today she wore a beautifully tailored Scotch tweed to fit her slim figure. It had a skirt with wide, stitched-down pleats and a jacket with breast and hip pockets and she teamed it with a pink silk blouse. As she pinned her broad-brimmed hat into place, she said, 'I must get some extra non-perishable food in. The government said we could.'

But Grace shook her head. 'You've left it too late. That was back in July. We can't do it now the emergency has started.'

Mary looked crestfallen. 'Oh dear, it seems we've all been burying our heads in the sand, hoping it would go away.' She sighed. 'I'll just get one or two bits extra then, shall I?'

'Don't forget the blackout material for curtains and you can get thick brown paper from the stationers to make the frames.' Grace issued her orders. 'And get me the *Daily Sketch*. There's bound to be picture of the King. And I want to see who's in the War Cabinet. I just hope Winston's back at the Admiralty.'

Rose winked at her mother. Gran was back on form.

'Bob'll help us with the blackout,' Peggy said, as she and Rose were about to leave for work. Peggy had been going out with Bob for just over two months and the family were used to his visits. 'I'll ask him to come round tonight, shall I?'

Grace shrugged. 'If you like, but he'll have to help his mam with hers, won't he?'

Bob Deeton lived with his widowed mother and Peggy had told them that she relied a great deal on her son. 'I don't know what'll happen if he ever leaves home,' she'd said with a wry smile. 'She'll fall to pieces, I reckon.'

The family had exchanged amused glances wondering if they should read more into Peggy's words than she was saying.

That evening, despite the seriousness of the task and all that it implied, there was great hilarity in the living room. Even Grace smiled as she watched Rose wielding a saw, cutting up battens and laths into the required lengths to make frames to fit each window in the house. Then she picked up the hammer and began to join the pieces together with nails.

'Ouch!' she cried and sucked her thumb. 'I thought you said Bob was coming to help, Peg?'

'He said he'd try,' Peggy said, 'but his mother is panicking about getting their blackout up. She's a real worrier. Here, let me have a go.' Rose gladly handed over the hammer.

Lastly they stretched several sheets of brown paper over the frame, pinning it in place. A lath nailed diagonally across the back of it held the frame rigid.

'How are you going to fasten it in the window frame?' Myrtle asked. 'It won't just balance there. It'll fall out.'

'Aha,' Peggy said triumphantly. 'I thought of that today and asked Bob how to do it. He told me to get these – ' she picked up a paper bag she'd put on the sideboard when she came in from work – 'cupboard door fasteners. We've to screw one of these to each corner of the window frames and they'll hold the blackout frames in place.'

'Holes in my window frames?' Grace was scandalized.

'It's the only way, Gran. I'm sorry.'

'That Hitler's going to have a lot to answer for before this is over,' Grace muttered, but said no more. It had to be done.

Peggy and Rose were struggling upstairs with a completed frame, giggling so much that they were in danger of dropping it, when a knock sounded on the front door.

'That'll be Bob, I expect.'

'Don't let go, Peg. I'll drop it. Shout to Myrtle. She'll let him in.'

But when Myrtle opened the door, a man she didn't recognize, dressed in an unfamiliar uniform, was standing there.

'Hello, love. My name's Joe Bentley. I'm the air-raid precautions warden for this area. You're showing a light at the back.'

'Oh – er – yes. Sorry. We're just putting up the blackout.' Myrtle opened the door wider and indicated her two sisters halfway up the stairs.

'It should have all been up earlier than this.' Joe hesitated. He was a friend of Tom Bradshaw, who lived on the corner next door to the Booth household. They often played darts together on a Saturday night in their local pub. He knew all about Tom's neighbours from bits he'd overheard Letty Bradshaw telling his wife as they sat together drinking a half of shandy. There was no man in this house, Joe remembered, and though the girls were doing their best, it must be difficult, he thought, without a handyman around the place.

'Tell you what,' he said, removing his helmet and stepping through the door. 'Let me give you a hand. We'll have it all up in a jiffy.'

As Myrtle closed the front door, he nodded towards

the stained-glass panel in the upper half. 'You'll need a curtain across this an' all, love.'

Within an hour, Joe had helped put up frames or curtains over every window and all light showing from the house was successfully blotted out. As he left, with their effusive thanks still ringing in his ears, he reminded them, 'You've done a grand job, ladies, but don't forget a curtain for this door.'

'We'll do it right away, Mr Bentley,' Mary promised.

'And whilst you've got your saw handy, Rose,' Grace said, 'you can cut me a piece of that lath about a foot long and then mark it from one end at five inches.'

'Right-o, Gran. What's it for?'

'The bathroom. From now on that's the depth of water we're allowed to have. I don't want anyone painting a black line round my bath, thank you very much.'

'Five inches! That'll hardly cover my—'

'Thank you, Rose, that'll be enough of that. And another thing – we'll have to share bath water.'

Now four pairs of eyes stared at her.

'Well, if you're thinking I'm getting into the bath with either Peggy or Myrtle, you've got another think coming,' Rose said firmly.

'Don't be silly!' her grandmother snapped. 'Not taking a bath *together* – just using the same water like we used to do in the old days. Children first, then mother and, lastly, father.'

'That'll be me in first then,' Myrtle said happily, adding with a smirk, 'and you last, Gran.'

Grace glared at her and sniffed. 'I was thinking you three girls could share one lot of bath water and me and your mother another. I'd go first, of course. It is my bath and my water.'

'Of course, Gran,' the three girls chorused and avoided looking at each other in case they should burst out laughing. Grace frowned, but said nothing, whilst Mary turned away to hide her smile. After years of being reminded that she and her family were living with Grace under sufferance, she felt as if she now had three allies. Well, at least two in Peggy and Rose. She wasn't too sure about Myrtle; she and her grandmother often shared a joke at the expense of the others.

'What are these, Gran?' Myrtle asked on the following Saturday morning when there were only the two of them left in the house.

'A luggage label with your name and address on it. Everyone's got to carry them until we all get our identity cards.'

Grace had taken charge of all the public information leaflets that were being issued. She listened carefully to the announcements on the wireless and, when she went out shopping, she read all the posters that were appearing around the city.

'Identity cards?'

'Yes, we'll get them in about a month's time. But until then you carry this.' Grace handed a label to her. 'I'll leave these on the table for the others when they come in.'

Myrtle eyed her suspiciously. 'I thought these were only for kids being evacuated?' Her eyes narrowed. 'You're not thinking of sending me away after all, are you?'

'Only if the bombing got really bad here.'

Myrtle's eyes widened. 'It won't, will it? Not in Sheffield?'

'Nothing's happened yet as they expected, Myrtle. London's still expecting to be bombed any day and then the enemy will target other major cities. And, don't forget, we're a major industrial city and much of our output from now on will be for the war effort, I've no doubt. And you just be careful in this blackout, Myrtle. It'll soon be almost dark by the time you get in from school and—'

'Coo-ee – anybody home?' A voice sounded in the yard followed by a knock and then the sound of the back door opening. Grace groaned. 'Not her, again. She's been round twice today already.' She raised her voice. 'Come in. Make yourself at home.' She dropped her voice as she muttered, 'You will anyway.'

Letty Bradshaw – dressed as always in her pinafore, her hair covered by a headscarf folded into a turban – lived next door in the corner house of the terrace with her husband, Tom, and her family. She'd given birth to five boys. Her eldest son, Walter, was married and lived in Walkley and now worked in the steel industry. The second, Simon, had joined the navy and was somewhere at sea. The third, Albert, known as Bertie, was living in lodgings in London and was 'summat in the city', as Letty, with pride and something akin to awe in her tone, told anyone who would listen. Only the two youngest, Sidney, aged ten, and Jimmy, aged eight, now remained at home. They were the tearaways of the street and any pranks were always laid at their door whether the boys were guilty or not. They were often spanked by their father, whilst still protesting their innocence of a particular misdemeanour.

Tom was not fooled. 'Happen tha's done summat else, though, that ah don't know about,' he would say and the boys would grin, knowing full well that there was plenty of mischief their father didn't know about. They would take their punishment like the men they would one day be.

'Can I borrow a cup of sugar, love?' Letty began, almost before she stepped into the living room.

'You can and you're welcome,' Grace said. Whilst Letty irritated her almost beyond endurance at times with her gossiping, Grace was shrewd enough to know that in the coming months – maybe even years – neighbours would need each other. And Tom Bradshaw – big and burly and strong – was the nearest male that the Booth household had. But with him came his wife. So Letty had to be tolerated. And Grace realized that with five boys, one already in the navy, Letty would have her own anxieties to face.

'"Needs must . . .",' Grace could often be heard to mutter under her breath on various occasions and putting up with Letty Bradshaw was one such.

'But,' Grace went on now, 'we might not be able to oblige for much longer.'

Letty gaped at her. 'Eh?' Then she spotted the little pile of luggage labels on the table and the one Myrtle was holding. 'Tha's not goin' away? Not bein' evacuated?'

'No, no, but we've all got to carry these until we get our identity cards. And in another month or so – November they say – we'll get our ration books.'

'Ration books?'

'That's right. A lot of foodstuffs will be on ration and I've no doubt sugar will be one of them. So that's why I say you're welcome to a cupful now, but soon we'll all be going short.'

'Eh, tha's a mine of information, Mrs Booth. Who needs t' papers or t' wireless when tha's around? An' wait till I tell my Tom he'll 'ave to stop 'aving sugar in his tea. He'll not like that.'

'Then he'll have to lump it, Letty, just like we all will. Myrtle, get Letty a cup of sugar, love, will you? I'll have to sit down. I've been on my feet all day.' Grace sat down in her armchair and eased off her shoes. 'Queuing's getting bad already.'

'Hast tha had a stirrup pump and a shovel delivered?' Letty asked, sitting down uninvited as if settling down for a nice long chat. Grace glared at her but said nothing, whilst Myrtle hid her smile.

'We have. I've put them down the cellar.'

'What a' they for?'

'If we get incendiary bombs.'

'Oh, my lor',' Letty cried and fell back in the chair. 'It's really goin' to 'appen, Mrs Booth.'

Soberly Grace looked at Letty and was the gentlest she'd ever been with her exasperating neighbour. 'I'm afraid it is, Letty.'

'Oh, Mrs Booth,' Letty said, with tears in her eyes as the thought that had already struck Grace came into the woman's own mind. 'What's goin' to 'appen to my lovely boys?'

Five

On the following Monday Myrtle came home in a panic. 'What am I going to do? They might close our school. They're shutting all the elementary schools until further notice.'

Grace looked up over her glasses. 'Whatever for?'

'Because they say there aren't adequate air-raid shelters. If they do, we've to go to each other's houses for a bit until they get something organized.'

'And how long's that going to last?' Grace had visions of hordes of unruly schoolchildren crowding into her best front room.

'I don't know, but they won't be able to teach us properly like that.'

'Quite right, Myrtle,' Grace readily agreed. 'I don't want a gaggle of your classmates here. If you need to see a teacher, you go to wherever they are.'

'It won't be ideal, but it'll be better that you're safe,' Mary put in. 'You can study at home until they get some shelters organized.'

'But they said it might be a *whole term*.'

'It's not the end of the world.'

Myrtle glared balefully at her mother. It seemed like it to her.

*

Peggy completed her training and became a fully fledged clippie. She loved her new job, especially dealing with the awkward customers, whom she cajoled into good humour with a smile and a cheery word. Even the prospect of standing on a cold and draughty platform when winter came, punching tickets, giving change with frozen fingers and working the late shift: none of it fazed Peggy. And Laurence Bower had teamed her with Bob. He knew that the couple were walking out together, but as long as 'love's young dream' didn't get in the way of their work, then he was happy to play Cupid; a rather old and bullish one at times, Laurence realized, but even he had a softer side that not all of those under his charge saw very often.

From the beginning, when Peggy came home in her uniform and regaled the family with stories of the training and her first days as a clippie, Rose was even more determined to join her.

'We've already been warned that it's bitterly cold in winter and boiling in summer,' Peggy warned her. 'It's dirty and dusty – and you wouldn't believe the trouble we're likely to get from passengers sometimes. And by the end of an eight-hour lump – that's what they call a shift – my feet are killing me.'

'But you love it, don't you, Peg?'

Peggy's eyes had sparkled and she couldn't deny it. 'Yes, I do.'

'Will Bob have to go? You know, be called up?'

As the first volunteers were disappearing from their neighbourhood and even one or two men from work had gone already, Rose asked the question.

Peggy shook her head. 'He says not. Mr Bower saw a list published in *The Times* in January—'

Rose gasped. 'You mean they thought there was a war coming back then?'

Grace, overhearing, sniffed. 'Of course it was always coming. It never really ended last time. That's what the papers say, anyway. And we've had leaflets already telling us what to do if there's an invasion.'

'You shouldn't believe all you read in the newspapers, Mother,' Mary said mildly as she glanced up at Peggy. 'Go on, dear.'

'Nobody listens to me,' Grace muttered and then clamped her lips together as if determined to say no more.

'Mr Bower kept the list,' Peggy went on, 'just in case it came in useful, and it includes tram motormen, so he thinks at least they'll be exempt.'

But Grace's efforts to remain silent didn't last many minutes. 'Unless they volunteer, of course. And you know what fools men are.' She glanced up at Mary, silently reminding her that her husband, Ted, had been a gallant volunteer, but look where that had landed them all. 'You mark my words, they'll all go flocking to get themselves killed and we'll be left with silly young girls to drive our trams.'

Rose's eyes widened. 'Do you really think so, Gran?' She clapped her hands. 'Oh, I do hope you're right. I'll ask Mr Bower in the morning and get my name put down.'

The family all laughed at Rose's enthusiasm, not taking her seriously for a moment, but the very next day Rose cornered the inspector when he came into the canteen.

'Mr Bower, if a lot of the drivers leave, will you be

training up women to take their place, because if so I'd really like to be considered?'

'Whoa, whoa there, Rose. Hold your horses, love.' He peered at her closely. 'I thought you wanted to be a clippie like your sister.'

'I did – I *do*, but learning to drive a tram would be so much more exciting.'

'It's not about excitement, Rose. It's about keeping our passengers safe.'

'But *will* you be training girls?'

Laurence shook his head. 'I really don't know yet, lass. Management haven't said owt.'

'But if they do – *please*, Mr Bower.' She pretended to pout, but her eyes were full of mischief as she said, 'You know I always give you an extra spoonful of your favourite mashed potato.'

Laurence Bower wagged his forefinger playfully at her, trying hard to keep a stern expression on his face, but failing miserably. 'Don't think extra helpings are going to coerce me into giving you a new job. You're a bad 'un, Rose Sylvester. A real bad 'un.' Now he was grinning broadly, but then his smile faded and he became serious. 'I know you want to be a clippie like your sister. She's a good lass, bright and excellent with money. At the end of the day, her ticket takings are rarely wrong and she's calm in a crisis. We get a few awkward customers, y'know, but she can handle them.'

He regarded Rose thoughtfully. He was already on the lookout for a new batch of recruits. Maybe he could take a chance on Rose. 'Look, I tell you what, I'll see if I can get you on training up to be a clippie.'

'Oh, Mr Bower, *thank* you.' Rose flung her arms around his neck and kissed him soundly on the cheek.

''Ere, steady on, lass. What if someone sees us?'

Rose giggled deliciously. 'Well, it wouldn't be the first bit of scandal in the depot, would it?'

Now that women were being trained as conductresses, rumours were always rife about tram drivers and their clippies getting a little too close to each other. But when you thought about it, Rose said, they spent more hours with their work colleagues than they did with their families. And look at Peggy and Bob, though at least neither of them was already married.

Laurence found himself smiling; you couldn't help it for long when Rose Sylvester was around. For a lot of reasons she'd make a good clippie, and her passengers would love her. He just dreaded the moment when her ticket takings would be counted each night! Now, though, he chuckled. 'Well, there's never been any gossip about me and I don't want there to be, even though I'm a widower and thought to be fair game by some of the older women. So keep your kisses for your boyfriend, there's a good lass.'

'Haven't got one, Mr Bower,' Rose said cheerfully.

'I can't believe that. I'spect you're keeping them all at arm's length until Mr Right comes along, eh?'

Rose stared at him and the smile faded from her face.

'What? What have I said?'

'N-nothing,' Rose stammered, but he had. Mr Right, he'd said. And now the full force of the truth hit her like a sledgehammer. Mr Right – *her* Mr Right – had come along.

The only problem was – he was in love with her sister.

*

That night, in the single bed set close to Myrtle's in the small attic room, Rose lay awake staring into the darkness, trying to come to terms with her devastating realization about her feelings for Bob Deeton. He was so kind and caring. He was good-looking too – at least Rose thought so. With light brown hair and hazel eyes. He had a stray curl that flopped onto his forehead and Rose longed to stroke it back into place. She even found his shyness endearing. He was nothing like one of those conceited, full-of-themselves young men and she liked that. But he wasn't hers, he was Peggy's, and so Rose must treat Bob like the brother none of them had ever had. She'd laugh and joke with him but she'd be careful never to let him – or anyone else – see how much she cared for him.

It wasn't going to be easy, but she'd do it. For her sister and for him. If Peggy was the one he wanted, then she just hoped her sister would make him happy. Instead, Rose vowed, she'd give up all thoughts of Bob Deeton and concentrate on being the best clippie Mr Bower had ever had.

'I won't have to have a medical, will I, seeing as I already work for the company?'

'I think it would be best, Rose,' Laurence Bower said. 'It's a very different job from working in the canteen.'

Rose shrugged. She was confident that she would pass A1. She'd rarely had a day's illness in her life, except for the usual childish complaints in her school days. Since she'd started work she'd never taken a day's sick leave.

The doctor was a dour man, who spoke little and when he did it sounded as if he was permanently angry.

'Have you brought another woman with you as chaperone?' he asked when Rose entered the room where the medical inspections were being held.

'Eh?' Rose blinked in surprise and then she smiled impishly. 'It's all right, Doc. I don't mind.'

'But I do,' he snapped. 'I don't want some foolish young woman making a complaint about me.' Rose opened her mouth to protest angrily, but he ignored her and went to the door, opened it and asked the secretary seated outside to come in. The woman was clearly embarrassed, but did as she was asked, standing awkwardly in the corner whilst Rose was examined. The doctor listened to her chest, speaking only to say, 'Breathe in' or 'Breathe out.' He tested her sight and her reflexes. He examined her feet closely and then weighed and measured her.

'You may get dressed,' he said curtly as he sat down at his desk, picked up his pen and began to write. When she was ready he merely nodded and said, 'You may go.'

'Have I passed?' Rose asked eagerly.

'You'll be informed,' the doctor said stiffly. Rose left the room, raising her eyes skywards as she passed the woman now seated back at her desk. The woman smiled and gave the tiniest of nods to show that she understood and empathized. Rose went back to the room where eight other women who had also applied to become clippies were waiting for their turn to be examined.

'He's an old goat,' Rose said, as she sat down beside a girl who didn't look old enough to have left school, let alone become a tram conductress. She looked nervous and agitated, twisting her fingers together in her lap. Rose took pity on her. 'Like me to come in with you? He seems to want another woman there when he's examining someone.'

Relief flooded the girl's face. 'Oh, would you? My husband would have come, but he's away in the army.'

Husband! Rose nearly fell off her chair and before she could stop herself, the words were out of her mouth. 'You're married?' Nor could she stop the surprise in her tone. The girl must have been used to such comments, for she smiled shyly and said, 'I'm older than I look. I'll be twenty next month. We – we got married in April this year.' Now she looked away, as if embarrassed, and avoided meeting Rose's gaze. Instead, she murmured, 'My name's Alice. Alice Wagstaffe.'

'And I'm Rose Sylvester. Pleased to meet you.'

When Alice was called in to see the doctor, Rose got up too and followed her in. 'I thought I'd save the secretary the trouble of coming in again.'

The doctor glared at her for a moment, grunted something unintelligible and then got on with his examination of Alice, ignoring Rose completely.

'Phew!' Alice said, as they stepped out of the room a little while later. 'Thank goodness that's over. But now we've got the mental tests to get through.'

'They'll be dead easy,' Rose said confidently as the nine women were taken to a large room, where the secretary was waiting for them. She smiled as the applicants filed in.

'My name is Mrs Kerr. Please sit down.' She waved towards the chairs set around a large table in the centre of the room. Then she handed out sheets of paper and pencils.

'Write your name at the top, please.' She sat down

at the end of the table and began to read out sums, giving only a short space of time between each question.

'156 tickets at 7½ pence . . . 67 at a ha'penny . . . 942 at 2½ pence . . .' There were twenty such sums to do quickly. Rose was the first to finish and sat with her arms folded. She felt as if she was back at school and looked up expectantly for the teacher's praise, but more sums were to come. Additions, subtractions and more multiplication. When all the candidates had done as many as they could manage, the woman collected the papers, smiled at them briefly and left the room, saying, 'I'll be taking each one of you individually for an interview. Please wait here until you are called.'

'By 'eck,' a middle-aged woman said as the door closed. 'I didn't reckon on all this. I couldn't do them sums for toffee. What about you lot?'

One or two others nodded agreement, but those who had found the arithmetic tests quite easy – Rose amongst them – said nothing. They didn't want to sound boastful. One by one they were called out of the room and were away for about ten minutes. When Rose's name was called, she followed Mrs Kerr into a smaller room. Behind the desk, set in the centre of the room, sat a man of about forty dressed in an inspector's uniform. Mrs Kerr introduced her. 'Mr Marsden, this is Miss Rose Sylvester.' Then she gestured towards the chair where Rose should sit, turned and left the room, closing the door quietly behind her.

The man didn't smile at her, but his voice was deep and pleasant as he said, 'Just a few questions, Miss Sylvester. We usually set a written questionnaire, but because of the urgent need for staff we've had to cut out some of the usual tests. We need to speed up the process. Do you still live at home?'

Rose explained the circumstances of her family life, ending, 'My sister, Peggy, is a clippie.'

He gave a brief nod, but made no comment and Rose felt a little foolish. Perhaps it had sounded as if just because her sister was already employed as a conductress she thought that she too should be taken on. For a moment Rose was flustered as she added quickly, 'What I mean is I know what the job entails, the shift work and such.'

'Of course. And you work in the canteen, so you already know a lot of the drivers, don't you?'

At the thought of Bob Deeton, Rose felt sudden, unexpected tears prickle her eyes. 'Yes,' she said huskily. 'I do.'

'Then I think you'll do very nicely, Miss Sylvester. I'm putting you forward for training and, subject to you doing well on the course, we'll be pleased to take you on.'

Rose stood up and held out her hand. 'Thank you, oh, thank you. I'll not let you down.' The man seemed a little startled by her effusive thanks, but he shook her hand and, at last, gave a little smile.

As Rose rode home on the tram, she watched the clippie. She'd paid little heed before, but now her eyes followed the girl's every movement and she listened to the merry banter between the conductress and her passengers. That, of course, would be no problem for the ebullient Rose!

She alighted at the tram stop on Northfield Road and ran down the hill towards her home. She burst into the house and danced round the kitchen table, grabbing hold of Peggy and whirling her around too, singing, 'I'm going to be a clippie – I'm going to be a clippie.'

When they'd collapsed against each other, laughing

and breathless, and Rose had calmed down a little she told Peggy, Grace and Mary all about the medical, the arithmetic test and her interview. 'And I'm to report tomorrow morning for training.'

'Well done, Rose. It's what you've always wanted.'

Rose's expression sobered. 'It is, Mam, but I do realize that, if it hadn't been for the war, I might never have been taken on. Mr Bower doesn't think I've the makings of a good clippie, but I think his hand's been forced by the urgent need for more drivers and conductresses.'

'Well.' Mary smiled. 'You'll just have to prove him wrong, love, won't you?'

Six

When Rose stepped into the training room the following morning she found several of the girls and women
who'd been interviewed at the same time as her already
there, but there were others too whom she had not seen
before. Obviously, there had been more interview ses-
sions and now they'd come together for training. There
were twenty in all. Most of them were young, but there
were a few older married women who were there to
undertake war work.

'Rose?'

She turned to see the young woman she'd met the
previous day, Alice Wagstaffe. 'Oh, how lovely. You
made it too then.'

Alice nodded shyly and bit her lip. 'To my surprise,
yes.'

'Why do you say that?'

'Well, I – er – I've not been well lately. I thought I'd
fail the medical for a start – ' she smiled faintly – 'but
here I am.'

Rose linked her arm through the other girl's. 'You'll
be fine. Look, we'll sit together.'

They sat down at the desks and as Mr Marsden, the
inspector who'd interviewed them, entered the room,
the other women found places too. Rose glanced
around the walls at the posters and pictures of trams,
but then Mr Marsden's voice brought her attention

back to him and their instruction began. Firstly, he explained that their period of tuition was to be half the time they usually gave trainees. 'The war had impelled us to make changes,' he said, as he walked between the rows of desks, handing out a book of rules to each of them. 'It would therefore be helpful if you could do some work at home.'

The rest of that first day was spent with the inspector going through the rulebook, explaining the reason behind each regulation and its level of importance, but above all, he said, the comfort, welfare and safety of the passengers were paramount.

'The most difficult thing,' Mr Marsden explained seriously, 'is to deal with those members of the public who, shall we say, can be confrontational. Employees of the company must at all times remain patient, avoiding arguments and yet at the same time maintaining firm control of any situation. It isn't easy.'

'A good clip round the ear,' someone muttered, 'is what they need. I thought that was why we were called "clippies".'

Smothered laughter rippled around the room and even Mr Marsden's lips twitched; he couldn't have failed to hear the remark. But after that any tension there had been in the room evaporated and even Alice, sitting nervously beside Rose, seemed to relax.

'My head's spinning,' Rose said as the day ended and they trooped out of the training room. 'Let's go to the big canteen and get a nice cup of tea. It's where I used to work.' She lowered her voice. 'My mates will find us one.'

They entered the canteen to be greeted with good-humoured jeering from the girls serving meals, copious cups of tea and cakes. 'Here she comes. The traitor.'

But Rose only grinned and led her new friend to a table. 'Two teas, miss, please,' she said loftily.

'Huh!' Sally, up until the previous day her work mate, laughed. 'The cheek of the besom. What d'you think I am, Miss High 'n' Mighty. A waitress?' Rose and Sally fell into fits of giggles. She came to the table and put her hand on Rose's shoulder. ''Course I'll get you some tea. We're all pleased for you, 'cos we know it's what you've always wanted, but we'll miss you. This place won't be the same without you.'

'Thank goodness,' someone called from behind the serving counter, but Rose knew it was only banter. When Sally brought the tea, there were three cups on the tray. 'Mind if I join you? I want to hear all about it. I'm thinking of applying myself.'

'Oh do, Sal,' Rose urged. 'You'd love it.'

For the next half an hour the three girls chatted. 'I'll have to go,' Sally said reluctantly at last. 'Be seeing you and good luck.'

As they walked out Rose asked, 'You said you'd been ill, Alice. Are you sure you're quite better because you do look a little pale? This job's not going to be easy, you know.'

'I'll be fine. It – it'll take my mind off things.'

'Oh – your husband being away, you mean?'

'That – and . . .' She hesitated and then, taking a deep breath, confided, 'I had a miscarriage two months ago. I'm fine physically, the doctor says, but it's – it's just taking me some time to get come to terms with it. I – we – so wanted a baby. And now . . .' Her voice trailed away.

Rose squeezed Alice's arm, but didn't quite know what to say. She could only guess at the devastating hurt the girl was feeling. The hectic working life of a clippie would certainly take Alice's mind off her sadness, but Rose was worried that, despite what she'd said, the girl wasn't yet physically fit enough. The days would be long and hard, standing on the draughty platform of a city tramcar, wrestling with a swaying vehicle, locking horns with truculent passengers and making sure the correct tickets were issued and the right amount of money taken.

But Rose couldn't wait to get started!

The following morning's tuition began with a brief recap of the rules, over which Rose had pored the previous evening sitting beside Myrtle at the table, much to the younger girl's amusement. Rose had never been the studious type, but here she was burying her head in the rulebook and murmuring aloud. Myrtle grinned. 'Want me to test you?' she asked facetiously, but Rose nodded and said seriously, 'Yes, please, Myrtle. Would you?'

Myrtle blinked and teased her no more. Now she realized just how serious Rose was about her new job. And when Bob called to take Peggy to the cinema later that evening, he sat down and gave Rose some valuable tips.

'Mind you get on good terms with your motorman, or motor*men*, because you might not always be with the same one. They'll help you. They're a good bunch.'

Rose nodded and swallowed hard. How she wished it could be Bob who'd be her driver.

Now, as the trainees assembled once more, she sat beside Alice again. After they'd read through the rulebook yet again, Mr Marsden handed out a black box and a bundle of different-coloured tickets. 'Familiarize yourselves with the different tickets and remember you must call out all the stopping places as you approach and also the end of each stage.'

Rose's hand shot in the air. 'I'm sorry, sir, but I don't understand what you mean.'

'You call out the name of the stop,' Mr Marsden said patiently, 'and the end of the fare they've paid. For example, "End of one penny stage."'

'Oh, I see. Thanks.'

'Don't mention it,' he murmured, giving one of his rare smiles. 'That's what I'm here for.' He addressed the whole class. 'Don't be afraid to ask questions.'

'You're very patient,' one of the older women ventured and Mr Marsden's smile broadened. 'As must you be with your passengers. I've had plenty of practice.'

After hearing about bell pulling, emergency brakes and fare stages, there followed a session of ticket punching, which left the class in hysterical laughter. Mr Marsden calmed them down by having each one of them read aloud one of the rules from the book. 'You have to get used to speaking loudly and clearly.'

Rose read with confidence, but Alice was timid, her voice barely above a whisper.

'We'll work on it,' Rose promised.

Alice smiled weakly. 'I'll never manage all this. I think I ought to give up now.'

'Don't you dare,' Rose said. 'We're in this together.'

At the end of the afternoon, the trainees trooped to the clothing store, where a woman measured each one of them for their uniforms. Now they began to feel like real clippies.

'Isn't it funny,' Rose remarked, as they once again

found their way to the canteen, 'how a uniform makes you feel the part? It gives you confidence, somehow, though I don't know why it should.'

'Maybe it's because it gives you a certain authority. People know you're the one in charge. Most people will accept that, though a few won't, like Mr Marsden warned us.'

'You'll be all right, Alice.'

Alice bit her lip. She wasn't so sure. There was so much to learn: how to fill in all sorts of forms and reports and even how to read the duty boards on the walls of the depot, put up every Thursday night, which would tell them what their journeys and break times would be for each week.

'It's not a journey they call it, is it?' Alice said worriedly. 'What is it?'

'A detail.'

'Oh yes, that's it. And a break is a "relief".' She giggled. 'I expect it's called that because it will be a relief if you're having a bad day.'

Worst of all for Rose, though, was to learn that should there be any short-fall in the money handed in at the end of the day, the clippie had to make up any difference. 'I'll be paying them to come to work,' she moaned. And now it was Alice's turn to do the comforting. 'You'll be all right, Rose. You came out top of the class in the mental arithmetic tests.'

It was true, but the classroom atmosphere was very different to working on a swaying, tram crowded with impatient passengers.

Two evenings later Peggy asked, 'So how's it all going?'

Rose sighed. 'All right, I think. Today they took us

to get some practical experience. We went up and down this hilly side road – I don't know how many times. We took turns to stop the car. And then there was the phone to the main office in an emergency and all sorts of things I can't even remember now. Oh, Peg, I didn't realize there'd be so much to learn.'

Peggy laughed. 'I've had it said to me more than once that all we clippies have to do is to punch tickets all day, but I just smile nicely and hold my tongue.'

'I can't see Rose doing that for long,' Grace remarked. 'It won't be only tickets she'll be punching if anyone gets awkward with her.'

'She'll have to,' Peggy said gravely. 'The Company puts courtesy towards the passengers only second to regard for their safety.'

'Have you got your uniform yet?' Myrtle looked up from her homework.

'In a few days, I think.' Rose pulled a face. 'We've still got a few more days in the classroom yet. How you stick staying on at school, our Myrtle, I don't know. Not that we don't want you to,' she added swiftly.

'I might have to leave,' Myrtle said, 'now there's a war on.'

There was a chorus of 'no' from every member of her family and Myrtle hid her smile; it had been the response she'd wanted.

Rose came home with her uniform. It fitted her perfectly.

'Oh, you do look smart,' Mary enthused, and even Grace looked up from her paper and nodded as Rose paraded in front of them in her navy-blue jacket, skirt and peaked cap. She'd also been given a pair of trousers and a thick overcoat.

'Tomorrow we go out on a real live tram – under the supervision of a trained clippie, of course.'

Peggy smiled. 'That'll be me, then.'

'Eh?' Rose blinked at her. 'They won't let me go out with my sister, will they?'

'I asked Mr Bower today and he said he didn't see why not.'

Rose flung her arms round Peggy and hugged her. 'But you'll have to do everything I tell you,' Peggy warned. 'I'm no soft touch.'

And indeed she wasn't. The following morning when they reported for duty at the timekeeper's office, Rose glanced about her. She'd never been to this part of the depot before and the trams looked far bigger than they did out in the streets. But there was no time to gape, Peggy was already showing her how to put the heavy punch over one shoulder, the money bag over the other and then load the ticket rack with the multi-coloured tickets, each one clearly stamped with its value.

'Most clippies wear the punch from their right shoulder across their chest and resting on their left hip and the money bag the opposite way.' Peggy laughed. 'I'm awkward. I wear mine the other way on. Just try them out and see which suits you best.'

When Rose had settled the machine and the bag comfortably, Peggy said, 'Come on. We're lucky today, we've to pick up our tram here, but sometimes we have to travel into the city to start our detail.'

Bob was waiting for them by the navy-blue and cream-coloured tramcar.

'Morning, Rose. All set?'

Rose ran a nervous tongue round her lips. 'Ready,' she said, with more conviction than she felt.

As they boarded the car to begin their journey, Peggy proved to be a disciplined taskmaster.

'First, we make sure that the seat backs are positioned correctly.' The trams only travelled backwards and forwards – they couldn't turn round. The motorman controlled the tram from either end and the backs of the seats flipped over so that passengers could always travel facing forward. 'And make sure the cleaners have done their job properly.'

Rose followed Peggy up and down each aisle, glancing to each side. She loved the interior of the tramcar with its plush green-patterned seats in the lower car and red leather seats upstairs. On the lower deck at both ends stairs curved upwards behind where the motorman stood at the controls.

'Passengers should get on and off at the opposite end to wherever the driver is. And remember,' Peggy warned as they moved off, 'when the car's full, you put the rope across and shout, "Another one behind." You'll get some abuse, but just smile and never, ever, get involved in a slanging match with a passenger.'

For the first ten minutes Rose found it hard to concentrate; Bob was so close and she was hard pressed not to keep glancing towards him. But, as the car began to fill up with passengers, her mind was fully occupied in punching tickets, taking the correct fare and giving change. By their first relief, the huge money bag she'd been given was heavy with takings.

'This is killing my shoulder,' Rose moaned.

'You'll soon get used to it.' Peggy laughed as Bob joined them in the mess room for a welcome cup of tea.

'Let's just hope when you make your waybill out tonight, everything tallies.'

'It won't,' Bob said, 'but don't worry about it. Mr Bower is lenient with trainees.'

But Rose wasn't so sure. The job she'd hankered after wasn't as easy as she'd thought. She watched her sister with growing admiration. It was wonderful how Peggy seemed to know which poor old lady really needed a hand on and off the tram and which was putting it on. She hadn't known her older sister could engage in banter with the men and fend off the advances of the cheekier ones.

'Coming out with me tonight, darlin'?' one smartly dressed young man asked Peggy as he hopped on to the tram and refused to leave the platform to take a seat. 'Ah've got summat ah'd like to show thee.'

'Sorry, love. I'm washing my hair.'

Nonplussed, the young man winked saucily. 'What about ya mate here, then?'

'That's my sister and she'll be helping me wash my hair. Now, if you'd move down the car, love, and let the other passengers get on, we'll be on our way all the quicker.'

Rose could hardly hide her laughter, but then she was plunged once more into punching tickets for all those who had just boarded the car and remembering to shout out the next stop.

When they reached the terminus, Peggy reminded her to go down the line of seats, flicking the backs over.

'Clever, isn't it? And what's the other thing you must remember?'

'Oh heck – I don't know,' Rose moaned, looking so woebegone that Peggy laughed. 'To carry your gas mask, silly.'

'Not something else to hang round my neck!' Rose sighed and then grinned. 'But half the passengers getting on the trams aren't carrying their gas masks.'

'That's no excuse,' Peggy said primly. 'Mr Bower says we must set a good example.'

'I wonder how poor Alice is managing,' Rose thought while she counted out change as the tram swayed around a corner, only to be told that she'd given a penny short.

Alice, it seemed, had had a better day than Rose. Under the tutelage of an experienced and patient older man, she'd got the hang of everything very quickly. 'Although I nearly sat on one feller's lap when the car lurched. He didn't seem to mind, though.'

'I bet he didn't.' Rose laughed wryly.

'And my figures tallied,' Alice smiled triumphantly.

'Well done, you,' Rose said and added mournfully, 'I wish mine had.'

'See you tomorrow.' Alice smiled as they parted company outside the depot.

'That's the most cheerful I've seen her,' Rose confided to Peggy. 'She's had a bit of a hard time of it. But it looks like she's taken to a clippie's life like the proverbial duck to water.'

'And so will you,' Peggy said, linking arms. 'Come on, let's catch the tram home.'

As they sat down with a sigh and Rose eased her aching feet out of her shoes, she noticed that the conductress passed by them and didn't ask for their fares.

'Don't we pay?' Rose whispered to her sister.

'We never charge other staff and you're one of us now.'

Rose felt a warm glow. At last, she was a real clippie.

Seven

At the beginning of December Rose brought home a copy of *Picture Post*.

'Here you are, Gran, I thought you'd like to read this. The editor says we ought to spend at Christmas – not save.'

Grace frowned, but picked up the magazine and leafed through the pages. Then she began to read. After a moment, she chuckled. 'He's telling you to give National Savings Certificates or War Bonds as presents.'

'Read on, Gran.' Rose grinned. ' "Or on ordinary purchases", he says.'

'Encouraging a lot of folk, who can't afford it, to be extravagant,' Grace muttered. 'Well, you'll each get a War Bond from me, so that's that.'

'Eat, drink and be merry, that's what I say, and show Hitler he can't get us down.'

It had been a strange few months in the run-up to the first Christmas of the war. Whilst hordes of children had been evacuated from London and other big cities to the safety of the countryside, the anticipated bombing had not happened, so many had drifted back home.

'There, you see, I told you so,' Myrtle had said triumphantly. 'If you'd sent me away, I'd have been coming back by now.' Myrtle had flatly refused to consider being evacuated. 'It'll interrupt my education,' she'd argued. 'And besides, Gran says the cellar's safe enough.'

But there were other things over which the family had no choice. Blackout regulations were in full force and economies were already being advised. Rationing had not yet started, but was threatened for early in the New Year.

'Better make the most of it,' Mary said. 'We don't know what might be happening by another Christmas.'

'Oh, it'll all be over by then,' Rose said cheerfully.

'Peggy, would you like to invite Bob and his mother to have Christmas dinner with us?'

Before Peggy could reply Grace butted in. 'I think you're forgetting that this is my house and I'll say who we invite. I don't want a lot of strangers in and out of the house on Christmas morning. It'd be like Victoria Station. Can't we have a bit of peace for once?'

'Oh, but Mother, Bob and Mrs Deeton are all on their own. I thought it'd be nice for them – and for Peggy.'

'No doubt it would,' Grace said shortly.

'And I thought we might ask Mr Bower,' Rose put in, mischievously adding fuel to the argument. 'He's a widower and, from what he said yesterday, he'll be all on his own.'

'He's got a brother, who's a farmer in Derbyshire,' Peggy said. 'Someone said he usually goes there for Christmas.'

'He has – but his sister-in-law is ill in hospital and he says his brother's at his wits' end to cope anyway without having a visitor at Christmas.'

'Oh, why don't you invite them all?' Grace snapped. 'What about Letty and Tom Bradshaw from next door? I'm sure Letty would love to get her nose in.'

Rose's mouth twitched. She knew her grandmother was being sarcastic, but, impishly, she pretended to take the old lady seriously. 'Well, we could.'

Grace glared at her. 'You'll do no such thing.' She paused and then added, reluctantly, 'But I suppose you can ask the others. I don't like to hear of folks being lonely at Christmas.'

Though she would never have admitted it, it was Grace's biggest fear. Despite her constant grumbling about never having any peace in *her* house, in truth it was the last thing she wanted.

The only person who, surprisingly, did not seem too keen on the idea was Peggy. And Rose had mixed feelings. Though she longed to be near Bob, to talk and joke with him, she knew it would be a double-edged sword. She would have to watch whilst Bob made sheep's eyes at her sister and it would be like a knife through her heart.

A knock at the door on Christmas Eve revealed Laurence Bower carrying something wrapped in cheese-cloth. As he stepped across the threshold, he said, 'Mrs Sylvester, I hope you will accept this as a gesture of my gratitude for your kind invitation to spend tomorrow with you. It's a turkey from my brother's farm.'

'A turkey! Oh, how wonderful, but you shouldn't really, Mr Bower . . .'

'Please call me Laurence.'

'And I'm Mary,' she said, taking the bundle from him.

'I've taken the liberty of bringing the ingredients for the stuffing. I hope I'm not being too presumptuous.'

'Of course not. We were planning beef, but I was so worried it wasn't going to stretch to enough for all of us. This is a godsend. It really is. Thank you so much.'

'Please don't mention it. You won't believe how much I'm looking forward to tomorrow when all I was facing was another lonely day.'

'You're most welcome.' Mary laughed as she added, 'And not just because of the turkey.'

Grace and her three granddaughters looked up in surprise when they saw whom Mary was ushering into the room. 'Do sit down, Mr Bower.'

'Laurence, please.' He glanced at the two girls who were his employees and smiled. 'Just for Christmas,' he added with an impish smile.

'Would you like a glass of sherry?' Grace offered, deciding to play the gracious host. This man had been good to her granddaughters and she didn't want to appear churlish.

'No, no, I won't tonight. I have to go back to the depot – just to make sure everything's all right. It's been a busy day.'

'Hasn't it just,' Rose remarked with feeling. 'My feet are killing me.'

'How's she doing?' Grace asked Laurence, gesturing towards Rose.

'Very well.' Laurence couldn't keep the surprise out of his tone and the whole family laughed. For a moment, the man was embarrassed; he hadn't meant it to sound so obvious.

'I've surprised myself,' Rose said generously, 'never mind anyone else. And that first night when my ticket takings didn't tally, I thought I was going to be sacked before I'd hardly started.'

'There's not many it doesn't happen to the first day or two, but you've been spot on ever since and I hear very good reports from your motorman.'

Jack Wainwright was the tram driver with whom

Rose worked the most. He was a middle-aged, married man with two children. The older one – the boy – was already in the army, and Rose was acutely aware of the burden of anxiety Jack carried daily. His daughter was coming up to school-leaving age.

'I'm dreading her having to go out into the big wide world,' he confided in Rose. 'She's a shy little thing. I wish she had more of your spirit, Rose. Girls need it, especially now. Goodness knows what sort of a job they'll find her.'

Over the next few weeks Rose and her motorman talked a lot during their relief times and became good friends. She knew she could rely on him whenever she needed help or guidance. Laurence Bower could not have teamed her with anyone better. Now a pink tinge of pleasure coloured her face to think that Jack had spoken so highly of her to the inspector.

Christmas Day was a merry affair for the family. Peggy had brought down a box of Christmas decorations from the attic cupboard behind Myrtle's bed.

'These are starting to look a bit sorry for themselves,' she said, pulling out crumpled coloured paper chains. 'But I suppose they'll have to do for this year.'

'I've made some paper hats out of newspaper,' Myrtle said, holding up a Nelson-shaped triangular hat.

'Is that my paper?' Grace asked sharply.

'It's yesterday's, Gran, don't panic.'

'Less of your cheek, miss. I might not have finished reading it.'

'You read them from front to back every morning, Gran,' Rose said, sticking up for her younger sister.

Grace muttered and rustled the paper she was reading. 'That's as maybe, but she should ask first.'

'Sorry, Gran,' Myrtle said. She didn't want to fall out with the old lady. She and her grandmother had a special relationship; they shared the same wry sense of humour and could always be relied upon to drop in a sarcastic remark at any opportunity. Whatever was happening, it was Grace and Myrtle who shared an amused glance.

Hester Deeton and Bob arrived armed with little gifts for each member of the family. 'And I've made a cake,' Hester said uncertainly. 'I hope it'll be acceptable.'

'Acceptable, Mrs Deeton? It'll be wonderful,' Peggy assured her. 'We couldn't get all the ingredients to make our usual cake, though Mam has managed two puddings. There seem to be shortages already.'

'I'd put things aside from the summer. It's not hoarding,' Hester added swiftly, in case anyone should think she was breaking the advice the authorities were already handing out and what would soon become law when rationing started in earnest.

Laurence Bower arrived just before lunch with a box of chocolates. As he handed them to Mary he said, 'These are for all the family, but mind you pick out your favourites. You must have been working so hard to get everything ready for today.'

'I've had help. Mother still does a lot of the cooking and the girls are very good.'

'Still—' Laurence looked into Mary's eyes as he added softly, 'You deserve a little treat.' Laurence had never looked at anyone else since the death of his wife, but Mary was still a pretty woman with a slim figure and gentle brown eyes and Laurence found himself

57

experiencing feelings he thought had gone forever. He'd lived a solitary existence for the last three years, but now he wondered whether, at forty-five, he was foolish to resign himself to a life of loneliness. He sat beside Mary at the dinner table and joined in the merry banter. Even Hester, after two glasses of sherry and with spots of colour in her cheeks, relaxed and for a brief time managed to put aside the many anxieties which life seemed to hold for her. Bob, sitting between Peggy and Rose, was the life and soul of the party. After lunch, when they'd all taken turns to help with the washing up – all except Grace, who everyone insisted should put her feet up – it was Bob who organized games and quizzes.

For a few hours they were able to put aside all thoughts of the war, of its impending restrictions and dangers and, by late evening when the visitors left, every one of them declared it to be the best Christmas they could remember.

Eight

Only a few days after Christmas Letty came bursting in through the back door, tears streaming down her face. 'They've only gone and done it, the silly buggers. In't it enough that I've got one lad in danger, without them going an' all?'

Grace bent to put two cakes in the range oven and closed the door carefully. Straightening up, she said, with a sigh, 'What's them two rascals done this time?'

'Eh?' Letty blinked and then, as realization came to her, she shook her head. 'Oh, no, t'ain't the two young 'uns. Not this time. 'Tis Walter and Bertie.'

Grace stared at her for a moment and then guessing what had happened said kindly, 'Sit down, Letty, and tell me all about it.'

'They've only gone and volunteered, that's what.'

'Never? Well, they want their heads banging together, Letty. They'd no need to go yet. At least they could've waited until they were called up.'

'I know,' Letty wailed as fresh tears welled in her eyes. 'And t'daft part about it is, Walter might not've had to go at all. His firm's turning to some sort of war production, so they say. Likely he'd've been in a – what do they call it?'

'Reserved occupation.'

'That's it.' She paused a moment before adding flatly, 'Bertie might have had to go anyway, but he needn't

59

have gone yet. He could've waited. I mean, it's not like last time, is it? Folks aren't going round handing out white feathers, are they? At least, not yet.'

'What service have they joined? The navy, like their brother?'

"No. Walter's going in the army and Bertie's signed up to go into the RAF. He wants to be a fighter pilot.'

'Oh, well now,' Grace said, trying to lighten the woman's misery. 'If the Bradshaw boys have got all three services covered, the war'll soon be over.'

But poor Letty was not in the mood for levity and Grace's weak attempt at humour fell flat.

'They came home at Christmas. We all had a lovely time.'

'We heard,' Grace murmured.

'Oh dear, did we disturb you?'

'Of course not. It was grand to hear you all having fun. Besides, we had visitors and were making quite a bit of noise ourselves.' Grace would never have admitted it, but she had thoroughly enjoyed Christmas Day. She hesitated and then asked, 'Was that when they told you?'

Letty shook her head. 'No, it might have been better if they had, in a way. They let us all have a good Christmas and then dropped their bombshell. But it took all the pleasure out of it, you know.'

Grace nodded sympathetically. 'I can understand that. But they meant well, Letty. They didn't want to spoil the festivities. I'd say that was thoughtful of them.'

Letty sighed. 'I suppose you're right, but it was just – sort of – going from one extreme to the other.'

They talked for a while, Grace trying to instil in the distressed woman some pride in her sons' actions. After Letty had left, Grace sat in her chair deep in thought.

In the Great War, she had thought that volunteers were fools and she hadn't hesitated to say so. She'd believed that though everyone should do their duty for their country, they should at least wait until they were called up. But now she wondered if she'd been wrong. No one nowadays could be ignorant or naive about what might happen. The newspapers and wireless left no doubt as to the dangers ahead. This war was going to be so much closer to home. Their country was under threat. It was not going to be fought in some far-off land. Not this time.

And for the first time in her life, Grace couldn't help feeling a sneaking admiration for these brave young men, who were prepared to defend their freedom from a tyrannical oppressor.

'As if we haven't got enough to contend with,' Grace grumbled. 'What with all the rationing and now this. We won't even be able to get to the shops, ne'er mind queuing.'

Rationing of certain foodstuffs – butter, sugar and bacon – had started at the beginning of January and now, towards the end of the month, the weather had worsened and storms swept across the country. Four feet of snow fell and the city's transport system was badly affected.

'Do we even have to go into work?' Rose asked.

Peggy shrugged. 'I expect we'll have to report for duty – if we can get there, that is.'

Rose pulled a face. 'I don't fancy getting wet wading through piles of snow, just to be told the trams aren't running.'

As they all finished eating their evening meal, Mary

stood up. 'Right, Peggy, it's you and me on washing-up duties.'

'It's Myrtle's turn by rights,' Grace put in.

'She's got her homework to finish off for tomorrow morning,' Mary said.

Myrtle hid her smile and picked up her satchel from the floor as Rose began to clear a space for her. 'It'll be icy in our bedroom. We can't afford the coal to light a fire up there. You'd better do it down here tonight.'

'Does she have to?' Grace asked. 'I want to listen to the wireless tonight. You know I like to hear the news, especially on a Sunday when we don't have a newspaper.' The square wireless had been moved to stand on a small table beside Grace's fireside chair. It was she who operated it and determined what the family listened to.

'It won't bother me, Gran,' Myrtle said. 'Besides, I like to hear the news too. Our headmistress says we should take an active interest in everything that's happening.'

'By the way, Gran,' Peggy asked, 'did you find out if we've got to have a Morrison or an Anderson shelter?'

Grace shook her head. 'Neither. A man came yesterday and inspected the cellar. He says it'll be quite adequate—'

'Unless,' Myrtle murmured, 'we get a direct hit.'

Grace glared at her. 'I hadn't finished. If we get a direct hit, my girl, no Anderson shelter is going to save us. But we might just have a chance in the cellar if, the man said, we have it reinforced. And,' she added, with a grimace, 'we've to have a doorway knocked through from ours into the neighbour's cellar so that if either of us did get a direct hit, there'd be a way out. I've already been in touch with a builder. He's sending two men tomorrow. He reckons it won't take long. A couple of days at the most. So, I expect I'll have to put up with Letty Bradshaw joining us, as well as Hitler's bombs, because if there's an open door there'll be no stopping her.'

'Now, now, Mother, Letty's not so bad. And don't forget, her lads have cleared the snow for us.'

Grace sniffed. 'A right pair of tykes, they are.'

When the snow had begun, Sidney and Jimmy had appeared at the back door and asked if they could clear the steps and the short pathway leading to the road and the stretch of pavement in front of Mrs Booth's house.

'We've done our mam's,' Sidney told her. 'Tha can 'ave a look. We'll keep it clear for thee if tha wants.'

'And how much is that going to cost me?'

'Sixpence a time, missis,' Sidney said promptly.

'Thruppence,' Grace bargained. The two boys glanced at each other and Sidney sighed. 'Seein' as you're our neighbour, all right then. But don't you tell t'others in street. It'll be sixpence to them.'

So Grace kept a pile of threepenny bits on the mantelpiece to hand to the boys every time they cleared the paths.

'Saves us the job,' she murmured as she stood in the doorway, her arms folded across her chest, watching the boys work. 'And it keeps that pair of scallywags out of trouble for an hour or two.'

In fact, it kept the Bradshaw boys out of trouble for several days as they cleared several of their neighbours' pathways.

'Not so bad?' Grace repeated now, responding indignantly to her daughter. 'I feel sorry for her that her eldest lads have got caught up in the fighting – I'll not deny that – but it still doesn't stop her being the biggest gossip in Sheffield. You lot – ' she nodded towards her family – 'just be careful what you're saying in front of her, that's all. And I expect she'll have those little ruffians with her.'

Ignoring her mother's grumbling, Mary said, 'We ought to get an air-raid pack put together and leave it near the cellar door. We've had leaflets about it.'

'Have we had leaflets?' Grace said sarcastically. 'They talk about not wasting paper, but all these information leaflets are the biggest waste of paper I know.'

'How else would folks get advice, Mother?'

'The wireless.' Grace was rarely short of an answer.

'They use that an' all,' Rose said, 'but people don't remember it like they do when they've got it in print.'

'Then they could write it down.'

'And what would they write it on, Gran?' Myrtle said cheekily and was rewarded with one of Grace's steely glares. 'You get on with your homework, miss.'

But as the older woman opened Saturday's newspaper yet again, Myrtle saw Grace's mouth twitch as she tried to prevent a smile. 'Actually,' Grace said, coming back to the original topic of conversation, 'we ought to do a lot more than just have a pack ready. We need to get the cellar prepared properly.'

'What do you mean, Mother?'

'We might be down there for several hours at a time. We'll need to sort out bedding and warm clothing. Food in tins or jars and drinking water, which we'll have to change regularly. Thermos flasks we can leave at the ready in the kitchen and fill them up when the sirens start.'

'My word! You have been giving it some thought.'

'Torches and batteries,' Grace went on. 'I'd like to take a wireless set, but I've only the one, so I'll have to do without that. And I suppose,' she added reluctantly, 'we'll have to sort out some sort of toilet arrangement.'

'Oh no!' Myrtle was adamant. 'If you think I'm going to the lav with those two little tykes from next door listening, you can think again. I'd sooner dash across the yard – bombs or no bombs.'

Grace and Mary smiled. 'Well, I can't help agreeing with you, Myrtle, but we'll have to see.'

'I'll make a list,' Mary said, 'and we can start collecting all the things we'll need.'

'And don't forget some books and games to keep those little rascals from next door quiet. And my newspapers. Don't forget to take my newspapers.'

'How are we going to read in the dark?'

'There's an electric light down there, but if that fails, we'll use candles. It's surprising what light candles give off, if you can get enough of them.'

'You've got an answer for everything, Gran,' Myrtle murmured in admiration.

A little while later a knock sounded at the front door.

'Oh Gawd,' Grace muttered morosely. 'That'll be him again. Has he been daft enough to trudge through all this snow? Never gives up, does he, even though it's obvious she's not interested in him. I hope he doesn't stay long. I want the news at nine.' Mary and Peggy were still washing up in the kitchen. Grace sighed. 'You'd better let him in, Myrtle.'

The girl glanced up sullenly. 'Why do I always have to be the one—?'

'I'll go.' Rose turned from where she'd been folding the tablecloth and putting it away in the sideboard drawer. She paused for a moment and stared at her grandmother. 'What – what d'you mean, Gran, Peggy's not interested in him?'

'She's not exactly acting like someone head over heels in love, is she? She must have heard the knock and yet she's not coming rushing through to answer it, even though she must know it's him.' Grace sniffed. 'Like we all do.' Then a wistful smile played briefly on the old woman's mouth. 'Even I can remember what it was like when I fell in love with your grandad. Besotted, I was. Almost made myself ill with the excitement of it all. But then, he was a very handsome man – tall and dark-haired and—'

'Oh, Gran, Bob's good-looking, he . . .' Rose began and then stopped, appalled that she might have given herself away by extolling Bob's virtues. Instead, she muttered, 'I'll go, seeing as no one else seems to want to.'

As she went into the narrow hallway, her mind was in a whirl. She had never thought for one moment that Peggy might not be in love with Bob. Rose couldn't imagine anyone not being, but maybe . . .

'Hang on a minute while I put the light out.' She opened the door and smiled a welcome, forcing a light, teasing note into her tone. 'Now fancy seeing you. Whatever brings you here, Mr Deeton? As if we didn't know.'

Bob grinned shyly as he stepped across the threshold. 'Is she home?'

'She's in the back just finishing the washing up. I bet you could do with a cuppa.'

'Ooo, I could. Ta, Rose.' He stamped the snow from his boots. 'I reckon it's getting colder.'

Rose closed the door and switched the light back on. 'Let me take your coat.' She shook the snow from it and hung it on one of the pegs on the wall. 'Gran's paper said that the other night was the coldest for years. Parts of the Thames were frozen over. Can you believe that?'

As Bob handed her his trilby, Rose added, 'My, we are smart tonight. Were you hoping to take her out?'

'I was, but the weather's too bad. I don't want to drag her out in this. Maybe later in the week, when the snow's cleared a bit.'

'Come through.' Rose opened the door into the living room and ushered him in. 'Sit by the fire and get warm.'

Bob nodded to Grace and Myrtle. 'Evenin', Mrs Booth. Hello, Myrtle. Busy with your homework?'

Myrtle glowered and lowered her head. She was now in the fifth form and determined to do well in her School Certificate exams, which were scheduled to take place in June.

'Myrtle, say hello to Bob,' Rose prompted.

Without looking up the girl muttered, 'Hello to Bob.'

'Ee, she can be right mardy sometimes. You keep a civil tongue in your head, young Myrtle,' Rose admonished her younger sister, but she was smiling as she said it. Indeed, she was keeping a smile firmly fixed on her face. 'I'll just get our Peggy. I'll take over with the drying if they've not finished.'

As she moved towards the door into the small back kitchen, Mary appeared, 'All done. Oh hello, Bob. Peggy, love,' she called over her shoulder, 'Bob's here.' There was a pause, but Peggy did not appear. 'She's just putting the pots away. She'll be here in a minute,' Mary explained.

'I'll do it,' Rose offered and left the room.

Pushing the door closed behind her, she hissed, 'Peg, what's the matter with you? Bob's waiting for you.'

'So? He can wait a minute whilst I put the pots away, can't he?'

'Well, if it was me—' Again Rose bit back the words. Oh, she was going to have to be so careful.

Peggy sighed as she closed the cupboard door and took a last look round the kitchen. Everything was neat and tidy. 'I'm coming.'

Back in the living room, Bob half rose to his feet as the two girls came in, his eyes alighting on Peggy's face. Rose's heart twisted painfully as she saw the adoration in his eyes directed at her sister. Why couldn't it be me? she was thinking, but she turned away, sat down at the table beside Myrtle and picked up a book. The printed words danced before her eyes and she couldn't concentrate on the story as she listened to what Bob was saying.

'I'd thought we might go out but the snow's still deep in places where folks haven't cleared their fronts. Anyway, I just thought I'd pop and see how you all were.'

'I don't expect you did much "popping",' Grace muttered. 'It's nearly a mile to your place, isn't it? It must have taken you an age in this weather.'

Bob grinned. 'Not quite a mile, Mrs Booth, and yes, it was a bit slow going.' He glanced at Peggy and the unspoken words hung in the air. But it was worth it to see Peggy.

A few days later, when most of the snow had cleared and the city's transport was running normally once more, Bob called again on the Friday evening. This time he suggested a trip to the cinema. 'But I'm not sure where we can go,' he said as he hovered near the door.

All places of entertainment had been closed on the outbreak of war.

Myrtle glanced up from her books. 'They should all be open again by now. They started reopening as early as last September. They were only closed for a couple of weeks when war was declared.'

All eyes turned to look at her.

'How d'you know that?' Grace asked.

'There was an advert in your newspaper. Obviously – ' sarcasm crept into her tone – 'you don't read it very well.'

'Less of your cheek, young lady.'

Bob's face brightened visibly. 'That's all right then. Shall we go, Peg?'

'If you like.'

'You might sound a little more enthusiastic,' Rose couldn't stop herself saying.

'Perhaps you'd like to go somewhere different,' Bob said.

'*Aladdin* is still on at the Lyceum,' Myrtle said with deliberate wide-eyed innocence. 'Or you could go dancing.'

Peggy ignored her and smiled. 'Of course I'd like to go out, Bob, but I'd really like to go to the Regent cinema. There's Robert Taylor and Hedy Lamarr in *Lady of the Tropics*. I'd love to see that.'

'Then that's where we'll go.'

'Have I time to change?'

'Of course, but you look fine as you are,' he added gallantly.

Myrtle rolled her eyes and exchanged an amused glance with her grandmother.

'Don't be too late home, darling,' Mary said. 'You're on early in the morning, aren't you?'

Before she had time to respond, Bob said, 'I'll make sure she's home in good time, Mrs Sylvester. I'm on the same shift.'

'As ever,' Rose muttered under her breath and thought, I reckon Bob bribes Mr Bower to keep him as Peggy's motorman.

As the door finally closed behind the young couple, Grace muttered, 'What's she doing, stringing the poor lad along? I can't make her out.'

'I think she's very fond of him,' Mary said, her knitting needles clicking rhythmically.

Grace snorted. 'Fond, indeed. That's hardly enough for marriage, is it?'

'Not all love is whistles and bells and crashing cymbals, Mother.'

'Isn't it?' Grace pretended innocence. 'Then it should be. I just hope she's not leading him on and then going to hurt him. He's a nice, steady sort of lad.'

Unseen by the rest of the family, Myrtle raised her eyes to the ceiling. How dull, she was thinking, how *un*romantic. She buried her head once more in her copy of *Wuthering Heights*, relishing the passion between Catherine and Heathcliff that almost singed the pages of the book. Now here was true love.

'Peggy's very quiet and reserved,' Mary said. 'She doesn't say a lot.'

'More's the pity,' Grace countered. 'Now, if it was our Rose here, we'd all soon know if she was in love. She'd be even more scatterbrained than usual.'

Rose managed a grin, but inside her heart was breaking. Oh, don't hurt him, Peggy, please don't hurt him.

Nine

'So how are you enjoying life as a clippie?' Peggy asked.

'It's great, but I hadn't realized it was going to be quite so much hard work. My feet are killing me by the end of a shift and you don't get much time to look around, do you? I was so looking forward to seeing more of the city we pass through, specially when we go to the outskirts and you can catch a glimpse of the countryside.'

'But you do see all walks of life, don't you?'

Rose laughed. 'You can tell what people are by the time they travel on the tram and the way they're dressed; all the factory workers very early in the morning, then the office workers and shop assistants along with the kids going to school.'

Peggy pulled a face. 'Children are the worst. The little devils are always playing with the seats upstairs, crashing them backwards and forwards in their sockets. The times I have to run upstairs just to stop them.' She cast her eyes to the ceiling in mock despair.

'Then you get the shoppers. They're the best. You hear all kinds of snippets of gossip and, despite their worries, they're mostly a cheerful bunch. But it's the posh ladies that make me laugh. I can hardly keep a straight face when one of them looks down her nose at me and then sits down in her fancy clothes on a seat that a few hours ago was occupied by a coal miner.'

'Just watch out for an inspector getting on,' Peggy reminded her. 'It'll always happen when you haven't gone upstairs to get the latest fare or when the kids are yelling and running up and down on the top deck.'

'Who? Mr Bower?'

'He's just one, and some of the others aren't so understanding of mistakes, believe me.'

The two girls were enjoying comparing notes. 'I'm so lucky having you, Peg, to show me the ropes.' Impulsively she gave her sister a hug. 'Thanks.'

'Oh, I'll keep you on the right track.' At her unintentional pun, both girls dissolved into laughter.

To Rose's surprise, Mr Bower was unstinting in his praise. 'I was wrong about you, Rose,' he was generous enough to admit and he said as much to anyone who would listen. 'I thought you were a flighty piece, but you've settled in right well.'

Rose blushed at his praise. 'I love the work, Mr Bower. I knew I would.'

'So, you don't mind the cold mornings and the late nights, the awkward passengers and all the motormen flirting with you.'

Rose laughed. 'I was used to that working in the canteen. I can handle them.'

'Ah, but I worry about you young lasses.'

'You don't have to be concerned about me, Mr Bower.'

She saw the man glance at her, doubt etched into his face. She could almost read his thoughts. Peggy's the steady one, but I'm still not sure about you. Rose turned away lest he should read something in her eyes that she didn't want him – or anyone else for that matter – to see.

Alice, too, had settled in better than she herself had expected. She and Rose met up in the canteen now and again and sometimes Peggy was able to join them. The three became friends at work, but they did not socialize together. Maybe it was because Alice was married and, even though her husband was away, she seemed reluctant to go out without him. 'Derek wouldn't like it,' she said primly, when Rose asked her if she'd like to go to the cinema with her.

The war news in the early part of 1940 was depressing. In April the enemy invaded Norway and Denmark and when, at the end of May, Belgium and Holland fell, it seemed only a matter of time before France would be overwhelmed.

'But our boys are over there,' Rose said, wide-eyed with fear, as Grace read out snippets from the papers. 'Walter's probably there.'

The answer came only a few days later when the great evacuation of troops from Dunkirk's beaches began. Now every member of the household was fighting over Grace's newspaper to read the latest developments. On 31 May the front page of the *Daily Express* showed an artist's impression of a bird's eye view of the fighting. 'Look,' Grace jabbed a finger at the paper. 'See how they've got the English and the French trapped with their backs to the sea.'

'What are those meant to be?' Myrtle asked, leaning over Grace's shoulder and pointing at the tiny shapes of ships in the Channel.

'Boats taking the soldiers off the beaches.'

'And those?' Now she pointed to birdlike shapes.

'Planes – but whether they're meant to be the RAF or enemy planes strafing the beaches, I don't know.'

Mary sighed. 'Both, probably.'

'We've lost three destroyers already,' Grace murmured, 'but at least they're getting our boys back home.'

Though it was a defeat for the British army, the rescue operation was hailed as a miraculous victory. The soldiers arrived back to a rapturous welcome, the papers said. They were dirty – many of them had lost their boots, their jackets – but still they clung to their rifles. And they were hungry. The people of the south-coast towns where the ships landed the men turned out to wave flags and cheer them home, but most importantly they were ready with food and drink. The arrival of hundreds of thousands of soldiers back on British soil, snatched from beaches, which had been under constant attack from German dive bombers, caused Rose to say, 'Oh, I wish I was there to help. Now I understand what made the Bradshaw boys go.'

'Don't you get silly ideas into your head about volunteering,' Grace warned, suddenly afraid that her headstrong granddaughter would do something impetuous. 'Your job'll be dangerous enough if we get bombed.'

Rose blinked. 'We won't get bombed here, will we? Not really? Oh, I know we've had to prepare, just like everyone else, but—'

Her voice faded away as Grace eyed her. 'It wouldn't be the first time,' Grace said quietly.

'What?' Rose stared at her and then sank down into a chair. 'What d'you mean?'

'We were bombed in the last war.'

'Not – not here. Not in Sheffield.'

Grace nodded. 'Yes, here in Sheffield.'

'But – but I didn't think – I mean – how could their planes get this far?'

'It was a Zeppelin raid. There were twenty-eight people killed and a lot injured.'

'I – never knew. You've never said.'

Grace shrugged. 'We all wanted to forget about the war. The men who'd been to the Front would never talk about it. Your dad included. And we all wanted to put it behind us and believe what they said about it being the war to end all wars. This city lost a lot of men on the Somme and then, only just afterwards, we got bombed. No one was prepared – not really. They all thought the same as you're saying – that they couldn't reach us. But they did.' Grace fell silent, lost in her own thoughts. Rose waited, biting her lip to stop the questions from tumbling out. Grace would carry on in her own time and at her own pace. She wouldn't be hurried.

'Of course your dad and mam weren't married then. That was before he came home injured and your mam – oh well, enough said about that, I suppose.'

'Tell me about the bombing,' Rose whispered, morbidly fascinated. She didn't want to hear about their city being attacked and yet she had to know.

'The first bombs fell on the Burngreave Cemetery.'

Rose gasped. 'Where Dad and Grandad are buried?'

Grace nodded.

'But that's not far away from here.'

'I know. We – your mother and me – watched it from the bedroom window and then we realized they might come our way, so we went down into the cellar.'

'So that's how you know the cellar will be the safest place?'

Grace nodded again, this time her face grim with unhappy memories. 'And now Hitler's overrun France, he can get right to the coast just across the Channel. Not only can he invade the south coast, but his bombers can probably reach every place in the British Isles.'

Rose gaped at her grandmother. For once in her life, she could think of nothing to say.

Grace turned back to her newspaper. 'They've rescued over three hundred thousand men from Dunkirk,' she said. 'You can't believe it, can you? France is lost, but we live to fight another day. I do hope Letty's boy is all right. She hasn't been round for a couple of days. Maybe there's been bad news.'

Never one to shirk an unpleasant task, Rose said, 'I'll go round.'

She came back in only a few moments. 'Letty's in floods of tears – ' Grace looked up sharply – 'but it's all right. They've just had news that Walter's safe. He's down south somewhere – but back in England. They've been desperately worried for several days 'cos they knew he'd just gone out there. She says – ' Rose grinned in anticipation of her grandmother's retort – 'she's sorry she hasn't been round.'

Grace glanced up at her granddaughter. 'I know just what you're thinking. That I'm going to trot out one of my famous sayings. "It's an ill wind . . ." and all that, but even I wouldn't wish that kind of worry on anyone, let alone my neighbour. Oh, I know she irritates the life out of me some days and her two boys are little devils, but we could have a lot worse as neighbours, Rose.'

'Yes, Gran,' Rose said dutifully, stifling her laughter, especially when she saw Grace's mouth twitching as she tried to stop herself laughing too.

A fortnight later one of Grace's newspapers showed a picture of German soldiers riding on horseback up the Champs-Elysées.

'How dreadful,' Rose murmured, with tears in her eyes. She could picture such a scene happening here in her own city and shuddered at the thought.

Although the rescue operation from Dunkirk had been magnificent, there were sadly many casualties too and one amongst them affected both Rose and Peggy. Laurence approached them one morning when they reported for work.

'Alice won't be in today – probably not for several days. She's had news that her husband was killed on the beaches. Evidently, he was up to his waist in the sea, waiting for one of the little ships to pick him up, when an enemy plane strafed them.'

'Oh, poor Alice – I'll go and see her,' Rose said at once.

Laurence shook his head. 'No point. She's gone down south to stay with her brother and his wife for a week or two.'

It was a month before Alice returned to Sheffield and came back to work. After offering her condolences, Rose said, 'We all thought you might stay down there.'

Alice's face was pinched with grief and she looked thinner than ever, but she smiled bravely. 'I did think about it – all my family is there – but Derek's parents live in Rotherham. I thought he'd've liked me to stay near to them – at least for a while.' She paused and then burst out, 'The worst is knowing I'll never be able to have any children. It was all me an' Derek ever wanted. But now . . .'

There was nothing Rose could say. Words of comfort like, 'Oh, you'll meet someone else' would sound hollow and somehow insulting to her beloved husband's memory. All Rose could do was to keep an eye on her friend and be a sympathetic ear if ever Alice needed one.

Through the summer of 1940 Peggy and Bob continued to see each other outside their working hours, but the romance did not seem to progress. They went out most weekends, held hands in the back row of the pictures and kissed goodnight outside the front door when Bob delivered her home at the time demanded by Grace. He was the first young man Peggy had gone out with for any length of time. She'd been out once or twice with Walter Bradshaw when she was seventeen, but he'd met a girl from Rotherham and soon became engaged to her. Peggy had never felt as if she'd been jilted; their friendship had been just that and no more. She didn't weep into her pillow over Walter. But now she wasn't sure what it meant to be 'in love'. She read romantic novels but felt nothing of the passion for Bob which the heroines obviously felt for their heroes. She liked him very much, was fond of him even. She was comfortable with him. He was kind and courteous, considerate and undemanding, but her heart didn't beat faster at the sight of him or her pulses race when he kissed her gently. Being reserved herself, maybe Peggy needed someone more exciting, whilst Rose would have been ecstatic if Bob had even looked at her.

Myrtle, however, had no problem defining her sister's so-called romance.

'He's slow,' she voiced her opinion to Rose as they undressed for bed one warm August night. 'Everyone's blaming Peggy, but he's not exactly sweeping her off her feet, is he? If you ask me, he's as dull as ditch water and as slow as a tram on strike.'

'How dare you talk about Bob like that?' Rose flared in an unguarded moment.

'Ooo-er, touchy, aren't we? Fancy him yourself, do you?'

'Don't be daft,' Rose snapped, angry for having left herself open to Myrtle's shrewd remark. 'I just think he's a nice bloke who Peggy's not being fair to.'

'Whom.'

'What?'

'It's "to whom" she's not being fair, not "who".'

'Oh, go to sleep,' Rose muttered, jumping into her single bed and pulling the covers up and then immediately throwing them off again. 'It's so hot up here.'

'Well, at least it'll be nice and cool on your tram platform tomorrow.'

'D'you know what?' Rose said, changing the subject. 'Mam's volunteered for war work and there's a fair chance she might be sent as a clippie. She told 'em she'd got two daughters who were clippies. Or is it "whom", Miss Clever Clogs?'

'No, no, "who" is correct in that context.'

As Myrtle blew out the candle and climbed into bed, Rose smiled in the half darkness of the summer night. 'We only want you and Gran to sign up and we'd have a full house.'

But there was no sound from the next bed. Myrtle was one of those fortunate people who, the moment their head touched the pillow, fell fast asleep.

Rose was left staring into the darkness and praying

that by morning Myrtle would have forgotten all about her hasty retort regarding Bob.

Towards the end of the school summer term, Myrtle had taken her School Certificate and had passed with the highest grades possible in all her subjects. Her family was justifiably proud of her. During the holidays she took over more of the household chores when Mary became a fully fledged clippie too, but Myrtle's studies were not laid aside completely. Before the end of term she had ascertained the literature books she would need for the sixth form and, through the long, hot summer days, read all of them – and more.

The sound of the air-raid sirens was becoming part of the city's everyday life. There had been numerous false alarms and, even though there had been one or two minor raids, the public became blasé about the warnings and just carried on with whatever they were doing until they heard the sound of planes overhead.

'You must not ignore the sirens,' Laurence instructed his staff. 'You should get all your passengers to the nearest public shelter on your route whenever you hear the warning.' The motormen and the clippies did their best, but so many of their passengers refused to go into the shelters and grumbled if the tram stopped.

'It's nowt but a false alarm, love,' many a traveller would say. 'Just get us home.'

But one Thursday evening towards the end of August, Peggy and Rose returned home looking worried and agitated.

'Is Mam home?'

'Not yet. Why?'

The sisters glanced at each other and began to speak at once.

'She—'

'We—'

Catching their anxiety, Grace crumpled the newspaper she was reading onto her knee. 'What? Is there something you're not telling me?'

'No, no,' Peggy said at once. 'We just wanted to know she was all right, that's all.'

'Why shouldn't she be?' Grace's eyes narrowed. 'There *is* something, isn't there? Come on, out with it.'

'It's just that we thought she might have been on the route today near where the bombs fell.'

Grace's wrinkled face turned pale. 'What bombs?'

'Didn't you hear the sirens? Didn't you go down into the cellar?'

Grace looked sheepish. 'We thought it was another false alarm.'

'Well, it wasn't. Not this time,' Peggy said shortly. 'You should really be more careful, Gran.'

'And did you get all your passengers into a shelter?' Grace retorted defensively.

'They refused to go. Like you, they thought it wasn't serious. But when we heard the bombs dropping, they shot out of the car and down the nearest shelter like rats down a drainpipe.'

'I'm going back to the depot,' Rose said, 'to find out what's happened and where Mam is.'

'I'll come with you—'

'No,' Grace said. 'You stay here – with me, Peggy.'

The sisters glanced at each other and then looked back at their grandmother. Though she would never have admitted it in a million years, they could both see that Grace was frightened and fearful of news that might be brought to her door. She didn't want to be alone to hear it.

'Myrtle's here, isn't she?'

Grace ran her tongue round her dry lips and nodded. 'But she's only a kid. Besides, she's upstairs in her bedroom reading. She says she can't concentrate down here.' Grace smiled wryly. 'Says I keep talking to her. She's right. I do.'

'She'll be sat on her bed reading.' Rose knew Myrtle's habits.

There was a tense silence in the room until Grace said, 'Off you go, Rose. Go and find your mam.' Beneath her breath, she muttered, 'If you can.'

As Rose hurried out, Peggy said, 'I'll make a cuppa. Have you had anything to eat yet?'

Grace shook her head. 'We were waiting for you all to come home.'

'Then I'll get started on the tea.'

'Myrtle's got it all ready.' Grace looked up, reluctant to let her go, but when Peggy said gently, 'I'll just be in the kitchen,' the older woman nodded and picked up her newspaper again.

The waiting was terrible. Grace did her best to sit quietly. At her age, she told herself, she ought to be used to dealing with the tragedies that life brought. She'd lived through the last lot, hadn't she? She'd witnessed her neighbours and friends losing loved ones and had been there to comfort them as best she could when they'd received the dreaded telegram. She'd thought old age would bring tranquillity and the capacity to endure whatever life threw at her. But it hadn't. She could no more accept that she might see one or more of her family killed or injured in this new kind of conflict, which wrought terror amongst the civilian population, than she'd been able to come to terms with the carnage of the trenches. It was all a needless waste of lives, this time brought on by a megalomaniac.

Grace heard Peggy moving about in the kitchen, clattering pots and pans whilst she sat fidgeting in her chair by the fire, glancing up at the clock on the mantelpiece every few minutes. Myrtle, still blithely unaware of the anxiety of her family, read on in peace.

Downstairs, the waiting went on.

Ten

It was over an hour later that they heard the front door open and Rose's voice calling, 'Here we are, all safe and sound.'

Grace muttered a prayer of thankfulness and sniffed back her tears. It wouldn't do to let them see how worried she'd been. In this house of women, she was supposed to be the strong one, head of the house and all that. And then Rose and Mary were in the room and Peggy was hurrying from the kitchen to hug them both, not even attempting to hide her anxiety. 'Are you all right, Mam? What happened? Why are you so late home?'

Mary reassured her quickly, 'I'm fine. We got delayed, that's all, because of the line being blocked. That route will be out of action for a few days until they get the debris moved away and the track repaired.'

'Was it bad?'

Mary nodded, her eyes still wide with exhaustion and shock. 'As far as we know, no one was injured.' But she could not wipe the images from her mind. The sight of homes reduced to a smouldering pile of rubble; of a woman standing before a bombed house weeping openly; of a man tearing at a heap of bricks with his bare hands, desperation on his face. She'd still been shaking when she'd got back to the depot, but Laurence had taken her to the mess room at once and given her a tot of brandy. 'Medicinal purposes only,' he'd said gently. How kind he'd been, she thought.

'Sit down, Mam,' Peggy said now. 'Tea's nearly ready.'

'I don't think I could eat anything. And I must wash. I feel so grubby.'

As Mary left the room and went upstairs to the bathroom, the other three glanced at one another.

'She's had a nasty shock,' Grace said. 'You can see it in her eyes.'

'She shouldn't be working on the trams,' Rose burst out. 'It isn't right at her age. Why couldn't they find her some more suitable war work?'

'What?' Grace smiled. 'Sitting by the fire knitting socks like me. That's all I'm good for, but not your mam. She's only young. Oh yes—' Grace flapped her hand as Rose opened her mouth to protest. 'I know she maybe seems old to you. At your age, young Rose, anyone past thirty is over the hill, but believe you me, your mother doesn't see herself as old and she wouldn't thank you for insinuating as much.'

Rose grinned. 'Sorry, Gran. It didn't come out the way I meant it.'

Grace gave a snort of laughter. 'It often doesn't with you. Now, help your sister finish getting the tea, call Myrtle down and we'll sit down together to eat as soon as your mam's ready. And don't leave your jacket slung over the back of that chair. Hang it up in the hall where it belongs.'

A change of clothes, a wash and sitting down with her family had done Mary a power of good and she was soon laughing with the rest of them. But deep in her eyes was a haunted look of the tragedy she'd seen and the unspoken anxiety of what still might happen to her or her girls.

At the end of August 1940 Grace's *Daily Sketch* reported that after German bombers had failed to break the RAF's defences in south-east England, they were now turning their attention to London and other British industrial towns, cities, and ports. Attacks on the capital continued and soon came to be called the London Blitz. The whole country realized that it could be their turn next when Hitler threatened to raze British cities to the ground. Only the RAF stood between the British people and a ruthless enemy.

'Our Bertie's got what he wanted. He's a fighter pilot now,' Letty told Grace. 'God only knows where he is. Oh, Mrs Booth, I'm out of me mind wi' worry. Three of my boys in danger. It's more than a body can stand.'

There was nothing Grace could say to comfort her neighbour. The older woman was not one to gush with promises that couldn't be kept. It was no use telling poor Letty that her boys would be safe because in these dreadful days no one knew what was going to happen next. Grace did the only thing she could think of; she pushed a hot cup of sweet tea in front of Letty and handed her one of the family's precious ginger biscuits.

All the family were concerned about the Bradshaw boys. Peggy and Rose had grown up with them, had gone to school with them, had been chased by them, had had their pigtails pulled and their faces rubbed in the snow by them. Rose had played football and cricket in the street with them and Peggy had blushed when Walter had been the first boy to try to snatch a kiss.

But now the whole country depended on these young men and many more like them. Life was strange, Grace would muse in her quieter moments when she had the house to herself. Who'd ever have thought that those young rascals would one day turn into heroes?

Birmingham and Liverpool had been bombed repeatedly since August and, on the last day of November, one of the worst air raids of the war so far hit Coventry. Over one thousand civilians were killed and their beautiful cathedral was destroyed.

'We carry on as usual,' Laurence Bower told all his staff when the news reached them. 'It's likely that we will be the Luftwaffe's target eventually. My own belief – though I have nothing to substantiate it – is that those early minor raids were reconnaissance with a few bombs dropped for good measure. We are an industrial city and the enemy knows that. He'll have detailed plans, I'm sure. So, with that in mind, if anyone feels they really can't cope with the imminent danger—' His glance flickered briefly around his little band of women workers. He felt a fatherly protectiveness towards them and, if he could have had his way, he'd lay them all off whilst there was a definite threat of serious bombing hanging over them. But he couldn't. They couldn't run the city's tram system without women – not now. In fact, the situation was getting worse. Almost every day another of his male conductors or drivers felt it their patriotic duty to enlist and sought to be released from their reserved occupation. Consequently even more women were being taken on to fill their places. This war was a headache for Laurence in many ways. 'We will think no worse of you, particularly those of you who have children to think of,' he continued. Here his glance went to one or two of the married women whose children were still at school but were old enough to fend for themselves out of school hours. There were times now when Laurence felt very guilty that he'd been the one to suggest training women to work on the trams. But, he'd consoled himself, they'd have been employed in such roles by now anyway. All over the city – indeed the country – women were filling the jobs left by the men going off to war.

'If a bomb's got us name on it, Mr Bower,' Doris Ackroyd called out, 'then it'll find us whether we're on t'trams or at 'ome.'

There was a ripple of nervous laughter, but no one stepped forward to ask to be relieved of their duties and Laurence felt a glow of pride for their bravery. He nodded, torn by an inner conflict of emotions: relief that he would not have the nightmare of sorting out a new rota and training more recruits, but now with the added anxiety that some of the employees of the city's Transport Department might be injured.

'Did we ought to send Myrtle and my mother to the country?' Mary confided her constant anxiety to Peggy the day after they'd heard about a bombing raid on Liverpool.

'Gran won't go and I doubt you'd be able to per-suade Myrtle. I know she's still at school, Mam, but in normal circumstances, she'd be a working girl now. She's not a child any more.'

Mary frowned. 'No, I suppose you're right, but I do worry about them so. Can we be sure they'll go down into the cellar and – and even if they do, what if the house should be damaged? They'd be trapped down there.'

Peggy sighed. 'Mam, it's the sort of thing we've all got to cope with.'

'And what about you and Rose if a raid happens when you're on duty?' Her experience of being very near to a bomb exploding had unnerved Mary.

'We all know the rules. Mr Bower has told us often enough.' Peggy mimicked Laurence's instructions. ' "The safety of your passengers comes first and foremost." ' Mary smiled weakly as her eldest daughter went on, trying to reassure her. 'And both me and Rose have got a copy of the list we cut out of Gran's newspaper of where the public shelters are on the tram routes. What about you?'

'Yes, I carry it in my pocket and I've learned the location of the ones on the routes I usually work.'

'Then there's nothing more we can do.'

'Except hope and pray,' Mary murmured.

Later, when she reported for duty, Mary ran into Laurence and voiced her fears to him. 'I don't want to sound as if I'm making light of the raids we've already had because I'm not. Even the loss of one person's life is a tragedy, but the feeling seems to be now that we're in for a battering. What do you think?'

Laurence sighed. 'Sadly, Mary, I think you're right.' They stared at each other, sadness in their eyes, pondering what the next few days and weeks held for them all.

They weren't left wondering for very long. Early in December 1940 it was Sheffield's turn. Just when everyone was trying hard to plan for Christmas, to make the most of a festive time and to put their worries aside, even if only for a few days, the enemy unleashed a vicious attack on their city.

Eleven

The day had started out ordinarily enough.

'By heck, it's cold this morning,' Bob had greeted Peggy as they arrived at the depot at the same time. 'You'll want yer winter drawers on this morning.'

'Cheeky.'

Bob grinned and winked at her, but Peggy averted her eyes and busied herself with her tickets, making sure they were all in the right order.

'Come on then, let's get on our way. Folks won't want us to be late this morning in this weather.'

'Do they ever?' Peggy countered, but she smiled and followed him to the tram that was to be theirs for the day.

It was a busy day. After the workers came the shoppers, women prepared to queue for hours to feed their families. Others were shopping for Christmas, trying to find bargains to avoid their children being too disappointed in Father Christmas, but the privations of war were biting hard. Peggy wished she had a few hours off to wander around the city centre. The shops had made every effort to brighten people's spirits. Christmas decorations festooned the windows and, during the daytime, were brightly lit. But come nightfall all the lights would be put out, blinds and shutters drawn. The streets would be in relative darkness with only pinpoints of light for travellers to see their way.

By late afternoon Peggy was tired. She and Bob should have gone off duty, but the motorman, who should have taken over from Bob, had been taken to the local hospital on arriving at work. 'He was doubled over with pain,' Laurence told them. 'It sounds like appendicitis to me. He looked bad, anyway. So could you two carry on a bit longer? Just give me time to call in a relief crew.'

''Course we will,' Bob volunteered, without even consulting Peggy. She'd already been thinking longingly of sitting down in the chair beside the range to warm her cold hands, but she bit back a refusal and smiled thinly. She shrugged herself into her thick overcoat and climbed back onto the tramcar, blowing onto her hands to try to warm them.

'Where d'you think you two are going?'

Peggy turned to see Rose standing with her hands on her hips, grinning as she added, 'Taking a tram without the owner's consent? Fancied a night in the countryside, did we?'

Peggy smiled back, but then grimaced. 'Extra duty. Pete's gone off with suspected 'pendicitis.'

'Oh right. I'll see you later then.' Rose paused and then added, 'Have you seen Alice? I fancied a night at the flicks and I've finally managed to persuade her to come with me. She needs taking out of herself a bit. We're going to the Abbeydale.'

'What's on?'

Rose pulled a comical face. '*Young Tom Edison*. Alice likes a bit of culture, so I thought it'd suit her. But Mickey Rooney's in it, so it should be good. And there might be a comedy on with it.'

'The Abbeydale's quite a way to go for a night out. Mam'll worry if there's a raid.' Peggy glanced up at the sky. 'It's a moonlit night. You know what they say?'

'Bomber's moon,' Rose murmured. 'I know, but if I have to sit in the house another night watching Gran read a pile of newspapers for the umpteenth time – '

Normally Grace read just *The Star*, but since the start of the war she'd bought national newspapers too, a different one every day. 'I want a balanced viewpoint,' she'd told her family firmly before they could complain.

'– Myrtle poring over her books and Mam clacking her knitting needles, I'll go mad.' And the image of you and Bob together, she added in her own mind, but those thoughts she kept to herself.

'Just be careful, that's all. Promise you'll go to the nearest shelter if the sirens go. They'll make an announcement.'

As Peggy rang the bell and the tram began to move, Rose waved and called, 'I will.'

Mary was at home, having started work at five thirty that morning.

'Tea's almost ready,' she called from the kitchen when she heard Rose come in. Myrtle didn't look up from her homework and Grace was engrossed in the latest news from the war front. On the table beside her the wireless played softly.

'Do you know,' Grace murmured, 'the British launched an offensive in the Western Desert against the Italians and took a lot of prisoners? Over a thousand, they say.'

Rose glanced at them both with an amused smile

and then said loudly, 'Good evening, Rose, and what sort of a day have you had? Fine, thank you, and now I'm off to the pictures with Alice.'

'D'you think that's a good idea, love?' Mary said, coming in from the kitchen and catching Rose's last sentence.

'We'll be fine, Mam,' Rose said, as she sat down at the table to eat. 'Don't worry. Just you make sure the three of you go down into the cellar if there is any trouble.'

'We will. As Tom next door says, "We're goin' to cop it afore long, there's nowt so sure."'

'I'm very much afraid he's right,' Rose said, but as she went upstairs a little later to change out of her uniform, she pushed all thoughts of a possible air raid out of her mind. Instead, she found herself humming the song 'Whispering Grass', which had just been play-ing on the wireless. She was meeting Alice in the centre of town and then they would catch a tram out to Abbeydale Road. Rose smiled. That was one of the good things about being clippies: they'd have no tram fares to pay.

'Wow, just look at this place,' Rose said, as they stepped onto the mosaic floor of the foyer. 'I've never been here before.' When they took their places in the plush mahogany seats covered in green velvet, Rose stared around her, open-mouthed at the cream and gold decoration on the walls and ceiling. 'No wonder they call it the Picture *Palace*.'

'It's lovely, isn't it?' Alice said as the lights faded and they settled down to enjoy the film. They were soon engrossed in the story, thoughts of the war and all its sadness forgotten for a precious hour or two.

'Myrtle, help your mam with the washing up, there's a good girl,' Grace said as she turned the wireless off after the news finished.

'But, Gran, I've still got my biology homework to do.'

'Biology, indeed! What on earth good is that going to be to you, I ask?'

'It's human biology,' Myrtle retorted, not afraid to answer her grandmother back. 'It could come in very handy – if you have a heart attack. Miss Adamson says that, with the war and everything, we should all know a bit of basic first aid. We've all been given a copy of the British Red Cross *First Aid Manual*. And I've asked if I can sit an examination in the subject. It's fascinating.'

Grace glanced at her, an amused smile on her lips. She loved all her family, but this granddaughter was someone special to her. Myrtle was the only one who could answer Grace back and get away with it. Mostly, that is, because there were limits even for Myrtle. 'And does it tell you in this famous manual how to do the washing up?'

Myrtle laughed. 'Oh, Gran.' But with good humour she got up and went into the kitchen. 'Where's the tea towel, Mam?' Grace heard her say. 'I'll dry.'

But the pots didn't get dried, nor even completely washed, for at that moment the sirens began to wail.

They were on High Street heading out of the city centre, when they heard the sirens. Bob stopped the tram.

'Oi, you aren't stopping here, are you? I've got to get home to my kids.'

'Just a minute, madam,' Peggy said, 'while I have word with the motorman.'

Peggy hurried down the aisle to where Bob was standing, his left hand on the controller, his right still gripping the brake.

'What ought we to do? Get 'em all to a shelter like Mr Bower ses?'

Peggy shook her head. 'Keep going. I've got a car full and they're all going to play merry hell if we just stop and dive for cover.'

'All right,' Bob agreed, 'but let anyone off who wants to find the nearest shelter.'

Peggy nodded and hurried back to her post.

'We're carrying on, but if anyone wants to get off here and—'

'Thank Gawd for that.'

'Just get on with it. We're a sitting duck here.'

No one alighted and Peggy rang the bell for Bob to move on.

They heard the bombs falling, whistling through the air and then an explosion.

'By 'eck, that were a bit too close for comfort.'

'Watch out for the next one. It might—'

Whatever the man had been going to say was lost in a blast of noise and the splintering of glass. Several passengers shrieked in fear as the tram rocked and came to a halt as the one travelling in front of them stopped too.

Peggy was thrown to the floor of the platform and everything went black.

Twelve

'Quick, Mother, get down the cellar,' Mary cried. 'Myrtle, make sure the doors are locked and turn all the lights off. I've got the box. Oh, do come *on*, Mother.'

In the corner of the living room stood a box packed with last-minute items for a sojourn in the cellar. Mary picked it up and opened the door. She turned on the light to illuminate the steps leading downwards.

'That you, Mary love?' A voice drifted up from below, and behind Mary, Grace said, 'Oh no. Don't tell me Letty's there already. I reckon I'd sooner face Hitler's bombs.'

'Shh, Mother, she'll hear you.'

Grace sniffed. 'Don't care if she does. She might take the hint, though I doubt it.'

'Want any help, love?' Tom's deep voice now called.

'If you could just help Mother down, Tom ... Myrtle, do hurry up.'

But Myrtle was peering out of the front window, fascinated by the unfolding drama. 'They're dropping flares, Mam. They're lighting up the whole sky. Come and look.'

'I'll do no such thing,' Mary said. 'And neither will you. Get—'

And then they both heard the long-drawn-out ominous whistle of a falling bomb.

*

'Oh, now what?' Rose muttered as the screen went blank and the auditorium was plunged into darkness.

'It'll be a break in the film, I expect,' Alice said. 'It happens sometimes. They'll have to repair it. Fancy an ice cream while we wait?'

Several of the picture-goers began to whistle and catcall, but then the manager was standing in front of the screen and everyone fell silent.

'An air raid is in progress,' he said without preamble. 'Please make your way to the shelter below the cinema. We will serve soft drinks and ice cream free of charge as we will be unable to continue with the programme at the present time.'

They left their seats with the rest of the audience and filed in an orderly fashion towards the stairs leading down to the shelter – a spacious area beneath the cinema. There was plenty of room and the usherettes were already handing out refreshments. But Rose hesitated. 'I ought to go home or find out where Peg is.'

Alice grabbed her arm. 'You'll do nothing of the sort. You'll get yourself killed.' At that moment there was a resounding crash and the whole building seemed to shake.

Peggy wasn't knocked out for many seconds and instinctively she'd managed to cling to the rail to stop herself falling into the road. Coughing in the cloud of dust the explosion had caused, she hauled herself to her feet and staggered into the body of the tram. Not a window was left whole and one side of the vehicle had been badly damaged. She feared for the passengers who were sitting on that side. One or two were pulling themselves to their feet, others were sitting very still.

Outside, flames were already engulfing the buildings that had received a direct hit.

'Here, love, let me help you,' Peggy heard a deep voice say and saw a dark-haired young man in army uniform helping a lady up from the floor, where she'd been thrown.

'Please leave the car if you can,' Peggy shouted to her passengers. She couldn't see if anyone was seriously hurt, but she was fearful there must be casualties. All around her she could hear moaning and women crying. Thank goodness there'd been no children aboard when the blast had happened. She couldn't have borne having to lift a child out of the wreckage. She struggled forward, her eyes stinging, her breathing rasping, to find a woman collapsed on one of the seats. She tried to lift the woman, who was unconscious – or worse, Peggy thought, though she couldn't tell – when the soldier scrambled to her side. 'I'll lift her, love. You take her legs.'

'Oh my God,' Peggy breathed. 'They're covered in blood. Ought we to move her?'

'No, no, we'd better leave her there,' the soldier said. 'There's bound to be help arriving very soon. They'll know what's best to do. My basic first aid isn't up to dealing with summat like this.'

'I'll stay with her,' Peggy said, as she glanced up into the dark brown eyes of the soldier, 'if you could help get the rest of the passengers off the tram.'

He grinned at her, his eyes warm. A flick of dark hair flopped over his forehead, making him seem boyishly endearing. 'Of course,' he murmured, 'but don't go away, will you?'

Peggy felt her heart give a ridiculous leap. 'Th – thanks.'

It seemed ages until two members of an ambulance crew were climbing into the wrecked tram, though in reality it was only a few minutes.

'All right, miss, we'll take over now. You get yourself out. Can you manage?'

'I'll help her,' came the deep voice of the soldier from just behind her. 'Come on, love, give me your hand.'

She felt his warm, strong grasp guide her through the broken glass and splintered wood until she was standing safely on the road. But still he did not let go of her hand. The street was in chaos. Fire-fighting crews had turned hoses onto the burning buildings and policemen were urging people to go to the nearest public shelters as quickly as possible. It was an eerie, frightening scene. Huge flames licked the dark sky, illuminating the faces of the men of the rescue services. And above the commotion they could still hear bombs falling.

'Come on,' the soldier said, putting his arm around her. 'Let's get you out of here.' He put his face close to hers. 'You look as if you've got a little cut on your forehead and there's blood on your hand.'

Peggy looked down at her hands in a daze and then touched her forehead and felt the stickiness of her own blood. 'I'm all right, I must see to my passengers – see if I can help anyone else before I . . .' Suddenly, she was overcome by dizziness. She felt her legs begin to buckle beneath her, but his strong arms were supporting her and then suddenly she felt herself picked up and carried.

'Make way,' the soldier said. 'Let me through.' He set her down gently on the pavement, leaning her against a wall on the opposite side of the street to where the bombs had fallen.

'I'm all right – honestly. I must . . .'

'You sit there,' he said firmly. 'Your forehead's cut.

Flying glass, I expect. I'm going to get you a cup of tea. There's a cafe just along here. It's had its window blown in by the blast, but I've seen the owner bringing out cups of tea to the injured.'

'But I'm not injured,' Peggy insisted. 'Not really. I must . . .'

'Stay where you are at least until I get back with the tea. Promise?' His tone was gentle, but masterful, and for once Peggy was grateful to have someone take charge. She nodded, then leant her head back against the wall and closed her eyes.

'That's better. The colour's coming back into your face now. I thought you were going to pass out on me for a moment back there.'

Peggy smiled weakly. 'So did I. I'm all right now, but I'll do as you say if you're sure everyone is being attended to.' She ran her tongue round lips that tasted of brick dust. 'I – could do with a cuppa.'

Rose emerged from the basement beneath the cinema and thought she'd stepped into Hell. Dark, birdlike shapes droned against the moonlit sky, bringing death and destruction to her city. White frost lay on the streets, shining like a beacon to the enemy. Rose took a deep breath and began to run towards the city centre. She knew that was where Peggy would be. Every now and again she had to stop. Bodies lay in the road, but they were beyond her help. All around her bombs crashed into buildings, reducing houses and shops to piles of rubble in seconds. Already fires from incendiary bombs raged, but there were no firemen available to try to quench them. Cannon shells bounced down the road, sparking flashes of white. A stick of incendiaries pattered in a line down the street, and a bigger bomb whistled, was silent for a second and then hit the ground with a resounding crunch. But on Rose ran, her heart pounding, her legs trembling. The roads were icy. Rose slipped and slithered, but she ran on and on. She had to find Peggy – and Bob.

As she neared the city centre, she saw that shops had had their windows blown out and items from the displays lay in the middle of the street: clothes, handbags, shoes, even jewellery. Rose faltered as she saw a figure lying in the road, an arm raised in the air. It didn't move. She bit her lip, torn between the desire to help someone and her need to run on. With an inward sigh, she stepped over the rubble and scrambled towards the figure. As she bent over it, she realized it was a naked display dummy. She pressed her hand against her mouth. Hysterical laughter bubbled up inside her and then she sobbed with relief. Brushing the back of her hand impatiently across her eyes, she hurried on. Dust and debris and noise everywhere: she ran around a smouldering crater in the middle of the road. Ahead of her the centre of the city was on fire.

And then she passed an overturned tram lying on its side, its windows broken, the tram lines buckled and twisted. The sight spurred her on.

'Oh Peg, Peg, where are you?' she sobbed aloud, but deep in her heart were added the words, And Bob? Where are you?

On and on she ran, oblivious to the danger, her only thought to find her sister – and Bob.

It was just as the soldier was coming back along the street, picking his way carefully through the debris with two mugs of tea, that Peggy heard her name being called.

'Peggy – Peggy, where are you?'

Hearing the familiar voice and despite her promise to the soldier, Peggy struggled to her feet. 'Rose – Rose, I'm here.'

'Oh, thank God.' Rose scrambled her way to her sister and hugged her. 'Are you all right?'

At that moment, the soldier reached them. 'Good job I brought two cups – well, mugs. Here you are, miss. Drink this, you'll feel better. And you take this one, love. You look as if you've had a shock, an' all.'

Rose turned to look up into the soldier's face smiling down at her.

'This – this is my sister, Rose,' Peggy said, sipping the hot tea gratefully.

'Pleased to meet you, Rose, though I wish the circumstances were better. You all right?'

'Yes, yes, I'm fine.'

'What – what are you doing here? I thought you'd gone to the pictures.'

'I had. But when the raid started and everyone was going down into the shelter, I came out – much to Alice's disgust. She said I'd get killed, but I couldn't bear to think of you caught up in all this.'

'You should have stayed there.' Peggy remonstrated with Rose, though in truth she was glad to see her.

'I ran all the way here,' Rose told her. 'Bombs were falling all around.'

'Your guardian angel must have been working overtime,' Peggy said shakily.

Rose laughed as she put her arms around her sister and hugged her. 'More like the Devil taking care of his own.'

There were more whistles and crashes as bombs fell in the next street. The soldier put himself in front of them, spreading out his arms to protect them as flames burst skywards and firemen, silhouetted against the night sky, fought a losing battle.

'It's a devil that's unleashed this lot,' the soldier muttered and then turned his attention back to Peggy. 'You ought to get that cut on your forehead looked at.'

'I'm fine now, honestly. Thank you so much for your help. You've been wonderful, but I must find my colleague. I don't know where he is. I must have been knocked out for a moment and then I was so concerned about the passengers, I never thought to see what had happened to Bob.'

Catching her words, Rose spilled her tea as her hand trembled. Her eyes widened as she looked round wildly.

And there was no mistaking the panic in her voice. 'Bob? Oh, Peggy, where is he? Where's Bob?'

Thirteen

Rose set her mug on the ground and darted away, scanning the crowd that had now gathered around the disaster. No one seemed to care that the All Clear had not yet sounded. Folks were emerging from the nearest shelters and coming to try to help or just to gawp. The ambulance drew away with the first of the casualties and another took its place.

'You really should go to hospital,' the soldier, whose name Peggy still didn't know, insisted. 'Come on, let me help you.'

With his strong arms around her, Peggy allowed herself to be led towards one of the ambulance men, though she still protested, 'I'm all right, really I am. I must find Bob.'

'Your sister seems on a mission to do that,' he said. 'My name's Terry by the way. Terry Price. And yours is Peggy?'

She nodded.

'Now, lass, what's the matter with you then?' The ambulance man greeted her kindly. 'Were you a clippie on one of t' trams that was hit?'

Reminded by his words, the full realization of what had just happened hit her afresh and the man's face began to swim before her eyes. But Terry still had hold of her. 'I think she's in shock.'

Together they took her to the back of the ambulance

and got her on board. 'Lie down, lass, you'll feel better in a moment and I'll have a look at that cut on your forehead. It's a nasty one and there might still be splinters of glass in it.'

Peggy did as they bade her, but in a moment she was trying to sit up again. 'Bob. I must find Bob,' she murmured weakly and then fell back against the pillows and closed her eyes as nausea threatened to overwhelm her.

'Who is this Bob she keeps on about?' Terry asked.

'It'll likely be her motorman.'

'The driver of the tram, you mean?'

'Aye. Now, lad, if you're nowt to do with this young lady might I ask you to step out of t' vehicle so I can get on wi' me job. Thanks for your help.'

With obvious reluctance, Terry got out of the back of the ambulance, but he could not bring himself to walk away. Instead he looked around for anyone else who needed assistance, but all the time he kept his eye on the girl lying on the stretcher in the ambulance. He didn't want to let her out of his sight.

He was scrambling back into the wrecked tram when a voice hailed him. 'And just where d'you think you're going, soldier?'

Terry turned to see a policeman frowning at him.

'To find my kitbag and my cap – if I can. I was a passenger on this tram when it was hit. I was lucky I wasn't hurt and I've been trying to help those that were, but now everyone seems to be taken care of—' Again he cast a look towards where Peggy was being attended to. He still didn't know her second name or where she lived. He grinned at the constable. 'I thought I'd better retrieve my kit, else my sergeant will have my guts for garters.'

'I see – well, go carefully. I'll just wait here and see you safely off again.'

Smiling, Terry turned away. I reckon he thinks I'm going to loot folks' belongings, he thought. But nothing was further from the young soldier's mind. All he wanted was to find his own so that he didn't have to face the wrath of his sergeant.

Terry found his kitbag easily enough, but his cap was nowhere to be seen. He clambered back to the platform and jumped down. 'Can't find me cap, but at least I've got most of me stuff. Thanks, Officer. Anything else I can do to help?'

'I don't think so, lad.' They were shouting at each other to make themselves heard above the noise; aircraft were still droning above them, dark, raptor-like shapes against the moonlit sky; flames spurted and crackled from the burning buildings, punctuated by the sudden crash of falling masonry. 'Maybe it'd be best if you left now, raid's not over yet.' Still they could hear the sound of more bombs falling. 'That's if you're sure you don't need any medical treatment.'

'Not a scratch,' Terry said cheerfully.

The constable nodded towards the buckled tram. 'Then you was lucky.'

Terry glanced behind him and took in the devastation of which he'd been a part. 'I was,' he agreed soberly. 'D'you know if anyone was killed?'

'I don't yet, sir, no. But there are certainly one or two very seriously injured.'

Terry's glance went back to the ambulance that was just beginning to move away. 'D'you know where they're taking the injured?'

'To the Royal Infirmary, I expect, though I've heard

there's been a bomb in that area, so whether they'll get through, I don't know.'

'Thanks.' Terry moved away from the policeman and the tram, but he did not leave the area as the constable had suggested; he wanted to find Peggy's sister. Now what was her name? And then he remembered. Rose, that was it. He wanted to know more about the clippie called Peggy and he wasn't going anywhere until he did.

Rose had rushed away into the throng, dodging round people, searching desperately for Bob. It was dark, but the flickering light from the fires engulfing the buildings illuminated the scene. She glanced skywards briefly, searching for enemy planes; the blazing city was an open invitation for yet more destruction. She grasped the arm of a police constable. 'Have you seen the motorman from this tram?' She gestured towards the one she knew Bob had been driving.

'Who?'

'The tram driver? Have you seen him?' She almost shook the man's arm: he was being obtuse. Who else did he think she meant?

'I don't know him, miss.'

Exasperated, she snapped. 'He'd be in uniform. Surely—'

The constable was gesturing around them. Several tram workers had arrived on the scene. 'Take your pick, love.'

Her hand fell away as she muttered, 'Sorry – it's just—'

The man nodded sympathetically. 'I understand, miss,

but I haven't come across the driver of *this* vehicle yet, though the fire brigade are still searching the wrecked trams. There's more than just this one, y'know.'

Rose felt as if the breath had been knocked from her body. 'Oh my God. He's not still trapped in there, is he?'

As she plunged away from him, the man called after her, 'Leave it to the professionals . . .' But the girl had gone and the constable hadn't time to chase after her; he had more urgent work to do.

Rose stepped over debris, twisting her ankle but scarcely noticing the pain. 'Bob – Bob –' she was sobbing now – 'where are you?'

She reached the end of the tram where Bob would have been at the time it was hit. The vehicle was still upright, but there was glass and splintered wood everywhere.

'Where is he? Where's the driver?' she demanded of a fireman who was close by.

He turned and looked at her in surprise. 'Get away, miss. You shouldn't be this close. Some of them buildings are going to come down any minute.'

'But the tram driver? What's happened to him? Have you seen him?'

The fireman turned and shouted to one of his mates. 'Pete, you seen the driver of this tram?'

His colleague shook his head. 'But I heard that the clippie has gone to hospital.'

'That's my sister, but she's not badly hurt. It's Bob I can't find.'

'Your boyfriend, is he?' the first fireman said.

'No – no,' Rose stammered and knew she was blushing. 'But – but he's a – a friend of the family.'

'Maybe he's gone to hospital already,' the second

fireman volunteered. 'Alf – we're wanted to tek over that hose.'

'He's not here, love,' the first one said and added, 'but please step back. You're hindering us now.'

'Sorry,' Rose said, surprisingly meekly. As she turned away, the fireman called after her. 'I hope you find him safe.'

'Thanks.' Unbidden, tears blinded her. In a daze, she walked back to where she had left Peggy and the soldier, but now there was no one there.

'You all right, love?' Jack, the motorman she worked with the most, touched her arm. 'They've taken Peggy to the hospital. I came out to see if there was owt I could do, but I'd best get back to the depot now. They might be needing us for extra duties. This is going to throw poor Mr Bower's duty boards into chaos. I know you were off tonight, but he might need you an' all.'

Rose glared at him. 'I'm going nowhere until I've found Bob. You go, if you want to but I'm—'

'Bob Deeton, you mean?' Jack was grinning. 'He's sitting over there against that wall, large as life and twice as ugly.'

Rose gasped and followed the line of Jack's pointing finger. And then she was running towards him, her arms outstretched, not caring now who saw her. 'Bob – oh, Bob.' She threw herself down beside him, grazing her knees, and flung her arms around him, burying her face against his neck. 'Oh, thank God. I couldn't find you. Are you all right?' She drew back and scanned his face. 'Are you hurt?'

Bob was staring about him with a glazed look in his eyes. He hardly seemed aware of her.

'Bob?' she said again, more tentatively now. Something was wrong. He didn't have any visible signs of injury and yet he was dazed, not knowing where he was and seeming not to recognize her. Rose scrambled to her feet again and ran towards another ambulance that had just arrived. She pulled open the door of the passenger's side and almost dragged the man from his seat. 'Quick, you must come quick.'

'Steady on, miss. Let's get a hold on the situation first.'

'You're needed. Over here. The driver of one of the trams that was bombed is sitting against that wall and he doesn't seem to know what day it is or where he is.'

'Concussion, probably, and shock. Just let me get my bag out the back.'

'Hurry. Please hurry.'

She waited impatiently until the man retrieved his first-aid kit and then she led him, stumbling over the debris, to where Bob was still sitting, staring about him yet not seeing the devastation in front of him. All around them fires still burned and more explosions could be heard, though they were further away now. And then suddenly another incendiary fell quite close to them, shaking the ground and sending flames shooting into the air.

'Now, mate, let's have a look at you,' the ambulance man said calmly.

Rose knelt beside them and watched as the ambulance man deftly examined Bob.

'Better get him to hospital as soon as we can. Can you help me get him into the ambulance, miss?' He glanced back towards where his colleague was already helping another casualty into the rear of the vehicle.

'Of course. Tell me what to do.'

Together, they lifted Bob bodily from the ground. 'We'll have to carry him. He's not making any effort to

110

help himself. Put his arm round your shoulders and your arm round his waist. We might manage him that way, otherwise I'll have to fetch the stretcher.'

'We'll manage,' Rose said stoutly and followed the man's instructions.

How they managed it, Rose didn't know. Maybe her feelings for Bob gave her extra strength for he was a dead weight between them, but somehow they got him into the ambulance.

'Can I come with him?'

'Sorry, love, but unless you're hurt—'

'No, no, I'm not. I wasn't involved, but my sister was his clippie.' She nodded towards Bob, now lying on the stretcher. There were two other people already in the vehicle, one with an injured arm, the other with a rough bandage round a head wound that was bleeding profusely.

The ambulance man closed the back doors. 'We'd best get these folks to hospital.'

As the vehicle drew carefully away, Rose stood watching it and suddenly she was shaking from head to foot.

'Rose?' The soldier was pushing his way towards her. 'Hey, Rose.' He reached her side and put his arm around her. 'Did you find him? The bloke you were looking for.'

She nodded as tears began to roll down her cheeks. 'Yes,' she whispered huskily. 'They've just taken him away. He – he was dazed. He didn't know me.'

'And now you're the one in shock. Come on, let's get you another cup of tea and then we'll both go to the hospital.'

Fourteen

Terry couldn't believe his luck. When he'd got on the tram and the clippie had taken his fare, he'd noticed her soft brown eyes, her genuinely warm smile and the way her shoulder-length brown hair curled around her cap. What soldier worth his salt wouldn't notice such a pretty girl? And what was the saying his mother was always fond of quoting? It's an ill wind that blows nobody any good. Well, he'd not have wished the tram on which they were travelling to be caught in a bomb blast, far from it, but now that it had happened he could see that it had given him the chance to get to know the pretty clippie. And now, with an even bigger stroke of luck, he'd found her sister, who was obviously in need of a bit of company and support.

'We'll go to that cafe where I got the tea before,' he said purposefully.

Rose made no protest; she was feeling decidedly wobbly, so she allowed him to lead her across the street away from the tram.

'Mind the glass,' he said, still holding her arm. 'Here we are.' He pushed open the door and stepped into the cafe, which was, sadly, not the warm and comforting haven it normally was. The window had been blown out despite the criss-cross tape that had been plastered across it and glass lay all around. A jovial, balding man in a long white apron was sweeping the floor.

'Come in, come in. They've tried to get me to leave, but I'm not going nowhere. Tek more 'n Hitler to get me to leave me cafe. What can I get you? T' kitchen's not damaged, thank goodness. Mind where you sit though, love. Here, let me clean these two chairs for you in this corner.'

They sat down and ordered strong, sweet tea. 'Anything to eat?' Terry asked, but Rose shook her head. 'I couldn't. I just want to get to the hospital to see how Bob is. And Peggy,' she added, almost as an afterthought. She looked up at him. 'I'm sorry, what did you say your name is?'

'Terry Price. And yours is Rose and your sister's Peggy and your boyfriend's Bob. Am I right?'

Rose smiled weakly. 'Nearly. Only Bob isn't *my* boyfriend.' She pulled in a deep breath. 'He's – he's Peggy's.'

Terry felt as if his heart had dropped into his size ten army boots. 'Oh. I got it wrong then.' He looked across the table at her. She was a pretty girl too, but there was something about Peggy that had already captured his heart. This wasn't the sister he wanted, nice though she was. And if he wasn't mistaken, there'd been reluctance in her tone when she'd said that the young man she'd been searching for with such desperation in her eyes when she couldn't find him was, in fact, her sister's boyfriend. Of course, she'd've been concerned. Wouldn't any sister? But there'd been more to it than just that, he was sure. She'd been desperate to find him on her own account.

Casually, he asked, 'Serious, is it? Between them?'

'I expect so.'

'Don't you know? I mean, are they engaged or anything?'

'No – no. But they've worked together for some time now and they've been walking out together since just before the war started.'

Terry took a gamble. He laughed as he said, 'He's a bit slow on the uptake then. If she was my girl, I'd have a ring on her finger pretty smartish.'

Rose's head snapped up and two bright spots of colour burned in her cheeks. 'He's not slow. He's a lovely man. It's not him – it's our Peggy. She doesn't know when she's got someone – someone . . .' As if realizing she was giving herself away to this stranger, she dropped her gaze and concentrated on stirring her tea.

But it was too late. Terry had seen and heard all he needed to know. This Bob might think he'd got a girlfriend in Peggy, but it sounded very much to him as if the girl herself wasn't all that sure.

Terry smiled and said gently, 'Drink your tea and then I'll take you to the hospital and we'll see how they both are.'

If Rose hadn't been in such a dazed state, suffering from shock and lost in a haze of dreadful anxiety over both her sister and Bob, she might have heard the distant sound of warning bells and refused the soldier's well-meaning offer there and then.

And over the years Rose was to wonder if what followed hadn't all been her fault.

The hospital seemed to be functioning in organized chaos. Bombs had fallen very close to it and Terry and Rose had to take a circuitous route to reach the building. The staff, calm, unruffled and completely professional, were nevertheless going about their duties with an added sense of urgency. Wartime tragedies like this were sadly nothing new for them, though this was the worst they had experienced to date. They had all been trained to deal with such sudden and devastating emergencies and they also knew how to deal kindly, but firmly, with hysterical family members.

The staff nurse eyed Rose and Terry and decided that they could be trusted not to cause disruption. A soldier still in uniform and a girl who said she was a clippie even though she wasn't in uniform. Their training would have prepared them for just this sort of situation. 'Your sister is ready to go home. She's a bit shaky and she shouldn't go back to work for a few days. She'll also need to come in tomorrow to have her wound redressed. It took a couple of stitches, but we're keeping the young man in. We suspect he's concussed or he's in deep shock. One or the other – maybe both. The doctor's with him now. I'll know more tomorrow – oh, no, it's today now, isn't it? Come back later.'

Rose nodded. 'Thank you, I will.' She was calmer now that she realized Bob was in the best place and being taken care of.

'Like I say, your sister can go, but you'd better all wait here until the All Clear sounds,' the nurse added and then showed them where Peggy was sitting on a row of seats waiting to be taken home by 'someone responsible', as she had been instructed.

'Rose, am I glad to see you!' Her eyes widened as she realized who was with her sister. 'Oh! It's you.'

Terry grinned. 'Yes, it's me. Turning up like a bad penny.'

Peggy smiled tremulously. She was still feeling shaky and very close to tears. They sat together, but it wasn't long before Terry was helping to move trolleys, lending a supporting arm and comforting a crying child who couldn't find her parents in the confusion as more and more casualties arrived at the hospital.

When the All Clear sounded at about four-thirty in the morning, Terry said, 'Come on, I'll take you both home.'

He made a conscious effort to be circumspect, treating them both with the same kindly concern and trying not to show that his interest was in Peggy. Working in the city's public transport system, the girls knew the bus routes almost as well as their own tram routes and soon they were seated on a bus that should have taken them to the end of their street. But the devastation of their city in the pale morning light shocked them and, after only a short distance, the driver said, 'Can't get you folks any further. Sorry.'

'You can't *walk* all the way home, Peg,' Rose said worriedly.

'It's not far now,' Peggy said, 'only about half a mile.' But her voice shook and she put her hand to her head as if she was still feeling decidedly woozy.

Without another word, Terry picked her up in his arms.

'Oh!' Peggy was startled. 'You can't carry me all that way.'

Terry chuckled. 'Oh yes I can. We have to march miles with full kit. I'm stronger than I look.'

They passed piles of smouldering rubble, stepped over bricks and firemen's hoses, and carefully skirted craters. People were climbing over the debris, searching for their belongings. A child sat alone, staring into space, and an old man was weeping openly. They moved on, passing houses that had been reduced to a heap of wood and bricks in one night. Rose shuddered, imagining people still trapped beneath the collapsed buildings. She would have loved to stop and help the emergency services, who were already searching for survivors, but she couldn't linger.

A woman was sitting in an armchair perched precariously on top of a pile of wreckage, quiet and calm, just as if she were sitting at her own fireside.

Pausing, Rose said, 'Do you think she's all right?' Though she was anxious to get Peggy home – and to see if their own family was unscathed – nevertheless, she couldn't just walk past someone who might be in trouble. No more, it seemed, could Terry, for he set Peggy gently on the ground and climbed nimbly up to the woman. As he bent to speak to her, Rose and Peggy saw her give a wry smile and nod. Terry patted her hand and slithered back down the pile of rubble.

'She's fine. Just having a moment or two with her ruined possessions before she has to leave.'

As he picked Peggy up again, she said, 'What are all these poor folks going to do?'

'They'll set up rest centres for the homeless,' Terry said. 'Now let's get you home.'

'I hope they're all right,' Rose muttered and quickened her step. As they came to a street very near to their own, they saw that two houses had been completely demolished. Seeing the destruction and the smouldering crater, Rose began to run.

Fifteen

They'd been in the cellar for hours, when Letty suddenly piped up, 'Let's 'ave a sing-song. Drown out them buggers overhead, eh? Come on . . .' and in a raucous, tuneless voice she began to sing '*My ol' man said foller the van . . .*'

Half-heartedly, they joined in, all except Grace, who resolutely clamped her mouth shut. Sidney and Jimmy were sniggering in the corner of the cellar, trying to catch spiders to put into empty matchboxes, no doubt with the intention of making little girls at school squeal with fright. And then the Bradshaw boys would be in trouble yet again.

Letty was still singing about dillying and dallying when there was a whistle and a resounding thump that shook the ground beneath them. Above them there was the sound of breaking glass and a loud crash.

Letty leapt to her feet. 'The house, it's falling in on top of us. We'll be trapped. We'll be killed . . .'

Tom grasped her arm and pulled her back down. 'Calm down, Letty love. If it was t' house falling down, there'd've been a darned sight more noise than that.' He glanced at Grace. 'Reckon you'll have a bit of damage up there, though, love.'

'Ah well,' Grace said philosophically. 'As long as no one's hurt.'

But it was a vain hope.

When at last the All Clear sounded, they were all cramped and cold.

'Hot tea all round and bed for what's left of the night,' Grace said, shining the torch she always brought down into the cellar as she pulled herself up the steps and opened the door into the living room. 'Oh no!'

'What is it, Mother?' Mary asked, close behind her.

'I can smell something funny.'

'It's not gas, is it?'

'You all right, Mrs Booth?' Tom shouted from below. 'Want me to come up?'

'Just wait here a moment, Mother. I'll go and see what damage there is.'

The cold December morning was still dark, but as soon as Mary stepped into the room she felt the draught. 'I think the window's broken. Just be careful until I can put the light on. Wait there.' Her feet crunched on broken glass as she crossed the room carefully to the light switch. She flicked the switch a couple of times, but nothing happened.

Grace shone the torch around the room.

'Oh no!' Mary gasped. The room was covered in soot. The furniture, the walls – everything was blackened. The window was broken and glass was scattered over the floor, the table and chairs. The clock that usually stood on the mantelpiece was face down on the hearthrug.

Grace moved slowly into the room, glancing round her, her mouth a grim line. 'If I could get me hands on that ruddy 'Itler . . .' she muttered.

Myrtle climbed the stairs and stepped into the room.

'Be careful,' Mary said. 'We need to find another torch and light some candles. And I'll light the lamp. It's not gas you could smell, Mother, it's soot.' An oil lamp stood on the sideboard, always primed and ready should it be needed. Miraculously, it was still upright.

When the lamp was lit, Mary said, 'I'll check the front room. Myrtle, you check upstairs, but be careful.' The girl was standing by the table looking down mournfully at her books. They were all covered with a thin layer of soot.

Mary returned to say, 'Oh, Mother – I'm so sorry. Your china cabinet's been knocked over. I – I think nearly everything's broken.'

Grace stood by the table still glancing round her and shaking her head in disbelief.

'It's not too bad upstairs,' Myrtle reported. 'There's soot on the hearthrug in both your rooms, but it's not all over like down here. Mine and Rose's room is all right, because there's no fireplace in there. The only thing that's broken that I can see is Gran's mirror. There's a huge crack right across it.'

'Seven years' bad luck, then,' Grace murmured, still staring round, shocked and bewildered at the wreckage of her home.

Mary put her arm around Grace's shoulders. 'Come on, Mother. You go up and get into bed. I'll bring you some tea up.'

'What? When there's this lot to clear up?'

'You've had a shock – you ought to—'

'Mary, I know you mean well, but if you think I'm going to let that – that lunatic get the better of me, then you don't know me very well. Come on, the sooner we get started, the sooner we'll get it all cleared up.'

Grace set to work with an energy that surprised even her family. The only time her face crumpled and her shoulders sagged for a brief moment was when she stood in the front room and viewed the smashed remains of her treasured tea service.

'My parents gave us that on our wedding day,' she murmured. 'They didn't have very much and it must have taken them months to save up to buy it. I only ever used it the once.'

Mary put her arm around her mother and asked softly, 'When was that?'

'Your christening. After that, I was so afraid of a piece getting broken and spoiling the set that I left it safely in the cabinet and, when I could afford it, bought another to use on special occasions.'

'The willow pattern one?'

Grace nodded. 'Over the years pieces have been cracked and broken. We've only a few bits left now.' She sighed. 'So you see, I was right. That's what would have happened to my best set. But I needn't have bothered – Hitler's done it for me.'

Mary hugged her and whispered, 'They're just things, Mother. We're safe. That's what counts.' Her face clouded and her voice wobbled a little as she added, 'Just so long as Peggy and Rose come home safely.'

Grace took a deep breath and gave a weak smile. 'Yes, you're right.'

The three of them worked hard for an hour, sweeping and cleaning. And then they heard the rattle of the front door opening.

From the outside their house looked unscathed and, as Terry set her down gently outside their front door, Peggy felt the least she could do was to invite the young soldier in for a cup of tea after all his kindness.

'That's very kind of you,' Terry said, deliberately holding back his eagerness. 'As long as it's no trouble.'

Rose was already opening the door and shouting, 'Mam – Gran? Are you all right?'

'Mam would never forgive us if we let you go without a proper thank you,' Peggy said. 'Come on in. And be prepared,' she added, with a laugh that was still unsteady. 'We're a houseful of women, so don't say you haven't been warned.'

'I won't.' Terry grinned back at her as he placed his hand gently under her elbow to guide her across the threshold into the house.

'Oh my goodness, whatever's happened?' Mary came hurrying from the living room when she heard the front door open. She was still fully dressed from the previous day, but dusty from a long night spent in the cellar.

'Now don't panic, Mam. She's all right,' Rose tried to reassure their mother. 'Just a little cut on her fore-head and she's a bit shaky. She'll soon be as right as ninepence.'

'But how did you get hurt, Peggy? Oh—' Suddenly, she became aware that her daughters were not alone.

'Terry helped Peggy get her passengers out of the tram when it was hit—'

'Hit?' Mary's voice was high-pitched with fear. 'What do you mean – hit? Did another vehicle run into it? Oh my God!' Her eyes widened in fear as she realized exactly what Rose meant. 'The bombing. Your tram was caught in the bombing. But didn't you get to a shelter? Didn't you—?'

'Look, come and sit down and we'll tell you,' Rose said, taking charge and trying to quieten the panic she could hear in her mother's voice. 'I'll get the kettle on.

This nice young soldier could do with a cuppa before he has to face his sergeant. He's lost his cap in the confusion.'

'Oh, Rose, we can't. We've had some bomb damage. The place is in a dreadful mess.'

'Is everyone all right?' Rose asked, suddenly anxious. 'Gran? Myrtle?'

'Yes, yes, we're fine, but Gran's upset about the house. There's soot everywhere and several things have been broken.

'Can I sit down?' Peggy said suddenly and put her hand to her head. At once Terry's arm was around her and he half-led, half-carried her through to the living room and set her down in the armchair on the opposite side of the hearth to where Grace always sat. It still bore traces of soot, even though Grace had brushed it, but that was the least of their worries just now.

'Hello. What's going on?' Grace demanded, struggling to her feet from where she'd been on her knees sweeping the carpet with a dustpan and brush. 'What's happened?'

'That's what I'd like to know,' Mary demanded of Rose. 'Well?'

'Perhaps I can explain,' Terry said. He was still standing close to Peggy, watching her with solicitous eyes. 'The tram I was on, that is, Peggy's tram, was caught in a bomb blast.' Mary gasped, turned pale and sank into the nearest chair, not caring now if she was sitting on a layer of soot. Her legs just gave way as she heard how close her daughter had been to serious injury – or worse.

'Go on, young man,' Grace said.

'Not a direct hit, thank God, else I don't think either

of us would be here. Peggy was very brave.' His eyes softened as he gazed at her. 'She thought nothing of her own safety nor even of her injury.'

Peggy gave a wry laugh. 'To be honest, I didn't know I was injured until you got me off the tram. I was knocked to the floor and I think I must have passed out for a minute or two.'

'All she thought about was getting all her passengers, those who could move, off the tram.'

'Was anybody – seriously hurt?' Mary asked and added in a whisper, 'or killed?'

'There are several in hospital—'

'Bob's one of them,' Rose blurted out. 'He's in a right daze. Doesn't seem to know where he is or what happened. It might be concussion, the nurse said. We had to leave – bring Peggy home – but we can go back tonight.'

'Peggy's going nowhere tonight,' Mary said firmly. 'One of us can go up and see how he is.' She turned to Rose. 'Does his mother know?'

'I don't know. I'll go and see her later. I'll have to walk though. I've no idea what transport will be able to operate now – if any.' Hester Deeton, Bob's widowed mother, lived just under a mile away in the Walkley district. 'I hope she went into the Anderson that Bob built in the back yard.'

'We were in the cellar, but we heard all the noise. And then there was one dropped very close. The whole ground seemed to shake. It must have been that one that did all the damage.'

'It's just round the corner from here,' Rose said. 'You were lucky it wasn't any closer or . . .' She stopped and bit her lip. It didn't bear thinking about.

'I never thought one of you might be caught up in it.

Whyever weren't you in the public shelters, like Laurence – Mr Bower – instructed? And what about you, Rose? Where were you? How come you're with Peggy?'

Rose had the grace to look a little shame-faced. 'I – er – went to find Peg.' She omitted to add 'and Bob'.

Mary gasped. 'Didn't you go into the shelter? There's one under the cinema, isn't there?'

Rose avoided her mother's gaze.

'You didn't, did you? You went out in the middle of an air raid. Oh, Rose – what am I to do with you? If I'd known . . .' Mary shuddered and Grace muttered sagely, 'Good job you didn't know. I wouldn't have been able to do a thing with you until you'd known they were both safe.'

Terry looked up, caught the old woman's eye and winked broadly. 'Mothers, eh?'

Grace blinked, but instead of fixing him with a steely glare at such sauciness, she actually smiled. She liked a bit of spirit in a young man and he reminded her of her dear husband when she'd first met him: he'd had a similar cheeky grin and a roguish sparkle in his eyes.

'Well, I'm sorry we can't offer you tea, young man. We've nowhere to boil the kettle at the moment. But, Rose, you might be able to find a piece of cake in a tin in the kitchen cupboard. Go and look.'

When Rose came back into the living room a little while later with a tray of slices of cake set out on plates, proper introductions had been made and Terry was sitting beside Peggy still regaling Grace, Mary and Myrtle with details of the bombing. To Rose's amusement all three women appeared to be hanging on his every word. But then her smile died. Not one of them – not even Peggy – appeared to be giving a thought to Bob.

Sixteen

With a supreme effort, Rose managed to hide her feelings and her overwhelming desire to rush back to the hospital and demand to sit at Bob's bedside. She knew she wouldn't be allowed to do that anyway, but the need to go back there as soon as she could to see him was hard to rein in. Instead she handed round the cake, smiling, laughing, and trying to make her mother and grandmother forget what might have happened to them all. The damage that lay all around them was a constant reminder; a reminder too of what had happened to Bob. What if he was so badly injured she'd never see his wonderful smile again, never be able to enjoy saucy banter with him? Rose couldn't bear to think that he'd be changed by his injuries. She loved him just the way he was, even though that love must remain her secret. Soon she couldn't help bringing the conversation back to Bob.

'Peggy, do you want me to go round to his mother's? She might like some company.'

'Oh, Rose, would you? I'm sure Bob'd be so grateful. Thanks.'

'You're beginning to look better. The colour's coming back into your face,' Terry said.

Peggy pulled a wry face. 'I still feel dizzy.'

'You're bound to. Just take it easy.' He glanced

round the room, his gaze coming to rest on Grace, whom he'd guessed to be the head of the household.

'I'm not due back at camp until Sunday night. I could give you a hand here, if you like.' He grinned. 'Cleaning's one of my sergeant's favourite punishments. I'm quite a dab hand now.'

'That's very kind of you,' Grace said, 'but there are plenty of us. We'll manage.'

He shook hands politely with Mary and Grace, but it was Peggy whose hand he held a little longer than was absolutely necessary, Peggy's eyes he looked into a little too earnestly as he murmured, 'Take care of yourself.'

'I will.' Peggy was gazing up into his brown eyes and making no effort to pull her hand away from his. 'And – thank you so much for – for everything.'

'I'll see you out,' Rose said tersely, breaking up the tender moment. You should be thinking of Bob, she wanted to shout at her sister, not making cow's eyes at a complete stranger. 'Goodnight, Terry, and thanks again for all your help.'

'Don't mention it,' he said, picking up his kitbag, which he'd left in the hall.

As he began to walk along the street, Rose heard him whistling jauntily. The sound brought a smile to her lips and she shook her head. He was a likeable rascal – even their grandmother had been bowled over by him. But it was obvious to her that his interest was in Peggy and, to her dismay, Peggy had responded.

Rose sighed as she closed the door. Much as she loved Bob herself, she knew he had eyes for no one but Peggy and she couldn't bear to see him hurt. Plastering a smile on her face, she went back into the living room. 'Right, who's coming to the hospital with me to find out how Bob is for Peggy?'

Margaret Dickinson

'I will,' Mary said. 'But aren't you going to wait until this afternoon? Besides, there's work to think of.'

Rose made an impatient gesture. 'Mr Bower will understand. Besides, how d'you think the trams can keep running after last night? The whole city centre is devastated.'

'Maybe they won't, but they'll run what they can and it's not for you to decide not to turn up for work,' Mary said firmly. 'I think we should all get a bit of sleep now, have some lunch and then you and I, Rose, will report in for work. If we're not needed, we'll go to Hester's to make sure she knows about Bob and then we'll go to the hospital.' She paused and looked at Peggy. 'As long as you'll be all right.'

'She'll be fine,' Grace said. 'I'll keep my eye on her. Myrtle, hadn't you better be getting ready for school?'

The girl yawned. 'Do you think they'll be opening?'

'Well, you'll find out when you get there, won't you?' She turned to Peggy. 'And you, young lady, would be better in bed.'

'No, I'll stay down here for a while.' Peggy leaned her head against the back of the chair and closed her eyes. Mary fetched a blanket from Peggy's single bed and tucked it around her, but Peggy was already asleep.

'Right, Mam, are you ready?' Rose was fidgeting to be off. The sooner they reported for work, the sooner she could find out how Bob was.

'Like I said, a rest now, some lunch,' Mary said firmly, 'and then we'll go. Dear me, what a Friday the thirteenth this is turning out to be.'

'What about all this?' Frowning, Grace waved her hand around the room. 'I can't manage it on my own and Peggy's not fit. I wish I'd taken up that nice soldier's offer now.'

128

'I'll wash the paintwork down tonight,' Rose promised swiftly, 'but I think the wallpaper's spoilt.'

'I'm not redecorating yet just to have the same thing happen again,' Grace said, her fighting spirit restored. 'A good brush down and a wipe over will have to do for now. And I doubt you'll do much washing down tonight, Rose. The water's off. Let's hope that's only temporary. No doubt they'll come round with water carts.' Grace pulled a face. 'More queuing – this time with jugs and buckets. And all drinking water'll have to be boiled.'

'It could be a lot worse, Gran. At least our house is still standing.'

As Rose had rightly predicted, the duty board at the depot was in chaos. Poor Laurence had no idea which tram routes could operate – if any.

'I'm still getting information in. Nothing's running at the moment. There have been over thirty cars damaged beyond repair and about another thirty need major work on them. Then there are a lot more with minor damage – broken windows and the like – to say nothing of the poles and overhead cables. The centre of town is out of the question and even outlying routes have been badly affected.' He ran his hand through his hair. 'It's a nightmare. Look, you two go home, but keep in touch and I'll let you know when you're needed. How's Peggy?'

'Badly shaken. She'll not be into work for a few days. And I suppose you know about Bob?'

Laurence nodded. 'Let me know how he is, will you? I can't get up to the hospital myself yet. Maybe tonight.'

As they walked, Rose could sense that Mary was feeling the same horror that she'd felt at the sight of the carnage the night's bombing had left. When they arrived in the street where Bob and his mother lived, Rose breathed a sigh of relief. Bombs had fallen not far away, but thankfully not near their home. But when she rapped on the front door, there was no reply.

'Let's try round the back.'

They went down the alleyway between Mrs Deeton's home and the adjacent house and knocked on the back door. Still, there was no answer. Then the neighbour's back door opened and a man came to the fence and leaned on the top of it.

'Looking for Hester, a' yer?'

'That's right,' Rose said and stepped towards him.

'She's gone up t' hospital, lass. Her lad was injured in one o' them trams that was hit last night.'

'Oh, she knows. That's all right then. We'd come to tell her. We're on our way there now. Thanks very much.'

'No trouble, love. I hope you find him on the mend.'

'Yes – thanks,' Rose murmured and beneath her breath added, 'I hope so too.' Louder she said, 'Come on, Mam, we'd better get ourselves up there, else visiting will be over.'

But when they arrived at the hospital, it was to find that they were not allowed in to see him.

'Next of kin only, I'm afraid,' a nurse told them. 'I am sorry.'

Rose turned pale. 'How – how bad is he?'

'He has a head injury. We suspect a fractured skull, but we'll know more when we get the results of the X-ray.'

'Is his mother still with him?' Mary asked and the nurse nodded.

'Then we'll wait for her, if we may?'

'Of course.'

They went back to the entrance hall, through which Hester was bound to pass when she left. Whilst they waited, Mary said, 'I've known Hester a long time, you know. We were at school together.'

'Really, Mam? You've never said.'

'The Askews – that was Hester's name before she married – lived two streets away from us then.' Mary paused and bit her lip. 'If I was being snobby – and you know I'm not – I'd say that Hester married beneath her. Her husband was a hard worker, though,' Mary added quickly. She never liked to speak ill of anyone, not even if they richly deserved it. 'He worked at the steel works, but died following some sort of accident.'

'Wasn't he in the Great War, then?'

Mary shook her head. 'No, exempted because of the job he was doing.'

'But he died anyway.'

'Yes. Sad, isn't it?' Mary whispered and Rose knew she was referring not just to all the men who'd died in the previous war, but also all those who were dying right now. And this time the enemy were targeting the civilian population too.

They were trying to demoralize not only Londoners but the citizens of other big cities too. And one of those was their very own Sheffield.

'There she is,' Mary said suddenly, as the tide of visitors came flooding down the corridors and out through the entrance hall.

The little woman, shabbily dressed and clutching a shopping bag, came hurrying past them. Her face was creased with anxiety and she chewed her bottom lip nervously.

'Hester?' Mary stepped forward and touched the

woman's arm. The woman jumped and turned frightened eyes towards Mary, but recognizing her, her face relaxed a little.

'Oh, Mary, how good of you to come.' She turned to look at Rose, but it was obvious that she'd been expecting to see Peggy. At once the anxious look returned. 'I thought Peggy would have come. Oh dear, she's not hurt too, is she?'

'Only very slightly, but she's badly shaken. She's resting at home. But how is Bob, Hester? The nurse wouldn't let us come in.'

Mary guided Hester to the side of the hallway so that they could stand and talk without hindering those rushing to get home before the blackout, their journey hampered by the lack of public transport and the bomb damage. There was even the fear of unexploded bombs or, worse still, another visit from Hitler's Luftwaffe.

'They think he's got a fractured skull.' Tears filled Hester Deeton's eyes.

'Is he conscious?'

'Yes, but he's very dazed. Says he has no recollection of what happened.'

'We'll walk a little way with you,' Mary offered, linking her arm through Hester's. 'Is there anything we can do to help?'

'That's kind of you, Mary, but I don't think so. Only – only if Peggy could visit him as soon as she feels able. He's asking for her.'

Hester's words were like a knife through Rose's heart.

By the time they reached home Peggy was in bed and asleep.

'I told her that bed was the best place for her,' Grace said, setting down mugs of steaming cocoa on the table. 'I managed to boil some milk on the fire, so, come on, drink it while it's hot, 'cos I don't know how much longer we'll be able to enjoy cocoa. That's the last we had in the cupboard.'

Mary and Rose sipped it gratefully, cupping their hands round the hot mugs to get warm.

'It's bitter out and the blackout makes it worse somehow,' Mary said. 'I wish I wasn't back on duty quite so early in the morning.'

'I doubt either of us will be needed tomorrow or for a few days yet,' Rose said.

'But we must report in.'

'So – how was he?' Grace asked.

'We don't really know any more yet—'

'They wouldn't let us see him,' Rose burst out. 'Next of kin, but I bet they'd've let Peggy in if she'd gone.'

There was a note of reproach in her tone that the other two women could not fail to hear.

'She's not fit,' Mary said gently. 'She'll go as soon as she can.'

Rose buried her nose in her mug of cocoa. She wasn't too sure. She'd seen the way that Peggy had looked up at the soldier.

Seventeen

The knock at the door came early on the Saturday. Peggy, still in her dressing gown, was sitting near the kitchen fire. Mary and Rose had reported for duty though there was little they could do: most of the city's transport system was at a standstill. So, Grace, grumbling beneath her breath, was the one to open the door.

'Oh, it's you,' she smiled up at the dark-haired soldier. 'Come in, do.'

'I just called to see how Peggy is. And her young man,' he added, striving to be circumspect. He didn't want any of them guessing the real reason for his visit today, that he hadn't been able to get Peggy's pretty face out of his mind.

Grace held the door open wider and he stepped inside. She glanced up at him and smiled. 'You didn't find your cap then?'

Terry grimaced. 'No, I'll be for it when I get back to camp tomorrow night. That's if I can get there at all. I don't know what trains are running.'

'Surely not? You were caught up in a bombing incident. You can't be blamed for your cap going missing.'

Terry laughed. 'You don't know my sergeant. He'll likely think it's an excuse.'

'Well, you refer him to me if you have any trouble. I'll give him what for. Come on through. Peggy' – she raised her voice as she ushered him into the living room – 'are you decent? You've got a visitor.'

Peggy, who'd been dozing by the fire, opened her eyes and blinked. 'Oh! Hello.' There was no mistaking the blush that tinged her cheeks as she sat up and pulled the dressing gown more closely around her.

'Sit down, sit down.' Grace almost pushed him into the armchair that was usually her seat. 'I'm busy washing up.'

'Can I help?'

'No, no, you sit and chat to Peggy till I'm done.' Her eyes twinkled at him with a merriment that Peggy hadn't seen in her grandmother's eyes for a long time – if ever. If she hadn't known better, she'd've thought Grace was flirting with the young soldier.

When the door into the kitchen closed, Terry smiled at Peggy and asked softly, 'How are you feeling?'

'Much better. I ought to be back at work really.'

'You'll do no such thing. Besides, you're supposed to go back to the hospital today to have the dressing changed, aren't you?'

Peggy nodded. 'Mam's going with me when she gets home.'

'I could go with you.'

'Oh – well – that's kind of you, but I don't want to take up your time.'

Terry shrugged. 'I've nothing – else to do.' He'd almost said 'nothing *better* to do', but he'd altered the word just in time. He didn't want to push his luck too far, too soon. 'And anyway, there aren't many trams running. I've walked all the way here.

'You go and get dressed while I help your gran finish off in there and then I'll get you to the hospital somehow. And,' he added with more generosity than

135

he was feeling, 'you can find out how your feller's doing.'

Peggy gave a weak smile as she got up and went towards the door into the hall. Terry went into the kitchen to explain their plans. 'Now, Mrs Sylvester, where's a tea towel?'

''Tisn't Mrs Sylvester. I'm Mary's mother. It's Mrs Booth.'

'Oh, sorry.'

'You weren't to know.'

They'd finished the washing up together and were sitting by the fireside when Peggy came down. Terry rose to his feet at once. 'You look a lot better already, don't you think so, Mrs Booth?'

'Mm.' Grace eyed her granddaughter suspiciously. She couldn't tell whether this was because she was on her way to see Bob or because she was going out on the arm of a very handsome soldier.

Grace had the shrewd suspicion it was the latter.

They had to wait for Peggy's wound to be cleaned and redressed, so it was some time before she was able to ask about Bob.

'I'll wait outside,' Terry offered. 'They might let you see him if they know you were in the bombing too. And that you're his girl.'

When she joined him near the hospital entrance only a few minutes later, she shook her head. 'Visiting's just finished for this afternoon, but I did find out one thing. His injury's not as bad as they feared. They think he might have a hairline fracture of the skull, but it's nothing to worry about. He will be off work for a while, but there's certainly no permanent damage.'

'That's wonderful news,' Terry said, trying to inject genuine pleasure into his tone. Not that he wished the poor bloke any harm; far from it, but he wouldn't have minded Bob being out of the way for a little while longer. At least until he could wangle another leave, because Terry had made up his mind that he was going to try his luck with Peggy. In a way it was better that Bob wasn't seriously injured. Terry would have felt a heel if he'd nicked the bloke's girlfriend while he was lying in hospital. At least, this way, it would be a fair fight.

'Come on,' he said putting his arm around her waist. 'Let's get you home. I expect you're still feeling a bit wobbly.'

'I am rather,' she agreed. Making no effort to remove his arm, Peggy allowed him to steer her towards the bus stop. They waited ages until one appeared, but it could only take them part of the way. The city streets were so badly damaged that the public transport system – both buses and trams – was in chaos.

'I'll see if I can grab a taxi.'

'No – no,' Peggy insisted. 'If – if I could just take your arm and we walk slowly, I'll be fine.'

Terry smiled down at her and offered his arm, his heart leaping with hope.

Mary had arrived home by the time they got back, and Terry was still there when Rose came in.

'Oh!' She stopped in surprise when she saw all the family – and Terry Price – seated round the tea table. 'You're here,' she said unnecessarily.

'Terry's been very kind,' Grace said, getting up to fetch Rose's meal, which was keeping hot in the range oven. 'He took Peggy to the hospital and brought her home again.'

'What about Bob?' The question was more than just asking after him and they all knew it, but Peggy chose to ignore the further insinuation in her sister's question. How is he? the question implied, but also what about your boyfriend when you're sitting round the tea table all cosy with another feller?

Having washed her hands, Rose sat down and picked up her knife and fork. Her face was like thunder and she kept her eyes firmly fixed on her plate. The others had finished their meal and Mary turned to Myrtle. 'You may leave the table, if you've homework to do.'

Myrtle smiled and glanced from Peggy to Terry and then to Rose's furious face. 'Haven't got any,' Myrtle said promptly. 'Our school's been turned into a rest centre,' she went on to explain. 'When the head heard that all buildings which could take a lot of people were needed, all the staff volunteered to help the homeless. Our classrooms are housing people who've been bombed out. Some of them' – she paused dramatically – 'have lost everything but the clothes they stand up in.'

'And what about your lessons?'

Myrtle shrugged, 'Suspended for the time being. All the pupils have been running messages and helping to organize food, clothes and bedding for them.'

'You mean they're going to *sleep* there?' Rose asked.

Myrtle shrugged in a matter-of-fact manner. 'Where else?'

Rose blinked, but couldn't think of an answer.

'Well,' Grace remarked dryly, 'for someone who made such a fuss about schools closing when war broke out, you're taking this remarkably calmly.'

'This is different, Gran. People need help and it's quite nice to be doing something useful for once.

138

They're all so grateful to us for looking after them and folks from round about have been marvellous,' Myrtle went on. 'They've brought food and clothing to the school. Some women even brought prams for the babies. And two of the classrooms were turned into sick bays.'

'Now, you just be careful, Myrtle,' Mary began, but Myrtle dismissed her mother's worries with a wave of her hand. 'It was for people who'd got minor injuries. One family had been trapped in their cellar when their house collapsed. It took eight hours to dig them out.'

'I wondered why you'd gone out this morning dressed in your school uniform. I didn't realize until after you'd gone that it's Saturday today.' Grace shook her head and sighed. 'I've just lost track of the days.'

'So,' Myrtle went on, 'I'm helping out in the sick bay.'

Myrtle liked a bit of drama and now it looked as if there might be some at home as well as at her school. She'd no intention of going up to her room if things were likely to get lively. Myrtle's homework was useful when there were chores to be excused from, or she preferred to be on her own reading in bed rather than listening to what she considered the inane chatter of her sisters. Make-up, hairstyles and boyfriends had no appeal for the sixteen-year-old, though she admitted that Terry was handsome – very handsome. He was just the sort that she'd go for when she was older. But that would be when she was much older and she'd mind he had a better job than working on a city building site, which was where Terry at this very moment was telling them he'd worked until he'd joined up.

'I felt I had to do my bit this time round. My father

fought in the last lot. He volunteered when he was only seventeen – right at the beginning in 1914. Can you imagine that?'

Mary's face sobered. 'My husband volunteered too, but he was very badly injured. He – he was never the same again.'

'You should never have married him, Mary—'

'Mother – not in front of the girls.'

Grace waved her hand dismissively. 'They know my opinion about their father. Oh, he was a good sort – I'll never say different – but when he came back from the war he was a broken man.' She glanced at Terry. 'He never worked again – not properly – but he could still sire bairns for us to struggle to bring up.'

'Mother, please!' Mary's face reddened.

Terry touched her hand with a gentle, sympathetic gesture.

Oh, he's clever, Rose thought malevolently. Making up to Mam now, whilst still having his eye on the main chance. But I can see through you, Mr Price. I'm watching you. For some strange reason, it didn't even cross Rose's mind that if Terry were to entice Peggy away from Bob, then the field would be left open for her. All the girl could think was: Bob is going to be so desperately hurt.

'We were luckier,' Terry was saying. 'Dad came back without a scratch, though he did end the war with what they now call shell-shock.'

Mary's eyes filled with understanding. 'Ted had that too. That was almost worse than the physical injuries.'

There was silence around the table; Myrtle was still watching Terry whilst Rose was trying valiantly not to look at him.

At last he got up, thanked Grace and Mary for their

hospitality and said he must be going, but they could all tell that he was reluctant to leave.

'I'll call again tomorrow before I leave for camp,' he asked and then added politely, 'if I may?'

Rose opened her mouth to protest, but Peggy said quickly, 'Of course.'

Eighteen

'My, you look a mess. What on earth have you been doing?' Grace said bluntly when she opened the door to Terry the following afternoon.

Terry's eyes were dark, ringed with weariness, his uniform dusty, as he followed Grace into the living room and slumped into a chair at the table. But his gaze went at once to Peggy. 'I've been up all night.' His voice was hoarse, his words hesitant. Peggy's hand flew to her mouth. 'Oh no! Your family! They're not – they're not—?' She dared not say the word.

But Terry shook his head. 'No, they're fine. Thank God. No, I've just been out with the rescuers. Being in uniform, they let me help. We're been digging folks out from under their wrecked homes.' He paused a moment before saying flatly, 'Most of the time it was just bringing out bodies.' Then his tone was lighter as he added, 'But we did find several still alive. The best bit was when we found kiddies. Frightened and dirty, but still alive. That was the very best.' Now his voice was husky with emotion as he went on, 'But then I went to the Marples Hotel.' Peggy gasped and stared wide-eyed at him. 'It's dreadful there. A lot of people were sheltering in the cellars when it took a direct hit. They never had a chance. There's only a handful been brought out alive. It's – horrific.' They were all silent for a few moments, as if paying tribute to all those who had died.

'The centre of the city is destroyed. There's hardly a building untouched. Many are still smouldering. No end of trams are wrecked. I saw one lying in two pieces, its top deck completely severed from the bottom. Several are burned out and the wires are just a tangled mess. A lot of the big stores are in ruins and many lovely old buildings are gone forever and yet—'

'Yes?' Peggy whispered.

He smiled slowly. 'Folks are still trying to carry on. Men are walking to work – that's if they've work to go to when they get there. Rescue centres are springing up and the WVS are out with their vehicles, handing out cups of tea to the rescue parties and to the men who've already started on the repairs.' He shook his head. 'We took a hell of a battering on Thursday night, but he didn't destroy our spirit. I've never been more proud to be a Sheffielder.'

Grace pulled herself out of her chair. 'Would you like a wash in the bathroom, lad? If you don't mind carrying up a bucket of water. It's cold, I'm afraid, but you're welcome.'

'I don't want to use your water. You're having to fetch it from mobile tanks just now, aren't you?'

'We'll soon get some more.' She chuckled. 'Rose and Myrtle are the water carriers until the supply's back on. Up you go. There's clean towels in the airing cupboard. You'll see it. Help yourself.'

'I have to get back to camp tonight and I daren't be late.' Terry laughed wryly when he came downstairs again. He looked cleaner but his face was still grey with tiredness, his eyes haunted by the sights he'd seen. 'I'm going to be in enough trouble for losing my cap.'

'I could write to your sergeant,' Peggy offered. 'If it would help. Tell him what happened.'

Terry rested his hand on her shoulder. 'That's sweet of you, but I think he'll believe me. He knows I live in Sheffield and he'll have heard about the bombing.'

'Where are you stationed?'

Terry laughed again and tapped the side of his nose. 'Now, now, asking questions. Careless talk and all that. I'll be thinking you're a beautiful spy.'

Rose was about to get up to leave the room – she couldn't bear to watch the obvious flirting between the two of them – when another knock came at the front door.

Grace frowned. 'It's like the centre of town on a Saturday night,' she muttered.

Rose pulled a face and murmured, 'Not just now, it isn't, Gran.'

Grace buried her head in her newspaper.

A few moments later Rose ushered Laurence into the living room. 'I just called to see how Peggy is and to let you know the latest news. Work is progressing on restoring the tracks and overhead cables, but it's a slow job. They've already got a couple of routes open, but not ours, I'm afraid. A few buses are able to operate, but I understand that it's the electricity supply that's causing the major problem now for our trams and with so many cars beyond repair, we're trying to get replacements from other cities. Bradford and Newcastle may be able to let us have some, but I expect it'll be a while before we get them. So, a few more days off at least.'

'Not for you, I bet,' Mary said softly.

'Well, no, that's true. I feel I have to be at the depot in case I'm needed.'

'What about other members of staff?' Rose asked, her chagrin at Terry's continued presence forgotten for the moment in her concern for her colleagues. 'Was anyone hurt – I mean, worse than Peggy and Bob?'

Laurence's face was grim. 'I'm afraid so. In fact, two were killed. No one from our depot,' he hastened to add, 'but it feels as if we've lost members of our extended family.'

'What about Jack?' Rose asked about the motorman she worked with the most. 'I did see him that night but is he all right? And Alice? Is she safe? I – I left her at the cinema,' Rose added, feeling guilty now that she had deserted her friend.

'All fine, thank goodness, though I understand the street where Alice lives was badly damaged. No, Peggy and Bob were our only casualties.' He smiled at Peggy. 'How are you feeling now?'

Peggy smiled tremulously. 'Still a bit unsteady, if I'm honest.'

'There's no need for you to worry about coming back to work. There isn't any for you at the moment.' He stood up. 'I must be going.'

Rose glanced at Terry, almost willing him to say that he must go too, but he avoided meeting her hostile gaze. Terry knew exactly what Rose felt about him, but he wasn't going to let her spoil his plans. He was certain that Peggy's heart didn't belong to Bob and he meant to win her. His only problem was that he wasn't going to be here very often and Bob was here all the time.

As darkness fell Terry said, with obvious reluctance, that he would have to leave. 'I mustn't miss the last train.'

Peggy made as if to get up too, but Rose shot out of her seat. 'I'll see you out, Terry. The blackout and all . . .' She didn't want him stealing a furtive kiss from Peggy in the darkness of the hallway. In a flurry of goodbyes, she led him through the hall, drew back the blackout curtain and opened the door.

'Goodnight and thank you for everything you did for Peggy.' With unmistakable finality, she added, 'She'll be fine now.'

'Goodnight, Rose. I'll be seeing you,' he added, as he stepped across the threshold.

'Not if I see you first,' Rose countered. Her tone was deliberately jocular, but there was no mistaking the underlying threat beneath her words: stay away, it said.

As Terry walked along the road, he grinned to himself in the darkness and began to whistle 'We'll Meet Again'. Terry Price was not about to give up that easily.

As Rose returned to the living room, the wail of the sirens began.

Peggy's eyes widened. 'Oh no! What about Terry? We ought to call him back. Rose . . .'

Rose shrugged. 'He'll be too far away now.' She crossed her fingers behind her back as the lie slid glibly from her lips. 'He set off up the road at a run. He'd disappeared before I'd even got the door shut again.'

'Oh dear,' Peggy worried. 'I do hope he'll be all right.'

'Right, everybody,' Grace gave the order. 'Into the cellar.'

Nineteen

'D'you think they're going for the city centre again?' Peggy said, as they sat in the cold semi-darkness.

'The incendiaries were falling more to the north-east,' said Myrtle, who'd once again peered out of the window before reluctantly going down the cellar steps.

'Happen they're going for t' industrial area tonight then,' Tom's gravelly voice said.

'D'you think that's where they were meant to be going on Thursday and they got it wrong?'

It was a moment before Tom answered. 'Mebbe, lass, mebbe. But if you ask me, them Germans are far too clever to get it wrong. No, I reckon they intended to bomb us just like they did in London, Coventry and all t' other places they've been having a go at. And they'll keep on coming until they've blitzed all t' major industrial cities. You mark my words.'

They'd all have liked to contradict Tom, but not one of them could. Grace, from her avid reading of the daily newspapers and listening to the wireless bulletins, knew that he was unfortunately probably right.

As they all fell silent, listening to the bombing still happening in the distance, they knew that there'd be more folk killed or injured this night and many more made homeless or left without a place of work to go to in the morning.

*

'Do you want to go and see Bob this afternoon?' Rose offered when Peggy appeared bleary-eyed for a late breakfast. Mary and Myrtle had already left and Grace was wiping down the surfaces in the kitchen, tutting in disgust. Though, with only cold water from the rain barrel in the yard and what Rose and Myrtle could fetch, it was a thankless task. They heard the back door open and Letty's voice, complaining bitterly about the mess that Thursday night's bombs had left. 'I'll be months getting it right, Mrs Booth. Months.'

'None of us were hurt, Mrs Bradshaw. That's what we've got to be thankful for.' No one, not even Hitler, was going to defeat Grace for long.

'I could go to the hospital with you, if you like, Peg,' Rose said, her mind still on Bob.

Peggy bit her lip. 'I ought to go, but I don't think I could walk all that way. I still feel wobbly, and after a night in the cellar I feel so tired.'

'Then I'll go,' Rose said firmly, giving Peggy the benefit of one of her glares. Rose was good at glaring when she wanted to press home her point of view. It was a look, as Grace said, that could stop a clock. 'One of us from this family should visit, even if it's only to keep his poor mam company.'

'Yes.' Peggy sighed wearily. 'You go, Rose.'

'And I'll tell him you send your love, shall I?'

There was a moment's hesitation before Peggy said quietly, 'Of course.'

Rose was still feeling angry with her sister when she arrived at the hospital to find Hester Deeton waiting anxiously in the queue of people lining up to go into the wards when visiting time started. The poor woman looked so careworn and frail, though she couldn't be much older than Mary was. Rose's annoyance fell away in her concern for Hester. Then fear shot through her: was it Bob? Was he worse? She touched Hester's arm lightly, making her jump.

'I'm sorry, I didn't mean to startle you. Are you all right? You look so – so anxious.'

Tears filled Hester's eyes. 'Oh, Rose – how good of you to come. Have you brought Peggy?'

'No, I'm sorry. She's still feeling very shaken.' Not too shaken to be making sheep's eyes at a handsome soldier, Rose thought, but she pushed her uncharitable thoughts away. Perhaps she had made more of it than she should have done in her concern for Bob. Terry had been very kind, she had to admit that. She paused and then asked, 'How – how is Bob? He's not worse, is he?'

Hester smiled through her tears and shook her head. 'No, no, he's doing very well now. But it was such a shock, Rose, him getting injured like that.' She lowered her voice and leaned closer. 'I don't like folks to hear me say this – it sounds very selfish – but Bob's all I've got. I was so relieved when we found out that his job's a reserved occupation. I was over the moon. I don't mind telling you that, Rose, you'll understand; but other folks who've got family out there fighting, well, it doesn't sound very fair of me, does it?'

Rose squeezed Hester's hand and said huskily, 'I know what you mean, but any one of them would bring their boys back if they could.'

'But, you see, I never thought he'd get injured *here*.' Tears welled in her eyes again. 'I thought he was safe.'

'But he's going to be all right, isn't he?'

'Yes, but I'll never know another moment's peace when he's back at work.'

Now there was nothing Rose could think of to say to comfort the other woman. At that moment the signal came that the visitors could go in.

'You go, I'll wait here,' Rose said.

'No, no, he's allowed two visitors at a time now. We'll both go in.'

The ward was crowded. The beds had been moved closer together and there was also an additional row of beds, head to foot, down the centre of the ward. Dust and grime were everywhere, but apart from some minor damage, the hospital was intact.

Bob did look much better. He was sitting up in bed, watching the door with a smile of anticipation. It faltered a little when he saw it was only his mother and Rose. But Rose forced a cheery smile – wasn't it what she was known for? – as she approached the bed. When the usual greetings had been exchanged, Bob's first question was, 'Where's Peggy?'

'She sends her love,' Rose assured him, 'but she's still feeling very shaky.'

Bob nodded. 'Poor girl. Tell her not to worry. They might let me go home the day after tomorrow, then I'll come and see her.'

'You'll do no such thing,' Rose blurted out before she could stop herself. 'You're far worse than she is. No, no, she'll visit you. If not here, then at home.'

Bob grinned at his mother. 'Fiery piece, isn't she? Peggy always says there's no arguing with Rose once she gets the bit between her teeth.'

They chatted for half an hour and then Mr Bower appeared in the doorway of the ward. Rose stood up. 'I'll go,' she said, 'and let Mr Bower see you.' As she began to move away, Bob caught hold of her hand. 'Give Peggy my love, won't you, Rose?'

Rose swallowed hard but managed to smile brightly and nod. She couldn't speak. The warmth in his tone and the look of longing in his eyes were like knives through her heart.

In comparison with other cities, Sheffield's blitz didn't last long. It seemed as if Hitler had moved his attentions elsewhere and whilst Sheffielders would not have wished such devastation and tragedy on any of their countrymen, they couldn't help but be relieved that the heavy bombardment of their city seemed to have ceased for the moment. There was still the spasmodic raid – as there probably would be for however long the war lasted – but at least the concentrated bombing had stopped. But the fear remained, especially when they heard with horror that only five days later Liverpool had been the victim of what would come to be called the Christmas Blitz, which lasted for three nights. And then, two weeks later, the enemy dropped ten thousand firebombs on London in an effort to set the city on fire.

'They'll come back here,' Rose said dolefully. Usually it was Rose to whom the family turned to raise their spirits. But for once she wasn't feeling optimistic about the future. 'They'll want to finish the job they started and wreck our industries completely.'

'Tom was telling me that although they bombed the Vickers' factory, they missed the massive drop hammer.' Grace lowered her voice, almost as if she feared there might be spies listening. 'It's one of the best-kept secrets of the war, Tom says, and of course he should know. He works there.' Her voice dropped to a whisper. 'It's vital for the production of Rolls-Royce crankshafts for Spitfires and Hurricanes.'

'Really?' Rose's eyes widened. 'Then no wonder Adolf wants to wipe us out.'

Bob came home from hospital, and despite Rose's protests it was he who came to see Peggy. He sat beside her holding her hand, whilst Rose slammed the pots about in the scullery as she washed up after tea.

'What's the matter with you, girl?' Grace shouted at last. 'You'll break something if you carry on like that. Hasn't Hitler done me enough damage in this house without you starting?' The noise of clattering crockery stopped and, out of sight of the others, Rose leaned against the sink and closed her eyes, murmuring to herself, 'I can't stand this much longer. I'll have to leave. Get a place of my own.' They were brave words, but she knew she wouldn't. For one thing, her family needed her and for another, on her wage alone, she couldn't afford it. If it hadn't been Peggy who was causing Rose's heartache, she might have suggested that the two eldest sisters get a little place of their own to rent. But even then she knew that, despite Grace's constant grumbling, her grandmother wouldn't want any of her family to leave her. Especially now there was a war on.

No, there was nothing Rose could do to alleviate the pain in her heart. She drew in a deep breath and promised herself that she would bury her feelings for Bob, put a brave smile on her face and get on with her own life and stop mooning over her sister's boyfriend.

Just so long as that handsome soldier didn't come back.

Twenty

'Would you believe it?' Letty said, arriving at the back door on Christmas morning. 'Our Tom's taken t' lads to the football at Hillsborough. After all we've been through, all 'ee can think about is United playing Wednesday.'

'Best thing he could have done,' Grace said.

'Eh?' Letty looked startled. She'd wanted sympathy. She hadn't expected Grace to side with Tom.

'Those lads – little rascals though they are most of the time – are having to experience things no boys of their age should have to. We're living in dark times, Mrs Bradshaw, and this Christmas is going to be a miserable one for many Sheffielders. We're lucky, when you stop to think about it. At least all our families are safe—' Her voice softened as she added, 'And, God willing, your boys in the forces are safe too. They'll be making the most of Christmas, wherever they are, I don't doubt. And so should we.' Moved to an unusual feeling of friendliness towards her neighbour, Grace said, 'Now, you'll join us for dinner, won't you? Just bring whatever you can and we'll try to forget the war for a few hours, shall we? Mr Bower will be joining us again, though Bob Deeton and his mam are staying at home. Poor Hester. She's such a worrier. She thinks the day would be too tiring for him and Bob's too kind-hearted to upset her.'

Letty's face brightened at once. 'Oh, tha's good, Mrs Booth, as I was saying to Mrs Tanner only the other day, yourn is a lovely family.' She moved closer, her irritation with her husband forgotten for the moment. She had a juicy bit of gossip to impart. 'Hast tha heard about Mrs Leggett at t'bottom of t'street. She's expecting. Sixth months gone, so Mrs Tanner reckons and –' Letty's voice dropped to a conspiratorial whisper – 'her husband hasn't been home for nearly a year. Now, what dost tha think to that, eh?'

Grace could think of a very rude retort, but she held her tongue. Instead she said, 'None of my business, Mrs Bradshaw. Now have you got anything you'd like to put in my range oven?' Not for the first time, Grace was glad she hadn't got rid of the range that still dominated the living room.

Letty was not offended by Grace's brusque refusal to indulge in gossip; she was used to it, but she never stopped trying.

They all enjoyed Christmas more than they'd thought possible. They'd pooled their rations to make a feast and, surprisingly, there was laughter around the table even though the days just before Christmas had been traumatic for all of them. Rose unearthed some board games and she Myrtle and Peggy kept the boys amused in the afternoon, whilst the others sat in front of a roaring fire in Grace's best front room, chatting or dozing. Tom had insisted that he contribute a share of the coal, and the warmth – and the drop of brandy he'd been keeping for a special occasion – mellowed their mood and they were soon reminiscing about the 'good old days'.

'They'll come again,' Tom said stoically, his thoughts turning once more back to the present war, and Laurence agreed. 'We may be bowed in this city – in this country – but we're certainly not beaten.'

'I'll drink to that,' Tom said and raised his glass.

On the Saturday evening, a month after Christmas, Terry jumped off the bus at a stop on Crookes Road and, whistling jauntily, set off towards the 'house of women' as he'd come to call it in his own mind. He'd been lucky to wangle another leave so soon after the last one and he still felt guilty about telling his sergeant that his mother was ill following the bombing. When he'd arrived back at camp the last time he'd almost been put on a charge. Immediately after the bombing word had gone out that all leave had been cancelled and he should have returned to camp at once.

'But I didn't hear,' Terry had told his sergeant. That bit was true. 'Everything in the city was in chaos and I was helping dig in the ruins to find folk.'

Though his sergeant had eyed him suspiciously, he'd believed him. And he'd granted him this leave too only a month later.

'And where are you off to?' his father asked, as Terry smoothed his black hair and straightened the knot in his tie in front of the mirror above the fireplace. On arriving home, he'd changed out of his uniform and was now wearing his best suit.

'See my girl, that's where.'

'Eh?' Harry Price looked startled and his wife, Edith, had looked up from darning her husband's socks. 'Sylvia? You're taking Sylvia out?'

Terry shook his head.

'You took her out last time you were home.' Sylvia Thomas lived next door to the Prices.

Terry pulled a face. 'That was just before I met Peggy, Ma.'

'Oh, Peggy, is it?'

'Yes, and it was never serious with Sylvia. We've grown up together. She's more like another sister.'

'Amy's not going to like it,' Edith said. Terry's younger sister, Amy, was Sylvia's best friend. 'She's always dreamed of you two getting married and her being bridesmaid.'

'Well, it's not going to happen, Ma. Me and Sylvia are just mates. Why, I've never even kissed the girl.'

'Yes, you have. In a game of postman's knock last Christmas.'

'That doesn't count.'

'It did to Sylvia.'

'And have you kissed this Peggy yet?' his father asked bluntly.

Terry grinned. 'Not yet, but I intend to before this leave's over.'

'Then you'd best hurry up,' Harry chuckled, not taking any of this romantic nonsense seriously. 'You've only got another twenty-nine hours of your leave left.'

Terry was stationed in North Yorkshire and could get home relatively easily on a short leave, especially when he told the odd white lie. And hitching lifts was easy for a soldier in uniform. He was luckier than many of his fellow soldiers and he knew it. But they all expected to be posted somewhere else before long, possibly abroad. He wasn't going to think about that now; today he was going to see his girl and he vowed to himself that before he left her, this very day, she would know how much she meant to him.

'What's she like?' Despite her disappointment over Sylvia, Edith was curious. The neighbours – the Prices and the Thomases – had been friends for years and Edith wasn't sure how her friend, Mabel, was going to take this news. Mabel Thomas was a big woman in every way: in build, in heart and in laughter, but she was a devil when crossed. Edith shuddered. She didn't want to have to be the one to tell Mabel that Terry was seeing another girl.

Terry turned from the mirror. 'She's very pretty, Ma. Curly brown hair and lovely, soft brown eyes that melt your heart, and when she smiles she has dimples in her cheeks.' He pointed at his own cheeks to demonstrate.

Edith stared at him. He could remember everything about this girl in fine detail. He must be smitten. Her heart dropped as she thought of Mabel next door. 'Where did you meet her?'

'On a tram. I was going into town when the tram was caught in a bomb blast.'

Edith gasped and put her hand to her breast. 'Not the night of the blitz?'

'Aye, the Thursday night.' Terry spread his hands. 'But, as you can see, not a scratch.' His eyes darkened as he recalled the sights he'd seen that night and just afterwards. He was glad his parents and sister had been safe in the Anderson shelter they shared with the Thomases.

'Luck of the Devil, you've got,' Harry muttered. He was pretending to read his newspaper, but in fact he was listening to every word. He was mates with Percy, Mabel's husband, but now Harry was beginning to see just how this might affect their two families.

'I helped Peggy get the passengers out first and then I helped her. She'd got a cut on her forehead.' He touched his own hairline.

'Why did you need to help the passengers? Didn't the rescue people come?'

'She was the clippie, see, and her first duty – even before her own safety – was the care of her passengers. That's the sort of girl she is, Ma,' he added softly and neither his mother nor his father could miss the admiration in their son's tone. They glanced at one another, but said no more as he bade them goodbye and left. But once he was out of earshot, Harry shook his paper and muttered, 'Oh dear, Ma, I reckon we're going to have problems.'

Edith bent her head over her mending once more, wondering how she could avoid bumping into Mabel for the next couple of days until Terry was safely back at camp.

Terry knocked on the door, wanting to hammer on it in his impatience, but knowing that wouldn't go down well with the older generations. He smiled. It was a strange household and no mistake. He'd never encountered anything quite like it before. All these women of different ages and not a man to be seen. Still, perhaps it was just as well. He could charm most women of any age, but a man might be very different. Though he was wary of Rose. She wasn't backwards at coming forwards, as the saying went.

Peggy opened the door and there was no mistaking the pleasure in her eyes and in her smile, nor the pink that tinged her cheeks. 'Oh! Hello. What brings you here?'

'You, of course,' Terry said, removing his trilby and giving her a courteous little bow. 'I came to see how you are. I'm sorry I haven't brought you any flowers.

There don't seem to be many about. There's a war on, you know.'

Peggy laughed. 'Yes, I had heard.'

'Aren't you going to ask me in or has Rose forbidden it?'

Peggy pulled the door open wider. 'Don't be silly. Rose has nothing to do with who I see.'

'Glad to hear it,' he said, as he stepped over the threshold. 'Are they all at home?'

'No – no, only me and Gran.'

Terry was relieved: he was sure he could charm the old lady.

'So,' he asked again as Peggy led him through to the living room, 'how are you?'

'Much better. I'm going back to work tomorrow.'

'And Bob?' He felt compelled to ask and held his breath until she answered.

'Doing well. He's out of hospital, but he's not going to be allowed back to work for a while yet. They've got to be sure he doesn't get dizzy spells.' She laughed wryly. 'It wouldn't do while you're driving a tram.'

Terry smiled as he stepped into the room, his glance going at once to the old lady in the chair by the fire. She was partially hidden behind the newspaper she was reading, but, at the sound of someone entering the room, without looking up she said, 'The Australians have entered Tobruk.' She chuckled. 'There was no Union Jack available so they ran a bush hat up the flagpole. I like their style.' As she looked up to see who had come in, to Terry's relief, she smiled. 'Here again?'

He gave her a conspiratorial wink. 'Just passing, you know, and thought I'd look in.'

Grace smiled back. He didn't fool her for a moment and the young man knew it too.

'Are you all OK?' he asked. 'Mum said there'd been one or two more bombing incidents.'

'Just a couple since Christmas. No one killed as far as I know,' Grace said.

Terry turned to Peggy. 'I wondered if you feel well enough to come to the pictures with me?'

'Oh – I don't know if I should. I'm still officially on the sick list.'

'Surely no one would mind? Besides, it'd be a bit of a test to see if you're really fit enough to go back to work. Though what they'll find for you to do, I don't know.'

Oh, he's clever, Grace thought. She'd give him that. She lowered her glance, pretending to concentrate on her paper again.

'They've repaired a lot of the track already,' Peggy was saying. 'Several of the routes are running again. The system's steadily getting back to normal, though some of the repairs to track and overhead cables are taking longer than others.'

They both stared at each other remembering their shared experience of that dreadful night. 'So?' He smiled, changing the subject and trying to divert her thoughts away from terrifying memories. 'Are we going?'

'Yes, all right,' Peggy said. 'I'll just get ready. If I'm quick, we should catch the first house.'

As she hurried upstairs to change, Terry sat down on the opposite side of the fire to Grace. He was about to start a conversation with her, but at that moment the back door opened and Myrtle called out, 'I'm home, Gran.'

Terry's heart sank. He'd hoped they'd get away before any other members of the family arrived home. But he thought the schoolgirl wasn't much of a challenge, just so long as Rose wasn't with her.

Myrtle came into the room. Her eyebrows shot up in surprise when she saw him. She nodded curtly in greeting and then turned to her grandmother. 'I got all the shopping, Gran, but the meat's a bit pathetic. Scrag end. It's all I could get.'

'It'll do, love. Your mam's getting to be a dab hand at making a silk purse out of a sow's ear.'

At that moment Peggy ran lightly down the stairs and entered the living room. Myrtle's eyebrows reached her fringe this time as she saw that her sister was dressed for an evening out. She smirked as she asked pointedly, 'Going to see Bob, are you?'

Peggy flushed as she stammered, 'No, no, I – we're going to the pictures.' Her blush deepened as she saw Myrtle's disapproving glance go from her face to Terry's and back again. Then the younger girl shrugged and turned away, but not before Peggy had seen the gleam in her eyes. Peggy shuddered as she realized that the moment Rose stepped through the door, she'd hear about Peggy going out with the soldier.

And no doubt, not long after that, Bob would know too.

Twenty-One

'She's gone out with *him*.'

Rose closed the door, pulled the blackout curtain across it, switched on the hall light and turned to face her young sister. 'Give us a chance to get in the house, our Myrtle. What are you on about?'

'Him. Terry What's-his-name. Peggy's gone to the pictures with him.'

Rose stared at her for a moment before saying tartly, 'Has she indeed? We'll have to see about that, then, won't we, Myrtle?' And Myrtle smirked.

'Do Gran and Mam know?'

'Mam's not home till eight, but Gran knows.'

'And?'

Myrtle shrugged. 'She doesn't seem bothered.'

Rose snorted and marched into the kitchen. ''Lo, Gran. You all right?'

'Fine. Your tea's all ready. Keeping hot in the oven.'

'Thanks.' There was a slight pause before Rose added, 'What's this about Peggy going to the pictures with the soldier?'

Grace glanced up. There was no mistaking the belligerence in Rose's tone. Grace raised her eyebrows. 'No harm in it, is there? He seems like a nice lad.'

'No harm in it, you say? 'Course there's harm in it, Gran. Or could be. She's supposed to be Bob's girl. What if he finds out?'

162

Grace eyed her granddaughter over her steel-rimmed spectacles. 'He's unlikely to – unless, of course, you tell him.'

Rose reddened. It had been in her mind to do just that, but now she said lamely, 'Someone from work might see them and tell him.'

'They easily might,' Grace said. 'But not many of them would run tittle-tattling to Bob, especially – ' she added pointedly – 'whilst he's still recovering from the accident. Leave it be, Rose, there's a good lass. Things have a habit of working themselves out for the best without any meddling from others.'

Her tea forgotten, Rose sat down slowly in the chair opposite her grandmother, while Myrtle stood near the table, listening intently. She kept quiet. For once, it seemed, she might be privy to a family discussion instead of being sent out of the room. If she just kept quiet, the other two seemed to have forgotten about her.

'So he's charmed you an' all, has he?' Rose said softly.

Grace shook her newspaper. 'I don't know what you're talking about, Rose. Get your tea else it'll be dried to a cinder.' She glanced up. 'Myrtle . . .'

The girl held her breath. Here it came; Myrtle, go to your room. But instead, Grace said, 'Get your sister's tea out of the oven.'

Myrtle scuttled to do as she was asked, but left the door between the living room and the kitchen open so that she could still hear what was being said.

'You know very well what I'm talking about, Gran,' Rose spat.

Grace frowned. 'Don't take that tone with me, my girl. This is my house and I'll say who comes into it and who doesn't.'

163

'And don't we know it,' Rose muttered.

'What did you say?' The two women, two generations apart, glared at each other, neither willing to back down.

Rose was heartily sick of having the fact that they were living in this house by Grace's charity rammed down their throats. They were never allowed to forget that they owed the roof over their heads to her. And in her turn Grace had often longed to have her home to herself. But now they both knew they were trapped in a situation that was unlikely to alter. And they both knew the reason, though it would never be voiced aloud.

Grace was getting old. Whilst she was still active and well able to care for herself at the moment, now was not a good time for the family to leave and seek a place of their own, even though, with three wages coming into the house, they could probably afford to do so. Besides, both Rose and Grace were thinking exactly the same thought: Mary would never hear of such a thing.

Rose was the first to drop her gaze. 'Nothing, Gran.'

Grace pursed her lips and said no more, though she'd heard what her ungrateful granddaughter had said. There was nothing wrong with her hearing, even if they all thought she was in her dotage.

Myrtle came back into the room, carrying the hot plate carefully. She set it on the table. 'Come and get it, Rose, while it's still hot.'

With a sigh, Rose got up. 'Well, I think it's wrong anyway. And I shall tell our Peggy so when she gets home.'

Grace laughed wryly. 'I've no doubt you will. But just remember, Peggy's of age. She's twenty-two next month. She can do what she likes and none of us can stop her.'

There was a pause before Rose said slyly, 'But like you've just said, Gran. This is your house and you could stop him coming here – *if* you wanted to.'

'But I don't.'

'So – what about Bob?'

'Ah, so now we're coming to it. Just tell me something, Rose. Is it your sister you're concerned about? Or Bob?'

Rose, her knife and fork suspended momentarily in midair, stared at her grandmother for a long moment. Then, without answering, she bent her head and began to pick at the meal in front of her.

All of her sudden, her appetite had deserted her.

When Myrtle realized that the conversation was at an end – for the moment – she went up to her bedroom to start her homework. But half an hour later, when she heard the front door open and close and knew her mother had come home, she slipped quietly down the stairs and sidled into the room, trying hard not to be noticed.

'Did you know?' Rose demanded before her mother had taken off her coat and hung it on the clothes pegs in the hall.

'Just let me get near the fire, Rose love. I'm freezing.' As she moved into the living room, Mary added, 'Know what, love?'

'About Peggy and the soldier?'

Mary blinked and stared at her daughter. 'Rose, what on earth are you talking about?'

Impatiently, Rose said, 'Terry. He's been here – *again* – and they've gone to the pictures.'

Mary frowned. 'I see.'

'No, I don't think you do. What about Bob? Nobody seems to care about Bob and how he's going to feel.'

'You seem to care enough for all of us,' Grace muttered.

Rose swung round on her and opened her mouth, but closed it again when she felt her mother's warning touch on her arm.

'I've told her,' Grace went on, pretending not to have noticed Rose's reaction, 'that Peggy's a big girl now and she can do what she likes.'

Rose bit her lip, stemming another outburst, promising herself that she wouldn't tell her mother everything that Grace had said; Mary had already had to put up with remarks about her and her family living in Grace's house for years. Rose wouldn't add to that burden. But she'd reckoned without Myrtle.

'Like Gran always says,' the girl said softly, 'it's her house and she's the one to say who comes into it and who doesn't.'

Mary turned her gentle eyes on her youngest daughter, guessing exactly what had been said.

'Haven't you got homework to do, Myrtle?' Rose snapped and then turned back to her mother, patting her hand. 'I'll get your tea, Mam.'

Myrtle trailed back upstairs, wishing she'd kept quiet. Now she wouldn't hear any more. But she needn't have worried; the subject as far as the three women downstairs were concerned was closed, yet it lingered in each of their minds.

Just what was Peggy thinking of?

Peggy was thinking how nice it was to have Terry's arm around her shoulders. They were sitting in the back row of the darkened cinema, amongst all the courting couples, the only light coming from the flickering screen. Very slowly she turned her head to look at him and found him staring at her. The cinema was only about a quarter full, most unusually for a Saturday night. They'd made their way through the unlit streets, clinging to each other as they stumbled over bomb-damaged paths. Grotesque shapes loomed in the darkness; half a building left standing, furniture teetering drunkenly on sloping floors and the house next door reduced to a pile of rubble. Fitful moonlight illuminated the scene briefly and Peggy couldn't recognize the streets she'd known so well that she could have found her way around the city centre blindfolded. But not any more. Not since Hitler's bombers had paid them a visit. They'd headed for a cinema they'd heard was still open and now they were sitting close together in the darkness, hardly aware of the fictional romance being played out on the screen.

'You're lovely, Peggy,' Terry whispered. 'Do you know that?' He traced the outline of her face with his finger and then leaned closer. His kiss was gentle and endearingly hesitant, not bold or demanding. Her heart felt as if it was doing somersaults in her breast and her knees trembled like a young schoolgirl experiencing her first kiss. It was not the first time Peggy had been kissed, but it was the first time she had felt like this. Now she understood what all the romantic novels talked about, what the lovers on the screen portrayed. It was the feeling she should have when Bob kissed her, but she didn't. She had never in her life felt like this before.

Peggy put her arm around Terry's neck and kissed him in return.

*

'I won't come in. I don't think I'll be very welcome.'

'Don't be silly. Of course you will.'

They were standing outside the front door of Peggy's home. The night was pitch black and because there were no streetlights, not even a chink of light showing from any of the houses, they were safe from prying eyes.

'Not by Rose. No, darling, I'll go.'

They'd walked home through the blackout, stopping every so often to kiss and hold each other close. Words were unnecessary between them; they both knew they were falling in love and there was nothing they could do about it, even if they'd wanted to. And they didn't.

Terry kissed her again gently and then with a growing ardour. He drew back and chuckled. 'I really had better go.'

'Oh, please, not yet, just another five minutes.'

He groaned and buried his face against her neck. 'I don't want to go at all, Peggy, but I must. I have to go back to camp tomorrow.'

'You'll write, won't you?'

'I'm not much of a letter writer, Peg. Sorry, but I hated school and bunked off as much as I could. So my learning's not up to much.'

They lingered over their last kiss, touching hands to the very last minute until he had to go, swallowed up by the black night and leaving her bereft and feeling so alone as she turned at last to enter the house and face the recriminations of her family. His final words to her were, 'I'll be back, Peggy darling. I promise I'll come back. Don't ever doubt that, will you?'

Twenty-Two

The house was silent, the fire banked down for the night and all the lights turned off. Peggy crept upstairs to the room she shared with her mother, undressed in the darkness and slipped into her own single bed. She lay there, staring wide-eyed towards the ceiling reliving every moment of her evening with Terry. His face was in her mind's eye; his dark hair, cut to army regulation shortness, his dark brown eyes, so soft and loving – yes, loving – and the way his whole face seemed to light up when he smiled. She could still feel his arms around her and the touch of his mouth on hers.

Sleep, when it came at last, was restless and filled with dreams of the handsome young soldier.

No one spoke at breakfast. Myrtle was a long time finishing her cereal, glancing around the table as if waiting for someone to speak, but no one did. Then she asked for a piece of toast.

Rose stared at her. 'You never have toast.'

'Well, I'd like some this morning. Please. It's Sunday.'

'What's that got to do with it?'

'I just thought I'd have a treat.'

Rose hacked at the loaf and almost slung the round of bread towards Myrtle. 'Here, toast your own. The fork's by the fire. And go easy on the butter.'

Myrtle got up from the table and went towards the range. Reaching for the toasting fork, she pinned the bread on the end and held it out towards the glowing coals.

Peggy rose from the table, went into the hall and put on the rest of her uniform before returning to say briefly. 'Bye. I'll see you all tonight.'

'Bye, love,' Mary said and Grace smiled and nodded. Pointedly Rose ignored her and turned instead to Myrtle. 'You can do me a round of toast while you're at it.'

As the front door closed, Mary looked up at Rose. 'Have you got a shift today?'

Rose nodded and pursed her lips. 'Yes, but I've no intention of walking to work with Peggy. Not while she's playing fast and loose with Bob.'

'Then,' Grace said, standing up and beginning to clear away the breakfast pots, 'you'd better clear the air with her tonight. I'm not having this sort of atmosphere in *my* house.'

Rose and Mary exchanged a glance, but said nothing. There was nothing they could say.

Clearing the air, as Grace had demanded, escalated into a full-blown row between the sisters that evening. Not since they'd been children and had squabbled over a toy had there been such a falling out.

'Just what do you think you're playing at? Going to the pictures with him. What if someone from work saw you and tells Bob?'

Peggy's face flamed, but she stood her ground in the face of Rose's wrath. And it was wrath; the girl was incensed. 'Then it'll save me the job, won't it?'

170

Rose gasped. 'You don't mean it. You *can't* mean it.'

'Rose—' Peggy reached out, but Rose leapt back as if her sister's touch was abhorrent to her. 'Try to understand. I've never felt like this before. I'm fond of Bob, of course I am. But – but I've fallen in love with Terry.'

'How can you possibly say that? You've only seen him two or three times and—'

'Rose – I know.'

'You're a hussy and a – a–'

'Now, now,' Grace admonished, but Myrtle's eyes gleamed. She was sitting at the table, pretending to read, having declared it was too cold to sit in her bedroom. Now she was listening gleefully to every word.

Mary sat in her chair by the fire, her knitting lying in her lap. 'That's enough, the pair of you. Peggy, if you really mean what you say, then you should tell Bob yourself. That's only fair. He shouldn't hear rumours and gossip from anyone else.'

'I've no doubt my dear sister would love to impart a juicy bit of gossip,' Peggy said bitterly.

Rose turned pale. 'No, I wouldn't do that. *I* won't be the one to hurt him. You can do your own dirty work.' With that parting shot she flounced out of the room. They heard her footsteps running up the stairs.

'Oh dear,' Mary murmured, and Grace muttered, 'Never a moment's peace in this house with you lot.'

Peggy stood uncertainly by the table, fingering the chenille tablecloth nervously. 'I – I suppose I should go and see him, shouldn't I?'

'It would be best, dear,' Mary said with an outward show of calmness she was not feeling inside.

'But it seems awful to tell him something like this when he's – when he's not fully recovered.'

'There'll never be a good time, love.'

'But what if it sets him back? I'd feel awful.'

'It'll be worse if he hears it from someone else.'

Grace rustled her newspaper impatiently. 'If you have something unpleasant to do, do it sooner rather than later. That's what I always say.'

Peggy glanced worriedly at the clock on the mantelpiece. 'It's getting late now—'

'You're making excuses. Just go and get it done. Then we might all have a bit of peace. Though I doubt it, with Rose in that mood.'

Still Peggy hesitated. She hated hurting people and especially someone of whom she really was very fond. She took a deep breath. 'Yes, you're right. I'd better go and see him. I'll go straight from work tomorrow.'

As it turned out, she was obliged to go sooner rather than later.

'I've no work for you, love,' Laurence told her once he had greeted her and asked how she was. 'All the routes we've managed to get operational again are fully manned today.' He smiled. 'You go back home, Peggy lass, and get a good rest while you still can. I'll send word by Rose or Mary when there's more work for you.'

So, Peggy had been left with no choice. She had to visit Bob.

Hester Deeton opened the door. 'Oh, Peggy,' she exclaimed, stretching out her hand towards her in greeting. 'I'm so glad you've come. He's been asking me to find out how you are. I wouldn't let him come round to your house again. He was shattered by the time he got back last time. He's so looking forward to seeing you. Come in, come in. Let me take your coat. I'll make tea for all of us. Oh, it's so good to see you.'

Peggy felt her heart plummet even further. This was going to be even more difficult than she'd thought. When she entered the room and Bob's face lit up at the sight of her, Peggy's resolve crumbled. He was sitting by the fire, a blanket over his knees, though whether this was because he really needed it or he was pandering to his mother's fussing over him, Peggy couldn't guess.

He held out his hand and, after a slight hesitation, she put hers into it.

'How lovely,' he said, smiling. 'How are you, dear?'

Peggy's smile was hesitant. 'I'm fine. I went back to work for the first time yesterday, but this morning Mr Bower had nothing for me.'

Bob's face clouded. 'Do you think you should have even tried to go back so soon? You were hurt, to say nothing of the nasty shock.'

'I'm fine. But you're different. You'll need a fair time off work, I expect.'

Bob grimaced. 'I'll have to do what the doctor tells me, I suppose. When it's people's safety at risk, they'll have to be sure I'm fit. At least they've now found out for definite that I've not cracked my skull after all.' He grinned. 'Much too thick.' He paused, searching her face, but she avoided meeting his gaze. 'And how have you been – really? I'd hoped you might come and see me before now, because there's something I want to ask you—'

Peggy's heart leapt in fear. Oh no, surely he wasn't going to propose.

She opened her mouth to tell him, to forestall him

making matters even worse, but at that moment Hester came into the room carrying a tray. 'Here we are. Tea and biscuits.'

'Oh, thank you, Mrs Deeton.' The woman couldn't possibly guess that Peggy was thanking her as much for the interruption as for the welcome tea.

Peggy eased her hand from Bob's grasp and jumped up to help. She took the tray from Hester's hands and set it on the table.

'You be mother.' Hester laughed. 'You know by now how we both like our tea.'

Peggy smiled weakly, realizing that there'd be no chance on this visit to talk to Bob alone without fear of his mother interrupting. But as Mrs Deeton saw her to the door about an hour later, she leaned forward and whispered, 'I go round to my friend's next door on a Tuesday night for a game of whist. If you come round tomorrow night, you can have a bit of time on your own without his old mother being in the way.'

'Oh, Mrs Deeton, don't—'

'Now, now.' The woman patted her hand. 'I'm not so old that I can't remember what it's like to be young and in love.'

Peggy walked home through the blackout feeling like the very worst kind of traitor. If only, she thought, I'd realized sooner that I wasn't in love with Bob, I'd have been honest with him and all this heartache would have been avoided. But I didn't know. I really didn't know. Not until I met Terry.

Twenty-Three

'So?' Rose demanded, almost before Peggy had got through the door.

'No, his mother was there most of the time. There just wasn't the right moment.'

Rose snorted. 'There never will be the right moment.'

'I'm going round tomorrow night. Mrs Deeton goes to her neighbour's for the evening every week to play whist. I'll – I'll tell him then.'

'Mind you do.' Rose got up. 'I'm going to bed. I'm on early shift in the morning. Night, all.'

It had to be done, Peggy thought, as she got into bed herself. As well as worrying about Bob, Peggy was also tired from tossing and turning the previous night and the long walk she'd had that day. She fell into an exhausted sleep.

'I'm just off,' Mrs Deeton called out merrily as Peggy sat down opposite Bob in their living room.

'Sit here, next to me,' Bob patted the chair, but Peggy shook her head. 'Bob, there's something I have to say to you.'

'And I've something I want to say to you, but go ahead – you first.'

Peggy took a deep breath. She'd rehearsed this moment the whole day and yet now she was sitting opposite him, the words fled from her mind and she opened and closed her mouth like a goldfish.

'Come on, Peg, you can tell me. What's up? Because I can see there's something.'

'Bob, we've been friends for a long time now.'

'I hope we're more than friends, dear.' He was making this even more difficult than it already was.

'But we've been sort of thrown together – working together – seeing each other every day. I'm sure Mr Bower puts us on the same shift deliberately.'

Bob grinned. 'Of course he does.'

Peggy pulled in another deep breath. 'Oh dear, this is so difficult. Bob, I'm very fond of you, but I'm not in love with you. I – I thought it only fair to tell you.'

Bob's smile faded and the hurt in his eyes was almost more than she could bear, but she had gone thus far and there was no turning back. Whatever else she was – and her sister had plenty of names for her now – Peggy was not deceitful. Even if she never saw hide nor hair of Terry Price again, she knew now what real love was and it wasn't what she felt for Bob.

'Is there someone else?' he asked bluntly. ''Cos if it's someone from work I'll knock their bleeding heads off.'

Peggy was startled. She'd never heard Bob use bad language or even raise his voice. She shook her head. 'No – it's no one from work.'

'So – there is someone then.' He was red in the face with anger now and Peggy felt a twinge of fear, wishing suddenly that she wasn't alone in the house with him. Then she shook herself. This was Bob – good old dependable Bob, her work mate and colleague.

'Sort of,' she murmured at last.

'Who? Tell me who it is?'

Peggy lifted her chin. 'No, I won't. It doesn't matter. I'll probably never see him again anyway.'

'What do you mean?'

'What I say. He's in the army and—'

'Oh, I know who it is. It's that blasted soldier, who made himself so helpful the day of the bombing. I see why now. Knew him before that, did you?'

Peggy shook her head, but could not deny that Bob had correctly guessed the identity of the man he now viewed as his rival.

'He's been round your house, hasn't he? Rose told me when I was in hospital that he'd come to enquire how we both were. I never thought . . .' He ran his hand across his eyes. 'Oh, Peggy, don't you know how much I love you? I was going to ask you to marry me, if we could get engaged, and now . . .'

'Bob, I'm sorry, but I can't be anything less than honest with you.' She stood up. 'I'd better go. I'll see Mr Bower in the morning and ask him to put us on different shifts when you come back.'

'You needn't bother,' he muttered, viciously. 'I probably won't come back.'

'What – what d'you mean? Of course you'll come back to work once you're fit enough.'

Slowly he raised his face to look her in the eyes now. 'I might volunteer instead.'

'Oh no!' she breathed. 'You can't do that.'

'There's nothing left for me here. Not now. I might as well become cannon fodder.'

Anger surged through her. 'That's a terrible thing to say – to do. Think of your mother, if no one else.'

Bob dropped his head. 'She'll understand – when I tell her what you've done.'

'I see,' she said, sitting down again. 'So the blame's going to be laid at my door, is it?'

'Well, it *is* your fault. If you're throwing me over for some soldier.' He looked up sharply. 'That's it, isn't it? It's because I'm not in uniform. Going to start handing out white feathers, are you, like they did in the last war?'

'Bob, don't be silly. I don't want you to go at all. I don't want . . .'

'Oh yes, it's all about what you want, isn't it, with never a thought about anyone else? You've been spoilt – all of you have in that house. A house of women, that's what it is, with no man to show you what's what.'

She leaned towards him. 'So you want me to say that I'll stay with you, that I'll marry you, even though I know now that I don't love you as two people getting married should love each other. Is that what you want?' She was blazing herself now. Peggy was so like her mother. They were both placid and easy-going – to a point. But when that point was reached then they would stand their ground.

He stared at her for a long moment and then dropped his gaze. This wasn't the Bob she knew. Had she discovered a side to his personality that she'd never seen before or was it just because he was so dreadfully hurt that he was saying things he didn't really mean?

But a wise saying of her grandmother's came to her suddenly. 'You can never unsay things. Even if you say things in temper and try to make out you didn't mean what you said, there's always a ring of truth.'

Peggy bit her lip. Even though he was smarting, she knew that he had meant what he said. And so did she.

She was certain now that what she'd felt for Bob wasn't true love. A deep friendship, yes. She would always care about him, but, as she'd tried to explain to him, that wasn't love. And now, as he revealed a nastier side to his nature, she was even surer. At his next words, she began to despise him.

'Peggy – darling – you don't mean it. You can't.' He reached out and grasped her hands, holding them tightly, clinging to her. 'I'm sorry – I didn't mean what I said . . .'

She pulled her hands free. 'Yes, you did, Bob. Don't make it worse than it already is. I am truly sorry I've hurt you. I never wanted to do that and, yes, if I hadn't met Terry, then maybe we would have drifted into marriage, but isn't it better that we find out now?'

Bob shook his head. 'No, it isn't, because I still love you like I always have done.'

Exasperated now, Peggy shook her head, 'Then if you'd be happy for us to marry knowing that I don't love you in the same way, you're a fool.' She stood up again. 'I'm going.'

As she opened the door and fled from the room and the house, his final words, shouted after her, were ringing in her ears. 'I mean it – I'll join up, and when I get killed it'll be your fault.'

'I can see by the look on your face you've told him.' Rose set the tray of mugs of hot milk on the table with a crash.

'Mind what you're doing, Rose,' Grace snapped. 'You're spilling it. We can't afford to waste a drop.'

'Sorry, Gran.'

Grace's glance turned to Peggy's tear-streaked face. 'Well, it's done now.' Her tone gave no hint as to whether she approved or not.

Mary smiled comfortingly and touched her daughter's hand. 'If you really don't love him,' she said softly, 'then you've done the right thing.' She said no more, but privately she was thinking: if only I'd had the same bravery years ago. But then, she reminded herself, I wouldn't have my wonderful daughters, and I wouldn't be without any of them. She glanced round fondly, though her gentle smile faded as she saw the looks on each of their faces. Peggy was still tearful, her hands actually trembling. Rose's face was puce with anger and Myrtle was watching them all with a smirk. Of the three of them, it was Myrtle's expression which disturbed Mary the most. Time would heal the hurt and anger the other two were feeling, but Mary was sorry to see that her youngest daughter appeared to be revelling in the family quarrel. Mary sighed. 'Rose, you must see that Peggy can't go on seeing Bob, building up his hopes of – of something more.'

'No, I don't see. All I know is that she's hurt a lovely man just because she imagines she's fallen for some – some wide boy she'll probably never see again.'

'Terry's not a wide boy,' Peggy retorted hotly. 'He's a soldier doing his bit for his country.'

'And Bob's not, I suppose.'

'I didn't mean it that way. You know I didn't.' There was a pause before Peggy blurted out, 'Bob said some dreadful things – hurtful things.'

'I don't blame him. I would've too.'

'What did he say?' Mary prompted gently, but Peggy shook her head.

'You can tell us.'

'He – he said he'd been going to ask me to marry him.'

Rose spluttered, indignant on Bob's behalf. 'And you call that "dreadful"?'

'No – no, of course not, but then – after I'd told him – he said he was going to volunteer – become cannon fodder and – and that if he gets killed, it'll be my fault.'

There was silence in the room whilst they all stared at her. Even Myrtle's enjoyment of the situation faded as she gazed at Peggy in disbelief.

'That was cruel,' Mary said. 'You were only trying to be honest with him.'

'No, it wasn't,' Rose burst out. 'It's how he feels. It's how *I* would feel if the person I loved had just jilted me so heartlessly.'

Now Peggy raised her head defiantly and repeated the words she'd said to Bob. 'So you'd have me go ahead and marry him without loving him, would you?'

Rose glared at her, opened her mouth to speak, but the words wouldn't come. At last she said huskily, 'No, no, I wouldn't. But what I can't understand is why you've led him on all this time. Everybody views you as a couple. You work with him, you go out with him.'

'I haven't led him on,' Peggy said, her voice rising heatedly. 'I'm very fond of him and we had a good laugh together. I didn't know it wasn't love – not until—'

'Not until you met that bloody Terry Price.'

'Wash your mouth out, Rose,' Grace snapped. 'I won't have that sort of language in my house.' Once more, even in the midst of a heated quarrel, Grace reminded them of their place.

'Oh, what's the use?' Rose marched out of the room, slamming the door behind her and leaving her drink untouched.

'"The lady doth protest too much, methinks",' Myrtle murmured as she picked up her mug.

'I agree with you, Myrtle,' Grace said, picking up Rose's mug as well as her own. 'And "Waste not, want not".'

'Sit down, love, and have your milk,' Mary said to Peggy. 'You've done the right thing. You couldn't do any other and the worst's over now.'

Twenty-Four

But Mary was wrong, for more recriminations were to come. Rose ignored Peggy totally, refusing to speak to her or even to acknowledge her presence in the household. And to make matters worse, the following evening Hester Deeton knocked on their door. The little woman was tentative and nervous, but she had overcome her natural reticence to speak up for her son.

'Come in, Hester.' As Hester stepped across the threshold, Mary closed the door and drew the blackout curtain back into place. She switched on the hall light and was shocked to see the other woman's drawn face and anxious eyes.

'Is – is Peggy at home?' It was difficult to guess whether Hester hoped the girl was there or that she wasn't.

'Yes, she's upstairs. Come on through to the living room and I'll call her down. I'm sorry we don't use the front room.' Mary smiled wryly. 'We can't justify heating two rooms except on special occasions.'

'I hope you don't mind me coming round, but – I expect you know what's happened – Bob's in such a state. He's threatening to enlist. Oh, Mary – I couldn't bear it if he went and – and—' The poor woman couldn't even bring herself to finish her sentence, but Mary understood her meaning.

'Come along in. I'll make us some tea.'

'I don't want to take your precious rations.'

'Don't worry about that.' Mary opened the door into the living room, where Grace was sitting in her usual chair by the fire. She looked up as Mary ushered Hester into the room, not at all surprised to see who their visitor was. Grace sighed inwardly, but fixed a smile on her face and gestured towards the chair opposite. 'It'll be Peggy you've come to see, I take it.'

Hester nodded, perching nervously on the edge of the chair. 'I can't understand why she's thrown him over. He's a good lad – a steady lad.'

Grace narrowed her eyes as she took in the other woman's distressed expression. Mistress in her house and strict in her dealings with her daughter and grand-daughters, Grace was never one to shy away from criticizing them. But when reproach came from outside the family, Grace closed ranks and defended her own with surprising vigour.

'Hester, I've known you since you were a child, so I'm going to speak plainly to you. Peggy has been honest with your Bob. She's been his friend for some time as we all know, but she's realized she's not in love with him. Not in the way she ought to be to marry him.' She put her head on one side, holding the other woman's gaze as she asked bluntly, 'You'd rather she was honest with him, wouldn't you?'

Agitatedly, Hester fingered the handbag on her lap. 'Yes – no – oh, I don't know. It's just that he's so hurt, Mrs Booth, and threatening –' she plunged her hand into her copious handbag and fished out a handker-chief, dabbing her eyes that had begun to flood with tears – 'to join up. He's saying he doesn't care if he lives or dies.'

184

'Then he's being very weak-willed and cruel towards you as well as to Peggy. That's emotional blackmail.'

Hester gasped. 'How can you say such a thing? My Bob hasn't got a cruel bone in his body.'

'Neither has Peggy. She's being honest, that's all.'

'Now, Mother.' Mary, who'd hurried through to the kitchen after seeing Hester settled near the fire, came back with a tray of teacups and saucers. She turned towards Hester. 'We do understand it must have been a dreadful shock for Bob and for you too, but—'

'He was going to ask her to marry him. He'd planned to take her into town and buy a ring as soon as he's strong enough. But he says she's met someone else.' Hester looked from one to the other. 'Is it true?'

Mary and Grace exchanged a glance. 'We really couldn't tell you that,' Grace said swiftly as she saw Mary open her mouth to reply. 'Peggy's a grown woman.'

'Are you telling me you approve of what she's doing? Throwing my Bob over for a soldier she hardly knows? Who is he anyway? Have you seen him? What's he like?'

'We've no intention of prying into Peggy's affairs,' Grace said primly. Of course, she regularly pried into everything her daughter and her granddaughters did and wasn't afraid to comment if she wasn't suited, but she wasn't about to let Hester Deeton know this. Mary was staring at her mother as if she couldn't believe what she was hearing. She'd never witnessed this side of Grace before, but then, she reasoned, she'd never had cause to. Even when Grace had voiced fears about Mary's own marriage to Ted Sylvester, there'd never been the need to defend the family name in the face of outsiders' criticism. But now there was and Mary was quick to pick up what her mother was doing. A feeling of warm pride flooded through her. Sharp and critical her mother might be within the confines of their home, but Grace was ready to defend her young and Mary loved her for it.

'But she lives in your house,' Hester was arguing. 'Surely you want to know the company she's keeping?'

'I keep my eye on all my family,' Grace said tersely, growing impatient with the woman's pleading and with Bob's obviously – in her view – weak reaction.

'Then you can't approve of what she's doing.'

'I *approve* of her honesty.'

Hester blinked, unable to think of a reply. 'Well,' she said lamely, 'she's hurt my son dreadfully and I want to know why.'

'We've told you why.'

'I want to see her. I want to hear it from her lips.'

There was a silence between them all. Grace sighed. She could see that there'd be no budging the woman until she'd said her piece to Peggy. 'Call her down, Mary. Let's get this over with.'

From the kitchen came the sound of a whistling kettle.

'I'll just make the tea.'

'I'll see to that,' Grace said, heaving herself up out of her chair. 'You get Peggy.'

Instead of just calling from the hallway, Mary ran lightly up the stairs and entered the bedroom she and her eldest daughter shared. 'Peggy, love, Hester Deeton's here.'

Peggy's eyes widened. 'I don't want to talk to her, Mam. I can't face her.'

'You'll have to, love. It doesn't look like she's going to leave until she's seen you.' Swiftly Mary repeated the conversations that had already taken place downstairs.

Peggy got up reluctantly. 'Don't leave me alone with her, Mam, will you?'

'Of course not.' Mary put her arm round Peggy's shoulders. 'And your gran will be there too.' When Peggy pulled a face, Mary added, 'She's sticking up for you.'

'I'll believe that when I see it,' Peggy muttered.

But see it she did. As she sat nervously on a chair by the table and waited for the onslaught from Bob's mother, it was Grace who said, 'I've told Mrs Deeton that you're only trying to be honest with Bob and that your whole family are behind you. We realize you've hurt him, but it's better done now rather than later.'

Grace had taken the wind out of Hester's sails, for now the woman could think of nothing to say and all she could do was to stare reproachfully at Peggy.

'I'm so sorry, truly I am,' Peggy said, 'but what else can I do?'

'But why did you let yourself fall for this soldier?' Hester said at last. 'Why did you go on seeing him? Where's your loyalty to Bob?'

'I didn't ask for it to happen. I—'

At that moment the back door opened and closed, and Rose came in from the kitchen. Peggy's heart sank. Despite Grace's firm assertion to Mrs Deeton that the whole family were on Peggy's side, here was one member who was most definitely not.

Rose paused in the doorway and took in the scene before her; the anxious looks on each face, the silence that hung heavily in the air. She moved further into the room and sat down in a chair on the opposite side of the table to her sister. 'Mrs Deeton,' she greeted the woman, who nodded in response but did not speak.

'How's Bob?' Rose went on and realized at once that it was not the most tactful remark she could have made, but then Rose was not known for her diplomacy. It felt to the others as if she might be deliberately stirring an already bubbling cauldron of resentment.

Mrs Deeton dissolved into tears and Grace shot her granddaughter one of her famous looks. 'Hester has come to plead with Peggy, but we've told her that we all – ' there was a definite accent on the 'all' – 'feel that honesty is best.'

Rose bit her lip. She wanted so desperately to tell the poor little woman, sitting with her shoulders hunched and her head bowed as she sobbed into her handkerchief, that she agreed wholeheartedly with her. But she knew how strong Mary was on family loyalty, so in front of her mother she said nothing.

Now there was a long, uncomfortable silence in the room. There was nothing left for anyone to say and Rose guessed – correctly – that it had all been said.

At last Hester dried her tears and stood up, murmuring, 'I'd better go. I can see I'm doing no good here.'

Rose got up too and said, 'I'll walk home with you.'

Hester glanced at her gratefully, but said, 'You haven't had your tea yet. You've just come from work, haven't you? I don't want—'

'That doesn't matter. I'll see you home. There's no moon tonight. It's pitch black out there.'

'Well, I would be grateful. I don't like being out in the blackout on my own, and Bob . . .'

Tears threatened again and she turned away towards the door, only pausing briefly as she passed Peggy to say, 'I'm very disappointed in you, Peggy. I'd really hoped that one day you'd be my daughter-in-law, but now – because of you – I might lose my son as well. My only son – my only *child*.'

With that parting shot, she turned away, as Rose followed her out of the room without even glancing back at her family.

Twenty-Five

'Thank goodness we've got that over and done with,' Grace said, as they heard the front door close.

'Over for now, Mother, maybe,' Mary said softly, 'but not done with, I fear.'

'I wonder what Rose is saying to her,' Peggy murmured.

Grace snorted. 'Plenty, I shouldn't wonder. Where Bob Deeton is concerned, I get the feeling that Rose has forgotten the meaning of family loyalty.'

The three women glanced at each other. 'Do you think,' Peggy asked hesitantly, 'she's in love with Bob herself?'

Grace nodded and smiled wryly. 'I've thought so for some time, but now I'm sure of it. And there's something else – ' her smile widened as she added mischievously – 'won't Myrtle be mortified to have missed all the fun.'

Despite the uncomfortable half-hour they'd just spent with Hester Deeton, both Mary and Peggy dissolved into laughter.

As Peggy had predicted, Rose did indeed have plenty to say to Bob's mother and, as they walked along arm in arm through the blackout, she was saying it. 'If you think I agree with what Peggy's done, then you're wrong. I think she's behaved disgracefully and I've told her so.'

'That's not what your grandmother said. She says you all – the whole family – agree that Peggy's right to be honest, as she calls it.'

'Gran's always been strong on honesty. And Mam too.'

Hester sighed as she admitted, 'I've always brought Bob up to be truthful and, yes, I suppose they're right, but what I can't understand is why she waited this long. Why lead him on? That's what's so hard to take.'

Rose snorted derisively. 'She says she didn't understand what it meant to be in love. Not until she met – *him.*'

'This soldier, you mean?'

'Mm.'

They walked on in silence until Hester asked, 'What about you, Rose? Have you anyone special? D'you know what it's like to be in love?'

It was a moment before Rose could bring herself to reply, to keep her voice steady as she said, 'Oh yes, I know what it's like to love someone.'

'And does he love you?'

As they turned the last corner into the street where the Deetons lived, Rose's answer was harsh with bitterness at the unfairness of it all. 'No, it's as if he doesn't even know I exist.'

A few more paces and they were outside Hester's front door. 'Do come in. I'm sure Bob will be pleased to see you.'

The woman couldn't know that her words were like a shaft through her heart, and Rose laughed wryly. 'I don't think he will want to see any member of my family ever again.'

Hester hesitated. Maybe the girl was right and yet, at this moment, she needed Rose's strength. 'I just thought you might be able to persuade him not to go ahead with this foolish idea of joining up.'

Rose hesitated, torn between wanting to see Bob and yet dreading having to deal with him mooning over her sister. The longing to see him won as she said, 'All right, but I don't know whether I'll be able to do any good.'

As she stepped into the room a few moments later, Rose was surprised and even a little irritated to see how he looked. Bob was slumped in an armchair near the fire, with a blanket over his knees, gazing into the flames.

'Here's Rose,' Hester said unnecessarily and then added, as if it was the panacea for all ills, 'I'll make some tea. The dear girl walked home with me before she'd even sat down to have her tea. We mustn't keep her.'

'It's all right, Mrs Deeton,' Rose said, drawing off her gloves and removing her coat. The room was hot and stuffy. She wondered how they'd managed to get the coal to have such a roaring fire. She sat down opposite him and said brightly, 'How are you doing, Bob?'

Slowly he raised his head to meet her gaze. 'I was doing very nicely, thanks, until your dear sister dropped her bombshell.'

Rose spent the next hour commiserating with him and yet, at the same time, trying to instil in him some fight back. 'Look at it this way, Bob. You've had a lucky escape.'

'Eh? How d'you make that out? I love her, Rose, and you can't just turn it off with a flick of a switch.'

'I know.'

'Do you? Do you *really* know what it feels like to love someone who doesn't love you?'

'As a matter of fact, yes, I do. I've been in love with someone for some time now, but he doesn't even seem to notice me.'

'Who?'

Rose's mouth twisted into a wry smile, but she managed to say pertly, 'That's for me to know and you to find out.' Neatly she turned the focus away from herself. 'But we're talking about you, not me. What's this about you threatening to join up?'

'It's no threat. I mean to do it when I'm fit enough.'

'But you've no need to go. Tram drivers were on the list *The Times* published of reserved occupations before the war even started.'

'And how d'you think I'm going to feel, seeing Peggy every day at work? I'd rather not be there at all.'

'Mr Bower will put you on another shift.'

'Oh aye, I'm sure he would, but he'd lose no time in telling everybody why, an' all.'

'No, he wouldn't. Mr Bower's not like that. He can keep his mouth shut.'

'Mebbe,' Bob growled. 'But it'll get out.'

'So? She's the one who'll look the fool, not you.'

Bob sighed and shook his head. 'I'm not out to hurt her, even though she's as good as stabbed me in the back.'

Rose put her head on one side. 'Aren't you? Out to hurt her in return, I mean? Isn't that why you're talking about enlisting? Striking back at her by trying to make her feel guilty?'

Bob cast her a baleful glance, but couldn't deny her words. Even to Rose's own ears it sounded now as if she was defending her sister, when in fact she was livid with Peggy. And yet . . .

Rose leaned towards him. 'But if you go, you'll be hurting your poor mother far more than you're hurting Peggy.'

'She'll not care, you mean?'

'No, I don't mean that. Peggy's not *that* evil. She's fond of you – she keeps saying that. She doesn't want you to do something stupid just because of her. Besides,' Rose added with a grin, 'she's not worth it.'

Bob stared at her for a long moment and then looked away, dropping his head to stare into the fire once more.

Rose stood up. 'I'm going. Like your mam said, I haven't had my tea yet, but—' She hesitated briefly before adding, 'I'll come and see you again – that's if you want me to.'

Bob shrugged as if he couldn't care one way or the other. 'Yeah, come whenever you want.' And then, as if he suddenly realized how ungrateful he sounded, he added, 'You're a good sort, Rose.'

She left the house with a half-smile on her lips. It wasn't quite the compliment she had hoped to get from Bob, but it would do for now. If Peggy didn't want Bob, then Rose most certainly did and she was determined to seize her chance. As she walked home, Rose was deep in thought. Another of her older sister's cast-offs she thought wryly, yet she didn't care. Where Bob was concerned she had no false pride. She'd do anything to make him happy. It might take a long time, but Rose vowed to make Bob Deeton forget all about her sister.

*

The atmosphere in the household of women did not improve. Rose and Peggy only spoke to each other when they had to, and Myrtle continued to watch the proceedings with nothing short of glee, while Mary looked on helplessly, feeling as if her little family was disintegrating around her and there was nothing she could do about it.

Only Grace continued as usual, rising above what she considered petty family squabbles.

Through the early months of 1941, Grace still followed the war news avidly. In the middle of February, she read that an advance guard of the German Afrika Korps, commanded by Rommel, had arrived in Tripoli. A month later, during more night raids on London and the south-east, it was said that a deliberate attempt had been made to destroy Buckingham Palace, but although incendiaries were dropped the palace escaped a direct hit. She did not relay this to her family, for only a week earlier landmines had been dropped on part of their own city, when eight people had been killed and several injured. Did this herald another concentrated spring offensive on British cities? Grace wondered, but she kept her worries to herself. In March, too, the official call came for women to do war work. 'Reckon our family's doing its share,' Grace muttered as every day she was left on her own to cope with the privations of war whilst three of her family worked on the city's transport system, which was valiantly trying to get back to something like normality. Grace went to the shops almost every day, joining the endless queues in an effort to feed her family. Every day she collected wartime recipes from the newspapers and magazines. I might not be doing what they class as war work, she thought, but I reckon I'm doing my bit too. What was that song they used to sing in the Great War? 'Keep the Home Fires Burning' – that was it. Well, Grace told herself, that was exactly what she was doing.

Try as she might – and she did try very hard – Rose was unable to persuade Bob to change his mind about enlisting. This did not improve her temper or her resentment towards Peggy. And then a knock came at the door one cool wet afternoon at the end of April, which threw the family into even greater turmoil and forced even Grace and the gentle Mary to decide whose side to take. Only Myrtle remained neutral – watching rather than participating.

'You!' Rose said with undisguised belligerence. 'What d'you want?'

'That's not a very nice welcome for a soldier home from the wars, now is it?' Terry Price grinned cheekily at her, the laughter lines around his eyes crinkling.

'I doubt you've been anywhere near the war,' Rose snapped, 'or you wouldn't be able to keep turning up like a bad penny. You're not welcome in this house.'

Terry raised his eyebrows. 'And is that what the head of the house says?'

Rose stepped towards him, pulling the door to behind her. 'Look, we don't want you here. None of us. You've caused enough trouble as it is.'

Now the saucy grin slid from Terry's face. He frowned. 'Trouble? What sort of trouble?'

Forgetting, in her anger, to guard her tongue, Rose blurted out the truth and so gave her unwanted visitor just the ammunition he needed. 'Peggy's thrown Bob over, that's the trouble you've caused.'

Terry raised his eyebrows. As he murmured, 'Has she now?' and began to smile, Rose realized her mistake.

'Now why do you think she'd do a thing like that?' he said slowly.

'Just go away, you're not wanted here. We used to be a happy, united family before you poked your nose in where it wasn't wanted. Now we're all at logger-heads.'

Terry shrugged. 'Sorry, I'm sure.' There was a note of amused sarcasm in his tone, but suddenly he was deadly serious. 'Look, Rose, if Peggy tells me to go and means it, then I will. I've no wish to upset her or her family, but I need to hear it for myself. From her. OK?'

Rose was beaten and she knew it. There was no way that Peggy was going to tell him any such thing and so Rose had to content herself with one of her frosty glares. 'Whatever she says,' she hissed, 'you'll never get a welcome in this house from the rest of us. You can be sure of that.'

''Tisn't the rest of you I've fallen in love with.'

Rose snorted. 'Huh! Love! D'you really expect me to believe that, coming from someone like you?'

For a moment, the young man looked startled as if his own words had surprised even him. Then he shrugged his broad shoulders again and said, 'I don't really care if you do or not. There's only one person who needs to believe me. Where is she?'

With a tut of exasperation, Rose pushed open the door once more. 'Wait there. I'll get her.'

'Aw, Rose, it's cold out here.'

'Tough,' Rose snapped and slammed the door in his face. 'Peggy,' she yelled, 'get down here.'

Peggy appeared at the top of the stairs. 'What's the

matter?' She was surprised and worried too. It was the first time Rose had spoken to her in weeks.

'He's here.' Rose jerked her thumb over her shoulder. 'You'd better get rid of him.'

Peggy clung to the banister. 'Who? Bob? I can't see him, Rose.'

'No, stupid. *Him.* Your lover-boy soldier.'

Rose – even though she tried hard not to – couldn't fail to see the joy that flooded Peggy's face as she hurried down the stairs. 'Terry! Is it really him?' She flew to the front door, dragged it open and fell into his arms.

'Well, that's more like it. That's what I call a proper welcome. Aw, don't cry, darlin'. I'm here now.'

Rose couldn't walk away, couldn't stop herself watching as Terry fished a white handkerchief from his pocket and gently mopped Peggy's tears. Now she forced herself to turn away, a lump in her throat. If only . . .

She went into the living room, closing the door quietly behind her. Grace looked up from her newspaper. 'They're making inroads into Greece now. Do we know where Walter Bradshaw – the one that's in the army – is?'

'He's here.'

'Who? Walter Bradshaw?'

'Eh?'

Grace sighed. 'You're not listening to a word I said. Anyway, what's going on out there? I heard shouting.'

'Terry Price.'

Grace's eyebrows rose. 'And?'

Rose sat down heavily and rested her arms on the table. 'He – he says he loves her.'

'Does he now?' Grace sniffed. 'Ah well, we'll see, won't we?' And she went back to reading her paper, leaving Rose straining her ears to hear what was being said in the hallway.

But there was very little talking going on. Terry was holding Peggy close and kissing her. 'I've missed you so much, my love.'

Peggy clung to him, returning his ardent kisses in equal measure and whispering when they drew apart. 'I've been so lonely. It's been awful here.'

'Because of me?'

'Sort of.'

'I'm sorry. I didn't want to cause trouble in your family. I like them – specially your gran.'

Peggy giggled. 'Gran?'

'She's a wonderful old lady. Me and her, I reckon we could get on a treat – ' he pulled a wry expression – 'it's your sister who doesn't like me, isn't it?'

Reluctantly, Peggy nodded. 'It's because of Bob. I – I've told him, you see, and Rose thinks I should stick with him. I think she rather – likes him herself.'

'Then you'd think she'd be glad you've finished with him. You have, haven't you?'

Again, Peggy nodded.

'Then she can have him.'

'I don't think he's ready to start another—' She stopped not sure how to refer to her relationship with Bob. 'He was very upset when I told him. He – he was about to propose to me, but I got it in first.'

'I see.' There was a slight pause before Terry asked, 'What exactly did you say to him?'

She buried her face against his uniform and her voice was muffled. 'I told him I knew now that I wasn't in love with him. That I was fond of him – always would be – we've been good friends, but that I didn't love him in the way two people who plan to marry should do.'

Terry put his fingers under her chin and raised her face so that he could look into her eyes. Softly he said, 'I know we haven't known each other long, but is that the way you feel about me? I hope it is, Peggy Sylvester, because I know that I love you with all my heart and I want us to be married as soon as we can.'

'Yes, oh yes, I do love you, Terry. I know I do.'

They kissed again and he hugged her close. 'Get your coat. We'll go back to my place. My mam and dad are out tonight – down at the pub – and Amy, my sister, is next door with her friend. We'll have the place to ourselves.'

Peggy reached for her coat from the pegs and they crept out of the front door, closing it quietly behind them. They hurried up the road, clinging to each other and giggling like naughty school children playing truant.

Twenty-Six

'Who's the lass your Terry brought home last night, then?'

Mabel Thomas stood in the back doorway of Edith's scullery, her arms folded across her ample bosom. Edith, her arms elbow-deep in soapsuds from scrubbing the collars and cuffs of her husband's shirt, turned wide eyes on her neighbour.

'Eh? What are you on about, Mabel?'

'Last night when you and Harry was at the pub, your Terry brought a lass home. They was here until just before you came back. Sylvia saw 'em sneaking out like thieves in the night.'

Edith turned her face away, slammed the scrubbing brush down onto the innocent shirt collar and began to scrub with a vehemence she hadn't known was in her nature. I'll swing for that lad yet, she thought. She'd put off telling Mabel that Terry had a new girlfriend, but it seemed she'd been forced into a corner. Now Mabel – and her daughter – would have to know. And yet she was irritated by what Mabel was saying. Terry had a perfect right to bring his friends back to his home. She wasn't going to stop him doing that, not when he was in the army and could be going abroad at any minute into real danger. Oh no, she wasn't going to fall out with her own son, not when he was fighting a war. Not even if it meant war with her neighbours.

She sighed and dropped the brush into the soapy water with a plop. 'Sit down, Mabel, I'll make us some tea. Go through. I won't be a minute.'

When they were both sitting at the kitchen table, Mabel asked, 'So, what's going on, Edie?'

There was no use putting off the moment and straight talking was the best way to deal with Mabel. 'He's got a girlfriend.'

'I thought our Sylvia was his girlfriend.'

'Not in Terry's eyes, Mabel. He's fond of her, course he is. They've grown up together. Mebbe that's the trouble. He sees her more like another sister.'

'That's not how our Sylvia sees it, I'll tell you that, Edie. She's going to be heartbroken and your Amy's reckoning on being their bridesmaid when the time comes.'

Edith regarded her friend steadily. 'Has Terry ever given Sylvia cause to think that he wanted to marry her? Has he actually asked her?'

Mabel blinked. 'Not in so many words, no. But there's been an understanding, hasn't there? I mean, they've been out together, to the pictures an' that. And he's always round our place, isn't he? Well . . .' she paused and was obliged to admit, 'he used to be, anyway.'

The two women were silent. Edith didn't know what more to say. She didn't want to fall out with Mabel. They'd been neighbours and friends for more years than she cared to count, but it looked as if their friendship might be over now. And Harry would miss his trips to the local with Mabel's husband, Percy.

'Who is this new girlfriend, then?'

'It was the first night of the blitz – the day the city centre got bombed so badly. She's a clippie and our

Terry was travelling on her tram when it was hit. He helped her get all the passengers off and looked after her – and that . . .' Edith's voice faded away.

'Oh aye – "and that" all right.' There was another silence between them before Mabel said reproachfully, 'You could have told me, Edie.'

'I – oh, Mabel, I wanted to, but to be honest I was hoping it'd blow over, but now, well, it doesn't look as if it's going to.'

'What's your Amy say about it?'

'She doesn't know.'

'I think she does. She was at our house last night when they were watching out of Sylvia's bedroom window.'

Edith bit her lip to stop herself saying that the two girls had no right to be spying on Terry, but she let it pass. She'd have to deal with Amy later and she knew her daughter was going to be every bit as upset as Mabel.

'Well, my opinion of Terry has taken a dive, I don't mind telling you. Jilting our lass like this and without even having the decency to come and tell her himself.'

Edith's head shot up. 'He didn't see them as boy and girlfriend, Mabel. And I'm sorry if Sylvia did.'

'Oh aye, she did right enough. And what Percy is going to say, I don't know. He'll likely kick up a rumpus.'

Edith sighed. She didn't want any physical fighting. Terry – fit from his army square-bashing – wouldn't be afraid of taking on anyone. And her Harry – well built and strong – was still handy with his fists.

'Don't let it come to that, Mabel. Please.'

Mabel shrugged. 'Couldn't stop 'em even if I wanted to and I can't say that I do. Percy'd only be sticking up for his daughter's honour. That pair were up to no good in here last night, Edith. I wouldn't have such goings on in my house.' She slurped her tea, crashed the cup back into its saucer and heaved herself up. 'I'll leave you to think on, Edith, but if I was you, I'd have a word with that son of yours. Let him know just what he's done. Broken the heart of a good little lass, that's what he's done. And,' she added, wagging her finger in Edith's face, 'he wants to watch himself an' all. Them clippies have got a bad name for themselves. It'll not be the first time she's been with a feller – if you get my meaning – you mark my words.'

Edith watched her friend go. She did not see her to the back door or even move from her chair. The two old friends were used to popping in and out of each other's houses without invitation or ceremony. But for how much longer would that tradition continue now? Edith wondered as she remained seated at the table, cradling the now cooling cup of tea in her hands.

When Peggy went to work the next morning she sought out Laurence Bower.

'Bob's been signed off. He's coming back to work today, I think. Could you arrange it so that we're on different details? We – we've had a fall out and it'd be difficult working together. I know it's asking a lot, but – if you could.'

'I'm sorry to hear that, lass,' Laurence said. 'But, as it's none of my business, I'll see what I can do.'

'I made a mistake, Mr Bower,' Peggy confided. 'I didn't realize he was taking our friendship far more seriously than I was.'

'I have to admit we all thought of you as a couple.

That's partly why I always put you together when I could. Sorry, lass. Obviously, I haven't helped matters.'

'It's not your fault, Mr Bower,' she hastened to reassure him. 'I enjoyed working with him. We've been good friends and, yes, I suppose everyone thought the same as you, even,' she ended bitterly, 'Bob.'

'You've met someone else, I take it?'

Peggy bit her lip but nodded. 'A soldier – the one who helped me so much on the day our tram got caught in the bombing.'

Laurence wrinkled his forehead. 'Oh aye, I remember.' He paused and then asked, 'What does your family think about it?'

Peggy shrugged. 'Rose is fuming – she's not speaking to me – and I'm not sure about Mam and Gran.'

'Ah well, lass, these things happen. It'll all be the same in a hundred years' time as my old mam used to say.'

Peggy managed a thin smile at the quaint saying that she hadn't heard before, but somehow it gave her comfort. Whatever happened in their lives, the world would still go on turning as it always had.

'There's something else you ought to know. I hope it won't happen, but you ought to know about it. Bob's threatening to enlist.'

'Then he's a fool,' Laurence said shortly, though his impatience was not directed at Peggy. 'He's in a reserved occupation. He's no need to go.' He eyed her closely. 'Oh, I get it, he's trying to make you feel bad, is he?'

Tears filled Peggy's eyes as she nodded. 'But it's so unfair on his poor mother. She's a widow and he's all she's got. I can't understand him being so cruel to her.'

'Maybe he'll change his mind, but in the meantime

I'll make sure he's on a different detail to you, even a different shift if I can manage it.'

But Bob did not change his mind and, instead of returning to work, he went straight to the army recruiting office in the city and enlisted. He didn't even bother to hand in his notice to Laurence.

When Rose heard the rumours flying round the depot that Bob Deeton wasn't coming back – and they all seemed to know the reason why too – she came home in a vile mood. 'See what you've done?' She wagged her finger in Peggy's face. 'I hope you're satisfied now. If he's killed, it will be your fault. He'd never have gone if you hadn't thrown him over.'

Peggy turned pale. 'Can't you reason with him, Rose? Can't you stop him? You're round at his place now more than you're at home.'

Rose fidgeted uncomfortably. 'I'm only trying to help them. His mother's at her wits' end.'

'I'd better go round . . .'

'You'll keep away. You've done enough damage already.'

Grace and Mary overheard the sisters quarrelling, but neither said a word. There was nothing they could say.

The atmosphere in the Price household was no better. Amy stormed at her brother and beat his chest with her fists, until he caught hold of her wrists and held her tightly.

Above her wailing, he shouted, 'I haven't even kissed Sylvia – not properly – so how on earth she's got the stupid idea that we're getting married, I've no idea.'

Amy stopped her shrieking and stared at him. 'Yes, you have. At the New Year's Eve dance the year before last. We all saw you.'

Terry laughed. 'Her and half a dozen others. Get real, Amy. I've never led her on.'

'You've taken her out. Dancing and to the pictures. Don't tell me you didn't sit in the back row.'

'We didn't – and if she's said different, then she's lying.'

Amy gasped. 'Are you calling my best friend a liar?'

'If she's told you such stories, then, yes, I am. Amy, listen to me. I've always been good friends with Sylvia and, yes, I've gone out with her, but only as mates.'

'Well, she thinks it was more. A whole lot more.'

'Then I'm sorry – very sorry – and I'll go myself right now and tell her so. And her mam and dad too.'

'I think you'd better, but I reckon you're in for a bloody nose from her dad. Maybe from her mam too. I wouldn't fancy facing Mabel Thomas when she's in a temper.'

'I'll go now – get it over with.'

A tearful Sylvia opened the door to his knock. 'Is it true?' she demanded at once, without even a pleasant greeting. 'Have you got a new girlfriend?'

'Sylv, let me come in and explain. There's been a misunderstanding.'

For a brief moment, hope lit her eyes. 'You mean, you haven't? That we're still . . .'

'Let me come in.'

They sat on either side of the kitchen table, staring at each other for a long moment before Terry took a deep breath. 'Look, Sylv, we're friends – always have been and I hope we always will be, but you've read much more into it than it is. I'm sorry – real sorry – if you thought we were boyfriend and girlfriend, but we're not. Never have been, in my mind. Just mates, that's all we are. Blimey, Sylv,' he laughed, trying hard to get her to see his point of view. 'Don't you reckon I'd've been kissing the face off you and – ' now he grinned saucily at her – 'wanting a whole lot more.'

Sylvia gazed at him with a doleful expression. 'And is that what you got from her the other night in your mam and dad's house? A whole lot more?'

Terry's face darkened at once. 'That's none of your business.' His tone softened again. 'I'm sorry if you're hurt – if I've done anything to make you think there was something more between us than just being friends, but—'

At that moment, Mabel came in by the back door, loaded with shopping bags. 'This rationing is getting worse. How we're supposed to feed our families on—?' She stopped abruptly when she saw who was sitting at her kitchen table. 'Oh, it's you. Well, young feller.' She dropped her shopping bags onto the table. 'What have you got to say for yourself?'

Terry stood up. The tall woman was imposing enough without her girth adding to her aggression. 'Mrs Thomas,' he began, but before he could explain, Sylvia butted in. 'He's throwing me over for some floozy he's met.'

Terry glanced down at her, 'Sylv, I've just explained – I've never thought of us in that way. We're just friends. Have been since we were kids. You, me, Amy and Billy from down the road. I mean – ' he spread his hands in a helpless gesture – 'I really don't know how you could have thought it was anything more.'

Sylvia bit her lip. The tales she'd told Amy and her parents were now coming back to haunt her. If she said now half as much as she'd made up in the past, then Terry wouldn't hesitate to call her a liar.

But blithely unaware of her daughter's fantasizing, Mabel blundered in. 'From what she's said to us, it's been a mite more than just friendly, Terry Price. You've led her on. She's an innocent, I'll grant you, but you shouldn't have led her on to think there was more to it than you intended. You've hurt her and humiliated our whole family. What the neighbours are going to say, I daren't think.'

'I've not led her on, Mrs Thomas. It's all in her imagination.'

'You calling her a liar? 'Cos if you are, I'll get my Percy to deal with you.'

'Leave it, Mam. He's not worth it. Let him have his floozy. He'll likely get more than he bargained for if what they say about them clippies is owt to go by.'

'Now look—' Terry began, but Mrs Thomas grasped his arm and began to push him towards the back door.

'You'd better go, but you haven't heard the last of this yet, m'lad.'

Twenty-Seven

'It was just the same – exactly the same – as you said it was with Bob,' Terry told Peggy later when he met her as she came off her shift. The city's transport system was now more or less back to as normal. Terry linked his arm through Peggy's and they walked through the darkening streets together. 'Why can't a lad and a girl be just friends without everyone reading more into it than there is?'

Peggy sighed. 'That's just it. I'm beginning to think that they can't be.'

'Well, that's daft. Me and Sylv had a lot of fun together. We used to go out as a foursome. Me, Sylv, my mate Billy and my kid sister, Amy. She's Sylvia's best friend, so it's making life very awkward. I'm getting called everything from a pig to a dog.' Terry held his tongue about what Sylvia had said about Peggy. Rumours always ran rife about romances and affairs when a group of men and women worked together. But he didn't believe gossip, especially not about his girl. 'They're saying I've thrown her over. Peg, I was just friends with her – I promise you.' He squeezed her arm to his side. 'I've never felt about Sylvia the way I feel about you. You do believe me, don't you?'

'Of course I do, because – like you say – it's the same thing I'm going through with Bob. I mean, we kissed, but never – well, you know—' Her voice faded away and she blushed in the darkness. Terry stopped and drew her into the shadows of a doorway. He kissed her longingly. 'It was good last night, wasn't it? I know it was the first time for you and – if I tell you summat – promise you won't tell a soul?'

'Course not. It's our secret.'

'It was the first time for me an' all, but don't you go telling anyone. Twenty-two years old and never had a girl before – I'd be a laughing stock, especially with my mate, Billy. To hear him bragging, you'd reckon he's had half the girls in Sheffield.'

Peggy giggled. 'I've overheard some of the chaps at work talk like that – even the married ones – when they don't know I've been listening. But I reckon if a girl fluttered her eyelashes at some of them they'd run a mile.'

'Come on, I'll walk you home. You know I've got to go back tomorrow. I don't suppose there's any way we can be alone tonight, is there?'

'Can't we go to your place again?'

'No. Dad'll go to the pub as usual, but Mam – and Amy too probably – will be at home.'

'Our house is never empty. Even if the others were out, there's always Gran at home.'

'Mm. I don't suppose . . .'

Peggy shook her head firmly. 'If she even knew what we'd been up to last night, she'd throw me out.'

He stopped and kissed her again. 'Oh, Peg, you don't know how much I love you.'

When they parted at her doorway, Terry promised to get home on leave again as soon as he could.

'Write to me, please,' Peggy begged, but Terry only shook his head. 'All our letters are censored. I don't want prying eyes reading the sort of thing I want to say to you.'

'Can't I write to you, though?'

'Best not, but I'll be home again soon. I promise. But never forget – I love you.'

As spring gave way to a reluctant summer, the household of women settled into a routine, but it was not the old routine. Sheffielders had seen their homes destroyed in two nights of heavy bombing and few lives would ever be the same again. And they weren't the only ones whose lives were altered irrevocably. London, Southampton, Liverpool, Hull – even Belfast and Clydebank – they, and many more, had suffered appalling damage and loss of life. And certainly things would never be the same in Grace Booth's household.

'We'll never get over this,' she would mutter, but the family had no idea of knowing whether she meant the destruction of her city or the turmoil in her family that had been an unexpected result of that first night. The air raids had wreaked havoc in people's lives that went far beyond the obliteration of homes and workplaces. Many families had lost loved ones and the blitz would never be forgotten – or forgiven. And the ripple effect still went on. Through Rose, Peggy heard that Bob had received his papers and had left to go for basic training. 'He's been sent to somewhere in Scotland,' Rose informed the family, not speaking directly to Peggy but knowing she was listening. 'Why ever do they send them so far away?'

'To stop them nipping on the first train back home, of course,' Grace said.

'His mother is devastated.' Rose glared at Peggy. 'If

owt happens to him . . .' She left the accusation hanging in the air.

With both Terry and now Bob gone, both sisters felt very lonely and the tension between them prevented them being a comfort to each other as they might have been. And Mary was affected by her daughters' quarrel. She'd always hated confrontation of any kind. She tried to coax both Peggy and Rose to sort out their differences. 'It's affecting us all and I don't like it.'

'It's not me, Mam, it's Rose,' Peggy assured her. 'I've tried to talk to her, but she won't listen.'

Rose merely shrugged her shoulders and reiterated stubbornly, 'She shouldn't have treated Bob so badly.'

'Well, you seem to be taking over where she left off in that direction.'

Rose glared at her mother. 'All right, I admit it. I like him, I always have, but while she's around he won't look at me. All he wants to do is talk about Peggy, Peggy, Peggy. And his mother's nearly as bad, moaning about what a lovely daughter-in-law she thought Peggy would have been.'

'Oh darling . . .' Mary began, but Rose turned away and all her mother could do was put on her uniform and go to work. At least for a few hours the hectic routine of a clippie's life took her mind off her family's troubles. Rose was acting so out of character. She'd always been the one to laugh off any petty squabbles, but now she was the instigator of a deep rift between the sisters that was affecting the whole family. Mary sighed inwardly. Rose was so obviously in love with Bob herself and she must be hurting too, but Mary didn't know how to help her, how to help either of her daughters. Maybe Laurence . . . ? Mary quickened her step, hoping that she would bump into the inspector at dinnertime in the canteen. She knew that at least he would be sympathetic to all her woes.

Grace carried on as usual, determined not to allow anything to disrupt her routine.

During the second week of May she read of yet another dreadful bombing raid on London, but at the end of May she had a good piece of news to tell her family. 'They've sunk the *Bismarck*.'

Myrtle, engrossed in her schoolwork, looked up. She had end-of-term exams looming and now the excitement of her feuding sisters had settled down to frosty looks and long silences between them, she'd buried herself once more in her studies. 'The one that sunk the *Hood* a few days ago?'

Grace nodded grimly. 'They've been hunting her ever since.'

'D'you think it could be a turning point?'

'Who's to know?' Grace murmured as she read on.

'Was there much loss of life?'

'I expect so,' Grace said solemnly. They were silent for a few moments. Even enemy sailors were someone's father, husband or son.

'What a waste,' Myrtle murmured. 'I hope Simon Bradshaw's safe.'

'Oh, the one that's in the navy? Yes, I hope so too. But we've no idea that he was involved in that.'

'I know, but he's out there somewhere, isn't he? Somewhere at sea and in danger.' She sighed and turned back to her books whilst Grace turned her attention to the battle raging in Crete. This was, indeed, a war that involved most of the world.

Would it ever end? And who would be the victor?

*

The days passed and neither Peggy nor Rose heard from the men they were so anxious about and Rose's mood grew ever more fractious. 'You'd've thought Bob'd've written. He's not even sent word to his mother.'

'Maybe they're not allowed to.'

'Don't talk daft, Mam, of course they're *allowed* to.'

Grace rattled her newspaper. 'Don't talk to your mother like that.'

Tentatively Peggy ventured, 'Terry said that all their letters – and ours – go through a censor. They read everything. That's why he won't write.'

'I bet he's writing to his family,' Rose said spitefully, 'oh, I'm forgetting. You can't ask them, can you?'

'Now, girls, please stop this bickering,' Mary said. 'I don't like it.'

'And I won't have it,' Grace declared, frowning at them over the top of her paper. 'Not in *my* house.'

'Where does he live, this Terry?' Rose asked.

Peggy bit her lip. 'In a terraced road in Attercliffe.'

When Rose pulled a face, Peggy defended the Price family. 'His father works in the steelworks and his mother's very house-proud.' She didn't tell them that the Prices' house was much smaller than theirs. She lifted her head defiantly. 'His home is rather like the one where the Deetons live.'

Rose glared at her but couldn't – for once – think of a suitably cutting retort.

Summer seemed a long time in coming; May continued as April had been – very cool and dull. June brought the sun, but the family scarcely seemed to notice. Only Grace took her folding chair out into the back yard and lifted her face to its warmth.

Bob was the first to arrive home on leave towards the end of June. He sat opposite Grace beside the fire, twirling his army cap in his hands.

'So, young man, how was it?'

'Pretty tough, Mrs Booth, but I'm with a good bunch of lads, though I shouldn't think we'll all stay together when we get our postings.'

'D'you know where that'll be yet?'

Bob shook his head.

'And even if you did – ' Grace smiled – 'you couldn't tell me.'

Bob laughed. 'Something like that.'

'Good to see you smile again, lad,' Grace said, with her customary bluntness. 'I reckon joining up was the best thing you could have done.'

'My mam doesn't think so.'

'Well, no, she won't and I can understand why. Just look after yourself for her sake, eh?'

'I'll try.'

Grace laid her paper down on her lap and looked directly across the hearth between them. 'Now, Bob, while we're on our own, there's something I want to ask you. I'm being a nosy old woman, I know that, but I have my granddaughters' best interests at heart.'

Bob didn't know whether she was talking about one or two of her granddaughters, but he kept silent.

'We were all sorry about what happened between you and Peggy – I want you to know that – but it's happened and life goes on.'

'You don't think she'll ever come back to me then?'

'No, lad, I don't.' Grace's tone was surprisingly gentle. 'But where you're concerned it's Rose I'm bothered about.'

'Rose?' Bob was obviously startled.

Grace regarded him steadily with her head on one side. 'Surely, you must realize how Rose feels about you or have you been so wrapped up in Peggy that you haven't noticed?'

'Rose and – and me?'

'Oh yes, plain as the nose on your face how Rose feels about you. Always has done, I suspect, though she'd never have done anything about it if you and Peggy had stayed together.'

His cap twirled even faster between fingers that were obviously nervous now. 'Rose,' he murmured again and the expression in his eyes looked as if a light had been suddenly turned on inside his head.

'It's her you've come round to see, I take it,' Grace said pointedly.

'Er – well – yes. Of course. She's been a good friend to me since—' He paused and was thoughtful for a few moments.

'Bob – you're a good lad, a nice lad,' Grace said firmly and added, as only someone of her age and with her wisdom could have done, 'but it's time you forgot about Peggy, and you and Rose would make a nice couple. Oh, I know.' She held up her hand. 'I'm a meddling old woman, but at least she'd be someone to write to when you're away and to see when you come home.'

'Well – yes. That'd be – nice,' he agreed, with a faraway look in his eyes. Rose, Bob was thinking. If what her grandmother was saying was true, then . . . It'd be nice to have a girl waiting for him back home, to boast about to the other lads and to write to and get letters from her. And Rose was a nice-looking lass. Pretty, though not in Bob's mind quite as pretty as Peggy was. But he must try to forget about Peggy. She was lost to him. Even her family seemed to have accepted that now. So, when Rose came flying in through the door a few moments later, Bob stood up and smiled at her. 'Hello, Rose. I've got a seventy-two-hour leave. Would you like to come to the pictures?'

The look on Rose's face left the young man in no doubt that Grace was right. Rose definitely had feelings for him.

Rose's mood improved overnight.

'Whatever's happened?' Mary asked when she'd heard Rose speak to Peggy almost civilly and they'd both gone out of the door to walk to work together.

'She went out with Bob last night, that's what,' Myrtle said.

'Really? How did that come about?'

Myrtle shrugged and Grace buried her face in her newspaper, pretending innocence and ignorance by concentrating on reading a piece about Hitler's surprising invasion of Russia.

Not suspecting that her mother might have had a hand in the new developments, Mary continued to question Myrtle.

'She came home very late,' the girl told her mother, gleeful to be able to impart the news. 'It must have been after midnight. She woke me up. She was singing.'

'Singing? Oh, my goodness, had she been drinking?'

Myrtle ran her tongue round her lips. 'I don't think so; it wasn't that sort of singing. She was just humming under her breath. You know, as if she was really happy about something.'

'It'll make a nice change if she is.' Mary laughed wryly.

Behind her newspaper, Grace smiled.

Twenty-Eight

Early in September Terry came home again on leave. 'We'd better make the most of it, Peg. There's rumours that we might be sent abroad soon.'

'Oh no,' she breathed. 'Where to?'

He tapped her playfully on the nose. 'Now you know I couldn't tell you even if I knew, but I don't. We'll likely just get our orders at the last minute and be off, though the lads say we get something called embarkation leave.'

'What's that?'

'A last leave before we're sent abroad because no one knows when we might get home again.'

Though warm in his arms in the back row in a darkened cinema, Peggy shuddered. It sounded so final, 'a last leave' as if he might never come home.

'You will write to me if you go abroad, won't you?'

Terry shifted awkwardly, 'I told you, love, I'm no good at letter writing.'

'But just a line or two, just to let me know you're safe. Please.'

'All right,' he agreed reluctantly. 'Listen, Peg, my mate Billy down the road from us ses we can use his place to be on our own.'

'How – I mean, aren't his parents there?'

Terry shook his head. 'His mam died four years

ago. There's just him and his dad and he works nights at the factory. So we could have the place to ourselves.'

'Where's Billy then?'

Terry grinned. 'At one of his girlfriends'. I reckon he spends more nights away from home than he does in his own bed.'

'Oh, Terry, you know I'd love to, but – but I don't know. It seems to make it all sordid, somehow.'

Terry was silent for a moment, but then he smiled gently and traced the line of her cheek with his finger. 'All right, sweetheart, if you're not happy about it, we won't go there. Tell you what, I'll splash out and book us a hotel room, shall I? Would that be all right?'

'No, that's even worse, facing the knowing looks of all the hotel staff.'

'You could wear a wedding ring.'

'Then they'd wonder why we weren't in our own home.'

'I could say it's a special occasion. Your birthday or something.'

Peggy bit her lip. She so longed to lie beside him, to have his strong arms around her, to have him make love to her again . . .

'All right, we'll go to Billy's place,' she agreed at last, 'but only if you can be sure we don't bump into him or his dad. I'd be so embarrassed.'

Terry kissed her. 'I'll make sure.'

So, on the last night of his leave, Terry took her to his friend's house. Billy had gone to a lot of trouble to make his small bedroom an idyllic love nest for them. He'd put clean sheets on his single bed, fresh flowers in a vase on the dressing table and two candles to give soft, romantic lighting. He'd even treated them to a bottle of sparkling wine.

'Sorry I can't run to champers, mate,' he'd written on a note beside the bottle, 'but enjoy.'

'Isn't that sweet of him?' Peggy said, as she read the note out to Terry.

'He's a good sort, old Billy. We've been friends since when we was kids at school. I was never very good at school. Billy used to help me a lot.'

'When am I going to get to meet him?'

'Oh now, I don't know about that.' Terry laughed, pulling her to him. 'He's a devil with the ladies. I don't reckon I could trust him with you, even if he is my best mate.'

Peggy put her arms around him and kissed him. 'You trust *me*, don't you?'

'Of course, but I may be gone a long time.'

'But we'll write to each other . . .'

Terry's answer was to silence her with his eager mouth. He picked her up and carried her to the bed.

Peggy was lonely after Terry had gone and so too was Rose now. Her friendship with Bob seemed to be developing into something more – just as Rose had secretly hoped – but she was determined not to rush him. She wrote to the address he had given her and, much to her delight, Bob wrote back faithfully every week. But there was no word from Terry. Happier now with her own hopes beginning to come true, Rose thawed a little towards her sister. Deep down inside – though she would never admit it openly – she realized her own good fortune had followed on from the decision Peggy had made. If Peggy had still been going out with Bob, Rose would have had no chance.

'Why don't you go round and see Terry's family? You know where he lives, don't you?'

Peggy bit her lip. 'I don't think I'd be welcome.'

'Why ever not?'

Peggy hesitated before saying, 'Because he's got a similar situation to the one I was in. There's a family who live next door to the Prices – have done for years – so they're all friends. You know, the fathers go to the pub together, the mothers are in and out of each other's houses all the time and the two daughters are best friends.'

'And?'

'Terry and his best mate, Billy, who lives down the road from him, used to go out with the two girls as a foursome – just as friends. But the girl next door – Sylvia, her name is – read more into it than Terry ever meant. Just like,' she added bitterly, 'Bob did with me. Rose, we never meant to hurt anyone. It just seems that boys and girls can't be *friends*.'

'No,' Rose said slowly, 'it does seem that way.' There was a pause before she added, 'Why don't you write to him? He might write back if he got a letter from you.'

'He wouldn't give me an address to write to.'

'That's a bit odd, isn't it?'

Peggy shrugged, but said nothing. She was close to tears.

'I know, why don't you ask his mate, Billy?'

'I could, I suppose,' Peggy said slowly. 'But I've never even met him.'

'You know where he lives, though, don't you?'

Peggy avoided meeting her sister's gaze. She nodded but did not explain how she knew.

'Well, then,' Rose said, 'go and see him.'

It was a reasonable enough suggestion, but Peggy shied away from it. She was embarrassed to meet Billy, but at last when no word came from Terry and Rose continued to receive a letter every Wednesday morning without fail, Peggy plucked up her courage and decided to go to Billy's home.

Just over a month after she had said goodbye to Terry and there was still no word, Peggy took the tram to the part of the city where he lived. She hardly recognized it in the daylight – she'd only been there with Terry twice, once to his home and the other time to Billy's, but she'd made a mental note of the name of the street and the numbers of the houses. As she walked down the street, she kept her face averted from number eleven, where the Price family lived, and even more so from number nine, where she knew Sylvia Thomas lived. Thank goodness, she thought, that Billy lives right at the other end of the row of terraced houses and on the opposite side of the road.

As she reached number forty-six, she hesitated before knocking on the door that led directly on to the pavement. A rather large woman was donkey-stoning the doorstep of the house next door. She glanced up and grinned toothlessly at her. 'Now then, lass, you lookin' for that scallywag, Billy Parkin?'

The woman tried to get up, but when she seemed to have difficulty, Peggy stepped forward at once to help her. 'Ta, lass. Eh, I'm getting too old for scrubbing me step. Now then, let's have a look at you.' The woman squinted at her and then smiled. 'A' you one of young Billy's fancy pieces?'

Peggy shook her head. 'No, I – I just wanted to ask him something about a mutual friend. That's all.'

'Oh, aye.' The woman sounded very disbelieving. Then, as the cogs in her mind began to whirl – Peggy fancied she could almost hear them whirring – the woman smiled. 'Oh ah, I know who *you* are. You're young Terry's fancy piece.'

Now Peggy could not deny it and felt herself blushing as the woman went on, 'Oh aye, talk of the street it's been, since he threw Sylvia over for you. A clippie, aren't you?'

'Er – yes.'

'Aye well,' the woman nodded knowingly. 'We all know a thing or two about you young clippies . . .'

'Whatever you've heard,' Peggy began to protest, 'it's not true. Terry didn't—' But her words were cut short by the door of number forty-six flying open and a young man with tousled fair hair, and dressed only in trousers and a vest, grabbed her arm and pulled her unceremoniously into the house.

'I heard what the old busybody was saying through me bedroom window,' he said, slamming the door. 'I 'spect half the street heard. Nosy old parker.' He paused and looked more closely at Peggy, his bold gaze taking in every detail. A slow smile spread across his face. 'Well, I'll hand it to Terry, he's picked himself a corker and no mistake.'

Peggy smiled. 'Ta very much, I'm sure. You must be Billy.'

'The very same. Come on in. I'll make us a cuppa.'

'Is your dad in?' she asked nervously, following him through the front room into which the front door had opened.

'Yes, but he's in bed. He works nights, y'know. Ever since me mam died. He finds it easier that way.'

'I'm sorry. When – when did that happen?'

'Four years ago now, but he still misses her. We both do.'

'Of course.'

'What about you? Terry told me you've no dad.'

'No, he died when I was seven.'

'You remember him then?'

Peggy nodded. 'I've two sisters. Rose was a few days short of her fifth birthday when he died, but Myrtle was only a baby. She has no memories of him at all and Rose only a few.'

'It must have been hard on your mam. Three kiddies to bring up on her own,' Billy said, as he filled the kettle and set it on the stove.

'We've always lived with my grandmother – my mother's mother. It's her house.'

He set cups and saucers on the table. 'Sorry, I've no biscuits.' He grinned as he added the favourite saying of the day, 'There's a war on, y'know.'

'Yes,' she sighed, 'and Terry's somewhere in it. That's why I've come to see you, really. Have you heard from him? I've no idea where he is and he hasn't written and he couldn't – or wouldn't – give me an address so that I could write to him. Last time he was home he said something about being sent abroad, but he wouldn't say where or even when.'

Billy stood quite still by the table, moving the cups so that the handles pointed in the same direction. Slowly he looked up and met her gaze. He stared at her for what seemed an age to Peggy. Her heart started to thump. Had something happened to Terry and she hadn't heard? At last he said, 'Terry's not much of a one for letter writing.'

'That's what he told me, but I didn't think he meant he wouldn't write at all, especially – ' she bit her lip – 'when he got sent abroad. Billy, has he gone abroad? Do you know where he is?'

Billy avoided her gaze and shook his head. She wondered if he was telling her the truth. 'I thought you'd be together – in the same unit or whatever they're called. Terry said you joined up together.'

Now Billy answered at once. 'No, they separated us. After what happened to the Sheffield City Battalion in the last war, they don't like "pals battalions" any more.'

'Do you know if his parents have heard from him?'

He shrugged. 'He'll not write. Like I said, he's not one for writing letters.' He seemed about to say more, but then closed his mouth firmly, as if to physically stop the words escaping from his lips.

'I hope you don't mind me coming here. I didn't want to go to his home.' She smiled wryly. 'I don't think I'd be very welcome.'

Billy gave a rueful grin too. 'Probably not. But they got it all wrong. We was all only mates. It's as bad as saying I was going out with his sister, Amy, and I wasn't. Mind you,' he added, with a laugh, 'I expect her parents are relieved about that. I've got myself a bit of a reputation with the ladies.' He winked at her.

Peggy smiled too. She liked Billy. He was honest, she could see that already, and she could also see what the girls found attractive in him.

'But, yeah, you come round here any time you want.' He laughed and held up his hands, palms outwards. 'And I promise not to try it on. I wouldn't do anything like that with my best mate's girl. Mind you, I'm likely to be posted any time soon, so I may not be around for a few months.'

They drank the tea he'd made and talked a little longer before Peggy said she must go. He saw her to the door and said again, 'Come round any time.'

As she walked back up the street, she risked a glance at Terry's home. There was no sign of anyone, but as she turned away again, Peggy fancied she saw someone at the bedroom window of the house next door: a girl's face peering from behind the curtain.

Was that Sylvia? she wondered. The girl whose heart Terry was supposed to have broken because of her? Peggy turned her head away and hurried on.

Twenty-Nine

Two more weeks passed and the whole month of October was surprisingly warm and sunny. Bob wrote regularly but not a word came from Terry. Peggy became resigned to the fact that he'd meant what he'd said: he was no letter writer. And then the household was thrown into turmoil when, one Wednesday at the end of October, no letter arrived for Rose.

'Something must have happened to him,' she wailed. 'He never misses.'

'Darling, do calm down.' Mary tried to comfort her. 'It could have been delayed in the post or he could have been kept too busy to write.'

'Bob would *make* time,' Rose insisted tearfully.

Grace retreated behind her newspaper, muttering.

'How d'you think I feel, then, when I never hear from Terry?' Peggy said, but was rewarded with an angry glare from her sister.

'Maybe Bob's met a pretty girl and forgotten all about you,' Myrtle offered, biting into a piece of toast, spread thickly with butter.

'Mam, have you seen her?' Rose snapped, her anxiety making her irritable. 'That's nearly a week's ration of butter gone on one piece of toast. Can't you stop her being so greedy? She's the only one not bringing money into this house and she gets all the treats and extras.'

Myrtle stopped chewing. Then she shrugged. 'Then

I'll leave school and get a job. I'm sure I could keep up the family tradition and become a clippie.'

'You'll do no such thing,' Mary said and Peggy added, 'We all want you to stay on at school. You're the clever one, Myrtle. We're all so proud of you. Take no notice of Rose. She's just bad-tempered because there's no letter for her.'

'I'll make my own excuses, thank you very much.'

'Girls, girls, please! Stop this bickering. Myrtle, none of us want you to leave school, but you should be careful with the rations and only have your fair share.'

'Sorry, Mam.' Myrtle hung her head, hiding a smile. The girl knew exactly what she wanted to do now. Other girls at school were leaving as soon as they were old enough and going into some sort of war work. Their conversations were littered with their plans.

'My sister's joined the Women's Auxiliary Air Force. She looks so smart in her uniform.'

'Mine's gone into the Land Army. The work's hard, but she's having a great time in the country.'

So Myrtle had been thinking. She was in the Upper Sixth now and would stay on at school until she'd taken her Higher School Certificate the following summer. She'd be eighteen by then and if the war was still going on, she'd join one of the forces. She was sure that, after the war was won, there'd be every chance for her to go to university then. Myrtle had complete faith that Britain and her allies would win the war; the only question was, how long would it take? But she told her family none of this; they wouldn't approve. And now, she was thankful that her mother's attention had turned away from her to Peggy.

'You look a little peaky this morning, love. Are you all right?'

'I'm fine, Mam, just a little tired.'

Mary said no more. She knew the girl was fretting because she'd had no news of Terry. She didn't talk about it much because it was a sensitive subject, especially when Rose was in earshot.

The two sisters walked to work together, but said little to one another on the way. As they neared the depot, Rose murmured, 'I'll ask one or two of Bob's mates if they've heard anything.'

'Mm.'

Rose glanced at her sister. 'Are you sure you're all right? You look awfully pale.'

'My tummy's a bit unsettled this morning. Must be something I ate.'

Rose laughed. 'I shouldn't wonder. Goodness knows what they put in some of this tinned stuff we're getting now. Bye for now. I'll see you later.'

Peggy went towards the tram she was on that morning, but when she reached it and climbed up on to the platform, she felt a wave of sickness wash over her. She clung to the handrail and took deep breaths until the feeling subsided a little.

''Morning, Peg,' a cheerful voice hailed her. It was her motorman, William, who always insisted on the full use of his own name but always seemed to shorten the names of others, or give them nicknames. 'Ready for the off?'

'I – think so.'

'Hey, you OK? You look as white as a sheet.'

'I feel a bit queasy. I think it must be something I ate.'

'D'you want to go home sick, because you'd better do it now rather when we're half way round the route.'

'No – no, I'll be fine. It's going off now. We'd better be on our way or else we'll have Mr Bower after us.'

The day passed without further incident. She ate her mid-morning snack and felt much better, but the following morning she felt light-headed and nauseous when she got out of bed and had to reach for the chamber pot.

'Just a piece of dry toast, Mam,' she said when at last she arrived at the breakfast table looking tired and white-faced.

'You're working too hard,' Mary said. 'The early morning shift when we're all rushing to work is the very devil. Why don't you ask Mr Bower for a couple of days off and have a really good rest?'

'That won't bring her a letter, will it?' Myrtle put in. 'That's what's upsetting her. She's afraid he's got killed and that's why—'

'Myrtle,' Mary snapped. 'That's enough.'

If it was possible, Peggy turned even paler. 'No, Mam, I'll be all right. I was fine yesterday once I got to work.' Her smile was a little wobbly as she added, 'Takes my mind off things. And don't be cross with Myrtle because she's right. I am worried something might have happened to Terry.'

Mary was on the late shift that day and once the girls had all left the house for work and school, she began to clear the dirty pots into the scullery to wash.

Grace shook her paper with an angry rattle. 'Mary – that girl's pregnant.'

Mary almost dropped the teapot she was carrying. She turned to stare at her mother. 'Oh no, Mother, she can't be. I mean – Peggy wouldn't—' She stopped and bit down hard on her trembling lip.

231

'Oh yes, she would,' Grace muttered sourly. 'She was out very late at night with that lad. Up to no good, I'll be bound.' She lowered her paper and stared straight at her daughter. 'But I'll tell you something now, Mary. If she is pregnant, out she goes. I'll not have such shame brought to my house.'

That evening, when Peggy came home from work and went upstairs to the bedroom she shared with her mother, Mary followed her. She closed the door quietly and sat down on her own bed, waiting until Peggy had splashed her face in the porcelain bowl on the wash-stand and hung her uniform up on a hanger behind the door. As she pulled on a jumper and stepped into a skirt, Mary asked gently, 'How've you been today, love?'

'Fine – once I got to work. Like I said, must be something I ate.'

Mary ran her tongue round her lips that were suddenly dry. 'How – how long have you been feeling sick in the morning?'

Peggy paused in fastening her skirt and stared at her mother. Confusion, fear and the beginnings of shame flooded into her eyes. She sank down onto the bed opposite Mary and twisted her fingers together. 'About – about a week.'

'And when did you last have your monthly visitor?'

Peggy jumped up and tore the calendar from the wall, turning back the page. 'Oh no!' she breathed in an agonized whisper. She raised terrified eyes to meet Mary's worried gaze. 'I've missed one completely.'

'And was the last one you had *before* Terry went back?'

Peggy bit her lip and nodded.

'And you've not had one since?'

Peggy shook her head.

'And did you – sleep with him?'

Peggy closed her eyes and groaned. She covered her face with her hands. 'Oh, Mam, I couldn't help it. I love him so. And he was going away and might never come back, but I never thought . . .'

'No,' Mary said flatly, 'when you're young and in love, you never do stop to think.'

Peggy raised tear-filled eyes. 'How – how are we going to tell Gran? Whatever will she say?'

'She knows, or rather she's guessed. And – I'm sorry to say it – but she says she'll turn you out.'

'Turn me out?' Peggy was shocked. She knew her grandmother was strict and never missed an opportunity to remind them just whose house it was that they were all living in, but she'd never thought Grace would be so harsh.

'She wouldn't, would she? She wouldn't really turn me out? Where would I go?'

Mary touched her daughter's hand. 'If she does that, we'll all go. Somehow we could manage between us.'

'But that wouldn't be fair on Gran. I couldn't let you do that, not when she's getting older and will need help. No, I'll – I'll have to go.'

'I'll talk to her. And Rose and Myrtle will stand by you.'

But Mary was wrong. When they all sat together later that evening and Peggy admitted that she believed she was pregnant, Rose was vicious in her condemnation. Even Grace had not been so vitriolic.

'You dirty little slut! How could you bring shame on us all like that and with someone you hardly know?

My God, no wonder you haven't heard from him. He's just been using you as a bit on the side – a bit of fun – before he went to war. And now he's deserted you.'

Peggy hung her head and let the tears flow. She had no argument against Rose's accusations. Myrtle said nothing. She was watching their grandmother for her reaction. When the old lady continued to sit quietly in her chair near the fire, taking no part in the arguments raging around the room, Myrtle asked quietly, 'What are you going to do, Gran?'

There was silence, whilst all eyes turned towards Grace. Even Peggy lifted her tear-streaked face.

'I told your mother that if you were pregnant – and it looks very much as if you are – I'd turn you out.'

Peggy gave a sob, jumped up and fled from the room. There was silence after she'd gone until, yet again, Myrtle was the one to ask, 'And did you mean it, Gran?'

'Of course she means it,' Rose snapped. 'And if she doesn't, then *I'll* throw her out.'

'It's not your place, Rose,' Grace said quietly, but firmly. 'If there's any throwing out to be done, then I shall do it.'

Rose pursed her lips as if to stop herself saying any more.

Grace rose unsteadily to her feet. 'I'm going to bed. All this has made me feel very old and very tired. I'm disappointed in Peggy. I'd thought better of her.' She glanced at Rose.

'What?' Rose stared back at her grandmother and then colour flooded her face. 'Oh, I get it. You wouldn't have been surprised if it'd been me – is that it?'

'I never said a word.'

'No, but you looked it. Ta very much, Gran.' Rose

leaned forward. 'But I'll tell you summat. I'll never let a feller touch me – not even Bob – till I'm wed. So there. You can put that in your pipe and smoke it.'

'Aye,' Grace shot back, with a vigour she thought had deserted her. 'An' I'll believe that when I see it. When he comes back and begs you to show him how much you love him before he goes back to the war, back into danger, you'll give way. Just like I expect Peggy's done.'

'I don't reckon she'd've needed much persuading,' Rose said nastily.

'Oh, please, please stop arguing.' Mary cried as she put her head in her hands. 'Whatever are we to do?'

For a moment, Grace paused by the door on her way out. She looked back at her daughter. 'I'll let you know in the morning, when I've had time to sleep on it. Goodnight – though I don't expect it will be a good one for any of us.'

When Mary went up to bed too she found Peggy sobbing into her pillow. She sat on the side of the single bed and put her arms round her daughter. 'Come on now, love. You'll do yourself no good, nor the baby.'

At her words, Peggy sobbed all the harder until Mary was obliged to say firmly, 'Now, stop this. We'll work something out.'

Still hiccuping miserably, Peggy pulled herself up. 'Did Gran really mean what she said?'

Mary sighed. 'She's sleeping on it. She's going to let us know in the morning.'

'And Rose? What about Rose? I know she hates me for what I did to Bob, but—'

'You leave Rose to me. I'll handle her.' Mary, usually

such a gentle soul, could on occasions surprise her family. When something important happened, Mary revealed a backbone of steel. Peggy lay back against the pillows. As long as her mother stood by her, she thought, she didn't really need the others.

'Mam, I'm sorry I've disappointed you, but you won't desert me, will you?'

'I'll not lie to you, Peggy. I wish it hadn't happened. I thought I'd brought you up better than that, but, no, I won't let you be homeless. Whatever your gran decides in the morning, we'll deal with it.'

Grace was late getting up the following day and they all, including Mary, who was starting a run of early-morning shifts, had to leave before she appeared.

Rose marched ahead of Peggy, refusing to speak to her or even walk beside her to work. Only Mary remained faithfully at her daughter's side.

'How do you feel this morning? Still sickly?'

'A bit. I've just got this awful hollow feeling inside. Maybe, I'll lose it, Mam. It'd be for the best—'

Mary stopped suddenly, grasped Peggy's arm and swung her round to face her. Her face was blazing. 'Don't you ever – ever – let me hear you say such a thing again. All life is precious. My God, we should know that when we're losing so many fine young men all over again in another bloody war.'

Peggy gasped. Mary never swore, never raised her voice, and to see her so angry and almost shouting in the middle of the street was almost more of a shock than finding out she was pregnant.

'Mam, I—'

'If you've created a life, then it's your responsibility

236

to look after it. To love and nurture it *however* it's come about. Your situation isn't ideal, fingers will be pointed, and folks will whisper behind their hands. We have that to face. But face it we will because it's not the fault of the poor little mite you're carrying. You'll love it and care for it, even if we have to do it without its father. You hear me, Peggy?'

But without giving her daughter the chance to reply, Mary loosened her grip, turned and walked on. Openmouthed, Peggy stared after her for a few moments before hurrying to catch her up as they reached the depot together. She didn't want all the Sylvester women to be seen arriving separately. The gossip would start soon enough.

Thirty

That evening Mary and Peggy walked home together. Rose, though she was due to finish work at the same time, was nowhere to be seen.

'I expect she's gone round to Mrs Deeton's to see if she's had a letter from Bob.'

'D'you think she'll tell her about me?'

Mary sighed. 'I've no idea what Rose will do next, love. But she's the least of my worries just now. Let's get home and see what your gran has to say. We'll know what we've got to deal with then.'

Grace was sitting in her usual place by the fire, but her newspaper lay idly on her lap and the elderly woman was gazing into the fire. She didn't even look up as Mary and Peggy entered the room. Grace usually began the preparations for the evening meal, but tonight nothing had been done.

'Mother,' Mary said tentatively. 'Are you all right?'

Slowly, Grace raised her head. She stared at Mary for a long moment before saying, 'Are you? Are any of us?'

Peggy turned and left the room. Whatever decision Grace had made about her future, Mary would relay the message. She couldn't bear to stay in the same room and see the accusation, the disappointment in her grandmother's eyes.

Mary took off her coat and sat down opposite her

mother. With surprising spirit for one so usually meek and mild, Mary asked. 'Well, do we stay or do we go?'

'Who said anything about "we"? This only concerns Peggy.'

'I'm sorry, Mother, but if Peggy goes then we all go.'

Grace's mouth twisted in a wry smile. 'Putting a gun to my head, are you?'

'Not at all. This is your house.' She almost added, 'As you so often remind us,' but thought better of it. She didn't want to antagonize her mother further or cause an unpleasant argument. Instead, she went on, 'And you have every right to ask Peggy to leave if you feel she has brought shame and disgrace to the family. But, in turn, I am not about to desert my daughter. Yes, I'm as disappointed in her as you are, but I will stand by her and help her. She's not the first to have a child out of wedlock nor, sadly, will she be the last. In fact, with this war, there are likely to be a lot more girls finding themselves in her position.'

'I don't doubt it,' Grace muttered, 'but I hadn't expected my granddaughter to be one of them.'

'Nor had I, Mother. But she is and we've got to deal with it.'

'Rose won't go,' Grace said suddenly.

'What d'you mean?'

'You said, "We'll all go." Rose won't go. She's already said so.'

'When did she say that?'

'Dinnertime. She dashed home in her break to see if there was a letter from Bob.'

'And was there?'

'No. She'll've gone to see Mrs Deeton. She said she would go after work.'

'I thought as much.' Mary paused then continued, 'So – you discussed things with Rose, did you?'

'Yes. She guessed that you wouldn't stand by and see Peggy turned out, but she's made it quite clear that she'll stay with me. I think she's even more disgusted at Peggy than I am.'

'And what about Myrtle? I presume she's up in her room doing her homework. Have you discussed this with her too?' A note of sarcasm crept into Mary's tone. She couldn't help it.

'She wants to stay here too, mainly, I suspect,' Grace added with a wry smile, 'because of her school.'

'So, it's just Peggy and me who'll be leaving then, is it?'

'I haven't said anyone's leaving yet.'

Mary raised her eyebrows. She was used to her mother's teasing. This was no time to play games, but she had no choice but to wait patiently until Grace was ready to make her pronouncement. With some sort of perverse pleasure, Mary thought, her mother was enjoying holding all the cards. It put her – not Peggy – at the centre of the drama.

'She can stay,' Grace said at last, though her tone was grudging. 'We'll face it as a family, but don't let her think for one moment that I condone what she's done. She's brought shame to my house and I'll never forgive her for that. And she's to stay out of my sight. She can stay in her bedroom or the front room. You – or one of the others – can take her meals to her. I don't want to set eyes on her.'

Mary was thoughtful for a moment. Her mother had softened thus far, maybe as time went on . . . She could only hope.

When she relayed Grace's words to Peggy, the girl

shed more tears, partly at the harshness of her grand-mother's ultimatum, but partly too with relief. At least she would have a roof over her head and food to eat, even though her life shut away between the cold front room and her bedroom would be lonely.

'I'll spend as much time with you as I can,' Mary promised. 'And perhaps Rose will come round in time.'

'Pigs might fly,' Peggy murmured and tried to force a smile through her tears. She mopped her face, straightened her back and added, 'But at least I can carry on at work until I begin to show. No one need know until then.'

'Are you well enough? I mean, this morning sickness . . .'

'It's only first thing. Usually by the time I get to work, it's gone off. A piece of dry toast in a morning seems to help.' She smiled wryly. 'At least Myrtle can have my butter ration.'

Mary smiled and patted her hand. 'Get to bed now. You need the rest.'

Peggy grasped her mother's hand, her voice husky. 'Thanks, Mam. I—'

'Don't say any more, darling. We'll get through this together.'

Mary's hopes that Rose would 'come round' were not fulfilled. Rose sided wholeheartedly with her grand-mother and refused to speak to Peggy. She wouldn't even carry meals up the stairs or into the front room for her sister.

'I'll do it, Mam,' Myrtle said, holding out her hands to take the tray from Mary. 'You've got enough to do without running up and downstairs after her.'

Mary raised her eyebrows but said nothing as she handed the tray over. The young girl was intrigued by her sister's pregnancy. She wanted to know everything about it. 'I'm doing biology,' she said to explain her curiosity. 'It's useful.'

'Just so long as you don't go telling everyone at school that your sister's pregnant,' Rose warned on one of the rare occasions she even referred to Peggy's condition.

The following Wednesday, a letter arrived from Bob and Rose's face was wreathed in smiles once more. 'He's applying for leave. He might be home just after Christmas. Oh, I can't wait.'

And this time, Mary guessed, Rose would lose no time in telling Bob all about Peggy.

'Well, there's no doubt about it now. We'll win the war.' Grace announced triumphantly early in December, when most folk in the city were dreading the first anniversary of their own particular blitz.

'I never doubted it,' Myrtle said, carefully spreading butter thinly on her toast. Even she'd learnt to use their rations sparingly now. 'Not for a moment, but what's making you say it now?' Grace was actually smiling as she stared at the headlines in the previous day's late edition of the *Daily Mail*.

'Japan has declared war on us – and on America.'

Myrtle stopped eating and stared at her in surprise. 'And that's supposed to be good?'

'It'll bring America into the war. The Japs have bombed the home base of the US Pacific Fleet at Pearl Harbor in Hawaii as well as other American bases.' She shook her head, but was still smiling. 'How can they have been so silly? And Canada has already declared war on Japan.'

'Oh well, they call it a world war so I suppose everyone's got to be in it. But who's fighting who? That's what I'd like to know.'

'Well, I'll tell you . . .' Grace lowered her newspaper.

'Not now, Gran,' Myrtle said, springing up and gathering her school books together. 'Must dash. See you tonight.'

'I'll tell you then,' Grace called after her.

'Not if I can help it,' Myrtle muttered as she left by the back door. Though she was interested in world affairs, often read her grandmother's papers and listened to the news bulletins on the wireless with her, Myrtle didn't want to sit the whole evening whilst Grace expounded her knowledge and her views.

There was often band music on after the news, especially if Grace could be persuaded to tune into the programmes for the forces. Myrtle would much prefer to listen to that. Even Myrtle, studious though she was, enjoyed a little relaxation sometimes, especially since there was no fun to be had with either of her sisters now.

Christmas – the third of the war – was a silent affair in the household of women. Laurence had gone to his brother's home this year and the Bradshaws had gone to visit Tom's sister in Rotherham. So, much to everyone's relief there was no one they felt obliged to ask to join them for Christmas dinner. They exchanged gifts as usual but with little enthusiasm and Mary noticed that the ones Peggy had bought for her grandmother and for Rose lay unopened.

'Mother, may Peggy join us for dinner?' Mary asked tentatively.

'Certainly not. She's made her bed, she must lie on it.'

'That's what's caused all the trouble in the first place,' Myrtle said with a smirk.

Grace rounded on her. 'It's no laughing matter, Myrtle, and I hope you're going to learn from this.'

Myrtle's smile faded and her eyes narrowed. 'I'll never let any man wreck my life, Gran. You can be sure of that.'

'I'm pleased to hear it. Now, can we please get on with our Christmas dinner – such as it is. I want to listen to the King's speech on the wireless later.'

Mary was right. When Bob arrived home on leave early in the New Year, Rose couldn't wait to tell him just what Peggy – the girl he had believed himself so in love with – had done.

They were sitting in the back row of the cinema amongst all the other courting couples. Most of the young men were in army uniform like Bob, snatching one and nine's worth of darkness. When the lights went up in the interval before the big picture started, there was much shuffling and sitting up straight.

'I've got summat to tell you,' Rose whispered. 'Peggy's got herself pregnant.'

Bob turned to stare, open-mouthed, at her. At last, he spluttered. 'With him? That Terry Price?'

'Of course. Who else? She's not a whore – although that's what I call her.'

Bob sat rigidly still for a moment and then he jumped up and grabbed Rose's hand. 'We're going.'

'But we haven't seen the big picture yet.'

'Come on,' he insisted, dragging her to her feet and pulling her along the row, forcing all the other occupants to grab their belongings and stand up quickly.

'Watch where you're putting your feet, mate. That was my toe.'

'Sorry,' Bob mumbled.

'What's the hurry, mate? Is Hitler coming?'

A titter of laughter rippled along the row, but Bob blundered on until he was standing in the aisle.

'Bob, wait,' Rose called. 'I've dropped my scarf . . .'

'Never mind that, Rose. Come on.'

'Here it is, love.'

'Ta,' Rose said and grabbed her scarf, stumbling past the last few seats and joining Bob. As they hurried down the stairs and out into the street, she said, 'I don't understand what's the matter with you. It's nowt to do with you that our Peggy's got herself into trouble.'

'She hasn't "got herself into trouble", has she? It's his fault. By heck, wait till I catch up with him. I'll bloody kill him.'

Rose stood still on the pavement staring at him, oblivious to the fine drizzle that had begun to fall. She was still holding her coat and was too stunned by what she was hearing to think to put it on. She shivered, but hardly noticed. 'You're still in love with her, aren't you?' When he didn't answer her, she screamed at him. '*Aren't you?*'

Calmer now, he turned to face her. 'I'll be honest with you, Rose.'

'Oh please do,' she answered, sarcastically.

'I don't know how I feel. I've become very fond of you, Rose. You've been a brick.'

'I don't want to be a brick,' she snapped, half

wanting to stop whatever he was going to say and yet knowing she had to hear it. 'I want to be the girl you love, the girl you want to marry. There, I've said it and no doubt I've embarrassed you, because nice girls don't tell a man that they love them. They wait until he declares his undying love for her. But you're not going to, are you, Bob? Because you're still in love with Peggy.'

'I've told you – I don't know how I feel. All I know is that the girl I *did* love is in trouble and needs help.'

'And what can you do to help her? Marry her?'

Through the darkness the words came that shattered Rose's happiness. 'If he won't, then, yes, that's exactly what I'll do.'

Thirty-One

'Calm down, Rose, do. I can't understand a word you're saying. What's happened? Is it Bob? Is he hurt?' Mary was trying, but failing, to get the girl to speak coherently.

Rose was crying and raging hysterically.

Grace gave a huge sigh and shook her head. More trouble.

'Sit down. Here, drink this.' Mary thrust her own cup of tea into the girl's shaking hands, but the cup rattled so dangerously in the saucer that she took it back again and pushed Rose into the chair by the fire.

'Stop the noise, Rose,' Grace snapped and, though Rose glanced balefully at her grandmother, her hysterical crying subsided to a miserable hiccuping sob.

'What's happened? Hasn't Bob come home on leave?'

'Oh, he's come home, all right,' Rose wailed. 'He's in the front room right now.' Her voice rose a pitch higher. 'Proposing to Peggy.'

Mary stared at her and even Grace looked up and blinked. 'What?' they asked in unison.

'Proposing. He's asking her to marry him – because he wants to help her.'

Mary sank into a chair by the table, thinking the same words that Rose now voiced. 'He's still in love with her.'

247

Grace picked up her newspaper, but the words danced before her eyes. Here's a way out, she was thinking. If they marry quickly, no one need know.

'She'll not do it,' Mary said quietly.

'Oh, she will. What with us all against her – except you.' Rose cast an accusing glance at her mother. 'You should have let Gran turn her out, then she wouldn't have still been here.'

'If he's that serious, he'd have gone looking for her,' Mary said softly, unwittingly hurting Rose even more.

'It's your own fault, Rose,' Grace said unsympathetically. 'You shouldn't have gone blabbing about our family secrets.'

'It's hardly going to be a secret. The whole street's going to know soon. She can't stay hidden for ever – not with a howling baby.'

There was silence between the three women as they all strained their ears to hear what was happening in the front room. There was the clatter of footsteps on the stairs and Myrtle came into the room, carrying a book.

She stopped in the doorway and glanced around the room at the three solemn faces. Rose turned her face, red and swollen from her copious tears, away, but not before Myrtle had noticed it. Her eyes widened and her glance went to her mother's face. She closed the door quietly behind her and sidled up to Mary. 'What's happened?' she whispered, fearful that they'd had bad news.

Before Mary could open her mouth to reply, Grace said, 'Rose has been foolish enough to tell Bob about Peggy's pregnancy. He's in the front room at this very moment offering to marry her.'

Myrtle's mouth dropped open and her remark, 'He

must still love her then,' prompted further tears from Rose.

After what seemed an age to those waiting in the living room, they heard the sitting-room door open and then the front door opened and slammed. Rose jumped to her feet. 'That must be Bob leaving. He might've—'

'I'll find out what's happened,' Mary said. Myrtle, too, half-rose out of her seat, but Mary said at once, 'You stay here.'

Mary opened the door into the front room quietly to find Peggy, wrapped in a blanket against the chill of the room – Grace had decreed that coal could not be spared for another fire in the house. 'She can stay in bed,' Grace had muttered hard-heartedly.

'Peggy, love?' Mary said softly, a question in her tone. Peggy was staring straight ahead of herself, yet seeing nothing. Mary moved further into the room and closed the door behind her. She crossed the space between them and sat down on the sofa next to Peggy. She took her hand. 'Oh, darling, you're as cold as ice. Let's go back up to your bedroom and you can get into bed.'

But Peggy didn't move. Instead she said, 'He offered to marry me, Mam. To make an honest woman of me and quieten the wagging tongues. He – he said he'd be willing for everyone to think the baby was his.'

'It takes a big man to offer something like that.' There was a pause before Mary whispered, 'What – what did you say?'

'I told him that I appreciated his offer – more than he'd ever know – but that I couldn't possibly do that to him. He – he tried to persuade me, Mam, but it wouldn't be right. I don't love him.'

'He obviously still loves you, though.'

Peggy sighed. 'I'm not sure if he does now.'

'How d'you mean?'

'I said, "What about Rose?" and he said that he'd grown really fond of her and – if this hadn't happened – then he thought they might have made a go of it, given time.'

Mary chafed Peggy's cold hand. 'She's heartbroken.'

Peggy nodded and said huskily, 'I guessed as much. Now she's never going to forgive me, is she? It was bad enough before, but now . . .' She left the words unspoken for there was no need to say more.

'So – you've definitely refused him?'

Peggy nodded. 'I couldn't do that to him, Mam. We'd both have a miserable life. I'd sooner face the disgrace.'

Mary patted her hand. 'Well, for what it's worth, I think you're right. He might fancy himself as a knight in shining armour riding on a white charger to rescue a damsel in distress, but it wouldn't last. Marriage is hard enough when two people do love each other. As time went on, he'd become resentful.'

Peggy nodded and lowered her head. 'Oh, Mam, I'm so sorry.'

'We'll get through it,' Mary said with more positivity in her tone than she felt inside. 'Come along now, up to bed with you and I'll bring you a hot drink.'

In the living room Rose was sitting stony-faced. When she'd heard the front door slam behind a departing Bob, her instinct had been to leap to her feet and run after him, but willpower and an innate sense of pride kept her sitting in the chair.

Grace cleared her throat. 'Sounds like that didn't go the way he wanted then,' she murmured.

'She wouldn't refuse him, would she?' Myrtle asked.

'No,' Rose said harshly. 'She'll not refuse such an offer. She'd not be that daft.'

'But she loves Terry. What if he comes back? He doesn't even know about the baby yet, does he?'

Neither Grace nor Rose could answer her.

All three listened to the sounds outside the room: the front-room door opening and closing, the sound of two pairs of footsteps mounting the stairs and entering the bedroom above them. Mary came downstairs a few moments later and three pairs of eyes looked up at her questioningly as she came into the room.

'She's said no.'

'Why?' Rose was the first to ask. 'It's the answer to everything.'

Mary shook her head as she sat down. 'Not in Peggy's eyes, it isn't. Nor – if it comes to that – in mine.'

'I see. So you'd prefer to face the shame and disgrace, would you?' Grace asked.

Mary turned to her mother and lifted her chin boldly. Though the older women had now said Peggy could stay, Mary knew very well that she could change her mind at any time.

'Mother – she doesn't love Bob and he's only doing it because he once loved her. He thinks it's the gallant thing to do.' Swiftly she related all that Peggy had said.

'I don't believe her – or him,' Rose said bitterly. 'If he had any feelings for me, he wouldn't be asking my *sister* to marry him, now would he? I bet she's made it up to try and make me feel better.'

'I don't think Peggy would do that,' Mary said quietly.

Rose glared at her mother as she said slowly and deliberately, 'You didn't think Peggy would get herself into trouble, did you?'

To that even Mary had no answer.

As they were locking up, banking down the fire and preparing to go upstairs to bed, Mary and Rose were the only ones left downstairs.

'You should go and see Bob,' Mary said. She was saddened by the dreadful quarrel between her daughters, who had once been so close and loving towards each other. She'd never dreamed anything like this could possibly happen. But it had and, as their mother, she was trying to comfort both of them. 'Ask him outright why he did it.'

Rose pouted and wriggled her shoulders. 'I don't care if I never see him again.'

'You don't mean that.'

'Anyway, he's going back tomorrow.'

'Then you should try to see him before he goes. Don't part on bad terms. You're on the late shift tomorrow. You could catch him before he leaves in the morning.'

When Rose still didn't answer, Mary added softly, 'Think about it. You might regret it if you don't even try.'

Rose had a sleepless night, but by the time the first light of dawn was creeping through the windows she'd realized her mother was right. Although it hadn't been put into words, Rose knew her mother was hinting that if anything happened to Bob, she'd spend the rest of her life regretting that she hadn't at least tried to put things right between them. She knew her dreams of marrying him one day now lay in tatters, but deep down she didn't want to part on bad terms with him. She'd never forgive herself if he were killed.

Thirty-Two

Hester was still up when Bob arrived home at last.

'Where've you been? I've been so worried. Come near the fire and get warm. Oh, Bob, you've been drinking. I can smell it on your breath.'

'Just a pint or two,' Bob mumbled. He was by no means drunk, but he had had more than the pint or two he was admitting to his mother. He shivered as he slumped down into a chair and held his hands out to the fire. 'Mam, I think I've done something very stupid.'

Hester's eyes widened and she couldn't prevent a little gasp escaping her lips. 'Oh, Bob, what have you done?' She scanned his face anxiously. There were no cuts, no bruises. It didn't look as if he'd got into a fight.

'Peggy's pregnant,' he said flatly.

'Oh no! Is – is it yours?'

Bob shook his head. 'No – it's that blasted soldier she met. But he's gone away and never been in touch with her. He's deserted her, Mam, I'm sure of it. So – I've offered to marry her.'

Hester thought she must be in the middle of a nightmare. Any moment she would wake up and find that this was all a horrible dream. But it wasn't. 'But *why*? If it's not yours . . .'

'I was very fond of Peggy. I just can't bear to think of her having to face the shame and disgrace of being an unmarried mother. When Rose told me—'

'*Rose* told you? She never said a word to me and she's been round here several times to see if there was a letter from you.' She paused and then realized exactly what Bob had said. 'You *were* fond of her? You mean, you're not now?'

Bob ran his hands distractedly through his hair. 'I don't know. I was in love with her – at least I thought I was – but when she went off with another man, well, it rather killed a lot of what I felt for her. And yet . . .' He sighed heavily as if he couldn't quite analyse what his feelings for Peggy were now. 'And I've become so close to Rose. Oh, Mam, what am I to do?'

Hester bit her lip. 'It was a foolish thing to do, but that's just like you, isn't it, Bob? You're too soft-hearted for your own good.' She sighed. 'Has Peggy accepted your gallant offer?'

'No.'

'Then what's the problem? You've been let off the hook. You've had a lucky escape.'

'But what about Rose? I must have hurt her terribly.'

'Yes, I'm sure you have, Bob, because if I know nothing else in all this, I know that Rose loves you.'

Hester Deeton, still in her dressing gown, opened the door to Rose's frantic knocking the following morning.

'Is he here? Can I see him?'

As she looked closer at the woman, Rose could see that she had been crying.

'Oh, Rose, he's gone.'

'Can I come in?'

'Of course, dear.'

When they were seated in the kitchen, Rose said, 'I

suppose he told you about Peggy? About him proposing to her?'

'Yes, he did and I told him he'd been a fool. He went off early this morning in such a foul mood.' Hester's eyes filled with easy tears. 'He hardly said goodbye.'

'What time was his train due to leave?'

Hester glanced at the clock. 'About now.'

Rose jumped up. 'I'll go to the station. If the train's late leaving – and they often are these days – I might just catch him.'

She rushed from the house and ran up the road to catch the nearest bus or tram to the centre of town. Then she ran to the station she knew Bob was leaving from and hurried onto the platform. A train was just pulling out. She pushed her way through the throng towards it, searching the carriage windows lined with soldiers' faces, waving goodbye to those still standing on the platform.

'Stop, stop the train!' But she knew it was hopeless. It was already gathering speed and disappearing up the line.

As the crowd started to disperse and leave the station, Rose stood on the edge of the platform, tears streaming down her face.

'Did you miss the train, lass?' a porter asked. 'There's another one in an hour.'

Rose shook her head. 'No,' she said shakily. 'I missed seeing someone off.'

'Aw, then I'm sorry. Train were late leavin' anyway.'

She turned away and walked slowly to the exit and up the road, back towards Mrs Deeton's home.

'Did you catch him?' was Hester's first question. Sadly Rose shook her head. 'The train was just pulling out of the station when I got there.'

'Oh, love, I'm sorry. Come on in and I'll make us a cuppa – or are you rushing off to work?'

'No, I'm not on duty until two.'

When the tea was made, they sat on either side of the table.

'I still can't understand why Bob proposed to Peggy.' Hester shook her head in bewilderment.

'Because he's still in love with her and he wanted to help her – to make an honest woman of her.'

'No – no, you're wrong there, Rose. I don't think he is in love with Peggy any more. When he got home last night – and I'm sorry to say it, but he was a little the worse for drink – he said he thought he'd just done something stupid. I thought he'd been in a fight or something, but then he told me.' She sighed. 'I've always known my son was soft-hearted, but I never thought he was soft in the head, an' all.' She paused before asking gently, 'What about you?'

'He's hurt me dreadfully by this. I really thought he was getting over Peggy and – well – that given time we might . . .'

Hester reached across the table and touched Rose's hand. 'If it's any consolation, Rose dear, he said he'd become very close to you and that was why he thought he'd acted impetuously without thinking it all through first. Still, at least Peggy had the sense to refuse him.'

Hester couldn't help feeling relieved. She'd always feared that her son would make some girl pregnant and would have to marry her. She'd done her best to bring him up properly, but she realized that times were very different now. Young men going off to war and thinking they might never come back had their needs. They didn't want to die never having known what it was like to make love to a girl.

'Rose, you're a dear girl and I'm so sorry you've been hurt.'

'I'm not giving up on him just yet – not completely.' Rose raised her head and met Hester's worried eyes. 'You see, I've loved him for so long, even when he was going about with Peggy, but of course I'd never have done anything about it. Not then. I'd never have tried to steal my sister's boyfriend –' she smiled wryly – 'even if I could have done.'

'What a complicated mess, but maybe it'll all come right after all.'

'I'll write to him and when he comes home again—'

'Oh, my dear, didn't you know? Didn't he tell you? This leave was what they call an embarkation leave. When he gets back to camp, he's being posted. He didn't know where to, but it could be abroad.'

'Peggy – is there something you want to tell me, lass?'

Laurence Bower met her as she stepped carefully off the tram platform at the end of her shift about a month after Bob's surprising proposal. During the weeks since he'd gone, life at home had been even more unbearable than before. She kept to her bedroom or the front room but, because of the winter weather, she'd spent most of her time huddled in her bed, with just the hot-water bottles her mother brought up to her. She hardly saw any other member of the family. Even Myrtle seemed to be avoiding her now. Evidently her younger sister had collected all the knowledge she needed for her biology project, Peggy thought wryly. Rose, she learned from Mary, was writing to Bob every week, just as before, but now there were no replies. Just as there was still no word from Terry.

'Who told you?' Peggy asked the inspector flatly. 'My dear sister, I suppose.'

'No one's told me anything, lass. I can see it with me own eyes. Me and the wife had two sons.'

Peggy blinked. 'I didn't know you had any family.'

Laurence smiled wryly. 'No, well, I tend to keep my private life just that. Private.'

'Are they – I mean – do they live with you?'

'They're both in the forces. John – the older – is in the RAF and Matthew's in the Royal Navy. He doesn't get home much and I never know where he is from one week to the next. He's not allowed to tell me, of course, but he gives me a hint now and again.' Laurence chuckled, though Peggy could now see the ever-present worry deep in his eyes. 'In his last letter he said it was bitterly cold, so I'm guessing they're somewhere near Iceland.'

'And your other son?' Peggy prompted.

Now Laurence sighed deeply. 'John's a fighter pilot. He gets home occasionally on what he calls a "flying" visit. Pardon the pun!'

There was silence between them until Laurence said softly, 'So, you see, I do know what's what. A few weeks back you were white and sickly every morning and now – ' he nodded towards her waist – 'if I'm not mistaken, that skirt's getting a bit tight on you.'

'So – I've to leave, have I?'

'I don't want to lose you, but it's not the sort of job to be doing when you're carrying a bairn, lass. I'm thinking of you and your baby.'

'And the reputation of the company too.'

'Oh, sod the company,' Mr Bower said with surprising alacrity. 'They'll neither know nor care – the big bosses, I mean. Only, if you was to have an accident or if we get another bombing incident—'

Peggy smiled ruefully. 'That was what started all the trouble.'

'Eh?'

'The first night of the blitz when my tram got hit. That was when I met Terry.'

Laurence blinked. 'Oh! Then – then your bairn's not Bob Deeton's?'

'No, Mr Bower, it isn't. And if that's what folks are going to think when the gossip gets around – and get around it's going to – I'd be grateful if you'd quash any rumours that it's Bob's.'

'Oh – well – of course, if that's what you want, lass.'

'I don't want Bob blamed for something that's not his fault.'

'No – of course not. I see that.'

She sighed. 'And you're right. I'd better hand in my notice. If you've suspected my condition already, then it's not going to be long before others start asking questions and I don't want it to get to that.' Though what, she thought, I'm going to do at home all day, I don't know. I'll be climbing the walls before long.

But Mary had other ideas. The morning after Peggy had come home from her last shift, Mary opened the bottom drawer of her dressing table and presented Peggy with knitting needles, several balls of white wool and knitting patterns for first-size baby clothes. 'I've set up my sewing machine in the front room on the table. I'll get you some bits of material off the market. You should be able to make some tiny clothes for next to nothing. Thank goodness I've taught you all to sew and knit, even though Myrtle turned up her nose at having to learn something practical.' She shook her head thoughtfully. 'I just wonder if we've done the right thing about her, you know. Filling her head with ideas

260

of going to university. What if she doesn't pass her exams well enough? What's going to happen then?'

'I don't think you've any worry there. She's cleverer than me and Rose put together. There you are, see. Is "cleverer" a proper word?'

'Don't ask me.' Mary smiled. 'I'm only good at looking after people, especially little babies. And now I'm going to be a granny.'

'You sound as if you're looking forward to it.'

'I am.'

'But you didn't want it, did you? Any more than I did.'

Mary sat down on the bed and took Peggy's hands. 'It was a shock at first, I admit, but I never want to hear you say you don't want your child. Every child should be a wanted child, no matter how they come into the world.'

Tears filled Peggy's eyes. 'But it's not that straight-forward, is it? Maybe I should have accepted Bob's offer. My child is going to have a dreadful life being branded a – a bastard.'

'Peggy! Don't use that word. It's horrible.'

'But that's what it's going to be. That's the name it's going to get called.'

'Not in this house,' Mary said with asperity. 'Not in my hearing, anyway.'

Peggy smiled wryly. 'Not even by Gran?'

Mary was adamant. 'Not even by your grandmother.'

Rose received no letters from Bob, but at least she could visit his mother, who was hearing from him regularly.

'Does he mention me?' Rose asked hopefully, but was always disappointed when Hester shook her head.

'I have got the right address for him, haven't I? Perhaps my letters are getting lost.' But when she checked the address against the one Hester was also writing to, it was correct. 'Then it's obvious,' she said sadly, 'he doesn't want to hear from me.'

'Wait till he comes home on leave,' Hester tried to comfort her. 'I'm sure you'll be able to sort it all out then.'

Rose glanced at Hester, but said nothing. But the words were in her mind: what if he doesn't come back? And even if he did, it could be months before she saw him again.

'Has he definitely gone abroad? Do you know?' Rose studied the address to which they both sent their letters. Hester shrugged. 'There's no way of telling when you just write care of something. I haven't got a clue what all those capital letters mean. I expect they forward them on.'

'How long do his letters take to get here?'

'Eh?'

'Does Bob put a date on when he writes them?'

'Oh, I see. You mean if they take a long time, then maybe he is abroad.'

Together they studied the date on the last letter Hester had received from her son.

'I don't think that's come from overseas,' Rose said.

'Then maybe he's still here in this country and if so, he might get home on leave. We can always hope.'

But Rose hadn't much hope left to cling to.

Mary kept Peggy busy. The girl did what housework she could. She cleaned the front room and the bedrooms

– even Grace's when she was safely out of the way shopping.

'I've joined the library,' Mary said one evening when she arrived home with an armful of books, 'so you've no excuse to be bored. Oh, how lovely,' she exclaimed, as she dropped the books on to the table in the front room and picked up the tiny white baby jacket Peggy had just finished knitting. 'Doesn't it look tiny?' She glanced at Peggy's increasing girth. 'I hope it'll still fit when he arrives.' Just recently Mary had begun to refer to the baby as 'he'.

'You're sure it's going to be a boy then?'

'Of course it is. There are enough women in this house already.'

Peggy sighed. 'Whatever it is, they won't want to know it.'

Mary changed the subject quickly. 'Mr Bower was asking after you today.'

'That was nice of him. Did you ask him how his sons are?'

Peggy had told Mary about Laurence's family.

'I didn't like to. He's never mentioned it to me. He's a very private man, isn't he? I didn't want him to think we'd been gossiping about him.' Mary was disappointed that Laurence hadn't confided in her. After all, he'd listened with such patience to her woes more than once and she'd thought they were growing close.

'Is there – is there much gossip at the depot about me?'

Mary shrugged. 'Well, if there is, I don't hear it.' She glanced out of the window. 'I'll get the tea and then we'll go for a little walk. You must keep getting some fresh air and exercise. It's been so cold for most of the month, but it's April next week. It should be getting warmer soon.'

'We'll go when it's dark, Mam. I don't want the neighbours staring. I'm getting so big now even a loose coat doesn't hide my bump any more.'

'They'll know soon enough, Peggy. You can't keep the baby locked away in here forever.'

'If only I could hear from Terry.'

'Have you been to see his friend again?'

Peggy shook her head. 'I can't see the point. I don't want to put Billy in an awkward position. He's a good friend to Terry.' Perhaps, she thought, if he hadn't been such a good friend in letting Terry and Peggy meet at his house, she might not be in this predicament now.

'Don't you think you ought to tell Terry's family?'

'No!' Peggy was adamant. 'If he'd wanted to keep in touch with me, he'd have written.'

Mary frowned but said no more. She believed that Terry's family had a right to know about the child, even if they decided they didn't want anything to do with it. Perhaps, when he was born, Peggy might feel differently.

Thirty-Three

'Your Peggy ill, is she?' Letty came through the back door holding a cup of sugar she'd borrowed earlier in the week.

'Credit where it's due,' Grace had remarked to Mary. 'She never used to be good at returning what she'd "borrowed", but since rationing started she does. I'll say that for her.'

Grace turned from the sink where she was peeling potatoes. She gave Letty one of her glares, took the sugar and turned away without answering.

Nonplussed, Letty went on. 'Only Tom ran into your Mary and Peg out for a walk last night in the blackout. Funny time to be taking a walk, we thought. It's still cold at night, even though it's meant to be spring. And in the dark too.' There was an even longer silence before Letty added, 'I haven't seen 'er going to work lately either. I mean, I know she does shift work, but I usually see 'em coming or going. I've seen t'others, but not Peg, so I wondered . . .'

I bet you did, Grace thought sourly. She was tempted to turn round and give the woman the rough edge of her tongue, but she couldn't. She couldn't deny the truth and she couldn't hide it forever. It would all come out soon enough. Maybe it would be better to tell their loquacious neighbour and get it over with. But her innate longing for privacy still held Grace back from

265

confiding in Letty. With a sigh she said at last, 'She's not been well. She'll be better soon, but being a clippie is not the sort of job you can do if you're under the weather.'

'Oh, I see,' Letty said, disappointed that that appeared to be all Grace was prepared to tell her. Letty had the shrewd suspicion that there was a lot more to Peggy's mysterious illness than Grace was letting on. 'Well, I hope she's soon feeling better.'

'She will be,' Grace said shortly. In about a couple of months' time, she added silently, and then no doubt you'll all know the truth.

Another pause, as if she was waiting for more, but when nothing further was forthcoming, Letty sighed and said, 'I'm just off into town. D'you want owt?'

'That's kind of you to offer,' Grace said, deliberately softening her tone. She didn't want to fall out with her neighbours. You never knew when you might need their help, she told herself, though she was dreading the time when Letty would gleefully spread the gossip about that uppity Mrs Booth's family. It was bound to happen: Letty Bradshaw would not miss such a golden opportunity. 'But I'll have to go myself later. I can't expect you to do all the shopping for a family this size.' Soon to be one more, she thought regretfully. Skilfully, she turned the conversation to Letty's own family. 'By the way, how're yours lads in the forces? Have you heard lately?'

Letty's face crumpled and suddenly Grace realized that maybe, just now, the woman's interest in her neighbours' affairs had as much to do with taking her mind off her own worries as with being a notorious gossipmonger. 'We've heard from Walter and Bertie last week, but there's been nothing from Simon. I'm worried sick, Mrs Booth.'

'It must be difficult for them to send off letters when they're at sea for weeks on end. I'm sure you'll hear soon.' Grace didn't add 'one way or the other', though she was thinking it.

Mary enjoyed her work as a clippie, nearly as much as Rose did. She loved the banter with the passengers – even the grumpy ones. The cold weather didn't bother her and she'd always been quick at mental arithmetic.

'You're a natural,' Laurence told her when he joined her one day in the canteen and sat down opposite her. Ignoring the amused glances of the canteen staff, he lowered his voice to ask, 'How's Peggy?'

'Surprisingly well, considering she's shut up in either the cold front room or in her bedroom,' Mary said dryly, with a sudden need to have someone of her own age to confide in. Even in the crowded household, Mary sometimes felt very lonely.

Laurence raised his eyebrows. 'Really? Is that her choice?'

Mary pressed her lips together as sudden tears threatened. Seeing her distress, Laurence said, 'Oh, Mary – my dear.'

At the kindness in his tone, the tears spilled over. Laurence fished in his pocket for a clean, white handkerchief and passed it to her. She mopped her face, aware that the canteen staff were watching them, yet trying to look as if they weren't.

Shakily Mary said, 'How silly of me. I'm not normally the weepy sort.'

'You're having a very trying time. We all are, but you have an extra burden to bear now. What's this about Peggy keeping to her room?'

'It's my mother. When – when we first found out about Peggy being pregnant, Mother threatened to throw her out. If she had, I'd have gone too. I have to stand by her, Laurence – sorry, Mr Bower—'

'It's all right,' he reassured her swiftly, 'there's no one to overhear. Though,' he added in an attempt to lighten her mood, 'we are getting one or two inquisitive looks from the staff. But never mind them – go on.'

'She relented enough to say Peggy can stay, but she won't speak to her or even have her in the same room. And Rose is as bad.'

'Oh dear, I am sorry.'

Mary blew her nose and promised to launder and return his handkerchief. Laurence shrugged as if it was of no matter.

'And I'm sorry to burden you with my worries when you have enough of your own.' Hastily, for fear he should think Peggy had betrayed his confidence, she added, 'With all the responsibility you shoulder at work.'

'Mm.' Laurence met her gaze and appeared to be considering something. At last, he said softly, 'I don't expect Peggy told you because I know how discreet she is, but I have two sons both serving in the forces.' He went on to tell Mary exactly what he'd told Peggy, but tactfully Mary didn't display any foreknowledge.

'How dreadful for you to have no one at home to share your worries,' Mary said sympathetically. It was common knowledge that Laurence was a widower.

He smiled and murmured, 'It is hard, but now perhaps I could talk to you sometimes.'

'Of course.'

'And don't you be afraid to ask me if there's any way in which I can help. Promise?'

'I promise.' Suddenly Mary didn't feel so lonely any more.

It was whilst they were out walking one evening at the beginning of June that Peggy felt the first signs of labour pain.

'We must get you home,' Mary said anxiously, but Peggy was doubled over with a spasm.

'You all right, lass?' A man's voice came out of the darkness. Mary's heart sank for she recognized the voice: Tom Bradshaw. He was the last man on earth she'd have wished to encounter just at this moment. Now Letty would soon know and the news would spread up and down the street like wildfire. But beggars can't be choosers, she thought, and they needed help. He was a strong, well-built man and could probably have carried the heavily pregnant Peggy all the way home if necessary. But all the girl needed was a strong arm.

Tom, it seemed, had summed up the situation quickly. 'Here, love, lean on me. Going to the hospital, is she?'

'No, no, we need to get back home.'

'Ah, I see. Want me to get the midwife for you, Mrs Sylvester?'

'No, no – I . . .' What on earth was she thinking? Word would be out soon enough now, if it wasn't already. Her daughter needed help and they needed to call the midwife quickly. Mary took a deep breath. 'That's kind of you, Mr Bradshaw, but I'll send one of the girls.'

He nodded. 'Time you called me "Tom", I reckon, don't you? We've lived next door to one another long enough now and shared some scary moments just lately.'

Whilst Grace had held all her neighbours at arm's length, the war had pushed them closer together and now her family was going to need all the friends they could get. Whilst she feared that Letty would revel in the telling of Peggy Sylvester's downfall, Mary was not one to reject kindness. And Tom Bradshaw was being kind.

They arrived at the front door of their home and he insisted on helping Peggy into the house and up the stairs to her bedroom.

'There, lass, you lie there and your mam'll send one of your sisters for t'midwife.'

As Mary went downstairs with Tom, he paused at the front door. 'Mary, lass – I can call you Mary, can't I? – you don't need to worry about me telling t'wife about this.' He smiled. 'Letty's a grand lass and a good wife and mother, but I know she likes to be the first with a juicy bit of gossip. But not this time.' He put his forefinger to his lips. 'She'll not hear this from me, though I am afraid it'll get out soon enough.'

'It will, Tom, but thank you. You've been very kind.'

'If you do need any more help, just knock on our door. Promise me now?'

Mary nodded, her eyes filling with tears at his unexpected thoughtfulness.

Once she had let him out of the front door again and drawn the blackout curtain, she hurried through to the living room. 'Rose – go to the phone box' – she scrabbled in her handbag to find a piece of paper on which she'd written the midwife's name, address and telephone number – 'we need the midwife right now.'

She held out the paper, but when Rose made no move to get up, Mary said impatiently, 'Rose – did you hear me? We need the midwife. Peggy's gone into labour.'

Slowly Rose looked up from the book she was reading. 'She got herself into this mess without my help, she can deal with it herself now.'

Mary stared at her, appalled by her daughter's callousness. Myrtle, sitting at the table with her homework, was wide-eyed. 'Is the baby coming, Mam?'

'Yes, yes. We must get the midwife.'

Rose dropped her eyes and pretended to carry on reading her book, though her heart was thumping.

Myrtle jumped up and held out her hand for the piece of paper. 'I'll go. I'll need some money though, Mam.'

'Oh yes, of course. Sorry.' Again, Mary delved into her handbag and brought out a handful of change. 'There, that should be enough.'

Myrtle rushed out of the back door; it was quicker than fighting with the blackout curtain over the front door. They heard her footsteps pounding across the small back yard and then the crash of the back gate. Mary was still staring at Rose's bowed head as if she couldn't believe what she had just heard. Quietly she said, 'I'm ashamed of you, Rose.' Then she turned and hurried back upstairs to Peggy.

In the living room, the silence grew heavier between Rose and her grandmother. The girl's face had flamed red with shame and even the older woman was silently struggling with her own mixed emotions. Upstairs her great-grandchild was about to come into the world and yet she could not bring herself to make it welcome.

Myrtle arrived back breathless and anxious. 'Her husband says she's out on another call and he doesn't know when she'll be back. Gran, what shall I do?'

'Go upstairs and tell your mother. She might have the name of someone else.'

Myrtle ran upstairs, two steps at a time, and burst into the bedroom her mother and Peggy shared. She stopped in the doorway, shocked by the scene before her. Peggy was writing in agony on the bed, her knees pulled up, her legs spread apart. Beads of sweat glistened on her forehead.

'The baby's coming so fast. How long will she be, Myrtle?'

'She's out and her husband doesn't know when she'll be back.'

Peggy threw back her head in a yowl of pain and fear.

'Did you leave a message? Did you tell him it was urgent?'

Myrtle nodded, but her gaze was riveted on her sister. 'What can I do to help, Mam?'

'Go round to the Bradshaws—'

'The Bradshaws!' Even at this moment, Myrtle was surprised. Surely, her mother didn't really want any member of that family here at a time like this?

'Ask for Mr Bradshaw. He helped us home just now. He'll help us.'

'Right,' Myrtle said and ran downstairs again, through the living room towards the back door.

'What's happening?' Rose asked.

'As if you care,' Myrtle shot back at her, but she

kept on moving, through the kitchen and out of the back door again.

As a loud scream sounded above them, both Rose and Grace glanced at the ceiling and then at each other.

Myrtle was back in minutes, followed by Tom and Letty Bradshaw. Grace raised her eyebrows, but said nothing as Myrtle led the two of them up the stairs. 'I've had five myself,' Letty was saying, 'there's nowt to it.'

But when she entered the bedroom and saw Peggy's agony, even Letty Bradshaw paled. 'Oh lor'. Tom – ' she grasped her husband's arm – 'you'd better get an ambulance. I can't cope wi' this.'

Tom lumbered down the stairs again and out of the front door, leaving the curtain undrawn and the door wide open in his haste.

'Oi,' came the familiar shout from the local air-raid precautions warden who, as luck would have it, was walking down the street, pushing his bicycle. 'What about that light, Tom Bradshaw?'

Now Tom had no choice but to let the world know what was happening inside his neighbour's house. 'Lass is having a bairn and it don't look too good. Midwife's not available and we need an ambulance.'

'Right, then,' Joe Bentley said. 'You get off to the phone box. I'll see to the light.'

As Tom ran up the road, the warden approached the Booth household. He stepped inside, closed the front door and pulled the curtain across the door. Opening the door into the living room, he was surprised to see two women sitting there, reading quietly as if nothing was happening. Even he could now hear the screaming from upstairs.

'Need any help? Tom's gone to phone for an ambulance, but he'd left the door wide open and a light showing.'

The older woman looked up. 'Going to fine us, are you, Mr Bentley?'

Joe Bentley shook his head but pursed his lips as he said, 'Not on this occasion, Mrs Booth – in the circumstances. But just mind you're more careful in future.'

As a piercing scream sounded again Joe Bentley winced, but the two women just carried on reading. He turned away, shaking his head as he made his way back through the hall and let himself out of the house.

'There's nowt so queer as folk,' he muttered to himself.

He waited outside the house until he saw Tom hurrying back up the street.

'There's – no ambulance – for about – half an hour,' Tom panted as he reached Joe. 'I don't reckon that lass's chances, or the bairn's, if she doesn't get some proper help real quick.'

Whilst the two men stood helplessly outside the house, wondering what more they could do, upstairs Letty had taken charge. 'Myrtle love, go downstairs and get the kettle and some pans of water boiling. Now, Peggy, prop yourself up. Breathe in and out steadily, lass, it'll help with the pain.'

'Mam, oh, Mam, it hurts so . . . Aaah.'

'It's a big baby,' Letty whispered to Mary, 'that's 'er trouble. She's going to be torn summat terrible if that midwife or t'ambulance don't come quickly. Go down and see if Tom's come back.'

Mary found the two men still standing outside the house.

'Tom, did you get an ambulance?'

'It'll be half an hour at least, lass.'

'Oh no!' Mary breathed. 'She's in so much pain and Letty thinks the baby's getting distressed too. Whatever are we going to do?'

'Letty will know what to do, love,' Tom tried to reassure Mary, but in truth he was not feeling so confident inside. His wife could deal with straight-forward births – none better – but get a bit of a complication, then Letty wasn't qualified.

'D'you want us to fetch anyone else, Mrs Sylvester?' Joe enquired.

Mary shook her head helplessly. 'I don't know who to fetch.'

'A doctor, maybe?'

'I suppose so.'

'Right, I'll go and see 'f I can knock one up.' Joe reached for his bicycle and was soon pedalling up the street.

'I must get back. See if there's anything I can do,' Mary murmured.

'You do that, love, but I'll be right here if you want owt doing.'

'Thank you, Tom.'

'Think nowt on it, lass. Now off you go.'

When Mary hurried back upstairs and opened the bedroom door, it was to hear Letty encouraging Peggy to relax and breathe deeply. Then her glance went beyond the writhing figure to the far side of the bed. Myrtle was standing there, holding her sister's hand and repeating every word that Letty said. But in the young girl's voice there was the tone of authority.

'Come on, Peggy, try to do what Mrs Bradshaw's telling you. The baby can't get out if you're all tensed up and you're making the pain worse. Breathe deeply in – out – in – out. And try to relax your whole body. That's better.' Myrtle glanced up. 'Is that right, Mrs Bradshaw?'

Letty nodded. 'You carry on, lass. She's takin' more notice of you.'

Mary moved closer to the bed. 'Is there anything I can do, Mrs Bradshaw?'

'I reckon it's high time you called me Letty, don't you?' She paused and then added pointedly, 'Mary?'

Mary smiled weakly. 'Yes. And I'm very grateful to you – Letty.'

Letty turned her attention back to Peggy. 'Do you feel the urge to push, love?'

'I don't know,' Peggy wailed. 'It hurts so.'

Letty spread the girl's legs wide apart. 'Try a little push – just a gentle one. That's it. Head's showing. Now pant.'

Peggy began to breathe deeply again.

'No, no, Peg,' Myrtle said. 'Pant. Like this.' And she demonstrated, sounding just like someone who'd run a mile.

But Peggy threw back her head and screamed, making no effort to do what she was being told.

'Oh dear,' Mary wrung her hands and tears filled her eyes. 'Whatever are we to do? If only someone would come.'

Above the noise her sister was making, Myrtle spoke sternly. 'You can stop that noise right now, Peg. Pant, can't you?'

Peggy stopped her wailing and glanced at her younger sister in amazement, but as another strong contraction gripped her, she opened her mouth to scream.

'Push, lass,' Letty instructed.

Peggy gritted her teeth and grew redder in the face as now she tried to follow Letty's instructions.

'You're doing well, but you've got to take your time, else you'll be torn.'

'I just want it out,' Peggy squealed.

'You've got to think of the baby,' Letty said.

'I don't care about the baby,' Peggy screamed. 'I don't care if it dies, I just want it all over with.'

Shocked, Mary, Letty and Myrtle exchanged horrified glances.

Myrtle looked down at her sister and said, 'I won't hear such talk, Peggy. This little baby deserves a life just like anyone else. Now do what you're told and get a move on. Poor little thing must be fed up of being in there.' She glanced across at Letty. 'When should she push?'

'When she feels a contraction coming. Here, lass, put your hand on her stomach, you can feel the muscles start to tighten. That's when there's a contraction coming.'

'Yes, oh yes – ' Myrtle's face lit up – 'I can feel it. Oh, isn't it wonderful?'

Peggy groaned and wriggled. 'Not from where I am. Oh – oh–'

'Now push, Peggy,' Myrtle instructed.

Peggy bent her chin to her chest, gripped her thighs with both her hands and strained to expel the baby from her. She grew red in the face.

'The head's come out,' Myrtle shouted triumphantly. 'Oh, I wonder what it is?'

'It'll not be a boy,' Mary murmured, watching everything that was going on, but not required to do anything. 'We're a family of women.' Then she added again, this time with a wistful note of longing, 'It'll not be a boy.'

Peggy drew in a deep breath and with one long, drawn-out growl pushed the baby into Myrtle's waiting hands.

'Oh, oh, look, Mam, it's a boy. It *is* a boy.'

'What?' Mary moved to the bedside now and looked down at the tiny baby with something akin to wonderment on her face. 'Oh, Peggy – it is a boy. How wonderful!'

Wryly Peggy said, 'Boy or not, he's still a little bastard.'

The baby lay still, not moving and making no sound.

Myrtle bit her lip. 'Shouldn't he be crying?'

Now Letty stood helplessly by the bed. 'I don't know what to do now, Mary. I've never had to go any further than actually seeing it born. There's always been a midwife there by now.'

'It says in the books,' Myrtle said, 'that if they don't cry, you have to hold them up by the ankles and slap them to make them breathe. Peggy—'

'Leave it,' Peggy said weakly. 'It'd be for the best.'

Myrtle looked to her mother for help, but Mary was just gazing down at the child as if turned to stone.

Gently, even though the child was still attached to the mother by the umbilical cord, Myrtle picked him up by his ankles and smacked him sharply on his tiny little bottom. When he did not respond she repeated the action. To both Mary and Letty, who were holding their breath, it seemed a miracle when the infant let out a thin, almost disgruntled wail.

'Now what do we do?' Mary said. Amazingly, both Mary and Letty seemed to be looking to Myrtle to take the lead.

'I know you have to cut the cord and then the afterbirth has to come away,' Myrtle said.

'But how – what do we do?'

'I – don't know.' Now even Myrtle was at the end of her book learning.

They stood helpless at the bedside, more urgently in need of qualified help than before.

Thirty-Four

Tom waited alone, pacing up and down in agitation. Even out here in the street, he could hear the poor girl's screams coming from the back bedroom. 'We're going to lose 'em both at this rate,' he muttered, anguished and feeling so helpless.

He heard the swishing of bicycle wheels and turned to see Joe careering down the street towards him. Tom raised his voice, not able to bear waiting even another minute. 'Any luck?'

Joe applied the brakes and skidded to a halt at the side of Tom. Panting hard, he shook his head and his words came in gasps. 'Doctor's – out – too.'

Tom jerked his thumb over his shoulder. 'Reckon that poor lass is going through it.' He shook his head. 'I don't reckon her chances – or the bairn's – at this rate.'

Just when the situation looked desperate and the two men were giving up hope of any help arriving in time to save Peggy and her child, they heard the sound of a tinkling bicycle bell. Pedalling up the road came a shadowy figure in a dark uniform. The woman braked sharply as she saw them standing by the side of the road. 'Is this where there's a baby coming?'

'Aye, it is, Nurse, and you'd best hurry. Lass is obviously in trouble.'

Now they all heard a piercing scream that rent the night air and then an unexpected and ominous silence.

'Oh my God,' Tom muttered, his face bleak.

The nurse leaned her bicycle against the wall, unclipped her bag and hurried inside. Nurse Catchpole was a middle-aged woman, with a calm and reassuring manner, and yet she wouldn't stand any nonsense. She'd heard the screaming when she'd arrived and as she climbed the stairs and walked into the bedroom, she was opening her mouth to say, 'Now, you can stop that noise. You're not the first to have a baby and you won't be the last.'

But in the silence three pairs of frightened eyes filled with relief when they saw who had entered the room. Only the young mother lay with her head turned away, quiet and still now.

'Mrs Bradshaw – fancy seeing you here,' Nurse Catchpole said with a hint of sarcasm. 'Have you delivered Baby?'

Letty moved out of the way as the midwife took her place at the side of the bed.

'No, actually, it was this young lass, here. The bairn wasn't breathing, but Myrtle picked him up and give him a couple of smacks and he cried.'

Nurse Catchpole glanced across the bed at Myrtle. 'Well done, my dear. You've probably saved the little man's life.'

'She needn't have bothered,' Peggy muttered morosely.

'Now, now, Mother, we won't have any of that talk,' the midwife said briskly and turned her attention to cutting the cord and encouraging Peggy to cough to expel the afterbirth. She wrapped the child in a towel and handed him to his mother, but Peggy turned her head away, refusing to take him or even to look at him.

'Here, let me,' Myrtle said. 'Please.'

With a sigh, not liking the way the baby's mother

was behaving, Nurse Catchpole had no choice – for the moment – to do anything but hand the baby boy to his young aunt. Then she turned to Mary and Letty. 'Now downstairs with you and bring me plenty of hot water and clean towels.'

More than a little thankful, both women left the room, knowing that both Peggy and the baby were in safe hands.

'Normally,' Nurse Catchpole said quietly, when the two women had gone, 'I'd ask the grandmother to stay, but it seems you're the capable one, my dear. Now, when I've washed Mother, I'll show you how to bath Baby. Have you any clothes for him? What's his name, by the way?'

'I don't know.' Myrtle glanced at Peggy, but the girl, now freed from the terrible racking pain, was lying with her eyes closed, deliberately taking no part in the proceedings.

Nurse Catchpole raised her eyebrows and asked no more questions.

When Peggy had been attended to, the afterbirth having come away cleanly, and she was washed and lying sleepily in clean sheets, the nurse bathed the baby tenderly, giving Myrtle clear instructions how to hold him.

'Tiny babies need to be kept warm – they don't generate their own heat for some weeks.'

Myrtle nodded. 'I read that.'

Nurse Catchpole's eyes twinkled. 'You seem to have done a lot of reading, my dear.

Was it because you sister was expecting?'

'Partly, but I do human biology at school.' She

wrinkled her forehead thoughtfully. 'I think it's my favourite subject. That and English literature. I love reading.'

'Well, both those subjects would be useful if you wanted to become a nurse.'

'Do you think I could?'

'It's a vocation, Myrtle. You have to really want to do it. It's hard work – but very rewarding.'

'I'd never thought about nursing,' Myrtle said, taking the tiny baby, now washed and wrapped warmly in little baby clothes and a shawl which Peggy had knitted during her lonely hours in the front room. Myrtle held the baby gently, feeling the new life moving against her. 'They all think I should try for university.'

'No reason why not. With a degree you'd be certain to get into nurse's training.'

Myrtle was gazing down at her nephew in wonderment, a tender smile on her mouth. The midwife watched her for a moment, wishing that the infant's mother would take such a loving interest in her newborn baby.

'Now, if you're ready, we can let the grandmother come back. Is there anyone else? What about the father? Is he – here?' Sarah Catchpole hesitated. There were so many times nowadays when the father was away fighting the war, or had been wounded or even killed. The nurse had to be very careful how she phrased her questions these days.

Myrtle raised her head slowly. There was no point in trying to deceive the nurse; she'd find out soon enough.

'There is no father.' Myrtle gave a wry smile. 'Well, of course there is. Somewhere. What I mean is –' she took a deep breath – 'my sister isn't married.'

'Ah, I see.' Sarah's tone was full of understanding. Sadly she recognized the circumstances only too well. Just recently, she seemed to have been delivering more illegitimate babies into the world than legitimate ones. She blamed the war. It had always happened, of course, and always would, but just now the number of unmarried mothers had definitely increased. Now she understood Peggy's reaction to her child. No doubt the poor girl had suffered untold accusations from her family.

'So,' Sarah went on in her matter-of-fact manner, 'who else is there downstairs?'

'Mam'll come up and,' Myrtle added, 'Mrs Brad-shaw.' They exchanged a smile, but the amusement died as Myrtle went on. 'But I don't think my gran or my other sister, Rose, will take any notice of the baby. They haven't been speaking to Peggy since they found out. They've made her live in the front room or up here in her bedroom. It's my gran's house, you see. She rules the roost. We're here on sufferance.'

'Where's your father?'

'He died when I was a baby. He was wounded in the Great War and we've always lived with Mam's mother.'

The midwife sighed. The complications in this household were worse than she had thought. Far worse.

'I'll come back in a little while to get him to the breast.' Sarah smiled down at Myrtle. 'I can see the little chap is in good hands.'

'He's so tiny,' Myrtle said. 'He's all right, isn't he?'

'He's fine – thanks to you. If he'd been left much longer not breathing, we might have had trouble. You did very well, dear.'

Myrtle blushed a little and felt a glow of pride. It was the very first time she'd ever been praised for doing something useful. The family encouraged her with her studies, but never let her do anything practical. For the first time Myrtle felt needed and it was a lovely feeling.

As the nurse put on her coat and picked up her bag, she said, 'I'll see the others as I go out. Tell them they can come up now – if they want to.' She glanced at Peggy. 'Let her sleep. She's had a difficult time. Hopefully, she'll feel differently when she wakes up.'

Then nurse ran lightly down the stairs and into the living room. She paused in the doorway, taking in the scene before her. An elderly woman sat in her chair near the range, reading a newspaper. At the table, a girl – presumably the other sister of whom Myrtle had spoken – also sat reading. Only Mary and Letty Bradshaw looked at her and got slowly to their feet.

'Are they – all right?' Mary asked tentatively.

'They're both fine. She has a fine, healthy baby boy.'

The woman sitting near the fire slowly raised her head and met the eyes of the midwife. 'A boy, you say? It's a boy?'

Sarah nodded. 'It is. A strong, lusty baby – thanks to your youngest granddaughter, who probably saved his life.'

She glanced at Mary. It seemed that neither she nor Letty Bradshaw had said a word to the other two women in the room. They hadn't even told them what sex the baby was. Sarah sighed inwardly. She felt for the young mother upstairs. The girl had made a mistake, yes, as many before had done and many more after her would do. Nothing shocked the midwife, but she was saddened when a new life was not treated with joy and welcoming arms.

'Myrtle?' Grace raised her eyebrows. 'What did she do? Talk it into taking its first breath.'

'She did exactly what the book says. She held it up and smacked it sharply. It shocks Baby into breathing. Now I must go. I've two other calls to make, but I'll be back later to see if we can get him put to the breast.'

As she turned to leave, Sarah noticed the girl sitting at the table shudder with revulsion, but the great-grandmother was still staring, as if mesmerized, at her.

'I'll leave you to it, then.'

Mary followed her. 'I'll see you out.'

'No need,' Sarah said cheerily. 'You'd do better to go back upstairs and help that young lass. And,' she paused with her hand on the door knob, 'you'll need to persuade your eldest daughter to take notice of her baby – or we're going to have trouble.'

'I'll – try,' Mary said weakly.

'You'll do more than try, Grandma,' the midwife said sternly. 'That little life depends on his mother.'

As the front door closed behind the midwife, Letty said, 'I'll be getting off, too, if you're sure there's nothing else I can do to help you.'

Mary shook her head. 'You've been very good. Thank you.'

Despite the fact that she knew the whole street would shortly be regaled with the goings-on at the Booths' house, she was grateful to Letty and more especially to her husband.

'Please thank Tom for me, won't you? I don't know what we'd have done without him – without you both.'

Letty smiled. 'That's all right, love. I'll see you later. I'll go out t'back way.'

I'm sure we will, Mary thought wryly as she closed the door behind the second visitor to leave. As she returned to the living room, she was surprised to see Grace levering herself up out of her chair. 'Are you going to bed, Mother? I'll bring you some hot milk.'

'No need just yet. I'm going to see my great-grandson.'

Mary's mouth dropped open and it fell even wider when Grace turned and said, 'Come along now, Rose. You're to come as well.'

'I don't want to—'

'You'll do as you're told. Mary, lead the way.'

A few moments later, Mary quietly opened the bedroom door, followed in by Grace and a very reluctant Rose. Myrtle was still cuddling the baby rocking him gently as she talked softly to him, her head bent over him.

Peggy appeared to be still asleep.

Grace moved towards Myrtle and stood looking down at her great-grandson for what seemed to the others to be an age, in which no one spoke and the only sound in the room was the baby's snuffling.

Then Grace pulled up another chair and sat down in front of Myrtle. 'Let me hold him.'

Myrtle stared at her and then, with obvious reluctance and not without a little trepidation, she handed the baby into Grace's arms.

There was a long silence in the room and then, to the amazement of them all, Grace began to smile.

'A boy! It's a boy!' she murmured with wonderment and incredulity in her tone.

'Mother?' Mary said tentatively, scarcely able to believe what she was seeing.

Grace glanced up briefly but then her gaze was fixed once more on the tiny infant in her arms. For the first time ever, Mary had seen tears in her mother's eyes.

She had never seen Grace cry before; not at her father's funeral nor at Ted's. She had not shed a tear at any of the births of her three granddaughters. She had merely regarded them steadily, sniffed and turned away. But now a smile trembled on her mouth, tears brimmed in her eyes and her voice was husky as she said yet again, 'It's a boy,' as if that explained everything.

Mary's puzzled frown faded as understanding dawned. 'Oh, after all the girls, you mean?'

Grace nodded, but her gaze never left the tiny infant lying in her arms.

'We've never had a boy in the family – not for years. Not on my side of the family. My mother only had two girls and my sister died when I was little. Diphtheria, I think it was. I don't even remember her.'

With her gaze still firmly fixed on the mite, she asked, 'What are you going to call him, Peggy?'

'Mm?' Peggy roused herself. She was so very tired and wished they'd all go away and leave her alone. And they could take the baby with them too.

'What are you going to call him?' Grace persisted. 'He must have a name.'

Peggy closed her eyes. 'Call him what you like. I don't really care.'

'Peggy, how can you talk like that?' Mary was devastated to hear the callousness in her daughter's tone. She had always been ecstatic at the birth of all three of her daughters, even though it had been yet another mouth to feed in an already stretched house-hold. She couldn't understand what was happening. She shook her head in disbelief. Peggy was rejecting her son and yet Grace was cuddling the little chap in her arms and demanding that he be given a name. Was there no end to the surprises this day was bringing? Firstly, the help of their neighbours, which had been most welcome but totally unexpected, and then Myrtle. Who would have expected Myrtle, of all of them, to take command of such a difficult situation? Young though she was, there was a self-confidence about Myrtle that none of the others possessed.

Mary's wandering thoughts were brought back to the present by her mother's voice. 'Then he'll be called Frederick after my father.'

Mary's eyes widened as she stared at her mother. 'But you – you said you didn't want anything to do with him.' The words were out of her mouth before she could stop them. 'You said—'

'I know what I *said*, but it's different now the little chap's here. And maybe,' Grace went on, analysing her feelings, 'it's because he *is* a boy. I don't know, but all I know is that he's brought the love with him. He's my great-grandson and – ' her head shot up and her gaze met Mary's squarely – 'even if he is a bastard – ' Mary flinched at the cruel word, but the sting was taken away by her mother's final words – 'he's ours. You hear me? He's *ours*.'

Peggy groaned and turned over. The decision had been made, taken out of her hands by, of all people, her grandmother. She'd fully expected Mary would try to persuade her to keep the child, but she'd never in a million years have expected that Grace would be the one to do so.

Rose was still standing uncertainly in the doorway. She had only come up here because her grandmother had demanded it. Now she turned away, muttering, 'I'll make us all a drink.' She was shocked by Grace's sudden capitulation. They were all in there now, almost drooling over the baby. Myrtle had a silly, smug look on her face

289

as if she'd delivered the child single-handedly. And with
everyone – including the midwife – telling her that she
had saved the baby's life, she'd become even more
conceited and unbearable. Rose almost stamped down
the stairs. Well, she wasn't going to give in, she wasn't
going to take any notice of the child. He was still a
bastard and had brought shame and disgrace to their
home.

And to make matters even worse, there was still no
word from Bob.

Thirty-Five

When Hester Deeton opened the door to her knock, Rose saw at once the anxious frown on the woman's face. Hester looked worried most of the time, but this was something more serious. Rose's heart leapt in fear.

'What is it? Has – has something happened?'

'He's been wounded,' Hester said, as Rose stepped inside and they moved through to the back room, talking as they went.

Rose gasped and felt the colour drain from her face. Wounded, Hester had said, not killed. 'How – bad?'

'In his leg. He's being sent home – back to England. Seems he was abroad after all.'

'But he'll be all right? He'll recover?'

'Sit down, Rose. Here – read his letter. You'll know what he says then.'

'Are you sure?' Rose asked, not wanting to seem impolite, but her hand was already reaching eagerly for the envelope Hester held.

Dear Mam, the letter read,

> *I hope this finds you better than I am at the moment. Now you're not to worry. I've got a small wound in my left leg, but it's not serious. Anyway, it'll take a while to heal so they're sending me back to Blighty as the lads out here still call home. Of course, I can't tell you where I*

291

am but it's a bit like Blackpool beach in summer.
I should be back home soon and I'll let you
know then where I am. I'll send some money for
you to come and see me . . .

The letter ended with affectionate instructions for her to 'take care of herself' and 'I'll see you soon'.

'His wound doesn't sound too serious,' Rose said.

'No, but I know my Bob. He always makes light of things. The thing is I know he's doing it, so I worry all the more about what he might *not* be telling me.'

Hester Deeton would fret whatever anyone said, Rose thought. A born worrier always found something to be anxious about, even when there was nothing. But now there was plenty. Even Rose, who normally sailed blithely through life, had turned into a worrier these days. Hadn't they all, with this dreadful war darkening their waking hours and disturbing their sleep?

'Where do you think he is? Blackpool beach in summer? Hot and sandy, I think he's trying to tell us.' Rose said. 'Do you think he's in the desert? Gran's been reading bits out of the newspapers about Libya and Egypt.'

'Possibly.' Hester chewed her lip. 'Will they really send him all the way back home if he's out there?'

'I don't know. Probably, because conditions can't be very good . . .'

Hester's hands fluttered nervously and Rose realized she was only adding to the little woman's worries.

'He – he doesn't mention me at all,' she murmured sadly, changing the subject.

'No, love, but then he's not referred to Peggy either.'

'True, but—. Oh, I don't know what to think.'

'Let's get him back home first and then you can talk

it through with him.' Hester regarded the girl, her head tilted to one side. 'You still love him then, I take it?'

Rose pursed her lips to stop the tears starting, but they filled her eyes anyway. 'Oh yes,' she whispered. 'I've never stopped and I don't suppose I ever will now. I mean, if I can go on loving him when he was going out with my sister and then – then when he asked her to marry him, I don't think –' she laughed bitterly – 'I've got much hope of getting over him, do you?'

'Well, I'm glad. I just hope he comes to his senses and sees what a lovely girl you are. I'm sorry to say it, love, 'cos she's your sister, but he's better off without her. And as for marrying her and taking on another man's child, well, I wouldn't have liked that, knowing it wasn't my flesh and blood.'

Rose thought about her own family. She was now the only one refusing to have anything to do with the child, except, strangely, the child's own mother. Peggy was still turning her face away from little Freddie and she only submitted to him sucking noisily at her breast because Sarah Catchpole was stern with her.

Rose ran her tongue round her dry lips. 'She – she's had the baby.'

'Has she? Is it – are they both all right?' Hester was not so cold-hearted that she'd wish any harm to either of them.

Rose nodded. 'Except Peggy won't have much to do with him.'

'That sometimes happens. It's a big thing to have a baby, you know, and I expect she feels it even more because . . .' Hester stopped, embarrassed by what she'd been going to say.

'You don't have to consider my feelings, Mrs Deeton. I know very well how she feels. Because I won't have anything to do with him either. I don't even want to touch him. He's the cause of all the trouble.'

Hester regarded the moody-faced young woman for a moment before she said gently, 'That's where you're wrong, Rose love. A boy, is it? Well, it's not the little feller's fault. He didn't ask to be born, did he?'

Rose frowned, but did not answer. What was it about the birth of a baby? Even if it'd been born on the wrong side of the blanket, as the saying went, folks seemed to go all dewy-eyed when the baby arrived.

As she left, Hester said, 'You can come with me when I go to see Bob if you want to.'

'No – no, not the first time. I'd like to see him, of course I would and I will, but you go on your own first time and see how things are. You – you can tell him I send my love and see what he says.'

Hester nodded. 'All right then, if you're sure.'

Rose wasn't – she wanted to fly to his side wherever he was – but she forced herself to nod and say, 'It'd be for the best.'

Reaching home, she opened the front door to a wall of noise. The baby was screaming, yet at first Rose couldn't tell where the noise was coming from. Then she realized with surprise the sound was coming from the living room. Was Peggy up then? She opened the door to see Grace sitting in her usual place, but on her lap was the baby kicking and screaming until he was red in the face. He was surprisingly strong and vigorous for only two weeks old. Grace was on her own; Mary was at work and Myrtle at school. Of Peggy – who should have been here – there was no sign.

'Oh, Rose!' Grace looked up with relief. 'Give us a

hand, will you?' she said, raising her voice above the noise. 'The midwife brought a bottle and all the para-phernalia round. Peggy's not producing enough milk to keep the little chap satisfied. He's a big baby, so Nurse said we must supplement him with a bottle. I've mixed it just like she showed me and tested it for heat, but he just screws up his face and won't even try.'

'Where's Peggy?'

'Upstairs. He's been crying all morning and she just leaves him lying in his cradle. She's not natural, that girl. Here, you have a go.' Grace held out the bottle inviting Rose to try to pacify him.

'Me?' Rose was scandalized. 'Oh, no, Gran. I don't want anything to do with him.'

'Rose, you're going to have to help me. I can't manage him. He won't take the bottle and the poor little mite's starving.'

'Then get Peggy to look after him. He's her child.'

'She won't,' Grace said flatly. 'It's the baby blues or whatever they call it these days. It'll go eventually, but in the meantime this little chap needs looking after.'

Rose clicked her tongue with exasperation, annoyed because neither Mary nor Myrtle was here. They loved to nurse Freddie, tickling him gently and talking to him.

'He smiled at me,' Myrtle would say triumphantly.

'Wind,' Grace would mutter.

'No, no, he smiled at me, Gran. I know he did.'

'Oh, give him here,' Rose said impatiently now.

She held the baby in her left arm, rocking him gently, and reached to take the bottle from Grace. Suddenly the noise stopped, before she had even offered him the bottle. Surprised, Rose glanced down at him and found herself looking into the biggest, darkest pair of blue eyes she could ever remember seeing. He was gazing up at her and even though the tears were still flooding from his eyes, Rose could have sworn a smile flickered on his tiny mouth.

'Thank goodness for that,' Grace muttered. 'Get him fed, for heaven's sake.'

Rose sat down and gently touched the teat of the bottle to the baby's lips. He opened his mouth and began to suck greedily at once.

'Goodness, he's really hungry,' Rose murmured.

'That's what all the noise was about. I'll say that for him, he only cries when something's wrong. He's not a whingeing baby.'

'Aren't his eyes a deep blue?'

Grace sniffed. 'Babies' eyes are usually blue when they're born, but they change. Terry had black hair and brown eyes, didn't he?' She nodded towards Freddie. 'He'll take after him, I expect.'

Rose snorted. 'He needn't bother. The less reminders we have of *him*, the better.'

The baby guzzled away happily, his tiny fingers curling round Rose's hand that held the bottle. The warm, feather-light touch was like an electric shock. Unbidden, an overwhelming love for this tiny mite flooded through Rose. Hester Deeton was right; it wasn't Freddie's fault he'd been born. He was so little, so helpless, and his life depended on all of them.

'Oh, Gran . . .' Tears blinded Rose's eyes as she gazed down at him lying in the crook of her arm. She blinked rapidly. 'Look at his chubby little legs and his tiny fingers. He's lovely, isn't he?'

Grace regarded her granddaughter thoughtfully, witnessing the change taking place in Rose's heart. In her long life Grace had rarely been moved to tears. She was a hard-working, determined Yorkshire woman, who'd known deep sadness and tribulation as well as times of great happiness, but she'd never been the weepy sort. Yet at this moment as she watched Rose fall in love with her nephew – and yes, there could be no other explanation for it – Grace felt a lump in her throat and tears prickle her eyelids. In a few minutes, holding him in her arms and ministering to him, Rose had become besotted with the little chap and his willing slave. Grace cleared her throat and said gruffly, 'You need to wind him.'

'Oh. How do I do that?'

For the next half an hour, Rose fed, winded and changed Freddie's nappy under Grace's instruction. And when Mary and Myrtle arrived home, they stood open-mouthed in the doorway of the living room as they saw Rose walking around the table, singing softly and rocking the baby to sleep.

Thirty-Six

'Wonders will never cease,' Mary remarked to Grace later that night when they were alone in the living room, the last to go to bed. 'Whatever brought that on?'

Grace chuckled. 'I – er – made out I couldn't manage him.' Mary stared at her mother in disbelief as Grace went on. 'He was screaming blue murder when Rose walked in. I was just about to feed him, but I pretended I couldn't get him to take the bottle. I told Rose she'd have to help me. She resisted a bit at first, but when she took him in her arms and fed him – oh, Mary, I wish you could have seen it. It was just like you say – a wonder. A miracle.'

Mary gaped. She'd never heard her mother wax lyrical and become so sentimental. It was indeed amazing what the arrival of this tiny baby had done to them all. All of them, that is, except the one who really mattered. The baby's own mother. She said as much now with a sigh. 'If only Peggy would feel the same, but she flatly refuses even to look at him properly.'

Grace was still shaking her head over Rose. 'I could hardly believe what I was seeing and then – ' she laughed again – 'did you see poor Myrtle's face when she saw little Freddie in Rose's arms? If ever I saw jealousy written on someone's face, it was on Myrtle's.'

'Oh dear,' Mary said worriedly. 'Everyone's falling for him except his mother.'

Grace shrugged. 'She'll come round and, in the meantime, there's plenty of us now.'

Indeed there were and it almost came to fisticuffs when they were all at home and time for Freddie's feed came around.

'It's my turn. You did it at breakfast,' Myrtle said, 'and I wasn't here at lunchtime. When I get home from school's the only time I have.'

'But it's my day off. I don't get much chance at all with all the different shifts I have to do,' Rose countered.

'Now, now,' Mary remonstrated gently, knowing she'd have to forgo her own turn. Never mind, she thought, I'm the one who has to get up in the night to him. But it was no hardship to her, not even when she was on the early shift. She loved the quiet hours in the middle of the night when she had the baby all to herself. Peggy could not be persuaded to take her turn even then. She was feeding him less and less and her milk was drying up. The bottle was now in greater use than ever, much to Nurse Catchpole's disgust.

'And don't forget.' Myrtle was playing her trump card. 'I brought him into the world. I was the one who got him breathing.'

'Oh please, Myrtle? Just this once. I must get to bed soon. I'm on earlies. You can do his last feed.'

'But he doesn't wake up until eleven sometimes and Mam makes me go to bed before then.' She gazed at the baby. 'Oh, all right then,' she agreed sulkily, 'but it's my turn tomorrow night, no matter what.'

'Agreed,' Rose said happily and went into the scullery to mix the baby's bottle. With a sigh, Myrtle opened her books and tried to concentrate on her homework instead of watching Rose feeding Freddie. But when

Grace put the wireless on for the six o'clock news, she gave up and sat gazing at the baby and listening with only half an ear to the bulletin.

As the news ended and Grace switched off the set, the door opened and Peggy stood there. It was the first time in months that she had ventured into the living room. Her glance flickered round the room and came to rest at last on her grandmother, who slowly lifted her head and met Peggy's gaze. There was an unspoken question hanging in the air. It seemed as if everyone was holding their breath, waiting to hear what Grace – the undisputed head of the household – would say.

Grace turned her head away, picked up her newspaper and opened it as she said casually, 'Come and sit down, Peggy.' It was the first time Grace had spoken directly to her granddaughter since she'd heard of the girl's pregnancy. And now she added, 'It's high time you stopped playing the drama queen and concerned yourself with the welfare of your baby. Now, Rose, hand him over. Let Peggy finish giving him his feed and then she can change him.'

'Oh, but—' Rose began, but catching her grandmother's stern glance, she handed Freddie into his mother's arms and held out the bottle. Feeling himself in strange and – it had to be said – unwilling arms, Freddie began to whimper.

'Cuddle him, Peggy,' Rose instructed. 'And talk to him. He likes to be talked to.'

Peggy looked up and the two sisters gazed at each other. It had been a long time since there had been any form of communication between them too. Rose knelt down and guided Peggy with the feeding of the baby. Mary watched. Holding her breath and praying that perhaps now was the turning point. Grace, pretending to read her paper, was also watching. Only Myrtle frowned with ill-concealed jealousy.

Rose's conversion was complete, so much so that she couldn't help enthusing about the baby to anyone who had the patience to listen. She didn't even hide the fact any longer that her sister had had an illegitimate baby.

'Oh, Alice, you should see him. He's beautiful,' she told her friend as they sat together during a lunchtime break. 'And he's growing so fast. The tiny little clothes that Peggy knitted for him before he was born are already too small for him. I can't believe he'll be a month old the day after tomorrow.'

'I'd love to see him,' Alice said softly. 'I'll come round some time if your sister wouldn't mind.'

'Peggy? She won't care one way or the other. She hardly takes any notice of him, except when we make her feed him.'

Alice gasped. 'What? What d'you mean?'

Rose sighed and confided, 'Well, I have to admit that before he was born none of us wanted him. We all felt the shame of Peg getting herself into trouble.' Rose's face twisted with regret. 'I was the worst. I wouldn't speak to her – wouldn't even lift a finger to help when she went into labour. Oh, Alice, I feel so ashamed about how I acted.'

'So you should be,' Alice said, with startling alacrity. 'Poor little mite – it wasn't his fault.'

'No, I know,' Rose agreed. 'And we're all trying to make up for it now.'

'If she doesn't want him,' Alice said, tears filling her eyes, 'then she should let him go to someone who will love him as he deserves. She should let him be adopted.'

Rose stared at her, aghast at the suggestion. 'Oh no
– no, we'd never let that happen. Oh no, he's ours. We
all love him to bits.'

'Except,' Alice said quietly, 'the one person who
should love him the most.'

Rose couldn't wait to visit Mrs Deeton when she heard
that Bob was back in England and that his mother had
visited him in a southern hospital.

'Come in, dear.' Today Hester was smiling, the worried
frown cleared, albeit temporarily, from the woman's
face.

'How is he?' Rose couldn't hold back the question
any longer. 'How badly is he hurt?'

Hester laughed, but she understood the girl's anxiety.
Hadn't she gone through agonies of uncertainty over
the last few days until she had been able to see her son
for herself?

'He's fine.'

'Really?' Rose couldn't really believe that any soldier
who'd been wounded on active service could be 'fine'.
But one thing she was certain of – Hester would not
minimize her son's condition.

'He is wounded in the leg, like I told you, and it's
going to take some time to heal. That's why they've
brought him home – back to England, I mean.'

'Where was he? Did you find out?'

'The Western Desert – just like you guessed. Bob
says we're a couple of dimwits. We should have known
he was abroad by the address he gave us to write to.
He couldn't tell us in so many words, but he tried to
give us clues.'

Rose chuckled. 'Blackpool beach!' She paused and then asked, 'Will they bring him nearer home? Where is he now? Can I go and see him?'

For a moment, Hester's face clouded and she avoided meeting Rose's gaze. 'I – don't know. They – they only let close relatives visit at the moment.'

Fear gripped her as Rose stared at the woman. 'Are you telling me the truth?' she asked, her anxiety making her blunt.

Hester was affronted. 'Of course I am. Rose, you have to understand. These hospitals are so busy. They can't allow all and sundry to visit the patients.'

'So – that's what I am, is it? All and sundry?'

'Oh dear, I didn't mean it to sound like that. Rose, dear, please try to understand. And to answer your earlier question, Bob is hoping to be moved back here. To Sheffield.'

'So I could see him then?'

'I expect so.'

Rose was mollified a little, but there was still a note of doubt in Hester's voice. There was something she was holding back, Rose was sure of it.

'Did you give him my message?'

Hester nodded, but again she wouldn't meet Rose's gaze.

'And?'

Hester sighed. 'Oh Rose, I'm sorry, it was Peggy he wanted to know about.'

Rose's heart sank. How could there be any chance for her, when Bob was still hankering after her sister?

'You told him about the baby?' Rose asked flatly.

Hester bit her lip, but was forced to nod.

'And?' Rose said yet again.

Tears filled Hester's eyes as at last she made herself meet Rose's gaze. 'He – he asked me to go and see her and to – to tell her he's still willing to marry her.'

As she stared at the mother of the man she loved so very much, Rose felt as if her heart was breaking into tiny pieces.

Thirty-Seven

'You see,' Hester went on hesitantly, realizing how much she was hurting this lovely girl, who had now sunk down into an armchair near the fire. Despite the warmth of the kitchen, Rose was shivering. She'd turned white. 'He thought Peggy might have changed her mind – now the child has been born and she's facing life as – as an unmarried mother. There must be such a lot of gossip amongst your neighbours.'

When Rose didn't answer, but just continued to stare blindly ahead of her, Hester murmured, 'I'll get you a cup of tea. You've had a nasty shock and I'm sorry to have to be the one to tell you. But it's better to be honest – better you know now, isn't it?' Hester was echoing Peggy's words, used months earlier, but then neither she nor Bob had wanted to hear such honesty. Now, though, it seemed that they expected Rose to accept it.

Still Rose didn't move. She felt as if she'd been pole-axed. She could think of nothing else except – he doesn't want me. He still loves Peggy.

The cup clattered in the saucer as Hester handed her a cup of hot, strong, sweet tea. Rose drank it thirstily. Feeling the hot liquid course through her, the colour returned to her face and she began to feel calmer, but now a heavy, hollow feeling settled in the pit of her stomach.

'Rose, I'm so sorry. I don't agree with him, you know that. And I told him so. Told him he was being a fool. But Bob has this overdeveloped sense of – chivalry, I suppose you'd call it – of doing the right thing.'

'I suppose that's one of the things I love about him,' Rose said and then added, 'do you want me to tell her?'

'I can't expect you to do that. It's not something I want to do, I promise you, but Bob's asked me and besides—' She broke off and then, her mind veering away, she added, 'Peggy might not believe you.'

Rose gave a snort of wry laughter. 'Oh, she'll believe me. *Especially* she'll believe me because she knows it's the last thing I want to happen.'

They sat for another hour, until it began to grow dark outside the windows.

'I'd better put the blackout up before it gets too dark to see what I'm doing. I used to rely so on Bob to do all this sort of thing. He made them for me at the beginning of the war.'

'Let me help you.'

When all the panels were in place and Hester had switched on the light, Rose said, 'I must be going. They'll be wondering where I am and it'll soon be time for Freddie's bath and feed.'

Hester stared at her. 'Why should that involve you?'

Rose hesitated and then smiled sheepishly. 'Oh, Mrs Deeton, I never thought it would happen. I didn't want it to and, for a long time, I fought against it.'

'What?'

Rose sighed heavily. 'I couldn't help it. None of us could. We've all fallen under his spell, you see.'

Hester frowned. 'Rose, you're not making any sense.'

'Freddie. We've all fallen in love with the little chap

– all, that is, except Peggy. She won't have owt to do with him.'

'Oh – the baby, you mean. I'm sorry to hear that because, however much the rest of you love him, he needs his mother.'

Rose nodded and pressed her lips together. She couldn't understand her sister now. Once they'd been so close. Near in age to each other, they'd shared everything. But since Peggy had fallen in love with Terry, had dumped Bob and then got pregnant, Rose felt she didn't know her any more.

'I must go,' she said again and kissed Hester's cheek. 'I'll come again to see you, even if – if Bob doesn't want to see me.' Her voice cracked a little, but she cleared her throat, lifted her head and said bravely, 'And I'll give his message to Peggy, I promise. Don't you worry about it any more.'

Hester's worried face cleared and she smiled. 'Oh thank you, dear. It would be such a help.'

'So, madam.' Rose stood just inside the door of the bedroom where Mary, Peggy and now the baby, too, slept. 'How long is this nonsense going on then?'

Peggy, sprawled on the bed reading, didn't look up. After weeks and months of her sister ignoring her, Peggy resolved not to answer Rose.

Rose took three strides to the side of the bed and whipped the book out of Peggy's hand. 'Just you listen to me, Peg, for once. I've got a message for you . . .' Now she had her sister's attention. 'But first I want to know when you're going to get a grip and look after your child.' When there was still no answer, Rose raised her voice, 'Come on, let's be knowing.'

Peggy shrugged with a couldn't-care-less attitude. 'He's fine. There are plenty of you to fuss over him.'

Rose bent down, her face close to Peggy's. 'It's not any of *us* he needs. It's you. His mother.'

'You didn't want him before he came, so why all the fuss now?'

Rose straightened up. 'It's like Gran says. They bring the love with them.'

For a brief moment, Peggy looked uncomfortable and Rose knew she was getting through, piercing the armour which the young, reluctant mother had built around herself.

'Peg,' she said more gently, 'he needs you. And we all want you to take over. Oh, we'll want a cuddle now and again – just try stopping any of us – and we'll help you. We don't mean to leave it all to you, but you should be the one getting up to him in the night when he cries, the one who feeds him and baths him. Oh, Peg, you should see him when he's in his little bath, he kicks and splashes as if he's enjoying it already.' Her voice quavered a little as she added, 'You're missing so much, Peg. Won't you try? Please?'

After a long pause, Peggy said, 'I can't. I don't want him. I'm thinking of putting him up for adoption. So it'd be best if I don't get close to him.'

Rose's mouth dropped open. 'Adoption?' She was appalled. 'Oh no. No! We won't let that happen.'

'You won't be able to stop it. As you rightly point out, he's my child. No one else's, not even,' she added bitterly, 'Terry's. His name couldn't be put on the birth certificate because he wasn't here to agree. So Freddie's a bastard – an *unwanted* bastard.'

Rose turned and ran from the room, clattering down the stairs and bursting into the living room. She stood in the doorway for a moment, meeting the startled gaze of her mother. Myrtle looked up from her books, but Grace continued to stroke the face of her great-grandson as he slept in her arms. Quietly she said, 'Not so much noise, Rose, I've just got him to sleep.'

'She doesn't want him – won't have anything to do with him. She's planning to have him adopted.'

Now three pairs of eyes stared at her.

'She can't.'

'We won't let her.'

'Never!'

They all spoke at once, with Grace having the final say. 'I'll have her put away first. Declared insane, if that's what it takes. Unbalanced after childbirth.'

'Mother, you wouldn't.' Mary was shocked.

Grace glanced back to the child sleeping peacefully in her arms. 'If she tried to take Freddie from us, I wouldn't think twice.'

Rose stepped into the room and closed the door after her. She sat down opposite her grandmother. 'Good old Gran.' She was smiling now.

Grace smiled and glanced up. 'Not so much of the old, young lady. I might be a great-grandmother, but I can still make myself useful, even if it's only looking after this little chap.'

'You couldn't manage him that time when I got home from work. You were only too ready to hand him over.'

Grace chuckled and, as her eyes twinkled with mischief, Rose saw a glimpse of the younger woman her grandmother must have once been when life had been good and she'd been happier.

'You reckon?' Grace said softly.

At the realization of how she'd been coerced into

taking notice of her nephew, Rose began to laugh. 'You old rascal!' As she wiped the tears of merriment from her eyes, she added, 'Do you think the same trick would work on Peggy?'

'I very much doubt it.'

Rose sobered immediately as she remembered that, amid all the shock of Peggy's pronouncement, she'd completely forgotten to relay Bob's message to her.

She sighed. 'There's one thing that might make her change her mind. I've got a message for her from Bob.'

Thirty-Eight

'I don't think you should tell her,' Grace said, after Rose had explained what Hester Deeton had told her. 'She doesn't love him, but she might be tempted to take up his offer and it'd be wrong.'

'I gave my word to Mrs Deeton,' Rose said firmly. 'You know me, Gran. I can be a nightmare, you know it – I know it. But one thing no one can ever say about me is that I'm not completely honest.'

Mary stared at her daughter with a mixture of pride and pity. 'You'd still do it even though it'll break your heart if she does agree to marry him – and, Rose, she might well do so now. There's such a thing as being too honest for your own good, love.'

'I know, Mam, but that's not me, is it?'

'I wouldn't tell her, if I was you,' Myrtle put in. 'She's had her chance before and said no. Why should anyone give her a second chance? Besides, *he* might come back.'

'No chance. Even if he's – he's still – you know, OK, he's never written, never been to see her when he's been on leave. And he must have had leave during all this time.'

'Not necessarily, if he's been sent abroad,' Grace said. 'It's often months, years, before they can come home.'

'Unless they're injured.' Mary murmured. 'Then they

come home. Have you heard just how badly Bob is hurt? Did he mother say?'

'It's a wound in his leg, but it won't heal properly so he's been sent back to England. He was in the desert, it seems, though Mrs Deeton had no idea.'

'Ah, I've been reading all about that,' Grace said. 'There's a right scrap going on out there. Rommel was advancing at a rate of knots—'

'I've heard about camels being called the "ships of the desert" but I didn't know their speed was counted in knots,' Myrtle said facetiously.

Grace glared at her, but went on, 'Anyway, the Eighth Army have halted him. It was touch and go, the papers say, and it's not over yet.'

'But once he's well again Bob'll have to go back, won't he?' Mary asked, her mind on matters closer to home.

'I expect so,' Rose said heavily. Then she heaved herself reluctantly to her feet. 'I'd better go and tell her. It might make her change her mind about how she treats little Freddie.'

Within the space of half an hour, Rose entered the bedroom for the second time.

'You again!' Peggy said morosely. 'Now what?'

'There's something I forgot to tell you. Bob's back in this country and Mrs Deeton's been to see him.'

Peggy glanced up, obliged to say, 'How is he?'

'D'you care? *Really* care?'

'Rose, I'm not quite as heartless as you make me out to be, I—'

'Aren't you? When you won't even look at your own little baby boy and you're talking about giving him away to strangers. I'd call that heartless.'

For a moment Peggy looked ashamed, but the expression was fleeting as she hardened her heart. 'What's the message?' she asked bluntly.

'Mrs Deeton was going to come and see you herself, but I said I'd save her the trouble. Bob's renewed his offer to marry you. He – he thinks you must be going through it with all the gossip and – and bringing up the baby on your own.'

Slowly Peggy raised her head. 'But I thought you and he were going out together now?'

'I thought so too,' Rose said bitterly, 'but it seems he's still hankering after you.'

There was silence in the room until Rose couldn't stop herself prompting some sort of response. 'Well?'

'I'll think about it,' Peggy said and picked up her book again.

Rose almost stamped down the stairs in her frustration. 'My lady will give the matter some thought,' she announced. 'And in the meantime, I suppose we just carry on looking after Freddie.'

'Of course we do,' Grace said firmly and with a note of finality added, 'and if I have my way, we'll continue to do so.'

'Myrtle, are you doing anything on Saturday afternoon?'

'No. My exams are all finished and we break up in a couple of weeks. Why?'

'I want you to come out with me.'

'Where are we going?' Her face brightened. 'To buy baby clothes?'

Rose smiled. 'Well, we might on the way back.'

'The way back? Where from?'

Rose lowered her voice. 'Look, Myrtle, can I trust you to keep a secret?'

The girl blinked. 'Of course you can.'

'I'm planning to go and find Terry Price's family. It's high time he was told what's happened and faced up to his responsibilities.'

Myrtle drew in a sharp breath and her eyes widened, then, as the idea took hold, she smiled. 'You're right, Rose, but are you sure this has nothing to do with thinking that Peggy might change her mind and agree to marry Bob?'

Rose glared at her. 'You're a bit too sharp for your own good, our Myrtle. You'll cut yourself one of these days.'

But Myrtle only grinned and said, 'Course I'll come with you. It should be fun.'

'I don't call it fun,' Rose said primly. 'But he should be told.'

'D'you know where they live?'

'Oh yes. I made it my business to find out when Peggy first started seeing him.'

'Right then. Saturday afternoon it is.'

They found the street in Attercliffe easily enough, but Rose wasn't sure whether it was number nine or number eleven where the Price family lived.

'It's on the left-hand side from this end, I know it is.'

'How d'you know?'

'Never you mind.'

Myrtle laughed. 'What did you do? Follow them home one night?'

'No, I thought about it, but I was afraid they'd spot me. No, I've been asking round my mates on the trams

314

and the buses that work the Attercliffe routes. They found out for me.'

'Quite the little detective, aren't you? You'd make a good spy, Rose.'

Rose wriggled her shoulders. 'Well, we needed to know what was going on.'

'Huh! I could have told you that. You only had to look at the pair of them to see it in their faces.'

They walked a little way down the road until they hesitated outside the two houses.

'So,' Myrtle said, 'which door are we knocking on?'

'I don't know. Pearl wasn't sure of the number – she just knew it was this street. Oh, come on,' Rose added, deciding quickly. 'It won't matter if we get the wrong one. The neighbours'll soon tell us where they live.'

They knocked on the door of number nine and waited for what seemed an age until a young woman of twenty or so opened it. Behind her another girl, about the same age, hovered.

'Yes?'

'We're trying to find where Terry Price lives.'

The girl opened her mouth, but before she could speak the one behind her piped up. 'Yes, this is where he lives. What d'you want with him?'

'Who are you?'

'His sister.'

The girl who'd opened the door was blinking rapidly and colour had suffused her face.

Rose smiled. 'You must be Amy then,' she said, speaking directly to the girl who had admitted to being his sister.

For a moment, Amy looked surprised, but she moved

forward, pushed the other girl out of the way and stood facing Rose with her arms folded. 'So?'

'Is your mam or dad in?'

'No.'

Rose felt as if she was getting nowhere fast. 'We want to know how Terry is.'

'Why?'

'Because –' now it was Myrtle who spoke – 'when he was home on leave at the time of the blitz, he met our sister, Peggy, and they started seeing each other.'

The other girl, still standing behind Amy and peering over her shoulder, made a noise that sounded suspiciously like a sob, but Myrtle pressed on. Whatever the news was going to be, they had to know the truth. They had to know what had happened to Terry Price. But if that girl's reaction was anything to go by, then it could be bad news. The worst. 'But we haven't heard a word from him for months and—'

Rose put her hand on Myrtle's arm and murmured, 'Hang on a mo, Myrtle.' Raising her voice again, she asked, 'Is he all right?'

Amy stared at them for a brief moment before saying, 'We don't know.'

'So, haven't you heard from him either?'

Amy shook her head.

'But – but if anything had – I mean – happened to him, then you'd have heard from the War Office, wouldn't you?'

Amy shrugged. 'Dunno.'

'But hasn't your dad tried to find out?'

'No point. If owt happens to him, we'll hear. Like you say.'

'But aren't you worried?'

''Course we are,' Amy snapped. 'Anyone who's got

family in the forces is worried out of their wits. Billy's dad down the road gets a letter most weeks off his lad, but if it's a day or two late, he's climbing the wall.'

Myrtle saw the girl standing behind Amy dig her sharply in the ribs. Amy turned and glared at her, but said no more.

Rose didn't seem to have noticed as she went on, 'And your mam? Isn't she worried because Terry hasn't written?'

There was a brief hesitation before Amy said casually, 'Not much of a one for letter writing is our Terry.'

Rose smiled wryly. 'That's what he told Peggy, but we thought he might have written to you. To his family.'

'Well, he hasn't. He could be dead for all we know.'

Rose gasped. She knew herself to be straightforward and not afraid to speak the truth, but this girl was shockingly blunt. For once Rose didn't know what to say. So it was Myrtle who said, 'We need to get in touch with him. Is there an address we can write to?'

Amy's eyes were suddenly wary. 'I've no idea.'

'Peggy needs to write to him. There's something she has to tell him.'

Amy stared at her and the girl behind her gave a little squeak, her eyes wide, her hand over her mouth. Then Amy spoke. 'Oh aye, just to tell him she's met someone else, I suppose, and she's dumping him. Well, that'll be all right by us and by him an' all, I shouldn't wonder. If he'd wanted to carry on seeing her, he'd have written, now wouldn't he?'

Her tone was smug now as if she'd got what she wanted, but it was Myrtle who dropped the bombshell and, at her words, even Amy's mouth dropped open, whilst the other girl began to cry.

'It's not that. She's had his baby and he needs to know.'

'But he can't – I mean – he wouldn't. He – he's—' There was another, longer pause whilst Amy seemed to be searching for something to say. 'He's engaged,' she announced triumphantly at last. 'To Sylvia here.' She jerked her thumb over her shoulder towards the girl still standing behind her, but now weeping openly. 'So you needn't think you can go putting the blame on our Terry, 'cos your sister's little bastard is nowt to do wi' him or wi' us.'

With that parting shot, Amy slammed the door in their faces.

'You don't believe her, do you, Rose? About him being engaged, I mean.' Myrtle asked as they walked slowly away.

'Course I don't. Our Peggy's been an idiot, but she's no liar. No, it's Mr Terry Price who's the liar and the cheat. Just wait till I get my hands on him.'

'If you ever do. Those two girls are hiding something. I know they are.'

In the house, their ears pressed close to the door, Amy and Sylvia listened to the departing footsteps.

'They've gone,' Amy said at last, straightening up. 'And good riddance.'

'Oh, Amy, d'you think you ought to have said those things? I mean we're not engaged and oughtn't you to have told them the real reason he's not written to their sister?'

Amy whipped round on her friend. 'I thought you was in love with our Terry?'

'I am – I am, but – but . . .' Sylvia bit her lip. 'What if they go to Billy's dad and start asking him questions?

318

He'll most likely give them an address so they can write to Billy. Because, even though they're not together, Billy does know where Terry is. And – ' she dug her friend in the ribs – 'so do we.'

'Mm – yeah – maybe I made a mistake there, mentioning Billy and his dad.'

'And you shouldn't have made out he might be dead,' Sylvia went on. Normally she was the quieter, more docile one of the two friends, always looking to Amy to take the lead. But for once she disapproved of what her friend had done. 'You'll wish it on him.'

Now it was Amy whose confidence deserted her. 'Don't say that, Sylv. Please don't say that.'

'Well, let's just hope they don't think of going to Billy's home, that's all.'

Amy peeped out of the window. 'No, we're all right, they've gone up the road.'

But if Amy could have heard the two sisters talking as they reached the top of the street, she might not have felt so confident.

'D'you think we should find this Billy's dad they talked about?' Myrtle was saying.

'Not today,' Rose said. She nodded back towards the house they'd just left. 'I reckon those two will be peering out from behind the curtains to see what we do. No, we'll come another time and come in from the other end of the street.'

'But we don't know where he lives.'

'True, but Amy nodded her head down the street when she spoke about him, so I reckon it's down there somewhere. Come on, Myrtle, we'd best be getting back. And remember, not a word to anyone, not even our mam.'

'I won't, Rose. But I don't reckon we should leave it there, do you?'

'I don't intend to, Myrtle. Believe me, I don't intend to.'

Thirty-Nine

Rose went about her work with a heavy heart. Peggy had still not given her family any indication about her answer to Bob's renewed offer and she continued to refuse to care for her child. Rose managed to put on a brave act while she was on duty and not one of her passengers would have guessed at her secret heartache.

But Mr Bower knew. 'How's things, love?'

'All right, Mr Bower, ta for asking.'

'Would it be all right if I popped round to see Peggy and the little chap? I've been having a clear-out and I found some baby clothes the wife had kept all these years. They're still in good order. I wouldn't suggest it otherwise. But it seems a shame for 'em not to be used and some of the other girls – ' Laurence always referred to the clippies as 'girls' even though one or two were even older than he was – 'have been busy knitting for Peggy.'

Rose felt tears prickle her eyelids. 'Oh, that's so kind of you – and of them.' Word had obviously got around the depot, but instead of criticizing, the other women were showing their support by sending welcome gifts.

'Aye well, like I've always said, Rose, your Peggy's not the first lass to get caught and she'll not be the last.'

'We'll all be glad to see you, Mr Bower, but you'll have to excuse Peggy. She – she's not quite herself since she had the baby.'

'It takes some women like that. The wife was like that after our youngest was born. Took her months to really get over it. It's a big thing, y'know, to have a bairn and specially when . . .' He stopped and smiled in embarrassment.

Rose sighed. 'It's all right, Mr Bower, you needn't pull any punches, not with me.'

Mr Bower patted her arm. 'You're a good lass, Rose, and you've surprised me.'

Rose laughed. 'You mean you thought if anyone was going to get themselves into trouble, it'd have been me.'

'No, no, I don't mean that, lass, though I have to admit Peggy was the very last person I thought it'd've happened to. No, what I mean is you've turned out to be the best clippie we've got. In fact, I'd like you to take a new woman under your wing and show her the ropes. Her husband's been called up and, although she's a fourteen-year-old daughter, she's volunteered for war work.'

Rose felt a glow of pride. 'I'll look after her, Mr Bower, don't you worry.'

'I know you will and, Rose . . .'

'Yes, Mr Bower.'

'I just wanted you to know that I do admire the way you've never let your family worries interfere with your work. I've watched you and you seem to be able to put it all aside and concentrate. Your ticket takings always tally and you've a special rapport with all your passengers. They all love you. Well done, lass, well done indeed.'

As she walked home, Rose felt she was walking on air. At one time she had hoped that if women were to be trained as motormen – or motorwomen, she presumed they'd be called – she'd be considered. But now, with Laurence Bower's unstinting praise ringing in her ears, she decided that she would rather stay as a clippie anyway. All a motorman did was stand at the controls all day. He had very little interaction with the passengers. To Rose, now, that would be very boring.

'Mr Bower's coming round later after he's had his tea,' she informed Mary and Grace. 'He's bringing some clothes for Freddie. And now, where is the little man?'

'He's out,' Grace said shortly.

'Who with? Mam's at work and Myrtle's not home from school yet, so . . .' Her eyes widened. 'Not Peggy? Don't tell me she's . . .'

'Sadly, no. Letty's taken him out in the pram.'

'Oh, Gran, no. She'll be showing him to everyone. "This is Peggy Sylvester's little bastard," she'll be saying.' Rose mimicked Letty's high-pitched voice. ' "And I helped bring him into the world. I don't know what they'd have done without me and my Tom." '

Grace rattled her newspaper. 'Be fair, Rose, they did help us and she's been good since. And as far as I know, she hasn't done all that much gossiping.'

Rose snorted as she passed through the living room towards the kitchen. 'But she'll be making up for it now, you mark my words.'

But Rose was wrong. Letty was marching down the street pushing the battered perambulator in front of her with as much pride as if Freddie were her own grandchild. True, the neighbours who stopped to peer into the pram knew very well whose baby it was, but seeing Letty with the child was enough to quieten them. If the biggest gossip-monger in their midst could accept the circumstances of the baby's birth, then they would do

no less. In fact, Peggy and her family had Tom Bradshaw to thank for the stillness of his wife's tongue on
the matter.

On the night of the child's birth, when they'd arrived
back at their own home after all the excitement, Tom
had wagged his finger in his wife's face and said firmly,
'Now you listen here, Letty love. I know you and your
friends like a little bit of a gossip now and again . . .'
That was an understatement if ever there was one, the
kindly man had thought privately, but he didn't want
to be too hard on his wife. She was a good sort in many
ways and she'd come up trumps that night. 'That there
family has enough trouble on their hands. They've no
man in the house for a start . . .'

'They have now,' Letty had countered, smiling
broadly.

'Eh?' Tom had blinked, momentarily side-tracked.
'Oh aye, I see what you mean. Anyway, what I'm saying
is this, they need a bit of neighbourly support, not a lot
of tittle-tattling going on behind their backs.'

'I won't, Tom,' Letty had promised him solemnly.
'That family's always been nice to me. They've never
snubbed me like some of the snotty-nosed buggers
round here have.'

'There you are, then. They need our support now.'

Letty had nodded. 'And they'll get it, Tom.'

She had continued to 'pop' round to Grace Booth's
house whenever she could and she'd always been wel-
comed. And so it was that Letty was out wheeling
Freddie in the pram when Myrtle came running down
the street, anxious to be home in time to give her
nephew his tea-time feed.

'Oh, hello, Mrs Bradshaw. Is that our Freddie you've
got in the pram?'

Letty beamed. 'Now who else would it be, lass? The bairn you an' me brought into the world.'

Myrtle smiled. 'It'll be time for his feed soon.'

Letty turned the pram around and they began to walk back together.

'Your Peggy any better, is she?'

Myrtle shook her head. 'Still won't have much to do with him. She'll feed him now and again, but only if Nurse Catchpole calls and insists.'

'You should get your mam to take her to the doctor. It's natural for a new mother to feel a bit low sometimes after the birth, but this has been going on too long now. Summat ought to be done. Best thing you could do is to get her out in the fresh air. Encourage her to get some exercise. Best thing for her.'

'I think she doesn't want to come out and face the neighbours.'

Letty gave a click of exasperation. 'Silly girl. She's nowt to worry about.' Letty's grin widened. 'I'll see to that.'

'I'll tell Mam what you've said – and thank you, Mrs Bradshaw.' Myrtle smiled sweetly at her and neatly took over pushing the pram, manoeuvring it up the short front path and pulling it backwards up the steps to the front door. She parked it at the side of the hallway where it usually stood, pulled down the hood and gently picked Freddie up. 'There, there, my little man,' she crooned. 'Did you have a nice walk with Mrs Bradshaw? I bet you're hungry now, though, aren't you?'

The door from the living room opened. 'Oh, you've got him,' Rose said and there was no hiding the disappointment in her tone.

'It's my turn to feed him,' Myrtle said.

'That's all right. I'll do his last feed tonight after I've bathed him.'

Myrtle grinned. 'If you can prise him away from Mam, you mean.'

Rose pulled a wry face and then smiled. 'Too true,' she murmured.

'Where's Peggy – as if I need to ask?' Before Rose could say a word, Myrtle went on as she carried Freddie into the living room. 'Mrs Bradshaw says we should get Peggy out or take her to the doctor, or both.'

'She won't go.'

'I know that and I said so. I told her that Peggy couldn't bring herself to face the neighbours and do you know what Mrs B said?'

'I couldn't begin to guess.'

'She said she was a silly girl and she'd no need to be afraid of facing them – she'd see to that.'

'Did she really?'

Rose was thoughtful as she mixed the baby's bottle. As she handed it to Myrtle, she said, 'You know, I think Mrs Bradshaw's right. Peggy's done enough moping about in this house. It's high time she got out and mixed with folk again.'

Myrtle took the bottle and touched Freddie's lips with it. Eagerly he began to suck. When she could see that he was settled happily, Myrtle looked up at Rose. 'What are we going to do?'

'I don't know, but I'll think of something. Mr Bower's coming round tonight to see her. That might be a good start.'

'She'll not come down to see him.'

'We'll see,' Rose said, with a glint in her eye.

Myrtle smiled down at Freddie. 'Your Aunty Rose is on the warpath. Watch and learn, little one.'

Forty

'Come through, Mr Bower,' Rose invited, leading him into the living room and offering him the armchair on the opposite side of the hearth to her grandmother.

Grace lowered her paper and smiled at their visitor. She'd become quite fond of the quiet little man, who often seemed to find an excuse to call at their house. And now she thought she knew why. On his last visit she'd seen the way he looked at her daughter. Well, Grace thought, Mary could do a lot worse for herself, but whether Laurence Bower would be willing to take on their family of women was another matter. And then her smile broadened as she remembered. They were no longer just a female household now; they had Freddie. Tonight Laurence was carrying a large cardboard box, which he balanced on his knees. 'What have you got there, lad?'

Rose turned away, chuckling at hearing Mr Bower called 'lad', but then her grandmother had the advantage of age, which let her get away with saying things others dared not.

'Baby clothes, Mrs Booth. I found some the wife had kept. They're still in good order – no moth holes – though maybe they could do with a good wash. And then some of the girls at work have been busy knitting.'

'That's very thoughtful of you,' Grace murmured.

'I'll just fetch Peggy down,' Rose said.

Grace glanced up, raised her eyebrows in surprise, but said nothing.

Rose ran upstairs, determination in every stride. She flung open the door to see Peggy sitting at the dressing table idly brushing her hair. 'Right, mi lady, I've had enough of this. Mr Bower has come to see you. He's brought you some things for the baby and you're going to come downstairs and see him.' She grasped Peggy's arm.

'No, Rose, I can't. I won't.'

'You can and you will.'

Rose was stronger than her sister and though she tried to resist, Peggy found herself hauled to her feet and being propelled out of the bedroom. Briefly she tried to cling to the door frame, but Rose prised her fingers free and pushed her to the top of the stairs. 'Now, unless you want me to push you down, get going.'

'Rose, I—'

'Go!'

Mr Bower got up as the two sisters entered the room. Grace's face was a picture and Rose dared not meet her grandmother's gaze or she would have burst out laughing.

'Peggy, how nice to see you. How are you?' Mr Bower held out his hand.

'I'm – fine. Thank you,' Peggy murmured as she shook his outstretched hand.

'And the baby? A boy, I understand. Is he doing well?'

'Yes – yes – thank you.'

Laurence held out the box and explained what it contained. Peggy took it from him, but made no attempt to open it.

'Let's have a look, then, Peg.' Rose nudged her and Peggy smiled thinly, but undid the string and opened the box.

'Three little coats and hats to match,' Rose enthused. 'Aren't they lovely? Oh, and a beautiful shawl.' She held it up for everyone to admire.

'My wife knitted that just before John – our eldest – was born,' Laurence said rather wistfully as he reached out to touch the shawl.

'I've never learned to knit,' Rose said.

'Hasn't got the patience,' Grace sniffed.

'Oh look, do look, Peg, there are more little jackets and leggings to match.'

'Now Peggy here, she's a good little knitter,' Grace said and added pointedly, 'if she puts her mind to it.' Peggy had lost interest in knitting since Freddie's birth.

'I expect you've got a lot to do with looking after a little one now,' Laurence said. 'But if you ever did want to come back to work, even if it was only for part time, we'd be pleased to have you, Peggy.'

Peggy gaped at him. 'You – you'd have me back?'

'You were one of my best clippies, but, of course, if you don't feel you've the time.'

'Of course she's got the time,' Grace put in. 'We all take turns in looking after little Freddie. It'd do her good.'

Peggy glared at her grandmother, but the older woman took no notice.

'Right then, if you'd like to come down to the depot whenever you feel ready, we can discuss your hours.' He stood up. 'I'd better be going.'

'Oh, but you haven't had a cup of tea,' Rose said.

'Please don't trouble. I've only just had my tea and I

wouldn't want to take your precious rations. I'll say goodnight then, Mrs Booth.'

Grace nodded and smiled and then picked up her newspaper as Rose showed Laurence out. 'Give my regards to your mother,' he said. 'I'm sorry I've missed her.'

'She's gone shopping with Myrtle. No doubt they've had to queue for hours.'

Laurence pulled a sympathetic face and stepped out into the summer evening.

As she closed the door after him, she turned to see Peggy sneaking back up the stairs.

'Oh no, you don't, my girl. I want to talk to you. Get yourself back in there.'

'But—'

'No "buts". This has got to stop. Mam and Myrtle should be home in a minute and we're going to get this sorted out. Sit down at that table while I get their meal ready. Then we can talk.'

'What's there to talk about? I'm not going back to work, if that's what you think.'

'Mebbe not, but that's only the half of it.'

A few minutes later, on their return, Mary walked into a wall of uncomfortable silence in the living room and Myrtle, hearing Freddie wailing in the bedroom, dashed upstairs.

'Myrtle's just gone to see to Freddie, she'll be down in a minute.'

'I'll keep hers hot then,' Rose said, as she placed her mother's meal in front of her. Then she stood with her back to the fire and faced the room.

Mary picked up her knife and fork but made no effort to eat. 'What's the matter, Rose? Has something happened?'

'Not really, but it's going to. We'll wait for Myrtle. Eat your tea, Mam, while we're waiting, else it'll get cold.'

Peggy was still sitting at the table, fingering the tablecloth and avoiding meeting anyone's gaze. Grace folded her newspaper, took off her spectacles and rubbed her eyes. 'I hope this isn't going to take long. There's something I want to listen to on the wireless.'

'Hopefully not, Gran.' Rose said.

Myrtle wandered in as Mary finished eating. 'I've got him off. He should sleep till ten or eleven now until his next feed.' She glanced round, sensing there was something about to happen. She took her place at the far side of the table, as Rose placed her meal in front of her. Mary moved to sit in the armchair beside the fire. 'Right, Rose, what's so important?'

'Peggy – and her child. It's high time she stopped moping about and started looking after her baby – ' Rose ticked the points off on her fingers – 'helping around the house, going out and even going back to work part-time like Mr Bower's suggested.'

'Laurence?'

'He came round tonight to bring some baby clothes for Peggy and he said he'd be pleased to have her back even if she could only manage part-time.'

'Mam, I—' Peggy began, but Grace interrupted. 'Quite right, too, Rose. I couldn't have put it better myself.'

Mary was watching Peggy anxiously.

'I met Mrs Bradshaw out wheeling Freddie in the pram when I came home from school,' Myrtle put in. 'She said Peggy should go out to get some fresh air and exercise. And if that doesn't work, she should see a doctor.'

'So, Peg, what's it to be?' Rose said firmly. 'And whilst we're deciding what's to be done, have you made up your mind whether or not you're accepting Bob's proposal?'

'I've written to him.'

'And?'

'Thanked him – but declined.'

Inwardly Rose heaved a sigh of relief. It didn't really make it any better for her if Bob was still in love with Peggy, but at least she wouldn't have the heartache of him becoming her brother-in-law. The two sisters stared at each other until Peggy dropped her gaze.

'I'm glad to hear it,' Grace said. 'Now Rose is right. You should start and get back to normal, Peggy. We've all cosseted you for far too long. And I don't want to hear any talk of having him adopted. He's ours and here he stays, but you ought to start acting like a proper mother. Tomorrow morning is Saturday and Myrtle always takes him out in the pram on a Saturday morning. And you, my girl, are going with her.'

Peggy sighed and got to her feet. Without another word she went up to her bedroom, but unbeknown to any of the others, she sat down beside the cradle and gazed at her sleeping son for a long time. 'I'm sorry,' she whispered at last. 'It's not your fault. None of it.' Then she picked up a letter she'd received that morning and went back downstairs. She poked her head round the living-room door.

'Rose, can you spare a moment?'

The two girls went into the front room and Peggy closed the door behind them. 'Here, you'd better read this.'

'What is it?'

'A letter from Bob, in reply to my refusal.'

'Oh, I don't—'
'I want you to read it.'
Rose sighed and sat down.

Dear Peggy, Thank you for your letter and your
honesty and I'll be as honest back. I have to
admit to being relieved that you've said no. I felt
I had to make the offer. Once I loved you very
much and I was very hurt when you took up
with that soldier, specially as you hardly knew
him. Still, that's not my business and all I want is
that you should be happy. I still care about you,
but I don't think I'm in love with you any more.
So, all I can say is that I wish you the very best
and hope things work out for you. I'll always be
there for you as a friend *if you should need my*
help. I don't expect you will as you've all your
family rallying round. Specially Rose, she's a
good 'un. Please tell her I'll see her when I get
home.

He'd signed it, *Yours, Bob.*
Rose's mouth gaped open as she finished reading and
looked up at Peggy. 'He – he says he's not in love with
you any more. His mother said as much, but I didn't
really believe her.'
Peggy was smiling. 'No, he's not. I doubt he ever
was really. So, sister dear, he's all yours.'
'Oh well, now, I don't know. He doesn't say—'
'He says he wants to see you when he gets home.
That's a start, isn't it?'
Rose hardly dared to hope. 'We'll see,' was all she
said as she handed the letter back to Peggy and got up
to leave. Peggy touched her arm. 'Thanks, Rose, for

what you said in there. I will try to do better. I'll just have to make up my mind that Terry's not coming back and get on with my life – whatever that might be.'

'Oh, Peg!' Rose flung her arms around her sister. 'That's wonderful. We'll help. We'll all help you.'

'I know you will,' Peggy murmured, as she hugged Rose in return. 'You already have.'

Forty-One

Myrtle had taken her Higher Certificate in June. Con-centration had been difficult with a crying baby in the house and her desire to hold him at every opportunity. But the groundwork of revision for the exams had already been done before Freddie's arrival and when the results came out, she had passed all her subjects with the highest grade. Her place at Sheffield University, for which she'd applied the previous year, was confirmed.

Towards the end of August Peggy decided to return to work.

'You're going back far too early.' Mary pleaded with her to stay at home and care for her baby until he was a little older.

'I'll go mad if I stay in this house much longer. Besides, I'm not needed now he's finished breast-feeding.'

'Of *course* you're needed, Peggy. You're his mother.'

Peggy turned away. 'I'm seeing Mr Bower this after-noon. I'll ask him if he can just put me on part-time. I can fill in when someone's ill or they're short-staffed.'

Mary was not pacified and she confided her worries to Laurence.

'Can you tell her there are no vacancies? I know I'm asking a lot, but she really shouldn't be coming back to work at all, let alone so soon after having him.'

'Trouble is, Mary, we're very short-staffed. It's my

boss's policy not to stop the men from enlisting if they want to, but it's leaving me with a real headache organizing the rotas, I don't mind telling you.' He touched her arm sympathetically. 'My dear, I'm honoured that you've felt able to confide in me, but have you thought that maybe – because of how Peggy feels about the baby – to come back to work might be good for her.'

Mary stared at him. 'I hadn't looked at it that way,' she said slowly. 'Maybe you're right. She spent so long on her own when – well, before Freddie was born. Perhaps that's part of the trouble and to mix with other people again would do her good.' Mary sighed. 'But I still don't like her leaving her baby.'

Laurence smiled a little wistfully. 'It's not us, is it? Mothers going out to work. In our day, wives and mothers were the home-makers.'

Mary pulled a wry face. 'I had to go out to work because Ted was injured in the war and couldn't work – or – or wouldn't. I didn't know which it was.' She'd never confided this to anyone before – not even her mother – but Laurence was the sort of man she felt she could trust implicitly.

'I'm sorry,' he said, contrite that he might have implied she'd not cared for her family as she might have done. 'Times were hard then, my dear, and they are again now.' He paused, then added, 'So what do you want me to do about Peggy? I can lie through my teeth if you really want me to, but I think she'd know I was doing so. It's no secret that we're desperate for staff. And I'd be turning away a *very* good clippie.'

'No, no, I wouldn't want you to do that.' Mary sighed. 'Let her come back and we'll see how it goes.'

'I'll watch out for her. At least the bombing seems to have lessened just lately.'

There'd been isolated incidents, but nothing on the scale of what the city now called their blitz. The most recent had been at the end of July at Hunter's Bar, but, happily, there had been no injuries.

So when Peggy went to see Laurence, he said, 'You just tell me how many hours a week you want to work and on what days and I'll see what I can do. 'Would it help if I ensure either your mother or Rose is at home when you're at work?'

Peggy shrugged disinterestedly. She was tired. Freddie had been fractious during the night and even though it had been Mary who'd got out of bed to him, his crying had still disturbed Peggy's sleep. 'It doesn't really matter. Gran's always there and Myrtle's on her school holidays. She'll be there until she starts at the university.'

'She's done well, hasn't she? You must be very proud of her.'

Peggy's eyes darkened. She glanced at him, but said nothing, and Laurence realized he had said the wrong thing. Myrtle had been a credit to the family, but Peggy had brought them shame.

Alice Wagstaffe was the first person to greet Peggy on the morning she started back at the depot. 'Hello, Peg. What you doing here?' The smile faded from the young woman's face when she realized that Peggy was dressed in her clippie's uniform. 'You're not coming back to work, surely? Not when you've got a young baby?'

'He's driving me mad with his crying,' Peggy muttered. 'Besides, there's plenty of them at home to look after him.'

'But you're his *mother*.' Alice was scandalized. She

pursed her lips in disapproval. 'You don't know how lucky you are to have a lovely little baby. You should be at home with him.'

'That's none of your business, Alice.' Peggy walked away towards the tram where her motorman for the day awaited, leaving Alice staring after her.

'Put Freddie out in the pram near the front door. Poor little mite needs some fresh air,' Grace instructed. It was a very hot Friday morning in late August.

'Will he be all right out here?' Myrtle said worriedly, as she manoeuvred the pram out of the front door and down the steep steps. She placed it carefully so that she could see it through the bay window of the front room. She glanced anxiously up and down the street. 'Wouldn't he be safer in the back yard?'

'The sun's not on the back yard now. He'll be all right.' Grace laughed. 'Afraid someone's going to run off with him?'

'They might,' Myrtle said seriously.

'He'll be safe as houses,' Grace assured her and turned to go back into the house to prepare the evening meal for when three hungry clippie girls arrived home.

Myrtle eyed her grandmother. Houses weren't all that safe these days, not when Hitler's bombs rained down on them all, but she held her tongue. Instead she murmured, 'I'll do my reading in the front room. I can keep an eye on the pram then.'

'Reading? What reading? You've finished school.'

Myrtle bit her lip. 'It's for university. If you're doing English, you get sent a reading list.'

While Freddie slept peacefully in the sunshine and

Grace peeled potatoes and carrots and turned her nose up at the meagre ration of meat that had to last the family for two days, Myrtle settled in the quietness of the sitting room. She was soon engrossed in the story. She loved literature, but since Freddie's arrival biology lessons had taken on a new meaning and soon she would have to tell her family of a decision she had made concerning her future. She wasn't sure what their reaction would be, so she'd decided to leave it until she'd taken her exams. She hadn't wanted family rows disrupting her concentration. But her exams were over now and she still hadn't plucked up the courage to tell them. Soon it would be too late and she'd be on her way to university.

Absorbed though she was in her work, she nevertheless glanced up every few minutes, checking that the pram was still there. As she came to the end of a chapter, she stood up, left the room and opened the front door. 'Time you came in now, little man. Sun's going down and it's getting chilly.' With a smile, she stepped towards the pram and grasped the handle.

'Have you had a nice sleep, Freddie—?' she began and then gasped in horror.

The covers had been pulled back and the pram was empty.

For a moment she was frozen in shock. Then she glanced wildly up and down the street, but there was only Letty on her knees scrubbing her front doorstep. Myrtle was about to call out to her, but then she realized Grace might have fetched the baby in, but couldn't manage to bring the pram indoors. Myrtle flew back inside and into the living room. 'Gran – Gran, have you got him?' She stopped in the doorway, seeing her grandmother dusting the mantelpiece.

Grace glanced round as Myrtle, now rigid with fear, shouted, 'Where is he? Where's Freddie?'

'Out in his pram, of course. Where d'you—?'

'No, he isn't. The pram's empty.'

'Wha—' Grace dropped her duster and stumbled forward as if she had to see the empty pram for herself before she would believe it.

'A' you sure one of the others hasn't come home and taken him upstairs?'

'No, no, I'd have heard the front door. Oh, Gran, I looked out every few minutes. Honest, I did.'

They stepped outside and stood staring at the empty pram.

'There's Mrs Bradshaw. I'll ask her if she—'

'No!' Grace gripped Myrtle's arm fiercely. 'I don't want her knowing – telling everyone we can't look after him properly—'

'Gran – I have to. Everyone's got to know and the sooner the better. That's the only way we're going to find him.'

She pulled herself free and ran out of their gate, calling out, 'Mrs Bradshaw – Mrs Bradshaw—'

'Eh up, lass, what's to do?'

'Freddie—' Myrtle panted as she reached the woman. 'He's gone from his pram. Have you seen him? Have you seen anyone with him?'

'Oh my gawd!' Mrs Bradshaw scrambled to her knees and hurried towards where Grace still stood helplessly by the empty pram.

'I did see someone near the pram – a young woman – but me eyes aren't that clever these days and I thought it were your Peggy.'

Myrtle and Grace glanced at each other. Galvanized into action, Myrtle rushed into the house and up the stairs, two at a time, calling as she went, 'Peggy, Peggy – are you home?' She flung open the door, but the bedroom was empty. Just to be sure she checked the other two bedrooms and the bathroom too, but there was no one there.

Outside again, she shook her head at the questioning glances from both her grandmother and Letty.

'Could it have been our Peggy and she's carried him somewhere?' Grace ventured.

'Where?'

'I don't know. I'm just trying to think what might have happened.'

'Someone's taken him,' Letty said sagely. 'That's what. You hear about it, don't you?'

Grace sagged suddenly, leaning heavily against the doorframe. She closed her eyes and moaned. 'Oh, Freddie, my little Freddie. Don't say that, Letty. Don't say it.'

'Let's get her inside, Myrtle,' Letty said, suddenly concerned for the older lady. 'She looks as if she's going to collapse any minute. I'll make her some strong tea whilst you run up to the top of the street and see 'f you can see anyone carrying a baby.'

'How long ago was it you saw someone?'

'Ooo, only about ten minutes.'

But ten minutes was a long time, Myrtle thought, as she ran up the street. The woman could have got on a tram or a bus. Anything, in that time.

There was no one who fitted Letty's description of the woman in sight. Myrtle ran back towards her own home and then beyond it towards the other end of the street. Again, no one. There were people about of course, walking or waiting for transport, but no young woman carrying a three-month-old baby in her arms.

Frantic with worry and guilt, she hurried home. Letty was still busy in the kitchen.

'Gran,' Myrtle whispered so their neighbour could not hear. 'You don't think Peggy has taken him and – and—'

'What d'you mean?'

'You know she talked about having him adopted, I just wondered if—'

'No, no, she wouldn't. She's been so much better just lately.'

'It could all have been an act and she was just biding her time. Maybe she's found someone who'd take him and—'

'No, no, I won't believe it.'

'What's that, love?' Letty asked, appearing in the doorway carrying a tray laden with cups, saucers and the teapot. 'I can't find any milk, Mrs Booth.'

'It's outside the back door in a bucket of water, keeping cool,' Myrtle said. 'I'll get it.'

She returned moments later, but was too agitated to drink the cup of tea which Letty poured out for her.

'We should get the police?'

'Wait till your mother gets in.'

'But we can't just sit here, Gran. The sooner they know about it, the quicker they'll be finding whoever's taken him.'

Grace glared up at her, 'But if . . .' She stopped, realizing that Letty's antennae were on full alert.

'She's right, Mrs Booth.' Letty nodded. 'That first hour, they say, after a crime – any crime – has been committed is the most important.'

Grace sighed heavily. 'You'd better go and tell them, then, Myrtle.'

As Myrtle ran out of the house again and up the

road, Letty said sympathetically, 'I know how you feel, love. You don't want everyone knowing you couldn't look after your own great-grandson, but it's for the best.'

Grace closed her eyes and moaned inwardly. Letty had correctly guessed her feelings, but at hearing it put into words Grace cringed.

Forty-Two

Myrtle ran until she felt her lungs might burst. But on and on she ran to the nearest police station. The words for what she would say whirled around her mind, but when at last she almost fell through the doors and staggered towards the reception desk, the only words she could gasp out were, 'Please – help us. Someone's taken him.'

She was lucky that a kindly sergeant with children of his own was on duty. He could see at once that the girl was very distressed. He came out from behind the desk, took hold of her arm and led her to a nearby chair. 'Now, lass,' he said gently, 'what's to do?'

'Freddie. Someone's taken him out of his pram. It was outside the front door . . .' she was babbling, almost incoherently, to the patient sergeant. When she had said it all once, he made her repeat it more slowly, whilst he wrote down the details. When at last he had the full story, he was quick to summon help and as soon as the word went round the station that a child – a baby boy – had gone missing, stolen from his pram, four constables seemed to appear as if by magic. Quickly briefed by the sergeant, they put on their helmets and hurried out.

'We'll find him, love. Don't you fret.' The sergeant turned back to Myrtle. 'Now, are you his mam?'

'No, no. He's my nephew. He's my sister's.'

'And where is she now?'

'At work. At least—' Myrtle glanced at the clock on the wall behind the desk. 'She might have got home by now.'

'Then what we ought to do first is to go and see her. I'll be off duty in ten minutes when I'll be relieved from here and I'll come with you.'

'Letty's there. She saw someone pick him out of the pram, but she thought it was Peggy. That's my sister.'

'The boy's mam?'

Myrtle bit her lip as she nodded. There was still the unspoken fear at the back of her mind that it had been Peggy who'd taken him. At this very moment she might be handing him over to adoptive parents. She shuddered at the thought. Seeing her action, the sergeant said, 'What you want is a nice hot cup of tea. I'll see what I can do.'

Why was it, Myrtle thought impatiently, that all anyone could think of in a crisis was to make a 'nice hot cup of tea'? But she didn't refuse him. Her mouth was dry and her heart was still pounding as if it would leap from her chest. And there was no more she could do for the moment, except wait for the sergeant to be ready to leave.

After ten minutes, which seemed to the anxious girl to be more like ten hours, the officer was ready. 'My name's Sergeant Baxter,' he told her as they walked out of the station. He began to stride quickly along the street. Myrtle had to take little running steps to keep up with him, but both she and the sergeant were glancing about them as they walked.

'Now, lass, tell me who I'm going to meet when we get to your home. It'll save time with a lot of introductions.' By the time they arrived at the front door,

Sergeant Baxter felt he already knew each member of the household and even one of their neighbours, Letty Bradshaw. As Myrtle led him into the house, past the empty pram still sitting outside, and opened the door into the living room, they were met by raised voices. Rose was arguing loudly with her grandmother. Mary was wringing her hands, tears running down her face. Only Peggy sat quietly at the kitchen table, her arms resting on it. She was staring straight ahead, her face chalk-white. She seemed unaware of the commotion around her.

Myrtle pointed to each member of her family in turn and told him their names. 'And the one in the kitchen – that's Mrs Bradshaw from next door.' Letty was again making the obligatory cup of tea.

'Right, lass. You leave it to me, now.' The sergeant, a tall and commanding figure, stepped into the room and said loudly, 'Now, now, ladies, this won't help.' The talking stopped and the sergeant placed his helmet on the table and sat down beside Peggy. He pulled out his notebook. 'Myrtle has told me a lot already, but I need as much information as you can give me. What was the little chap wearing?'

Peggy continued to stare straight ahead as if she had not even heard the man speaking to her.

Mary wiped her tears away with the back of her hand. 'Come on, Peggy love, you have to help the sergeant.'

'It's my fault – it's all my fault,' Peggy murmured. Grace and Myrtle glanced at each other grimly. Surely they hadn't been right. It didn't seem credible that Peggy could have done such a thing, but here she was admitting it. But then, Peggy went on bitterly, 'I should

346

never have left him with a schoolgirl and an old woman.'

Grace leaned her head against the back of her chair and closed her eyes, whilst colour flamed Myrtle's face. They felt guilty enough themselves without hearing Peggy say it. But then, Myrtle thought, if Peggy had taken the child herself, she would be trying to put the blame on others to divert suspicion.

Mary, though her face was bleak with anxiety, put her arm round her daughter. 'That's not fair, Peg. It could have happened to any of us. I put him out there in the sunshine only last week.'

Letty came into the room, carrying a tray. 'Ah,' the sergeant said, 'now you must be Mrs Bradshaw. I understand that you saw—'

'Shouldn't you be out looking for him?' Rose interrupted tartly.

'There are four officers already scouring the streets and there will be more very shortly,' Sergeant Baxter said calmly. He turned back to Letty. 'I understand you saw someone take the little boy?'

Letty nodded, revelling in being the centre of attention for a few moments. 'I thought it was Peggy. It looked just like her, 'cos she was dressed in dark clothes. I thought it was her uniform.' She nodded to Peggy, Mary and Rose, who were all still dressed in their clippie uniforms.

'Can you give me a description of her facial features?'

Letty shook her head. 'No, she had her back to me.'

'Did you see which way she went?'

'Well, she didn't come past my door, so she must have gone down the street. But I didn't actually watch her, you know. I've got me work to do.'

Rose was agitated. 'Do you want me for anything, Sergeant? Because if not, I'm off out to look for him myself. I can't just sit here drinking tea.'

'If there's nothing you can tell me, miss, then yes, you go. The more people out there the better.'

Letty glanced at the clock on the mantelpiece. 'I'll get my Tom to go out. He'll be home from work any minute. And he'll round up all his mates.'

'The woman could be anywhere by now.' Peggy shrugged as if she thought searching the streets was futile. 'She could have got on a bus or a tram.'

'That's it!' Myrtle cried. 'The trams – and maybe the buses too – we'll get all the drivers and clippies to watch out. I'll go now.' She was out of the door before anyone could say a word or attempt to stop her. Not that anyone wanted to. Anything was better than sitting there helplessly.

'I'll go with her,' Rose said and hurried after Myrtle. As she reached the front door, she saw Myrtle in the street talking to Mrs Deeton. The girl turned, 'Oh, Rose, Bob's mam's come to see you. I'm off.' And again, without waiting for a response, Myrtle was running up the street.

'I can't stop, Mrs Deeton,' Rose said. 'I'm sorry. Someone's taken Freddie out of his pram. We're in a panic.'

'Oh, I am sorry to hear that. I just came to tell you that Bob's home and he wants you to come round.'

'Oh! Oh yes, I will as soon as I can, but I really can't—'

'Of course not, dear. Off you go.'

*

When Rose arrived, breathless, at the depot, Myrtle was already talking to Laurence Bower, gesticulating towards the trams. As she joined them, Rose heard Laurence say, 'Course we will, lass. I'll pass the word right away. Rose, I'm so sorry to hear what's happened. We'll do all we can to help. And I'll have a word with my opposite number at the bus depot at once.'

As they went home together, glancing about them anxiously as they walked, staring into each pram that passed by, Myrtle said, 'Rose, you don't think it was Peggy that took him, do you?'

'Eh?' Rose was so startled by the suggestion that she stopped walking and turned to face Myrtle. 'What on earth are you talking about, Myrtle?'

Swiftly Myrtle explained the dreadful thought she'd had. 'And it crossed Gran's mind too. I'm not the only one to think it. And you saw how she was just now – just sitting at the table while the rest of us are running round like headless chickens, out of our minds with worry. And she was quick to lay the blame at Gran's and my door. Oh, I know we are to blame, but Rose, I was sitting in the front room working and I glanced up every few minutes. Honest, I did.'

Myrtle was a tough kid and rarely cried, but now tears filled her eyes. Seeing them, Rose linked her arm through her sister's. 'Don't take on, love. Like Mam said, it could've happened to any one of us. I left him outside the butcher's the day before yesterday when I was queuing for our rations. He must have been out there on his own for half an hour.' She shuddered.

'Oh, Rose, what if we never see him again? What if—?'

'Don't, Myrtle. Don't say it.'

The thought was far too painful for either of the girls to contemplate.

'We'll find him if I have to get the whole of Sheffield looking for him. But we'll find him, Myrtle.'

'And if it is Peggy who – who—'

'I don't believe that for a moment, but if it is,' Rose added grimly, 'then I'll deal with her.'

Forty-Three

The night was long and filled with an overriding terror that robbed all of them of sleep. Grace refused to go to bed, but sat in her chair by the fire all night. Exhaustion made her doze off, but then she awoke each time with a jump and a startled look – until she remembered. Mary sat with her through the night, but she insisted that Myrtle should go to bed.

'I want to go out with Rose to look for him.'

Rose was adamant that she wouldn't give up searching until he was found.

'You can't do anything in the dark, love,' Mary pointed out sensibly. 'Nor you, Rose. It'd be better if you both got some sleep and went out again tomorrow.'

Mary didn't hold out much hope of them finding him. Whoever had taken their darling boy would now have him safely hidden away. She just hoped that whoever had him was looking after him properly.

At last, after much arguing, Rose and Myrtle accepted their mother's advice and went to bed, but it was only to lie awake whispering to each other through the long hours of darkness.

Morning came at last and Rose and Myrtle dressed hurriedly and rushed downstairs, bursting into the kitchen. 'Any news?'

Mary, red-eyed from a sleepless night and the tears she'd shed, shook her head. 'No. I've been to the corner and rung the station from the telephone box, but the duty sergeant said there'd been no news.'

'Was it Sergeant Baxter?'

'No, he's on duty at ten and he's coming round here.' She turned to glance at Rose, who was dressed in her ordinary clothes – not her uniform. 'I thought you were on the early shift today?'

'I'm not going in. I told Mr Bower yesterday. He understands,' she added swiftly as her mother opened her mouth to argue. 'Me and Myrtle are going out again today.'

'Just make sure you come home for meals.'

'We won't have time, we—'

But now Mary was firm. 'You not eating properly and making yourselves ill won't help find Freddie. Now, please, girls, do as I ask. Gran says she will get meals ready and wait here for any news. Letty and I are going out together.'

For the first time Grace spoke, her voice sounding frail. She looked as if she'd aged ten years in a night. 'Tom and all the men from our street were out until gone midnight and they're all staying off work today.'

'Steel works'll be shutting down then,' Rose said wryly, with a weak attempt at humour, but no one was in the mood for laughing.

After a quick breakfast, the girls set off. Letty arrived a few moments later and she and Mary took a bus into the city centre. What they could do none of them really knew, but they needed to be out, needed to be doing something.

To everyone's surprise and Rose's disgust, Peggy said she was going into work. 'You're wasting your time roaming the streets. She'll have him kept well out of sight now.'

Rose regarded her sister with narrowed eyes, but for now she held her tongue. So, only Grace, left at home, felt helpless and useless. The knock at the front door was a welcome interruption to an ominously silent house. How she longed to hear the girls laughing together or even arguing and, more than anything, how she yearned to hear Freddie's gurgling. Even his yelling would be welcome now.

'Oh, Sergeant, do come in. Have you any news?'

'I'm sorry, Mrs Booth, but the answer's no.' As they moved into the living room and sat down he added, 'We're thinking of going to the newspapers, but we wanted the family's approval first.'

'If you think it best,' Grace said slowly, 'then, yes, though I shudder to think what will be said about us. That we can't look after him properly.'

'There's always someone ready to find fault, love, but you shouldn't worry. If I had a pound for every mother who leaves her baby out in its pram, I'd be able to retire tomorrow. Now I'm glad I've caught you on your own because I'd like you to tell me a bit more about the little lad's mother. I noticed yesterday – though, of course, it might have been that she was in shock – that of all of you she was – well – the quietest.'

Grace glanced at him shrewdly. She bit her lip, but knew that she had no choice but to confide in him. Her granddaughter's shame was common knowledge in their street and probably beyond, but now it was to be gossiped about around the police station and possibly revealed to the newspapers, she hesitated. She'd always loved reading *The Sheffield Star*, but she didn't want her family's troubles splashed across its front page.

As if reading her mind, Sergeant Baxter said gently, 'We'll have to give the little chap's name, of course, and say where he lived, but there'll be no need to go into detail other than that.'

'Lives, Sergeant,' Grace snapped, anxiety and shame making her tone sharp. 'Lives.'

'I'm sorry,' the patient man said and took out his notebook.

For the next hour the two of them drafted out a suitable item for release to the papers.

'I don't know why we're bothering,' Grace grumbled, 'they'll still print just what they like and make it sound as salacious as possible.'

But the sergeant shook his head. 'No, you're wrong there, Mrs Booth. I know the editor at the *Star* very well and, with something like this, they only want to help. I shall see him personally and the piece will be very discreet, I can promise you that.'

'Hmm.' Grace glared at him. She wasn't convinced even though the sergeant added, 'It's the only way to get the word out there fast. We need people to come forward with any information they might have. Information that they don't even realize at the moment is important.'

Grace narrowed her eyes. 'What sort of information?'

'If they've seen a relative, a friend or even a neighbour with a baby that wasn't there before yesterday. Even if they've heard a baby crying that's unusual.'

'You mean if someone's suddenly acquired a baby?'

'Exactly. And we need to get a description of the woman Mrs Bradshaw saw out there. Someone might have seen her in the street, on a bus or a tram.'

Grace explained that Rose and Myrtle had enlisted the help of the public-transport workers in the city and the sergeant nodded his approval. 'That was a very good idea.'

They talked for a while longer and then the sergeant stood up. 'I must be getting back to the station and in touch with the editor.'

'You will let us know if—'

'Of course. You've no need to fret on that account. We'll keep you posted on any developments, I promise.'

Grace tried to smile. 'Thank you. You've been very kind.'

As she stood up to see him out, Sergeant Baxter touched her shoulder lightly. 'I do understand, you know. All of it. Better than you might think. I've children of my own and we've just found out my eldest daughter is pregnant.' He paused slightly before adding in a whisper, 'And she's not married either.'

'Then you have my sympathy, Sergeant. It's not easy and I have to admit that, when I first knew about Peggy, I threatened to throw her out. If I had, they'd all have gone. But when the little chap was born, well, we all fell for him – hook, line and sinker. They bring their love with them, Sergeant Baxter. You'll see.'

'Aye well, mebbe you're right, Mrs Booth. The missus is already coming to terms with it, but it's taking me a bit longer.'

'Minute you clap eyes on the little mite, you'll be bowled over. I guarantee it. If a hard-bitten old cynic like me can become putty in our little man's hands, then you've no chance, I promise you.'

Forty-Four

The rest of the family returned home that evening, footsore and dispirited. There was no news. Not one of them had seen or heard anything hopeful. And when Grace relayed her discussion with Sergeant Baxter, they didn't know whether the plan to go to the local paper was good news or not.

'So my name's going to be dragged through the mud, is it?' Peggy said. 'I'll likely get the sack now. Mr Bower's covered for me with the big bosses, but if they think I'm bringing the company name into disrepute—'

Rose whirled round on her. 'Is that all you can think about? Your bloody job?' She wagged her finger in Peggy's face. 'And I'll tell you summat else and all, Peggy. It's crossed our minds that you might have had summat to do with all this.'

Peggy blinked and stared at Rose. 'What – what d'you mean?'

'You talked about giving him away – having him adopted. We just wondered if you've done it.'

Peggy gasped and her eyes widened. 'No – no. How can you even think that?'

'Because *you* said it. That's why.'

'But you know I've been better with him just lately. Oh, I know I was funny at first, but I'd never do that.' Her chin trembled and tears welled in her eyes.

'Then why on earth did you go to work today? Why weren't you out searching for him.'

'Because it's all my fault. I didn't love him when he was born – and to be truthful, I'm still finding it hard. And now I'm being punished.'

Rose stared down at Peggy, who dropped her head into her arms resting on the table and began to sob. 'It's all my fault.'

Rose's anger evaporated. She sat down beside her sister and put her arm around her. 'If you think that, then I'm as much to blame. I wouldn't have anything to do with him at first, would I?'

'What if we don't find him? What if someone's – hurt him?'

'Don't. Oh, don't.'

Peggy buried her face in Rose's shoulder and they wept together.

Another anxious night passed, another day of tramping the streets in a futile hope that they might see someone with Freddie. At the risk of being asked, 'What on earth do you think you're doing?' they peered into every pram and pushchair they encountered. But proud mothers were only too ready to believe that their babies were being admired. At last, weary and losing hope, they returned home.

'Is Peggy home yet?' Rose asked.

'No,' Grace replied, pursing her lips. 'How she can go to work when—'

'We had all that out last night, Gran. Leave her be. It's her way of coping.' She was thoughtful for a moment. 'Maybe she's right,' she said slowly. 'Maybe we are on a wild goose chase. Like she said, whoever's got him's not going to be parading him through the streets, are they?'

'They'll have to go out some time,' Grace argued. 'Besides, we've got to keep doing something.'

'Yes, that's how I feel.'

Myrtle said nothing, but washed her hands at the sink in the kitchen and then sat down at the table. Grace placed a plate of food in front of her. The girl sighed. 'It looks lovely, Gran, but I really don't think I can eat a thing.'

'Just try, love. That's all I ask. Your mam was right. You've all got to eat and we mustn't waste it, else I'll have the Ministry of Food knocking at the door. Besides,' she added with a wry smile, 'it gives me summat to do all day.'

Rose sat down too and the two girls tried to eat.

'Where are Mam and Mrs Bradshaw?' Rose asked, picking at her food, but managing to eat a little.

'No idea, but they should be back soon.'

'Is Mr Bradshaw going out again tonight?'

'I don't know. Trouble is, she's not going to be out with him at night, now is she?'

'I suppose not.'

They heard the front door opening and closing and a moment later, Mary came into the room. Immediately all eyes turned towards her, but she shook her head as she said, 'No, nothing. And I take it there's no news here either.'

She took their silence to be a negative answer and sighed. As she sat down she said, 'I ran into Mrs Deeton today, Rose. Bob is still asking for you to visit him.'

Rose gave an impatient shake of her head. 'Doesn't he realize I've more important things on my mind just now?'

'It might do you good to get out for a bit. Why don't you go round tonight? There's nothing more you can do here.'

'But what if there's news? What if—?'

'I'll come running to find you,' Myrtle promised. 'I know where the Deetons live.'

'Have they found him?' were Mrs Deeton's first words when she opened the door to Rose.

Rose pressed her lips together and shook her head.

'Oh, my dear. Come in, come in. Bob's through here.'

He was sitting by the fire in an armchair, his injured leg resting on a footstool.

'Rose!' His face lit up at the sight of her and there could be no mistaking his delight in seeing her, but his expression sobered when he saw the bleak, desperate look on her face. 'I'm so sorry to hear what's happened. Is there any news at all?'

'Nothing.'

She sat down opposite him and tried to focus on him. 'How are you, Bob?'

'Much better, thanks. The leg's healing nicely now it's getting proper attention. Trouble is –' he made a weak attempt at humour – 'once it's better, I'll have to go back.'

Mrs Deeton placed a tray of tea and biscuits on the table and then made an excuse that she had something to do upstairs, though Rose realized it was a ploy to leave them alone together.

'How've you been, Rose? I mean, until this awful business with Freddie.'

She didn't answer immediately as she poured the tea

and handed him a cup. Then she met his gaze. 'Peggy let me read your letter to her. Did you mean what you said?'

The cup trembled slightly in the saucer as he took it from her. 'Every word, Rose. I know now that I don't love Peggy. I did once, but she obviously doesn't love me. Never did, else she wouldn't have gone off with that soldier so – so easily.'

Rose sat down but remained silent as Bob went on, stumbling to find the right words.

'What she did sort of – killed it for me. It wouldn't have been so bad if she'd said earlier that she wanted us just to be friends, but she let me think there was more in it. And then to – to get herself pregnant—' He stopped, fearing he was saying too much to the girl's sister.

'I know what you mean,' Rose said softly. 'When she jilted you, I wouldn't speak to her and then when we found out she was expecting, well, the whole family cut her off.' She smiled ruefully. 'All of us except Mam.'

'But things changed when he was born, did they?'

'Not immediately, but you can't go on being resentful of an innocent baby, can you?'

'I – suppose not.'

Rose blinked and stared at him. 'But you were willing to marry her? Willing to take him on as your own? Because that's what everyone would have thought. That Freddie was yours.'

'I know. And I was a fool to make the offer. It would never have worked. I couldn't ever have looked upon him as my own. I know that now. And always there would have been the shadow of the soldier between us. Peggy was right to say no. It wouldn't have worked. And thank God she did, because – ' he looked straight into Rose's eyes – 'I have feelings for someone else now.'

Rose stared at him and her heart sank. He'd met someone already. Someone who worked in the NAAFI or for ENSA or –

'Rose – you told me once you loved me. Is that still true? Or have I lost my chance with you because I was stupid enough to offer to marry Peggy?'

It was what she had longed to hear him say. For years she had carried the secret of her love for him and now, at what should have been the happiest moment of her life, it was clouded with the overriding worry of Freddie's disappearance. Nothing – not even hearing that there could be hope for her with Bob – could obliterate her terror that something dreadful had happened to their darling boy.

'Oh, Bob!' Tears filled her eyes and then poured down her cheeks. 'Of course I do, but just now I can't think of anything else except trying to find Freddie.'

He leaned forward awkwardly because of his outstretched leg and touched her hand. 'I understand,' he said gently. 'Drink your tea and then off you go because I can see you're like a cat on hot bricks. Go back home, but keep us posted, won't you, if there's any news? Whatever time of day or night it is, come and tell us.'

She finished her tea quickly and hurried away. There'd be so much to think about, to talk about, but for now nothing else mattered except Freddie.

Forty-Five

It was gone ten and Mary was trying to get both Myrtle and Rose to go to bed. Peggy was already in her dressing gown and filling her hot-water bottle in the kitchen. She didn't really need it, but its warmth was comforting.

'You look done in, the pair of you,' Mary said. 'Now, I really think you should go to work tomorrow, Rose, and Myrtle, you should start getting yourself organized for going to university.'

'Mam, I wouldn't be able to concentrate. I'd be a danger to my passengers.'

'Nor could I,' Myrtle said firmly. 'I can't even begin to think about that.' She avoided meeting her mother's candid gaze. 'Please – don't make me.' The girl's voice broke and she pressed her hand to her mouth.

'Very well then,' Mary said with a sigh. 'Now off you go upstairs and—'

A loud knocking on the front door made them all jump. Rose was the first to rush out of the room, flinging open the door, oblivious to the blackout precautions. Mary and Myrtle were close behind her and Grace had struggled out of her chair to follow them. Peggy stood in the doorway to the kitchen, hugging her hot-water bottle close to her chest.

'Mr Bower? What on earth are you doing here? Oh – what's happened? Is there news?'

The poor man seemed flustered by the pairs of eyes staring at him. 'I – er – just wondered how you all are.' He ran his tongue nervously around his lips. 'And I – er – just wanted a word with – um – your mother.'

Rose gave a click of exasperation and before she could bite back the words, blurted out, 'We've all got enough to think about just now, without you coming courting—'

She felt her mother's restraining hand on her arm. 'That's enough, Rose. You go in. All of you. I'll have a word with – Mr Bower.' She smiled at him, though the sadness and the anxiety never left her eyes, not even for a second. 'Please come in.'

The rest of the family turned away in disappointment. For a fleeting moment, when the knock had come at the door, their hopes had been raised, only to be cruelly dashed. Mary closed the front door and when they were alone in the hallway, she murmured, 'I'm so sorry about Rose's outburst. We're all overwrought and—'

'Never mind about that.' He, too, was agitated. 'Mary, I need to you to come with me. Now. Right away.'

'Oh, but, Laurence, I can't. I can't leave the family just now and, besides, I can think of nothing else but Freddie.'

'It's about Freddie. I think I might know where he is.'

Mary gasped, her eyes widened and her hand fluttered to her mouth, but before she could utter a word Laurence touched her arm. 'Don't tell the others. Not yet. I don't want to raise their hopes, because until we get there I can't be sure.'

'Where? Who—?'

'I'll explain everything as we go, but just hurry. It wouldn't be right for me to go on my own. Not – ' his mouth twitched with wry humour – 'as my dear mother would have said, "seemly".'

'I must just tell—'

'No, don't. They'll only ask questions or think we're – well, I don't know what they might think. Just come with me, Mary. Just trust me.'

She looked into his eyes and despite the desperation she and her family were feeling, she knew that she could trust Laurence Bower completely. She nodded. 'I'll come with you.' And in those few simple words was a world of meaning. She would go anywhere, any time, with Laurence. He only had to ask.

Quietly they let themselves out of the front door and once they were safely out of earshot of the rest of the family, he said, 'Sergeant Baxter's waiting a little way up the street with a car.'

'Where are we going?'

'Just trust me, Mary,' he said again. 'I may be entirely wrong, so don't get your hopes up.'

There was no time for more questions for they'd reached the waiting car and the sergeant standing beside it. He opened one of the rear doors for Mary and Laurence to climb in. Laurence sat beside her whilst the sergeant drove, but neither of them seemed willing to enlighten her. The journey passed in total silence, but she was comforted by Laurence reaching for her hand and holding it tightly. Sergeant Baxter wound his way through the streets of the city but at last he drew the car to a halt in a narrow, terraced street.

'Is this it, Mr Bower?'

'Yes, number thirty-three.'

'Right then. I'll park here and we'll walk down. And

so's not to frighten her, you and Mrs Sylvester go to the door. I'll stand to one side, out of sight when she opens it.'

'Laurence, what—?'

He squeezed her hand. 'It'll be all right, Mary. But we must just do what the sergeant tells us.'

They all got out of the car and walked a few yards down the street to find number thirty-three. Now it was Mary who was clutching Laurence's hand. The sergeant hung back, staying out of the sight of anyone who might open the door. With a nod from Sergeant Baxter, Laurence knocked on the door. They waited, Mary biting her lip, wondering what exactly was going on.

They heard a noise behind the door and then it opened a few inches and Mary gasped out loud to see who was standing there.

'She's gone out,' Rose reported to the family, when she'd opened the living-room door to find the hallway deserted. 'With Mr Bower. What on earth is she thinking of at a time like this?'

'You went round to see Bob,' Myrtle reminded her and earned herself a resentful glare from her sister.

'Now, now, you two,' Grace admonished. 'Myrtle, it's high time you were in bed.'

'I'm not going anywhere until Mam gets back.'

'Me neither,' Rose said and sat down beside the younger girl, siding with her. Peggy was sitting staring into space, still hugging her hot-water bottle. She couldn't believe what was happening. She'd fallen in love with Terry so quickly and so completely. She'd never thought for one moment that he didn't feel the same way about her. But he'd gone away and there'd been no word from him since. Nothing. Maybe he'd been sent abroad. Perhaps he'd been taken prisoner or worse . . . She shuddered. If that were true, then the only part she had left of their passionate love for each other was little Freddie.

Oblivious to Peggy's unhappy thoughts, Grace sighed. 'She could be ages,' she reasoned, but she no longer had the strength to argue with her granddaughters. She felt suddenly old, the terror of what might have happened to her beloved great-grandson eating away at her. To think that she had almost turned Peggy out into the street when she'd learned of her unwanted pregnancy, that she might never have had the joy of holding him in her arms, of loving him. It was all too much. She struggled to her feet. 'I'm going to bed.'

Mary stared at the frightened face of the woman standing in front of her and then it all fell into place. She knew now why Laurence had felt unable to come here on his own to follow up his suspicions, why he'd needed her – a woman – to be there and, also, why Sergeant Baxter had come too. And she understood too Laurence's reasoning. Why on earth hadn't she or her family thought of it? But such a thing would never have crossed their minds, yet now it seemed such a simple explanation.

'Alice!' she whispered. 'Oh, Alice.'

The young woman's eyes widened and she tried to shut the door again, but Laurence's sturdy boot was in the gap. 'It's all right, love,' he said gently. 'Just let us in.'

She hesitated a moment, but then, with a defeated

gesture, Alice turned away, leaving the door open for them to follow.

As she stepped directly into the front room, from somewhere further inside the house, Mary heard the cry of a baby.

Forty-Six

'You'll have to knock,' Mary whispered when, at last, they were back home and standing outside her own front door. She laughed softly, 'We went off in such a rush, I forgot my key.'

It was Rose, still fully dressed, who opened the door to see her mother standing there carrying a tiny figure, wrapped warmly in a blue shawl, in her arms. Laurence was beside her and behind them both stood a beaming Sergeant Baxter. Myrtle appeared, peering anxiously over Rose's shoulder and, from the top of the stairs, came Grace's querulous voice. 'What's going on? What's all the knocking? What's happened?'

Without a word, Mary handed the wriggling bundle into Rose's open arms. Holding him in the crook of her left arm, she gently parted the shawl.

'Is it him?' Myrtle whispered, afraid of the answer. 'Is it Freddie?'

Rose's eyes blurred with tears, but not before she had seen the round, smiling face of her little nephew. He gurgled and kicked his legs as if he recognized whose arms he was in and knew he was well and truly home.

'Yes, oh yes,' Rose breathed. 'It's Freddie.' She put him into Myrtle's arms as she shouted, 'Peggy! Peggy – come quickly.' Then she turned back and flung her arms around a surprised Laurence Bower. 'Oh, thank you, thank you.'

Sergeant Baxter cleared his throat. 'I think, Rose, we'd better all go inside. We'll have the warden after us in a minute for showing a light.'

'Oh yes, yes. Come in, do.'

When they were sitting in the living room and Freddie was lying happily in Grace's lap, the story began to unfold as the questions came tumbling out.

'How did you find him?'

'What happened?'

'Where was he?'

'Who took him?'

'Whoa, whoa, one at a time, ladies.' Sergeant Baxter looked as if he would never stop smiling. So much of his work as a police officer was fraught with sadness or the seamier side of people's lives. It wasn't often he witnessed such a joyous outcome to a case. 'It's all down to Mr Bower, so I'll let him tell you.'

All eyes turned to Laurence, who shrugged in embarrassment. 'It was nothing, really, but the day after little Freddie was taken Alice Wagstaffe didn't come into work.'

'Alice!' Rose exclaimed. 'Don't tell me it was her.'

Peggy, standing at the back of the room, gasped and put her hand over her mouth, her eyes wide. Rose glanced at her and frowned, but for the moment she said nothing. She turned her attention back to Laurence Bower, who was continuing his tale.

'And she didn't appear the next day either and there was no word from her. She lives alone now, you know, so I didn't think much of it at first because if she was ill she'd no one to ask to telephone us. And then I got to thinking. I remembered how she'd been so interested in Peggy's – um – er – pregnancy. And later, when she heard that Peggy was going through a bad time and that she wouldn't take any notice of the baby, Alice was incensed. I overheard her talking to some of the other girls in the canteen about it.'

'She took him, didn't she?' Rose blurted out. 'That's what you're leading up to, Mr Bower, isn't it? Alice took him. And I thought she was my friend. I – I –' Rose was filled with a sudden guilt. 'I confided in her. It was me told her that Peggy wouldn't take any notice of Freddie.' She groaned and covered her face with her hands. 'And I told her Peggy was thinking about having him adopted.'

'She was disgusted by the idea,' Laurence put in.

'I know she was. Why ever didn't I suspect her when he went missing? I should've guessed.'

Sergeant Baxter put his hand comfortingly on Rose's shoulder as he took up the tale. 'We had some information come in this morning. You know that Mr Bower passed the word round very quickly amongst all the tram and bus personnel? Well, they'd been keeping a sharp lookout and one of the clippies on the buses came to tell us that she'd seen Alice getting on her bus with a baby in her arms. She doesn't know Alice well and wasn't sure if she had a baby of her own or not. Anyway, thank goodness she thought it worth reporting it to us. I expect Alice thought that by using the bus, instead of a tram, she wouldn't be recognized.'

'But the city's transport workers are all one big family and she remembered seeing Alice working on the trams,' Laurence said and then added softly, 'but I think Alice is to be pitied rather than blamed.'

Rose looked up sharply. 'Pitied? For stealing our Freddie and putting us all through Hell?'

'She's at the station being questioned,' Sergeant Baxter murmured.

'And you're going to charge her with kidnapping?'

'That rather depends.'

'On what?'

'On what you all want to do.'

'What *we* want? Well, I'd lock her up and throw away the key.'

'Now, now, Rose, let's hear the whole story first,' Grace said, tickling Freddie under his chin until he giggled and squirmed delightedly. 'Go on, Mr Bower.'

'All Alice has ever wanted was to get married and have a barrowload of kids, as she put it herself. She even told me that when I interviewed her for a job. "It'll only be till this is all over, Mr Bower," she said, "and my Derek comes home, because then we'll be starting a family. Both me and Derek want kids." ' He paused for a moment and sighed heavily. 'But we all know what happened soon after that. Her Derek was killed at Dunkirk. I don't think she's ever got over it.'

There was silence in the room as they thought about the poor girl who'd lost everything.

'There's something else as well,' Rose said. She was reluctant to find any excuse for what Alice had done and yet it had to be said. 'When we first met, she told me she'd had a miscarriage. She's probably never got over that either, but it doesn't give her the right to steal someone else's child, though,' Rose muttered, still feeling guilty that she had played a part in telling Alice that Peggy didn't want her child, 'I suppose it does explain it a bit.'

Now Peggy moved forward slowly. 'Sergeant, I don't want you to charge her. She's had enough sorrow.

371

Freddie's safely back with us and we'll never let him out of our sight again.'

Sergeant Baxter nodded. 'It's not up to me, but I'll see what I can do, if you're sure.'

'I am,' Peggy said firmly, as she reached out to take her child from Grace's lap. 'And now, my little man, we'd better see about getting you fed.'

'I'll do his bottle.' Myrtle leapt up.

'I'll change him,' Rose offered.

'No, no, I'll do it,' Peggy said. 'I'll do it all.' Then she looked squarely at Laurence. 'Mr Bower, will you please accept my notice with immediate effect? I intend to devote all my time to caring for my baby – as I should have done from the start.'

Mary and Grace smiled at each other, but Myrtle's chin quivered. 'But you'll still let us help, won't you, Peggy? I couldn't bear it if . . .'

Peggy smiled at them all in turn. 'Of course, I'll be glad of your help.'

The sergeant and Laurence left, and the family of women took turns to cuddle Freddie and to marvel again that he had been found safe and well.

'Well, I'm ashamed to admit that I'm not much of a one for praying,' Rose said, 'but I've done a lot of it in the last two days and I'll be saying a huge "thank you" tonight.'

'Now, Myrtle, it's very late. You really should be in bed.'

The girl got up and then hesitated. 'There's just one thing I think I ought to tell you now. I've decided I'm not going to go to university.'

'Oh, Myrtle, why ever not?' Mary cried.

'But it's what you've always wanted.' Rose was astounded.

Myrtle nodded. 'It was – until Freddie came along. But now I've decided I want to go into nursing. I want to become a midwife.'

The others gazed at one another, for once completely lost for words. Myrtle, unfazed by their shocked faces, said, 'Goodnight. I expect we'll all sleep well tonight for the first time in days.'

'I'm not sure I will now,' Mary murmured, 'after that bombshell.'

Rose yawned. 'Well, I could sleep for a week, but there's something I have to do first.' She left the room briefly, then returned wearing her outdoor coat.

'You're not going out again?' Mary was disapproving. 'Not at this time of night. It's almost one o'clock.'

'I must. I promised to let Bob and his mother know any news. And this is the very best. It can't wait until morning.'

Mary looked helplessly towards Grace, but the older woman merely shrugged. 'It seems, my dear, that your chicks are all bent on scratching for themselves now.'

Forty-Seven

The Deetons' house was in darkness when Rose arrived. She hesitated. She didn't want to wake the whole street with her knocking. Nor did she really want to disturb Mrs Deeton, and yet she had made a promise she intended to keep. Mrs Deeton's bedroom was at the front, overlooking the street, whilst Bob's was at the back. Feeling her way down the passageway between the terraced houses, where not even a sliver of light from the moon penetrated, Rose crept into the back yard. Here she could see the vague outlines of the water butt and the building that housed the nessy, but she missed seeing the washing line strung across the yard and walked into it. It caught her forehead, not injuring her but making her jump. She swore softly under her breath and then looked up at the window above the back door. First she tried calling softly, but when there was no movement at the window, she felt around on the ground until her fingers closed over a few small stones, which she began to toss at the pane of glass. Rose had a good aim and each one rattled against the glass, then fell back to the ground.

After four attempts, she saw the curtains pulled back and the casement window pulled up. Bob stuck his head out of the window.

'Who's there?' he called softly.

'Bob – it's me. Rose.'

'Rose! Good Heavens, what are you doing here at this time of night? Wait a minute, I'll come down.'

'No – no,' she began, worried now that she had caused the injured man to tackle the steep stairs. But he had disappeared and she could do nothing but wait until the lock turned in the back door and opened to admit her.

'What is it, Rose? What's happened? Have you had news? Here, come near the fire, it's not quite out. I'll build it up—'

'No, no, I'm not stopping, but I had to come and tell you. Freddie's been found. He's safe and unharmed. Oh, Bob, we've got him back.'

And then they were in each other's arms, hugging and kissing and murmuring words of thankfulness and joy.

'Thank God, oh thank God,' Bob said. His mouth found hers and now his kiss became more demanding, much more than the elation they both felt about the child's safe return. She felt his passion and responded to it. At last, breathless, they drew apart, but only for him to lead her into the front room and towards the sofa. They sat down close together and he kissed her again, his ardour growing, his hand cupping her breast and then fumbling with the buttons of her blouse.

Rose yearned for his touch, longed to let him go further and make her his in every way. It was what she'd dreamed of for years, but the sudden memory of Peggy, heavily pregnant and facing the censure and disgust of all her family, made her draw back.

'No, Bob, no,' she said gently.

He stopped at once and muttered, 'I'm sorry.'

They sat together in silence, the only sound in the room their heavy breathing. When they had both calmed,

Rose said, 'I'm sorry, Bob. Truly, but I'm not that sort of girl. I – I can't forget what happened to Peggy.'

'I wouldn't hurt you, Rose. I wouldn't leave you pregnant, I promise.'

In the darkness Rose smiled wryly to herself. She wondered if those were the same words which Terry Price had used to Peggy.

'But would you respect me afterwards?'

'Of course. You're my girl and I trust you.'

'Am I, Bob? Am I really?'

'It's what I wanted to tell you – to ask you – when I came home from hospital, but with the news of Freddie – well, I couldn't, could I?'

'And now?' she whispered, her heart beating faster.

'Rose Sylvester, will you please, please, please, be my girl?'

'Yes, Robert Deeton, I will.'

They fell against each other, laughing, and when he kissed her again it was gentle and so reverent that Rose felt her resolve begin to crumble. Almost, but not quite.

It took the family a long time to get over the nightmare of Freddie's disappearance – if they ever really did. For weeks and months they still woke each morning with a feeling of terror, which didn't subside until they remembered that he was now safely back with them. No charges were brought against Alice Wagstaffe, though she was advised to seek medical help. Without waiting to see if the company would dismiss her, she gave in her notice.

'How's she going to live?' Peggy asked when Rose gave her the news, but Rose only shrugged.

'Who knows. That's her lookout.'

'She's moved away,' Mary said. 'She's going to her brother's in London, so Mr Bower said. He's away in the forces and her sister-in-law is on her own with three kids to look after.'

'Oh, aye. Is she going to kidnap one of them?' Rose said sarcastically.

'Her family know all about what's happened and are standing by her.'

'She's lucky not to get thrown into jail,' Rose muttered darkly. 'You were too soft, Peg. If it'd been left to me—'

'Well, it wasn't,' Peggy said shortly.

'Let's try and put it all behind us,' Mary said, trying to calm what might become a full-scale argument between the sisters. There was still tension between them at times. 'And get back to normal. I'm more concerned now about Myrtle. What do you all think about it?'

Rose and Peggy glanced at each other, but it was Grace who spoke first. 'I think it's an excellent idea. Our sort don't go to university. I've always thought she was getting a bit above herself with such ideas.'

'That's exactly why we are willing to support her.' Rose rounded on her grandmother. 'A good education ought to be available to everyone – not just a privileged few.'

'Quite right, Rose, and she's clever enough,' Peggy agreed. 'No one can deny that.'

'Nursing is a good career for a girl, though,' Mary said, 'but I never thought she'd be suitable. It's a vocation.'

'It's because of Freddie. Being there that night when

he was born. Having a hand in it – literally.' Rose laughed. 'It did something to her.'

'She ought to talk to her headmistress,' Mary said.

Myrtle waited outside the headmistress's office, her knees trembling. She'd always hated having to see the head, even when she wasn't in trouble. Even though she'd officially left school she felt it only courteous to inform her former head teacher of her momentous decision. Miss Cartwright had been instrumental in helping her get a place at university. The autumn school term had just started and the main hall was thronged with pupils rushing from one class to another. For a brief moment Myrtle wished she was back amongst them.

Celia Cartwright was an excellent head for the city school, strict but fair. Tall, thin and straight-backed with her grey hair pulled tightly back into a bun, she was an imposing figure as she walked the corridors. When the green light at the side of the door bade her enter, Myrtle opened it and went in, closing the door quietly behind her. Seated behind her large desk, Celia smiled at her. Myrtle Sylvester was one of her favourite pupils, though she would never have dreamed of showing it. The girl was clever and studious and the headmistress had high hopes that she would bring credit to the school.

Myrtle raised her chin and Celia recognized the determination in her face and demeanour.

'Miss Cartwright, I'm sorry if what I have to tell you is going to disappoint you, especially after you've helped me so much, but I've decided not to take up my place at Sheffield University.'

Celia gazed at her for a few moments before saying quietly, 'I'm sorry to hear that. Is it – is it family troubles?' Celia had heard about the birth of an illegitimate baby into the household and wondered . . .

'No, not at all.' Myrtle crossed her fingers behind her back as she said confidently, 'My family will support me in whatever I decide to do.'

'I see. And have you decided what that is?'

'Yes. I've decided I want to be a nurse.'

Whatever the headmistress had been expecting it certainly hadn't been this. 'A – a nurse,' she repeated.

'Yes, Miss Cartwright. In fact, I want to train to be a midwife and possibly a paediatric nurse too.'

The girl had obviously done her homework on the subject already. Celia blinked.

'I – see,' Celia said again, feeling the kudos that a girl from her school going to one of the top universities would have brought slipping away from her. She sighed inwardly. She prided herself that she always had the best interests of each of her pupils at heart. 'If you're really sure that that's what you want, Myrtle, then I will do everything in my power to help you, but I can't help feeling you'd be wasting a golden opportunity. A university education isn't open to everyone, you know.'

'I know and I appreciate your encouragement and the support my family have given me, but to be honest I was never really sure that that was what I wanted. You see, I've never known what I wanted to do as a career afterwards.'

'But a degree would open so many doors to you, my dear. You could almost do anything you wished.'

'But what I want to do is become a midwife.'

Again Celia sighed, but capitulated. There was a light in the girl's eyes that she'd never seen before and a look of determination on her face. She could see that it was the same determination that she herself had had when she'd known – yes, known – that she wanted to become a teacher. She'd faced a lot of opposition from her father, who'd wanted her to follow in his footsteps and become a doctor. Now Celia knew that she must not repeat her father's error by trying to persuade the girl standing in front of her to do anything other than what she wanted.

She smiled at Myrtle. 'Very well. I'll make enquiries. Luckily you've already studied human biology and your exam result was excellent. I think that's one of the subjects you might need. I'll let you know what I find out, Myrtle.'

As she left the office, Myrtle breathed a sigh of relief. The interview hadn't been as difficult as she'd imagined. She'd fully expected the headmistress to be angry with her for forgoing the chance of going to university.

Celia Cartwright sat at her desk deep in thought. She was remembering her own struggle, but never for one moment had she regretted her decision. And Myrtle Sylvester would succeed at whatever she decided to do. In her mind's eye, Celia could visualize a much older Myrtle, walking the corridors of the city hospital dressed in a matron's uniform. And slowly the headmistress smiled.

Forty-Eight

The family settled back into a routine, but it was not the same as it had been before Freddie's disappearance. Peggy stayed at home to care for him and to help Grace with the housework. Now she had more determination and no longer shrank from going out with Freddie in the pram. To her surprise and delight her neighbours greeted her with friendliness and kindness. Only one or two turned their faces away with a disapproving look or crossed the street to avoid her, but Peggy held her head high and walked on proudly.

Myrtle had a new-found purpose. She now knew what she wanted to do with her life and, as far as she was concerned, all that romantic nonsense could wait. It was bad enough seeing Rose moon about the place without wanting to get involved with boyfriends herself, as some of her contemporaries were already doing. No, Myrtle had her life mapped out and nothing and no one would divert her from her chosen course. Within days she was granted an interview with the matron of the Royal Infirmary. She was accepted as a probationer nurse to start in the New Year.

'She'll end up marrying a doctor,' Grace prophesied sagely and then glanced at her daughter, 'and you, my girl, could end up married to the inspector at the tram depot, if you're not careful.'

Mary blushed and murmured, 'Oh, Mam, I don't know what you're talking about.'

In the weeks following Freddie's safe return, Laurence Bower had become a frequent visitor, always making the excuse of wanting to know how the little chap did. But it wasn't long before he tentatively invited Mary out for an evening. And there was a new light in Mary's eye and a spring in her step. She was even to be heard humming softly to herself despite the hardships the war was still bringing.

At the very end of October 1942 Grace was jubilant to read of Montgomery's triumph at El Alamein, but her delight was short-lived.

'I haven't seen Letty for a couple of days,' Mary said, as they sat down to tea. 'Has she been round, Mother?'

Grace paused and looked up, meeting Mary's questioning gaze. 'No,' she said quietly. 'I think you'd better go and see them when you've had your tea. Because the last thing she told me was that her son who's in the army —' She hesitated and Mary said, 'Walter.'

'That's right. Well, he'd written home to say that now Monty was in charge they'd soon have Rommel on the run. I just wondered – seeing as there's obviously been a big battle . . .' Her voice faded away.

'I'll go round,' Mary said and, after they'd finished eating and Myrtle and Rose had offered to do the washing up, she left to go next door.

It was some time before her knock at the Bradshaws' back door was answered. An unusually solemn-faced Sidney opened it.

'Oh, Sidney,' Mary breathed. 'Have you had bad news?'

He nodded as he opened the door wider. 'Come in, Mrs Sylvester,' he said politely. Mary shuddered. It was so unlike the merry-faced little rascal. As she stepped into the Bradshaws' living room, she saw Letty sitting in a chair by the fire with Tom opposite her. Their faces were grey with sorrow and Letty's eyes were red and swollen. Mary sat beside her and took her hand. 'Letty?' But it was Tom, his voice husky with emotion, who answered.

'It's our Walter, Mary. He's been killed at El Alamein.'

'I'm so dreadfully sorry. Is there anything I can do?'

Tom shook his head. 'Nowt, lass, but thanks for the offer. Sadly we're not alone in our loss.'

'I know,' Mary said gently, 'but that doesn't make it any easier.'

Mary stayed a while longer, trying to comfort the grieving parents, but there was nothing she could say, nothing she could do to ease their loss.

'I just hope nothing happens to the other two,' she added, when she relayed the awful news to her family. 'It's bad enough having just one member of your family in danger, but all three eldest boys – it's unbearable. She must be terrified now that something will happen to Bertie or Simon.'

'Mr Bower's got both his sons in the forces,' Grace pointed out. 'Have you asked him how they are?'

'Not lately, but I will,' Mary promised.

The next day, when she met Laurence in the canteen, Mary told him of the tragedy the Bradshaws were suffering. Laurence was quiet for a long time, gazing down into his cup of tea and not touching the slice of cake Mary had carried over to their table.

'Laurence?' Mary prompted gently.

'It's Matthew. His ship was torpedoed. I – I got a telegram this morning saying he's missing.'

'Oh, Laurence.' Mary reached out and grasped his hand across the table, not caring who saw them. 'I am so, so sorry.' She paused, then added gently, 'Shouldn't you be at home?'

Laurence shook his head firmly. 'No, I'm better at work. Keep busy, that's my motto.' He gripped her hand tightly. 'But just – just knowing you're there . . .'

When Mary told them that evening, her family was saddened by the news.

'Poor man,' Grace murmured. 'And Letty's in a dreadful state. I went round this morning, but there's nothing anyone can do.' They were all silent, thinking for once how lucky they were that they'd lost no one from their own family circle. And yet, for Peggy, there was someone missing, though she didn't know the reason why. Had he deserted her or had he been killed? The fear haunted her sleep. And now there was an additional sadness. If he was dead, Terry would never know he had a son.

'Promise me, Rose,' Mary was saying, 'if there are more air raids, that you'll go to a shelter straight away. No more heroics running through the streets.'

'I promise – as long as you'll do the same.'

Mary nodded and turned her attention to the rest of her family. 'And the same goes for the rest of you. Down the cellar immediately. No more thinking it might be a false alarm.'

Early in December Rose said, 'Right, Myrtle, are you up for it?'

Myrtle blinked and stared at her. 'Up for what?'

Rose lowered her voice. 'To have another go at finding Terry Price?'

Myrtle shrugged. 'I don't think it'll do any good but, yeah, I'll come along.'

'Right then. We'll go this afternoon. Sunday afternoon should find most folks at home.'

'We're not going back to his house, are we?'

'No. I'm going to try and find this Billy that one of those girls mentioned.'

Myrtle grinned. 'I don't reckon she meant his name to slip out. The other girl dug her in the ribs the minute she'd said it. Did you see?'

Rose grinned. 'All the more reason why we should look him up.'

'He might be away in the forces.'

'True. But if Billy's parents are at home, they should have an idea where their son is and, if the two lads are good mates, they could know where Terry is an' all.'

They set off after dinner. 'Let's walk,' Rose said, 'I'm sick of riding on trams and you could do with the fresh air. Always with your nose in a book. I suppose it's nursing you're studying now, is it? You'll get round-shouldered if you don't watch out.'

But Myrtle only smiled.

It was a long way to the part of the city where Terry lived, but the two sisters chatted as they walked.

'So you and Bob are courting now, are you?'

'Looks like it,' Rose said happily.

'You don't mind having your sister's cast-off, then?' Myrtle said slyly. For a moment Rose almost snapped back at the younger girl's barb, but then, ruefully, she realized the words were true. Seriously she said, 'I've loved him for so long, Myrtle, even when he was going out with Peggy – or rather we thought he was going out with her. Of course, I kept quiet about it then, but, no, I don't really mind that much.' She laughed wryly. 'I've no pride when it comes to Bob Deeton, I'm afraid.'

'Does he still love her?'

'By 'eck, you don't mince your words, do you?' She was thoughtful for a moment before she said carefully, 'He did love her once, but I don't think he does now. I think what she did killed it.'

'Running off with another man and having his bairn, you mean? But he offered to marry her.'

'I know and he regrets that now.'

Myrtle snorted. 'Good job she didn't say "yes" then, wasn't it, for everybody's sake.'

Soberly, Rose said, 'Yes, it was.'

As they came to the end of the street where Terry and his family and his mate, Billy, lived, they paused.

Myrtle's final words on the subject were, 'Well, if you get yourself pregnant, just remember I could do with the practice.'

'Ta, very much, I'm sure,' Rose murmured, but her mind was now on how they could find Billy.

The street was deserted. Not a soul was out for a stroll and, of course, on a Sunday, there were no women cleaning their front-door steps.

'What do we do?' Myrtle asked. 'Knock on doors?'

'It looks like we'll have to. Come on.' She marched towards the house on the corner and rapped smartly on the door. No one answered, so she tried at the house next door. A small child opened the door and peered up at her with wide eyes.

'Hello, love. Is your mam or dad in?'

The child didn't answer, but merely stuck her thumb in her mouth and continued to stare at them.

'All right, love, we'll try next door.'

'I reckon we're on the proverbial wild goose chase,' Myrtle muttered as they knocked at the third house.

This time a tousled-haired girl of about fifteen opened the door, blinking at them as if she'd just got out of bed and the bright light was hurting her eyes. Maybe she had just got up, Rose thought.

'Sorry to bother you, but do you know where a lad called Billy lives?'

The girl yawned and stretched and Rose noticed now that she was still wearing her nightdress. 'Billy Parkin? Yeah, two doors down on this side. Number forty-six. He's not there, though. He's in the army.'

'Do his parents live there?'

'Just his dad. His mam died before the war started.'

'Will Mr Parkin be at home, d'you think?'

The girl shrugged. 'Probably, but he won't like having his Sunday afternoon nap disturbed. You'd do better to come back in about an hour. The fellers all like their Sunday naps.' She smiled and jerked her head backwards, indicating the interior of her own home. 'My dad's snoring his head off in the front room.'

As the girl closed the door, Myrtle said, 'What shall we do for an hour?'

'Go back to that church we passed. We can sit down. There'll be no one there now.'

They walked back the way they had come and entered the cool interior of the church, where they sat down with a sigh.

'Looks like this place got bombed, too,' Myrtle remarked as they noticed scaffolding down one side of the church and a tarpaulin covering a gaping hole in the roof. Then her attention turned back to her own discomfort. 'My feet are killing me. How you stand up all day on the trams, I don't know, Rose.'

'You get used to it. And you'll be on your feet a lot when you start nursing.'

The time dragged. They talked a little more and then fell silent, gazing round at the stained-glass windows and the plaques on the walls.

'D'you think Peggy will have Freddie christened?'

Rose grimaced. 'She's not mentioned it and some vicars are funny about baptizing an illegitimate child.'

Myrtle snorted derisively and the noise echoed round the church, making them both fall into fits of laughter. When she'd wiped the tears of mirth from her eyes, Myrtle said, 'That's a bit unfair, taking it out on the innocent child. It wasn't his fault, was it?'

'No, it wasn't. So, let's see if we can find out where Freddie's father is. It must be nearly an hour since we came in here. Let's go.'

They retraced their steps back to the street and knocked on the door where Billy Parkin lived.

It was answered after a few moments by a big man, dressed in his vest and with his braces dangling down.

'Hello, lasses, and to what do I owe this pleasure? Am I still asleep and dreamin'?'

Rose smiled and Myrtle giggled.

'Is this where Billy Parkin lives?'

The man's round face beamed. 'It is, lass, and isn't he the lucky one having two pretty lasses after him.'

'Actually,' Myrtle said, 'it's his mate, Terry Price, we're looking for.'

A deep chuckle rumbled in his cavernous chest. 'Aw, now that's a pity. And there I was wonderin' if I was about to meet my future daughter-in-law.' He gave an exaggerated sigh, but opened his door wider, inviting them to step inside.

'I was just about to mek a cuppa. Would you girls like one?'

'Oooh, yes please,' they both answered in unison. For once Myrtle didn't snigger at the traditional offer. The tea, when it came, was strong with a little milk but no sugar, and the girls drank it gratefully. It had been a long walk and a long wait.

They sat around Charlie Parkin's kitchen table. 'Billy's not here, I'm afraid.' His merry face suddenly fell into lines of sadness and for a moment both girls held their breath. Had they unwittingly stumbled into the man's grief? Had Billy been injured – or worse? At his next words, they breathed a sigh of relief. 'He's away in the army.'

'Is he – all right?' Rose asked, still tentative.

The man wrinkled his forehead. 'Far as I know. I get a letter about once a week. Obviously, he was all right when he wrote it, but they take a while to come through and – who knows?'

'I'm sorry,' Rose said sympathetically. He was such a nice man, she didn't want to be the cause of reminding him of an ever-present anxiety. But Charlie Parkin was smiling again. 'So what brings you looking for Terry?'

The two sisters glanced at each other before Rose took a deep breath. They'd talked about what to say, should they be asked this question. They would tell the truth – all of it. There were enough people now who knew that Peggy had had a baby and they'd told Terry's sister on their previous visit. No doubt his mam and dad knew too by now.

'Before he went away, he was seeing our sister,

Peggy. But he's never written to her.' She shrugged. 'Maybe he doesn't want to see her any more and if that's the case, then she'll have to live with it. We called at his house a few weeks back. But they'd not heard from him either. At least, that's what they told us.' A note of scepticism crept into her tone.

'We didn't want to go back there again,' Myrtle said. 'We saw his sister and another girl and they weren't – well – what you'd call friendly. They didn't even seem to know if he was all right.'

'But our Peggy wants to write to him,' Rose put in. 'There's something he ought to know.'

Charlie raised his eyebrows, his mind working quickly. He'd been around long enough to guess what that sort of phrase meant. He was just grateful it wasn't his Billy these two lasses were seeking. 'I – see,' he said slowly and in a tone that told the girls he knew exactly what they were implying. The big man sighed. 'Aye well, these things happen, love. I expect she's in the family way, is she?'

Rose nodded. 'She's had the baby. He's a beautiful boy and, even if it's over between them, we think Terry has a right to know.'

'You want him to contribute to his keep, I suppose.'

Rose bristled visibly. 'Certainly not. That's not why we're trying to track him down, I promise you. No, there's plenty of us to take care of our little man. We all love him. Gran, Mother and we three sisters. We'll look after him and – as far as we're able – he'll want for nothing. But—' Here she paused and put her head on one side as she regarded Charlie steadily. 'We feel that any man has the right to know that he has fathered a child – especially,' she added, slyly appealing to a man's ego, 'a son.'

'We realize,' Myrtle said, 'that the reason he hasn't written to her is most probably because he wants to end it, but we still feel—'

To her surprise Charlie raised his hand to stop whatever she had been going to say, 'That might not be the case, lass. I don't want to raise your hopes, mind you, 'cos you could be right. Terry's a good-looking lad, but you see the reason he hasn't written to your sister – or to anyone for that matter – is because the lad never learned to read or write.'

Forty-Nine

Rose and Myrtle felt they had been knocked down with the proverbial feather. They stared at Charlie, glanced with shocked faces at each other and then looked back at him once more.

'Never—' Myrtle began, appalled to think that in 1942 there were still grown people who could not read or write. Rose put her hand warningly on Myrtle's arm and the girl fell silent.

Charlie sighed and explained. 'He found it very difficult. Our Billy used to help him get by as best he could, and the school never bothered with him. They treated him as a dunce and he was – is, God willing – anything but. He's a bright lad. Strangely, he's very good with figures and with his hands. He'd make a good mechanic or an engineer, but if you can't read or write . . .' Charlie spread his hands in a helpless gesture.

'How did he get in the army?' Rose asked. 'Don't they have to be able to read and write for that?'

'They probably weren't too fussy when the war was starting. Glad of anyone who volunteered and there's always mates to help you out. He was maybe able to hide it – just like he did at school. And besides,' he added sarcastically, 'you don't have to be able to read to be able to shoot straight.'

'But didn't he have a job after leaving school and before going into the army?' Myrtle asked tentatively.

She couldn't begin to understand how it must feel not to be able to read.

'Him and Billy got a job together working on a building site. Billy helped him out.'

'But now,' Rose said slowly, 'he hasn't got Billy with him to read or write letters for him.'

Charlie shook his head sadly. 'They volunteered together – hoped to stay together – but it doesn't work like that now. In the last war there were so many pals' battalions – you know when relatives and friends all joined up together, stayed together and died together – that I think this time the authorities don't want that happening again, where communities lose a whole lot of lads together. It's not exactly good for morale,' the man added bitterly.

'So his sister and that other girl were probably telling the truth when they said they hadn't heard anything from him,' Rose said. 'They didn't even know if he – if he was all right.'

'These days,' Charlie said, 'no news is good news, as they say. You did know they're abroad, him and Billy?'

Both girls shook their heads.

'Oh aye, been gone just over a year. North Africa, they've been, though they're not together. Billy said in his last letter that he hadn't seen or heard anything of Terry. It was worrying him, I could tell. And of course they can't get back to England on leave, probably not until the Company they're in is shipped home. At least, that's what I've heard said.' He paused and bit his lip, deliberating whether to tell these girls any more. He didn't know who they were. He only had their word for it that it was the truth they were telling. He decided to take the risk. 'There is just one thing that perhaps you ought to know. The other girl you saw that day, it was likely Sylvia Thomas from next door. She and Amy Price are best friends. And – ' he paused and took a deep breath before adding – 'there's always been a sort of understanding between the families that one day Terry and Sylvia might – well, you know what I'm saying.'

'Yes, we do,' Rose said bitterly. 'It's just a pity our Peggy didn't know that before she agreed to go out with him.'

'Like I say, maybe it's more to do with what the families'd like rather than . . .' His voice petered away, but then he added more strongly, 'Terry's not a bad lad. I don't reckon he'd lead a girl on if he wasn't truly fond of her.'

'I hope it was a whole lot more than "fond" of Peggy, Mr Parkin,' Rose said firmly. 'Our sister fell hook, line and sinker for him. She hurt a really nice lad to take up with Terry Price and she'd never have let him – well, you know – if she hadn't been in love with him. She's not that sort of girl. None of us are.'

Charlie gazed at her, seeing the bright spots of colour in her cheeks, the glitter of battle in her eyes. She was a feisty one and he admired that way she was sticking up for her sister – the way they both were. Slowly he nodded. 'I believe you, lass. I believe you.'

'He seemed to believe us, but did you reckon he was telling us the truth?' Myrtle asked as they walked home. There was a note of scepticism in her tone.

'What? About Terry not being able to read or write? Yes, I think I did. There was a girl in my class at school and she used to get into such trouble. The teachers called her idle, lazy – you name it, they called her it.

And all the other kids used to laugh at her, but I tried to help her. I felt sorry for her. She used to say all the letters got jumbled up. She could manage to read a bit. Signposts and short sentences, but when it came to reading long paragraphs she just got lost. Maybe it was like that for Terry.'

'And what about this Sylvia?'

'If it's true, then that would explain why those two girls were so – so frosty.'

'But do you think they are engaged? That he was just having a fling with our Peggy?'

'I don't know, Myrtle, any more than you do.' Rose was becoming impatient now. 'How could I? Come on, let's get home.'

'But what are we going to tell Peggy?'

'Nothing. Absolutely nothing.'

'Not even about him not being able to write, because that explains—'

'It explains nothing. Even if he can't write himself, if he'd wanted to be in touch with her he'd have got someone to do it for him.'

'Maybe he's too proud to ask anyone else now Billy's not with him. I know I'd be mortified if I couldn't read or write. I wouldn't want *anyone* to know. For once, I sympathize with Terry.' Myrtle, whose whole life until now had been immersed in studying, couldn't imagine anything worse.

'You could be right, but I still don't think we should tell Peggy. It might raise her hopes. She's getting on nicely now. We don't want to upset her again.'

'What about Mam and Gran? Do we say anything to them?'

'Not at the moment. We'll just see what else we can find out.'

'But how?'

To that Rose had no answer.

As Charlie Parkin closed the door after his departing visitors, he was thoughtful. He was friendly with both the Prices and the Thomases. Harry and Percy were his drinking buddies, but now he was faced with a dilemma. Did they know about this lass that Terry had got into trouble? He didn't know if he should say anything to them. Harry Price had never said a word, but then perhaps he wouldn't. Charlie mulled over the problem for the rest of the day and by the time he went to bed that night, he'd decided to wait until he wrote to Billy again. He'd tell his son what had happened. Billy would know what to do for the best.

But as Charlie slept soundly that night, a telegram was already being drafted to arrive at his house early the next morning with the worst possible news. The loss of his only son would drive all thoughts of Peggy and her baby out of Charlie Parkin's mind for weeks to come.

Fifty

Peggy was indeed much better. Now she took on most of the housework, though Grace still liked to do the cooking.

'I'm not taking to my chair with a rug over my knees quite yet,' she said tartly.

But she was willing to pass on her cookery skills to her granddaughter. 'Your mam never had the time to learn. Always had to be out earning money for all of us.' She sniffed, thinking about her son-in-law. She was not one to speak ill of the dead and it was obvious he had been poorly, but she sometimes questioned silently whether if he'd stirred himself a bit and not sunk into self-pity he could have found work back at the bank. Her own husband would have helped him, she knew. Ted had been content to sit by the fire, being the wounded war veteran and letting others take care of everything, but he hadn't been too badly wounded to bring three daughters into the world, Grace thought sourly.

'You're getting quite a dab hand at pastry,' Grace told Peggy and the young woman turned pink with pleasure. Her grandmother didn't hand out compliments very often and praise from her was rare.

They were all able to sit down together to the evening meal, but just before Peggy was ready to serve, Mary said hesitantly, 'I hope you don't mind, but I've asked Mr Bower to tea with us. I – I should have mentioned it before, but ... Is there enough to go round?'

'I've made a meat and potato pie, Mam. If we all have a slightly smaller piece, it'll stretch.'

Grace muttered something under her breath that Mary took to be disapproval. 'It's all right,' she said hastily. 'We'll go out.'

'There's no need to do that,' Rose said quickly. 'We all like Mr Bower, he's been good to this family. If it hadn't been for him . . .' She said no more but they all knew what she meant. If it hadn't been for Mr Bower's alertness, they might never have found Freddie. Alice could have taken him to her sister-in-law's and they'd never have seen him again. 'And besides, after what you told us about his son being missing, the poor man probably needs a bit of company.'

But even Grace was smiling when, on his arrival, Laurence handed over his weekly ration of meat. 'I'm not much of a cook,' he said. 'It'd be better in your hands.'

'Then you must come for tea again, Mr Bower,' Grace said graciously, almost pouncing on the parcel. She and Peggy were clever with the cooking and never wasted so much as a scrap of food, but with a household of five mouths and a baby to feed, rations sometimes didn't stretch to cover a full week.

As he sat down, Laurence glanced around the table, his gaze coming to rest on Mary sitting next to him. 'I've had some very good news. Matthew is safe. There were several survivors from his ship and they were all picked up.'

There were cries of joy from all the family and beneath the table Mary squeezed his hand.

After the meal Myrtle volunteered to help Peggy wash

up. Mary and Laurence decided to go to the cinema, and Rose, they could all see, was itching to visit Bob.

He opened the door to her himself. 'Mam's next door playing whist. We've the place to ourselves.'

As he led the way into the front room, she noticed that he wasn't limping so much. 'Is your leg getting better?' she asked as she removed her coat and sat down on the sofa. She waited for the answer with mixed feelings.

Bob sighed. 'Yes, it is and I've had a letter telling me to report for a medical check next week.' He looked at her with soulful eyes. 'They'll send me back, Rose, if they think I'm fit enough.'

Rose felt a stab of fear run through her. 'Then you'll have to limp more.'

He grinned ruefully. 'It's no good trying to shirk it, love. If they spotted I was malingering, the penalties are severe and – not very nice.'

'Oh. So you'd sooner go back to the front to be shot at, would you?'

A dark shadow crossed his eyes and Rose regretted her hasty retort. 'I'm sorry, I didn't mean that the way it sounded. I just want you here at home – safe.'

'It's what everyone wants, Rose, but it can't be, not until we've won.'

'And are we going to win?' she asked softly.

'Don't you ever doubt it for a minute.'

And strangely Rose didn't. Whilst there were men like her Bob – and yes, she could call him her Bob now – she didn't have any doubt that eventually the war would be won. The only worry was – how many would lose their lives in the process?

*

The following week Bob came back from his medical inspection with a glum face. 'I've to report back for duty on Monday,' he said. 'Fancy, only a week to go to Christmas and I have to go back.'

Rose nodded. She'd been expecting the news. 'Will they send you abroad straight away?'

'Not sure,' Bob said. 'I've tried to keep up with the news in the papers, but—'. He pulled a wry face. 'It's very different when you're involved. There's a lot that's top secret that's never going to reach the press.'

'Don't tell Gran that,' Rose laughed. 'She thinks the newspapers are gospel.'

'Can you come round for your tea on Sunday night? Mam's going to church and then she'll go to Ada's – her friend next door.'

'Not to play whist on a Sunday,' Rose said, pretending to be shocked.

'No – no. They sit and listen to Vera Lynn. So, will you come?'

'Of course I will.'

After tea, when they'd done the washing up and Mrs Deeton had hurried off to church, Bob turned the lights off in the front room and they settled on the sofa in front of the fire. The soft, flickering light gave the room a warm, cosy glow and the war seemed very far away. And yet they couldn't forget it for long. In only twelve hours' time Bob would be on his way back to camp and to the war.

'We didn't ought to be using your mam's precious coal,' Rose murmured, feeling drowsy and content with Bob snuggled close, his arms wrapped around her.

Bob kissed her, his hands caressed her and she felt

her love for him overflow. At last Bob loved her and she'd make him forget Peggy.

'Rose – please – I might never come back,' he murmured against her lips. 'You say you love me, then show me. Let me make love to you.' His fingers trembled as he tried to undo the buttons on her blouse. 'Please, Rose.'

Rose stiffened and drew back, staring into his eyes reproachfully. In the firelight they were dark with longing. 'You know I love you, Bob. I loved you even when you had eyes for no one but Peggy . . .'

'That was a mistake. It's you I love.'

'Then if you do, you should respect my feelings, respect *me*.'

He drew away and slumped in the corner of the sofa, covering his face with his hands. 'I'm not good enough for you. Just a tram driver turned squaddie. You deserve someone better.'

She pulled his hands away and made him look at her. 'Now you're being an idiot. It's just that I don't want to end up like Peggy. Giving herself to a soldier and then him disappearing and her left with a kid and having to bear all the gossip and the disapproving looks.' Her voice dropped to a whisper as, ashamed of her actions now, she added, 'Even from her own sisters.'

'But I promise I'd be careful.'

'I bet that's what *he* said. But he wasn't, was he? Left her pregnant and then went off to war without another word. Besides – ' Rose bit her lip, torn between wanting to love him, wanting to give herself to him and the silent vow she'd made – 'I want to keep myself for my wedding night. I only want to go to bed with one man in my life – my husband.'

He stared at her. 'That's emotional blackmail. Holding out on me so that I'll marry you.'

She gasped, appalled that he could say such a thing – could even think it.

'Bob, that's a cruel thing to say.'

He groaned and covered his face with his hands again. 'I'm sorry – I'm sorry, Rose. But I'm so bloody scared. If only I hadn't been so stupid – rushing to join up like that – I could have remained a motorman. I needn't have gone at all and now – I don't want to go back.'

'Then don't.'

This time he dropped his hands himself. 'Don't be daft. I'd be arrested for desertion. My mam'd never bear the shame. They shot lads in the last war for that, you know.'

'But not now. You wouldn't be shot.'

'No, but I'd be slung in jail and branded a coward. Is that the sort of man you'd want to marry?'

Rose bit her lip. If she was honest, no, it wasn't. The men at work, who were of the right age for war service, were having to stand all sorts of snide remarks and innuendoes even though they were employed in a legitimately reserved occupation. She could see now that there was no way out, no alternative: Bob had to go back.

But still she couldn't bring herself to give way to him. The image of Peggy's expanding girth when she'd been expecting Freddie, the way most of her own family had – for a time – turned their back on her and the way she hadn't been able to venture out, to live a normal life, made Rose stand firm. 'I'm sorry, Bob. I want you more than you could realize, but I – can't.'

'Then let's get married – right away.'

'But you said just now—'

'Never mind what I said just now. Please, Rose, marry me. I want to think there's someone waiting for me. And I want to – to know what's it's like to – you know.'

In the half-light Rose blushed, but she snuggled closer, sure now that he wouldn't misinterpret her loving action. 'You do understand, don't you?'

He sighed heavily. 'Yeah, I suppose so.' There was silence between them before he said, 'So, Rose Sylvester, will you marry me? Please.'

'Yes, Bob Deeton, I will.'

They hugged each other and kissed and whilst passion flared between them once more, now he made no effort to go further than Rose wanted.

'When I get back tomorrow, I'll see my commanding officer and ask for compassionate leave to get married. Lads are doing it all the time and with me just back from sick leave, I don't reckon they'll send me straight back abroad. And in the meantime you apply for a special licence and, when you let me know that you've got it, we'll set a date.'

'Oh, Bob. Do you mean it? Do you *really* mean it?'

'Of course I do, and Mam'll be thrilled. She really likes you better than—'

Rose put her finger over his lips and whispered, 'We're not going to talk about that ever again. From this moment on she's your sister-in-law, nothing more. Got it?'

Bob grinned and some of the fear and foreboding left his face. 'Got it,' he promised and kissed her again.

Fifty-One

To Rose's disappointment, the whole family was in bed by the time she arrived home; even Myrtle was snoring softly when she crept into the bedroom. She'd hoped to make her startling announcement at once, but now it would have to wait until tomorrow. But at breakfast everyone would be rushing to get to work or to feed a hungry baby. No one would have time to listen to Rose's plans. The girl lay awake through the night, torn with mixed emotions. Had she really, as he'd said, blackmailed Bob into proposing to her? Had she been wrong to hold out against him? Should she have given way to him? Let him make love to her before he went to war again? She tossed and turned through the night, first berating herself for being such a prude, and then realizing that, no, she'd been right. What if she'd given in and Bob had been sent abroad the minute he returned to duty? They'd not have had time to marry – still might not have – and she might have been left in just the same predicament as Peggy. No, no, she argued with herself, she'd been right. And yet for the very first time she knew why Peggy had given way to her hand-some soldier. She'd seen for herself the adoration they'd had for each other in their eyes. And now she knew how that passion could be overwhelming, making the strongest person lose their way.

Peggy's tragedy was not that she'd given herself to

Terry, or even that she'd had Freddie, it was that Terry had disappeared without a trace, leaving her desolate and alone. At last Rose turned onto her side, her mind at peace now, knowing that, at least for her, she'd been right. At last she slept.

They'd decided that Rose wouldn't go to the station to see Bob off. He'd laughed ruefully as he'd said, 'I really might not go then. Besides, you have to get to work.'

With great forbearance, Rose decided to keep her secret to herself until the evening, but her moment was spoilt by Mrs Deeton, who in great excitement had come round to the house as soon as Bob had left. By the time she arrived Mary and Rose had already left for work and Myrtle had gone to the city library.

Only Grace, washing up in the kitchen, and Peggy, feeding Freddie, were at home.

'Isn't it exciting news?' Mrs Deeton said, as she sat down by the range and pulled off her gloves.

'Is it?' Grace said, as she came in from the kitchen, drying her hands on a towel. 'What's happened? Is the war over?'

'Sadly, no,' said Mrs Deeton, her smile fading for a moment as she relived the parting with her son only an hour or so ago. 'No – about Bob and Rose, I mean.'

'Oh, that!' Grace said and sat down with a sigh.

'Aren't you thrilled? A wartime wedding! It'll help lift everybody's spirits.'

'What!' Grace exclaimed and Peggy looked up, inadvertently pulling the bottle out of Freddie's mouth and making him whimper. With a hand that shook slightly, she placed the bottle on the table, put the baby over her shoulder and patted his back. Freddie burped obligingly, happily oblivious to the tension in the room.

'What on earth are you talking about, Mrs Deeton?' Grace snapped.

'They're getting married. Bob asked her last night and he's going to see his commanding officer when he gets back and —' the woman babbled on, revealing all the young couple's plans before Rose had had a chance to tell her family.

'I see,' Grace said grimly. 'She might have told us herself.'

'She hasn't had a moment, Gran,' Peggy put in softly. She turned and smiled at Hester. 'She was late in last night and it's chaos here every morning when they're all getting ready to leave. I expect she's planning to tell us tonight.'

'Oh dear, I am sorry. I've spoilt the surprise.'

'Well, we're delighted for them both,' Peggy smiled and added pointedly, 'Aren't we, Gran?'

Grace shot her a look and murmured, 'If you say so.'

For a moment Hester looked perplexed, seeming to remember suddenly that it had once been the girl sitting here with a baby against her shoulder whom her son had been so keen to marry. Hester's face turned pink with embarrassment and tears filled her eyes. 'I was so excited – so sure she'd have told you. I'm so sorry.'

'You're not to worry. In fact, we could make out we don't know, couldn't we, Gran? Act all surprised when she tells us. And Freddie won't tell her, will you, my pet?' Peggy brought him down from her shoulder and settled him in her lap.

The child gurgled happily in response and beamed at Hester.

'Oh, if you could, I would be grateful. It's only right that she should be the one to tell you all.'

'And we won't say a word to Mam or Myrtle, so the surprise will be genuine for them, won't it, Gran?'

'If you say so, Peggy,' was all Grace said again.

It was all Peggy could do to keep Grace from blurting out the news their early morning visitor had brought. As they all sat round the tea table, she was almost holding her breath and willing her sister to make the announcement so that she could breathe easily. But Rose, it seemed was in no hurry; she was waiting for the right moment.

'No Mr Bower to tea tonight?' Rose asked impertinently, her eyes twinkling.

Mary blushed. 'We're just good friends, Rose, so don't you go reading more into his visits than there is.'

'No sound of wedding bells then?' Rose persisted.

'Certainly not,' Mary said sharply, but the colour in her face deepened.

'Well,' Rose said quietly, 'that's where you're wrong because there are going to be wedding bells.'

They all stared at her. Only Grace kept her head down and continued to eat her tea, ignoring the conversation going on about her head. Peggy, keeping up the pretence, asked, 'What on earth are you talking about, our Rose? You don't mean that Mr Bower is getting married, do you?' She glanced surreptitiously and saw, to her amusement, that the colour had now drained quickly from Mary's face as she stared at Rose.

'Don't be daft. He's only got eyes for our mam. No, it's me and Bob. He asked me last night and I said yes.'

She hurried on, telling them all of the plans they'd made.

'Rushed, that's what it'll be. Folk'll think you're in the family way,' Grace muttered and cast Peggy a hard look.

'Well, they'll know different when there's no baby in a few months' time, won't they?' Rose snapped. 'I thought you'd be pleased for me.'

'We are.' Peggy touched Rose's hand. 'You're perfect for each other. And no, that's not what folk'll think because there's dozens of couples getting wed before their menfolk have to go away. I hope it works out and Bob gets the leave. Now we'll have to think what you can wear as a wedding dress.'

'I'm not going mad. We want to get married in church, though – Mrs Deeton's a big churchgoer, you know.'

'What about bridesmaids and the best man?' Peggy asked. She'd given up hope now that Terry would ever come back and she knew her own hopes of marriage were pretty thin. Who would want to take on a woman with a child – and a child born out of wedlock at that? Besides, sadly, very soon there would be a shortage of young men and many a girl would be left an old maid. And so Peggy determined to help her sister have the best wedding that they could afford and that could be got ready in time.

'I'm to see the vicar and do all that's needed to get a special licence, Bob said, and then write and let him know.'

'Will they give him leave?'

'He's sure so.'

'That's if they haven't sent him abroad again before you can get it all organized,' Grace said, sounding a note of caution to the building excitement. 'But I've no doubt his mam'll be pleased,' she murmured and avoided meeting Peggy's warning look. But she didn't give the game away that she and Peggy already knew.

It was Myrtle who had the last word. 'I'll be bridesmaid and Freddie must be a little page boy. He'll look so sweet.'

Fifty-Two

Christmas was almost overshadowed by the talk of wedding plans, which dominated the conversation now. They spent the day quietly.

'1942's nearly over and still there's no end to the war in sight,' Grace commented.

'Forget about the war just for a day, Mother. And then we've the wedding to look forward to. Life has to go on.'

Laurence and Hester joined the family, but this year, sadly, the Bradshaws felt unable to celebrate.

'Letty ought to make an effort for the two young 'uns,' Grace said. 'Still, it's not my business.' But Mary noticed that, sitting on their sideboards, were two unusually large gifts wrapped in last year's Christmas paper and labelled to Sidney and Jimmy.

The arrangements for Rose's wedding were made swiftly and surprisingly smoothly.

'Well, I'm certainly not short of things that are "borrowed",' Rose laughed. 'Bob will be in his army uniform, of course, but I didn't fancy getting married dressed as a clippie, so Louise from work is lending me her wedding dress and her veil. It's from just before the war and it fits perfectly – surprisingly.'

'You've lost weight since the war started, Rose,' Peggy teased her. 'You'll soon weigh less than me. By the way, I'll give you clothing coupons for a wedding present. You could get some white shoes and dye them afterwards in a more serviceable colour.' Nothing these days could be wasted. Peggy chuckled as she added, 'And you won't get away from the trams altogether. Some of the girls are planning to meet you outside the church and make an archway of ticket machines.'

Rose laughed. She didn't mind what anyone did as long as Bob turned up on the day.

'Letty is insisting she'll make the wedding cake.' Grace pulled a face. 'Though what it'll taste like, I daren't think.'

'Let her do it, Gran,' Rose said. 'It might help take her mind off things.'

'And Laurence is seeing a friend of his, who's a greengrocer. Flowers are in short supply, but he reckons he can make you a little posy.'

'What about me?' Myrtle piped up. 'I need a dress and a bouquet.'

'I've got length of blue satin material upstairs,' Grace murmured. 'I bought it in a sale just before the war.' She glanced at Mary. 'You can have that for Myrtle.'

'Thank you, Mother. I'll sort out a pattern and get sewing.'

'Folks are being very kind,' Grace said, unable to keep the surprise from her tone. 'One or two of the neighbours have already brought tins of fruit round.'

'What are we doing about a wedding breakfast?'

'Ham and potatoes and whatever vegetables we can get.' She glanced at Rose. 'You might have waited until summer, instead of February, then we could have had a nice salad.'

'Sorry, Gran,' Rose said cheerfully.

'What about pudding?' Myrtle, who always seemed to be hungry these days, asked.

'Tinned fruit and blancmange.'

'And cake. Don't forget Letty's cake.'

'As if we could,' Grace muttered.

But Letty's cake, when she brought it round in the evening before the wedding, was a triumph. 'It's not very big, Mary, but Mrs Booth said there wouldn't be many guests.'

'Oh, Letty, it's wonderful. However did you manage to make a fruit cake with all the rationing?'

'Begged and borrowed – but I didn't steal.' Letty smiled. It was the first time she'd felt like smiling again since they'd had the dreadful news about Walter. But life had to go on, Tom had told her. Despite the empty, hollow feeling in her stomach, Letty was doing her best. Concentrating on making Rose's wedding cake had certainly helped. 'The neighbours have been really good giving me fruit and sugar and eggs. Real eggs came from Mr Bower's brother. Did you know?'

Mary blushed a little to think that Laurence had been doing so much, even behind the scenes.

Saturday, 13 February 1943, dawned bright and amazingly warm for the time of year.

'Are you superstitious about the thirteenth?' Myrtle asked, as she helped secure Rose's veil.

'Not a bit.' Rose laughed. 'Though I might have hesitated if today had been a Friday. There, how do I look?'

'Surprisingly pretty,' Myrtle said, but she was laughing as she said it.

'Thanks, Myrtle. I can always rely on you to be scrupulously honest.' In truth, she was flattered by her younger sister's remark. Myrtle always told the truth.

The service was held in the church Hester attended regularly. The Booth family were not regular church-goers and Rose had known it would mean a great deal to her future mother-in-law if her son was married there. Afterwards all the guests travelled back to Grace's home. The front room had been opened up and a warm fire burned in the grate. The 'best' gate-legged table had been opened up and, with the table from the living room put next to it, everyone could just fit in. A long, white tablecloth covered the two tables, set with china and glassware borrowed from Letty and Laurence. Every piece of furniture had been polished until it shone, though there was no hiding the tell-tale sooty marks on the wallpaper, nor the absence of Grace's china cabinet and its contents.

'I'm sorry,' she apologized to all their guests, 'but Hitler smashed my best china tea set. I'd've used it today for Rose but – it wasn't to be.'

Rose was the picture of happiness and Bob looked proud and happy. There was a moment's awkwardness when he and Peggy came face to face outside the church, but she smiled and kissed his cheek, greeting him with the words, 'Hello – brother-in-law.' She'd taken the sting out of the moment and neatly reminded him of their new relationship.

'And how are you enjoying being a nurse, Myrtle?' Laurence asked the girl sitting next to him at the table.

When she turned to him, her eyes were shining. 'It's wonderful, Mr Bower. It'll be quite some time before I am a proper nurse, but I know I'm going to love it.'

'I thought I might have had another member of your

family as a clippie.' Laurence laughed. 'But I'm really pleased you've found your vocation, for that's what it is.'

'I know,' Myrtle said seriously. 'I was a bit worried that Mam and the others would be disappointed that I haven't gone to university.'

'They're very proud of you, my dear, no matter what you choose to do.'

'Thank you, Mr Bower.' Myrtle beamed at him.

Bob and Rose left in a flurry of good wishes. They travelled the short distance from the city into the Derbyshire Dales, where they had a blissful three days' holiday. Then it was time for Bob to return to camp.

'Do you know for definite what's happening?' Rose shivered, as she clung to him on the draughty railway station platform.

Bob shook his head. 'I may not be sent abroad yet, love, especially as I'm only just back from a long sick leave.'

'I understand why you've had to go back – really I do. But just limp a bit now and again.'

'Actually, I do get a bit of pain in my leg occasionally.'

'Then mind you tell the medical officer.'

'I'll see. I don't want to be thought a shirker.'

'No one will think that. Oh no, there's the whistle.' She kissed him hard on the mouth and hugged him tight.

'Rose – darling – I must go.' He prised himself free, picked up his kitbag and ran for the train, climbing aboard just as the doors were slammed and then it began to move. He leaned out of the window waving.

Rose stood with all the other people on the platform waving goodbye, her hand on her mouth, which still stung from the ardour of his kisses.

'That's the first time he's ever called me "darling",' she whispered.

Fifty-Three

'Are you going to live with Mrs Deeton then?' Grace asked when Rose returned home, trying hard to stem the flow of tears. She was missing him already and, with no idea of when she might see him again, the days ahead looked bleak. She comforted herself with the knowledge that at least she'd get letters from him. That was more than Peggy ever got.

Rose blinked and glanced at Grace. 'Eh?'

'I thought you'd be setting up home with Mrs Deeton now you're married. There's no room for the two of you here.'

'I – hadn't really thought about it.'

'Aye – I guessed as much. "Marry in haste . . .",' Grace said sagely, but for once had the tact not to repeat the rest of the saying.

Rose bit her lip. 'D'you want me to go? Make more room for you all?'

Grace narrowed her eyes as she looked at her. 'Not until he comes home for good. Then you'll need to get a place of your own or live with his mother.'

Rose nodded. 'Of course, Gran, but – but I don't want to live with her just now. I – I couldn't bear to leave you all.'

'Don't you mean Freddie?'

'We-ell . . .' Rose's eyes twinkled as, for the first time

since parting from Bob, the thought of her nephew made her smile.

Grace grunted. 'Looks like we're stuck with you then.'

With a sudden impulse Rose kissed the old lady's wrinkled cheek.

'Oh, get away with you, you soft 'aporth,' Grace said, but Rose could see she was touched by her granddaughter's gesture.

'But I will see his mam often, just to make sure she's not too lonely and worrying too much about him. She's a real worrier.'

Aren't we all just now? Grace thought, but said nothing.

To emphasize her gratitude, Rose said, 'You sit still tonight, Gran. I'll get the tea.'

She was just finished peeling the potatoes when she heard the front door slam and hasty footsteps in the hallway. Rose frowned, dried her hands and went through into the kitchen just as Myrtle burst in from the door to the hallway. Still panting from running home, she gasped, 'Where's Peggy?'

'Taking Freddie for a walk in the pram. Why, whatever's the matter?'

'Is Mam home?'

'Not yet, no.'

'For Heaven's sake sit down, girl, and catch your breath,' Grace said and repeated Rose's question. 'What's happened? Have you killed off half your patients?'

Myrtle sank into the chair opposite her grandmother. 'I've seen him.'

'Who?'

'Terry Price.'

Rose and Grace gaped at her.

'Are you sure it was him?' Rose said, finding her voice.

Myrtle nodded. 'He didn't see me. He was on the other side of the road.'

'Was he with anyone?' Grace asked sharply.

'Yes.' She glanced at Rose as if seeking permission.

'It's all right. You can tell Gran. We'll decide together what's to be done.'

'It was Mr Parkin. He was walking along the road with Mr Parkin.'

'Who's Mr Parkin when he's at home?'

'Gran – we've been trying to do a bit of snooping.' Rose sat down at the table. 'We went to Terry's home, but there were two girls there. We think one was his sister and the other, the girl who lives next door. Well, they were very unfriendly and unhelpful. They said they had no idea where he was – that he could be dead, for all they knew.'

'But one of them let slip about a mate of his called Billy, who lived in the same street as them.' Myrtle took up the story. 'So later on we went to see him.'

'And?'

Rose and Myrtle exchanged a glance before explaining to Grace how they'd found out the reason why Terry hadn't been writing to Peggy.

'That may be it,' Grace mused aloud. 'But you'd've thought he'd've got someone else to do it for him.'

'Didn't want folks to find out, I expect. Billy was the one who'd always helped him, but he's not with him now.'

'Mm.' Grace was thoughtful. 'Then I think,' she said slowly, 'that you'd better go and find Mr Terry Price as soon as you can. But not a word to Peggy, mind, unless there's some good news. She's just coming to terms with the thought that he's deserted her and she's beginning to look to the future. I don't want to get her hopes up for nothing. It could set her back to square one again.'

'We'll go tonight after tea.'

'I'll see to the washing up. And you could make the excuse you're going round to see Mrs Deeton, Rose. But what about you, Myrtle?'

'I've got a bit of reading to do before we have to attend some theory classes tomorrow, but I can do that in bed.'

Grace nodded.

The three of them were unusually silent over the tea table, but it didn't seem to matter. Freddie was fractious and was taking the attention of both Peggy and Mary.

'I think he must be teething. Look how red his poor cheek is.'

A little later Rose and Myrtle were able to leave the house without anyone even asking where they were going.

'Phew! That was lucky, though I wouldn't wish pain on the little man,' Rose said as they hurried up the street towards the nearest tram stop. This time they hadn't the time or the inclination to walk to the street where the Prices lived.

'D'you think we should try to see Mr Parkin first?'

'No – we're taking the bull by the horns. And if either of those two girls tells us he's not there, well, we know different now, don't we? Come on, Myrtle, best foot forward.'

When the tram pulled to a halt, they were surprised to see Laurence Bower on a seat near the rear of the car.

'This young feller's in training,' Laurence said. 'He

can't join up because of a heart condition, so I've just got to make sure he's up to this job.'

The young man was fair-haired, thin and a little pale. Rose smiled at him as Laurence made the introductions. Then the inspector asked, 'How's your mam? I haven't seen her as I've been out all day.'

'She's fine. Day off tomorrow for her.'

Laurence nodded. 'Me too. I think we're taking a trip into Derbyshire if the weather's good – though it might be a little cold.'

Rose hid her smile. No doubt Laurence Bower engineered their days off to coincide. Not that she blamed him; he was a nice man and she was delighted he and Mary were friends. Secretly, Rose hoped more would come of it.

They stepped off the tram with cheerful goodbyes to both Laurence and the trainee conductor.

'Now, which house was it?' Rose said as they entered the street.

'Number nine.'

But when they knocked at the door an older man, whom they presumed to be Terry's father, opened it.

'Is Terry at home?'

'He should be, love, but he lives next door. Not here.'

'Oh – right – thank you.'

'He's home on leave—' The man stopped as if suddenly realizing he might well be giving too much information away. 'Who wants to know?'

'We just want to see him, that's all.'

The man frowned, but there was nothing he could do about it now. He'd given the game away.

Rose and Myrtle turned away quickly, giving him no chance to ask further awkward questions. But as they knocked on the door of the neighbouring house, they saw the man was still watching them.

Amy opened the door, but when she saw who was standing there, she tried to close it again. Rose was too quick for her and put her foot in the gap. 'Oh no, you don't. Not this time. We know he's here and we mean to see him if we have to stand in the street shouting his name all night.'

'What's going on, Amy? Who is it?'

Having heard the commotion, Edith Price came to the door. She pulled the door wider and smiled uncertainly at Rose and Myrtle. 'Can I help you?'

'Are you Mrs Price?' When the woman nodded, Rose went on, 'We've come to see Terry. We believe he's home on leave.'

'Well, yes, but—'

'It's that girl, Mam,' Amy hissed. 'Don't let them in. They're threatening to make trouble.'

'Amy, what are you talking about? Oh!' As if suddenly realizing just who the girls might be, Edith's hand flew to cover her mouth. She stared at them for a moment and then her hand dropped away. She sighed heavily. 'You'd better come in.'

'Mam!' Amy protested but her mother said, 'I don't want the neighbours hearing what these lasses have to say. Better done inside. I'll call Terry down. He's just getting ready to go out.'

'With Sylvia,' Amy said pointedly as she turned away.

'Come in, both of you,' Edith said and the two girls stepped straight into the front room. Edith closed the door behind them and then led the way through to the kitchen, on the way passing the foot of the stairs. She paused briefly to shout, 'Terry, come down, will you? There's someone to see you.'

421

Fifty-Four

They stood in the kitchen, waiting awkwardly until footsteps thumped down the stairs and Terry came into the room. He stopped in surprise. 'Rose! Myrtle! Whatever are you doing here? Oh, it's not Peg, is it? Don't say something's happened to her?' He moved further into the room and, to their surprise, the concern on his face looked genuine. Before either of them could speak, Terry added, 'Is it her husband? Has he been killed?'

Rose gasped and Myrtle grasped her arm.

'Husband?' Rose snapped, recovering quickly. 'What on earth are you talking about, Terry?'

'Amy said . . .'

Over his shoulder Rose saw Amy begin to sidle from the room as if to escape.

'Where do you think you're going, Amy? Stay where you are,' Edith said sharply. 'I think you've got some explaining to do.' She turned back. 'Look, Rose is it, and—?' She looked at them expectantly.

'Myrtle.'

'Please sit down and I'll make some tea.'

Myrtle almost laughed aloud – tea again – but it would have been laughter bordering on hysteria. The moment was fraught with tension.

Again, Amy tried to leave, but her mother said her name again warningly and she remained where she was near the door, but as if ready to flee.

'I'll get Harry.' Mrs Price left the kitchen briefly and stepped into the scullery. They heard her open the back door and yell, 'Harry, come in a minute, will you?'

Through the kitchen window that looked out over the back yard Rose saw a tall, thickset man emerge from the washhouse at the bottom of the yard.

'What's to do, Ma?' he said, as he came into the kitchen wiping his hands on an oily rag. 'I was just putting the chain back on me bike. Dratted thing keeps slipping off.' He stopped as he saw they had visitors, 'How do, girls?'

'I'm making tea,' Edith said. 'There's summat going on here needs sorting. This is Rose and that's Myrtle. They've come to see our Terry.'

The man smiled and his eyes twinkled and, when he chuckled, it was a deep, infectious rumbling sound. Despite what might happen in the next few minutes, Rose couldn't help liking the man. 'Lucky Terry,' he murmured.

They waited until Edith had handed round cups of tea and sat down herself. 'Now, dears, how can we help you?'

They were friendly enough, Rose thought, but would that change rapidly in the next few minutes when they heard what she and Myrtle had to say. The sisters exchanged a glance and, with a little nod of agreement from Myrtle, Rose took a deep breath and began.

'I don't know how much you know, Mrs Price – Mr Price – but I'm going to start at the beginning. My sister, Peggy, was a clippie on the trams—'

'*Was?*' Terry repeated and now no one could miss the fear in his eyes. 'Oh, don't say—'

Edith touched his arm. 'Let her go on, love. Let's hear what they have to say.'

'On the first day of the blitz here, Peggy's tram was caught in the bombing and Terry was a passenger. He was great—' Rose believed in giving credit where it was due. The lambasting would come in a few minutes. 'He helped her get all the passengers out and took her to hospital afterwards. And then – ' her expression became more serious – 'he started calling at the house – to see how she was, he said. Then he asked her out, knowing full well she was going out with one of the drivers from work.'

'Peg said it wasn't serious. I'd never have started courting her if I'd thought for a minute she was serious about Bob. Is it him she's married?'

Rose turned to look at him, meeting his earnest gaze. He looked so honest, so sincere, for a moment she felt a quiver of doubt. There was real pain in his eyes. But then she remembered all that Peggy had suffered because of him and her resolve hardened. 'Peggy's not married to Bob – or to anyone else. She could have been, mind you, because good old Bob offered to marry her when she found she was pregnant – with *your* child.'

Both Rose and Myrtle were totally unprepared for what happened next. For a moment Terry stared at them and then the colour drained from his face and he swayed, looking as if he was going to pass out.

'Harry!' Edith said urgently. 'Help him.'

His father stood up quickly, scraping back his chair. He caught Terry by the shoulders and turned him around. 'Put your head in your knees, lad. There, that's it. You'll be all right in a minute. Pour him some more tea, Ma. Good and strong. Plenty of sugar. Lad's had a shock. As we all have,' he glanced at Rose. But there was no accusation in his tone. If anything there was sorrow.

When Terry had recovered sufficiently, the colour returning to his face, he sipped his tea, though his hands still shook. 'I didn't know. I swear I didn't know.'

Rose and Myrtle believed him. No man – unless he was an Oscar-winning actor – could have put on a display like that.

'But your sister knew,' Myrtle said softly. 'We came to see her and we told her Peggy had had your baby. We knocked on the wrong door, but she was next door with her friend Sylvia. For a start she refuted the idea that the baby was yours.'

'Oh, it's mine all right.'

Rose was impressed that he made no prevarication. He didn't even ask for dates to prove the child was his or even suggest that it could be Bob's. Her resentment against him was lessening by the minute.

Terry pulled in a deep breath and said firmly, 'Amy – come here.'

Slowly his sister came to stand beside him. He looked up at her, but rather than being angry, his voice was full of sadness when he asked, 'Why didn't you tell me what you'd heard? And why, when I came home, did you tell me you'd heard that Peggy had got married?'

Tears ran down Amy's face. 'Because the minute you got home you were all set to go and see her. To take up with her again.'

'There's no "again" about it. I never stopped loving Peg. I was devastated when you told me she was married. You know I was. I just want to know why you said that.'

'Because – because—' the girl spluttered, 'Sylvia loves

425

you. It's her you should marry. We've got it all planned. I'm going to be your bridesmaid and Billy was going to be your best man.'

Terry flinched. 'Poor old Billy isn't going to be anyone's best man, now, is he?'

Rose and Myrtle glanced at each other. 'Why? Has – has something happened to him?'

'You knew Billy?'

Rose's heart contracted. Terry was speaking in the past tense about his friend. She licked her lips. 'We met his dad when we came to try to find you. Billy was all right then.'

'He was killed just over three months ago.'

Rose gasped. 'That must have been only just after we saw his dad.'

'I saw you in town yesterday,' Myrtle put in. 'You were walking with Mr Parkin. That's how I knew you were alive and here.'

'Alive? What do you mean?'

Amy began to sidle away again, but Terry caught hold of her arm and held her fast. 'Oh no, you don't, miss. You stay here.' He looked back at Myrtle, the question in his eyes.

'Amy told us they'd heard nothing from you and that they didn't know if you were alive or – or dead.'

They saw his grip tighten and the girl squirmed. 'Ow, you're hurting me.'

'I'll hurt you, you little bugger. How could you have told such lies about me? You'll wish it on me.'

'Oh, Terry,' Edith cried. 'Don't say that.'

Harry Price frowned. 'You've got some answering to do, my girl.'

'It was for Sylvia,' Amy sobbed. 'She's loved him for years. Ever since they were little.'

'Well, I've never loved her. We've been neighbours and friends, that's all.'

'All? We used to go out as a foursome. You, Sylvia, me and Billy. I thought – we thought . . .'

'You thought wrong. You're either very silly or very evil. At this moment, I can't decide which and I have an overwhelming desire to throttle the pair of you. For God's sake, Amy, you're twenty-one. Grow up!' He thrust his face close to hers. 'Listen to me – from the minute I set eyes on Peggy there's been no one else. Got it?' Now he released his grip on the girl and almost flung her away from him. He turned back to Rose, his tone at once gentle again. 'Is Peg all right? Will she want to see me? And – and the child. What is it? Have I a son – or a daughter?'

Rose smiled, even more impressed by his eagerness. 'You have a beautiful son. He's called Freddie.'

'And Peggy? She's all right?'

'She is now. She's fine, though just after the birth she got very depressed.'

'And you think she'll see me?'

'I'm sure of it.'

Terry stood up. 'Then what are we waiting for?'

Fifty-Five

'Let us go in first, Terry, and break the news. If you just walk in, it'll be a dreadful shock.'

'All right, I'll wait outside. But don't be long – I can't wait to see her.'

Rose and Myrtle entered the house and walked into the living room. It was a peaceful scene that met their eyes. Grace was sitting in her usual chair by the fire, reading her newspaper. Mary was sitting opposite her, a pile of mending in her lap, and Peggy was giving Freddie his late-night bottle. The little chap was already falling asleep in her arms. Rose and Myrtle paused in the doorway.

'Either come in or go out,' Grace said. 'There's a draught.'

Myrtle giggled nervously. 'There'll be a draught in a minute,' she murmured.

'Shush, Myrtle,' Rose whispered and then cleared her throat and said, 'we've something to tell you.'

All eyes turned to her.

'Don't tell us,' Grace groaned. 'You're pregnant.'

'No, no, I'm not – as far as I know. But it is good news. Peggy—' She moved closer to her sister. 'There's someone outside, who's desperate to see you.'

Myrtle couldn't hold back the news any longer. 'It's Terry. He's alive and home on leave.'

The baby's bottle slipped from Peggy's grasp and she

might even have dropped Freddie if Rose hadn't taken him from her arms. He was now fast asleep, oblivious to what was happening around him. Just as Terry had done, Peggy turned pale and clutched at the table for support.

'Here? He's here? He's all right?'

'He's fine. Handsome as ever – the devil.' Rose laughed.

Peggy didn't move – she couldn't move. She just kept staring at Rose. It was Mary who laid aside her darning and got up. 'He's outside, you say. Then we'd better fetch him in. I'll go.'

A moment or two later, Terry followed Mary into the room and his gaze at once sought Peggy. 'Oh, Peg, Peg, I didn't know. I swear I didn't know.'

And then Peggy got up and they were flying into each other's arms, oblivious to anyone else in the room. He kissed her hair, her forehead and at last his lips sought her mouth. They clung to each other, swaying with overwhelming relief.

After a moment they broke apart, gazing into each other's eyes as Terry said huskily, 'Rose says I have a son.'

Happiness shone from Peggy as she nodded and turned to take the baby from Rose. Gently she placed him in Terry's eager arms. 'There you are, Freddie. Say hello to your daddy.'

It was an emotional moment for all of them. Mary was weeping openly, though they were tears of happiness, and even Grace surreptitiously wiped a tear from her eyes. Rose was tearful too and only Myrtle, grinning from ear to ear, was the one to say, 'I'll make some tea, shall I?'

*

After the rest of the family had retired to bed and Terry had put Freddie into his cot, he and Peggy talked into the early hours, stopping only every few minutes to kiss.

She told him everything that had happened and he explained why he'd never written. 'I should have let you write to me. I was such a fool. I should have swallowed my pride and got one of the other lads to read your letters for me. But, you see, I only ever trusted Billy and now he's gone.'

'I'm so sorry. He was a good friend to us both.'

'The very best.'

There was a pause before Terry said, 'We must get married right away. Before I go back.'

Peggy laughed. 'Is that a proposal, Mr Price? Because if it is, I really think you should do it properly. Nothing less than down on one knee.'

So in the early hours of the morning, in front of the dying fire, Terry got down on his knees and asked Peggy – his beloved Peggy – to marry him.

'Oh, yes, yes,' she agreed happily and flung her arms round his neck.

'I'll sort it all out in the morning. I'm sure we've time before I have to go back, though it might have to be a register-office wedding. Would you mind that?'

'Of course not,' Peggy said. 'In fact, it would be better – in the circumstances. How long have you got?'

'A couple of weeks,' he said and then hesitated before adding, 'It's what they call an embarkation leave. When I get back I'll be posted abroad again.'

Terry's news cast a shadow over their complete happiness, but they were both determined to enjoy every minute they had together.

'I don't know what Gran will say to another wedding so soon after Rose's.'

Terry raised his eyebrows. 'Rose is married?'

Peggy chuckled. 'Yes, to Bob.'

For a moment Terry was stunned, but Peggy went on to explain. 'She'd always been in love with him, but never said anything because she thought him and me – well, you know.'

'Did you ever have feelings for him? I have to know.'

Peggy shook her head vehemently. 'Only those of a dear friend, but I think he took it to mean more.'

'He was in love with you.' It was a statement rather than a question.

'He – he said so, but I'm doubtful it was real love.' She smiled. 'He soon transferred his affections to Rose – thank goodness!'

Terry held her close. 'So you're really mine.'

'Oh, yes, yes,' Peggy breathed, lifting her face to be kissed once more.

The wedding was a quiet affair: only Peggy's family, Terry's family and Charlie Parkin, who had agreed to stand in for Billy as Terry's best man. 'It's what he would have wanted me to do,' the grieving father said bravely.

'You want to go to the hotel me and Bob stayed in for our honeymoon.' Rose pulled a face. 'If you can call three days a honeymoon. But it's a lovely place. It's in Buxton. I'll give you the address.'

So whilst her family took care of Freddie, Peggy and her new husband set off for a few days' holiday in the Peak District. When they'd left, Edith and Harry went to Mary, who was holding Freddie up to wave goodbye.

'Mrs Sylvester,' Harry began, 'it wasn't a very good start, but I hope we can put it all behind us and be friends. We'd like to see Freddie now and again, if – if that's all right with you.'

'Of course it is. Here, would you like to hold him?'

'Will he cry, do you think?' Edith asked, but held out her arms eagerly to hold her grandson for the first time.

'Shouldn't do,' Grace put in. 'He's used to being passed from pillar to post.'

And indeed the little chap beamed at his new-found grandmother and tried to pull her hat off. They all laughed, Edith most of all. She didn't care what her hat had cost or how many clothing coupons she'd used to get it. If her grandson wanted it as a toy, then he could have it.

The days went all too quickly and the moment came when Peggy was standing on the draughty railway station platform waving goodbye to Terry and holding Freddie up high so that Terry could see him until the last possible moment.

As the train disappeared into the distance, Peggy held their son close and whispered, 'Come home safely, my darling. Come back to us.'

Epilogue

The war went on for another two years, but the Sylvester family were lucky. Both their young men came back both physically and mentally sound. Many didn't. Many never came home at all, their graves were in foreign countries or their names on a memorial somewhere. Many more came home physically wounded, some irreparably so. Others returned with unseen scars that would take a long time – if ever – to heal. Laurence's sons and Letty's other two sons also came home safe and well, though her mourning for Walter, her firstborn, would never end.

Terry and Bob were demobbed and returned to their loving wives, grateful to be alive and determined to build a future for their families. Bob got his old job back as a tram driver and Terry learned to read and write under Peggy's sympathetic tuition. He was taken on by one of the city's cutlery manufacturers and, as Charlie Parkin had told Rose and Myrtle, with anything manual he was a quick and able learner. Myrtle continued with her nursing career, and in time she fulfilled her head teacher's prophecy and rose to become matron in one of the big city hospitals. She never married, but her interest in children never waned and she was the instigator of many improvements in paediatric care. She embraced the coming of the National Health Service with fervour, seeing it as fairness for all walks of life.

The name of Matron Sylvester became a byword for strict but fair discipline and her hospital was held up as a shining example of how a hospital should be run.

Sadly Grace did not live to see her youngest granddaughter's success, but she was able to hold Peggy's daughter and Rose's firstborn, a son. As the years went on, Rose and Bob added two more children – both girls – to their family and Peggy and Terry had two more sons.

After the war ended Grace seemed to fade quickly. With only Mary still at home, it seemed as if there was nothing to keep her going. Whereas for years she had grumbled about her house being invaded, now it was too quiet. Mary and Laurence Bower married quietly and he came to live with them, to help Mary look after Grace until she died in the winter of 1951 from pneumonia.

Laurence retired and he and Mary enjoyed their final years together, helping out with Mary's grandchildren, but also taking time for themselves to enjoy trips and holidays that neither of them had ever had the chance to do before. They visited Laurence's two sons, who had both settled in the south of England. They also married and presented Laurence with grandchildren of his own.

Peggy and Rose remained close, living not far from each other on the outskirts of the city. Bob and Terry, after an initial wariness, became good friends. They both supported Sheffield United Football Club and could be seen, together with Charlie Parkin, Harry Price and Percy Thomas, on the terraces at all the club's home matches on a Saturday.

'I can never take Billy's place,' Terry had confided to

an understanding Peggy. 'But I'll look out for his dad. It's what Billy would have wanted.'

It had been Harry and Percy who had settled the two families' differences over Terry and Sylvia. After Rose and Myrtle's visit and Terry's hurried departure to see Peggy, Edith and Harry had looked at each other.

'Well, lass, looks like there's definitely nowt between our lad and Sylvia, then.'

'No,' Edith had agreed. 'How ever am I to face Mabel? It was bad enough before, but now . . .'

Harry had puckered his brow. 'Leave it with me, love. In fact, there's no time like the present . . .'

He'd got up that very minute, called for his mate from next door and suggested a walk down to the pub. There he'd told Percy what had just occurred. 'Missis is worried how your Mabel's going to take it.'

Percy had taken a long drink of his beer, wiped his mouth with the back of his hand. 'They've been a couple of silly, romantic lasses, that pair,' Percy had said, referring to Amy and Sylvia. 'Time they grew up and learned what's what. And you leave Mabel to me.'

What transpired between husband and wife no one ever knew, for the matter was never referred to again. Mabel came round to her neighbour's house the next morning to borrow a spoonful of tea leaves and chatted amiably about the weather as if nothing had happened. Edith, taking her cue, said nothing either. The only reference ever made was when Mabel brought round a gift for Terry on the morning of his wedding. 'Me an' Percy hope they'll be happy, Edith. It's nowt much, but it's the thought that counts they say.'

'Oh Mabel, it is,' Edith said, taking the present gratefully. 'It is. *Thank* you.'

Margaret Dickinson

As for Amy and Sylvia, they had both been in such serious trouble with their parents for the lies they'd told that their friendship was awkward, blighted by their own silliness. Whilst they never actually fell out, they both began to make other friends and to go their own ways.

Times were still hard, rationing was still in place for several years after the war ended, but the resilient Sheffielders began to rebuild their city and their lives. It would all take time, and many hearts would still grieve for what they had lost in the dark days of the war, but now, for those that were left, there was hope for the future.

Jenny's War
Margaret Dickinson

Is it possible for a ten-year-old girl to fall in love? Jenny Mercer thinks so. Evacuated to Lincolnshire from the East End of London at the outbreak of war, she is frightened of the wide open spaces and the huge skies. But the kindly Thornton family soon makes her feel welcome. And no one more so than Georgie, the handsome RAF fighter pilot who is caught up in the battle for Britain's survival. When Georgie is posted missing, presumed dead, Jenny is devastated.

More heartbreak is to come when Jenny's mother Dot decides that she wants her daughter home and Jenny is forced to come back to live in the city, which is now under almost daily attack from enemy bombers. Dot's 'fancy man', Arthur Osborne, treats Jenny kindly. But is Arthur only interested in the girl because she can be useful to him? No one will suspect a ten-year-old girl of being involved with the Black Market . . .

When the law comes a little too close for Arthur's comfort, the family flees the city and head towards the hills and dales of Derbyshire. There, Jenny is caught up in a life of deception. All she really wants is to go back to Lincolnshire. For Jenny has never given up hope that one day, Georgie will come back . . .

ISBN: 978-0-330-54430-6

Bello:
hidden talent rediscovered

FOR MORE ON

MARGARET DICKINSON

sign up to receive our

SAGA NEWSLETTER

Packed with **features, competitions, authors'
and readers' letters** and **news of exclusive events**,
it's a must-read for every Margaret Dickinson fan!

Simply fill in your details below and tick to confirm that you would
like to receive saga-related news and promotions and return to us at
Pan Macmillan, Saga Newsletter, 20 New Wharf Road, London, N1 9RR.

NAME

ADDRESS

POSTCODE

EMAIL

☐ *I would like to receive saga-related news and promotions (please tick)*

*You can unsubscribe at any time in writing or through our website where you can also see
our privacy policy which explains how we will store and use your data.*

www.panmacmillan.com